ROLEMASTER COMPANION III™

CREDITS

Designers: Darrin Anderson, Mike Carlyle, Don Coatar, Mark Colborn, Singh Khanna, Hywel Phillips, Art Ridley, Chris Stone, Tim Taylor, Michael Veach

Developer/Editor: Coleman Charlton

Interior Art: Paul Jaquays

Cover Art: Walter Velez

Cover Graphics: Bart Bishop

Art Direction: Richard H. Britton

Production: Larry Brook, Bill Downs, Kurt Fischer, Leo LaDell, Judy Madison, Paula Peters, Eileen Smith, Suzanne Young

Pagemaking: Coleman Charlton

Editorial Contributions: Kevin Barrett

Special Contributions: Terry Amthor, Deane Begiebing, Rob Bell, John Breckenridge, John Brown, Pete Fenlon, Heidi Heffner, David Johnson, Bruce Neidlinger, Jessica Ney, Becky Pope, Mark Rainey, Kurt Rasmussen, John Ruemmler, Swinky

Copyright 1988 © by Iron Crown Enterprises Inc. . . . All rights reserved. . . . No reproductions without author's permission.

Produced and distributed by IRON CROWN ENTERPRISES, Inc., P.O. Box 1605, Charlottesville, VA 22902

First U.S. Edition, Dec. 1988.

Stock # 1700
ISBN 1-55806-050-2

1.0 INTRODUCTION
1.1 DESIGNER NOTES 3
1.2 NOTATION 3

2.0 OPTIONAL PROFESSION "LAWS"
2.1 NON-SPELL USERS 4
    2.11 Bounty Hunter (DA) 4
    2.12 Assassin (DA) 5
    2.13 Bashkar (DA) 5
    2.14 Farmer (DA) 6
    2.15 Duelist (DA) 6
    2.16 Craftsman (DA) 7
    2.17 Cavalier (DA) 7
    2.18 Gypsy (CKR) 8
    2.19 Sailor (DA&CKR) 8
    2.1.10 Warrior (DA) 9
2.2 SEMI-SPELL USERS 9
    2.21 Crafter 9
    2.22 Noble Warrior (CKR) 10
    2.23 Chaotic Lord (CKR) 11
    2.24 Macabre (TT) 11
    2.25 Montebanc (MV) 12
    2.26 Moon Mage (CKR) 12
    2.27 Sleuth (TT) 13
2.3 THE "PROFESSIONAL" (TT) 14
2.4 CRYSTAL MAGE (CKR) 14
2.5 MAGUS (MC) 15
2.6 DREAM LORD (CKR) 16

3.0 OPTIONAL ARMS "LAWS"
3.1 SIMPLIFIED INITIATIVE (DA) 17
3.2 SURPRISE (DA) 17
3.3 SELF-RELOADING WEAPONS 17
3.4 NEW WEAPONS TABLE (CKR) 18
3.5 MOUNTED COMBAT (MV) 18
3.6 A SUPER-FAST COMBAT SYSTEM (MC) 19

4.0 OPTIONAL SPELL "LAWS"
4.1 GREAT COMMANDS (MC) 22
4.2 SPIRIT RUNES (MC) 23
4.3 RITUAL MAGIC (HP) 26
4.4 DIRECTED SPELLS (CKR) 29
4.5 INDIVIDUAL SPELL DEVELOPMENT (DC) 30

5.0 OPTIONAL SKILLS/STATS "LAWS"
5.1 QUICKIE STAT GENERATION (MC) 31
5.2 "MODS ONLY" DEVELOPMENT (MC) 31
5.3 INNATE STAT ABILITIES (CS) 32
5.4 LUCK (DA) 34
5.5 LEVEL INTENSIVE COMBAT (MC) 35
5.6 ELOQUENCE (MC) 35
5.7 SIMPLE POTENTIAL GENERATION (DA) 35

6.0 OPTIONAL C&T "LAWS"
6.1 TREASURE GENERATION (MC) 36
6.2 ARCANE ARTIFACTS AND ITEMS (CS) 36
6.3 REPLUSIONS (MC) 38
6.4 MONSTER MASHING (MC) 39

7.0 OPTIONAL MISCELLANEOUS "LAWS"
7.1 ARCANE SOCIETIES (TT) 40
7.2 SOCIAL STANDING (DA) 42
7.3 DEATH OPTIONS (MC) 43
7.4 LINGUISTICS ADDENDUM 44
7.5 USING THE RMCIII CRITICAL TABLES 44

8.0 BASE LISTS FOR RMCIII PROFESSIONS
8.1 MONTEBANC BASE LISTS (MV) 44
    8.11 Mystic Escapes 44
    8.12 Disquise Mastery 45
    8.13 Beguiling Ways 45
    8.14 Appraisals 45

8.2 CHAOTIC LORD BASE LISTS (CKR) 46
    8.21 Chaotic Weapons 46
    8.22 Chaos Mastery 46
    8.23 Chaotic Armor 47
    8.24 The Choatic Table 49
8.3 MOON MAGE BASE LISTS (CKR) 53
    8.31 Moon Madness 53
    8.32 Moon Mastery 54
    8.33 Metamorphose 55
8.4 NOBLE WARRIOR BASE LISTS (CKR) 56
    8.41 Noble Armor 56
    8.42 Noble Weapons 57
8.5 SLEUTH BASE LISTS (TT) 58
    8.51 Analyses 58
    8.52 Sleuth's Senses 58
    8.53 Escaping Ways 59
    8.54 Time's Sense 59
8.6 MAGUS BASE LISTS (MC) 60
    8.61 Power Words 60
    8.62 Runes & Symbols 61
    8.63 Signs of Power 62
    8.64 Linguistics 62
    8.65 Command Words 63
    8.66 Spirit Runes 64
8.7 CRYSTAL MAGE BASE LISTS (CKR) 66
    8.71 Crystal Power 66
    8.72 Deep Earth Healing 66
    8.73 Crystal Magic 68
    8.74 Deep Earth Commune 69
    8.75 Crystal Mastery 70
    8.76 Fiery Ways 71
    8.77 Brilliance Magic 72
    8.78 Crystal Runestone 72
8.8 DREAM LORD BASE LISTS (CKR) 74
    8.81 Dream Guard 74
    8.82 Dream Law 75
    8.83 Dream Lore 76
    8.84 Dream State 77

9.0 ARCANE NAVIGATORS' BASE LIST (TT)

10.0 ARCANE COVEN BASE LISTS (TT)
10.1 Allurement 79
10.2 Household Magic 79
10.3 Barrier Ways 80
10.4 Brewing Lore 80
10.5 Hearth Magic 81
10.6 Wax Magic 82
10.7 Mending Ways 83

11.0 ARCANE SPELL LISTS
11.1 Plasma Mastery (CS) 84
11.2 Nether Mastery (CKR) 84

12.0 CRITICAL STRIKE TABLES
12.1 Plasma Critical Strike Table (CS) 86
12.2 Acid Critical Strike Table (CKR) 87
12.3 Physical Alteration Crit. Str. Table (CKR) 88
12.4 Depression Critical Strike Table (CKR) 89
12.5 Stress Critical Strike Table (CKR) 90
12.6 Shock Critical Strike Table (CKR) 91
12.7 Disruption Critical Strike Table 92

13.0 SPELL ATTACK TABLES
13.1 Plasma Bolt Attack Table (CS) 93
13.2 Plasma Ball Attack Table (CS) 94
13.3 Nether Bolt Attack Table (CKR) 95
13.4 Nether Ball Attack Table (CKR) 96

1.0 INTRODUCTION

The ***Rolemaster Companion III*** (***RMCIII***) is the third of a collection of optional rules and spell lists for the ***Rolemaster*** fantasy role playing system. Optional is the key word here; a Gamemaster should carefully examine each section of material before using it in his world or campaign. This material runs the gamut from play aids that simply make the standard game mechanics easier to handle to **very high** powered spells and optional rules. Most GMs should not and will not use everything in ***RMCIII***; there is just too big a diversity in style and power level. Carefully examine each section of material before using it in your world or campaign.

The ***RMCIII*** includes a wide variety of material because different role players want different things from a role playing system. Some GMs run a low powered tightly structured game; such GMs probably find that much of the material in this product will not be appropriate for their game unless they modify and experiment with it. At the other end of the spectrum, some GMs run a high powered or loosely structured game; such GMs will probably use most of the material in this product and modify it and extend it and wish that there were more 75th level spells. Most GMs fall in between these two extremes; they will use some of the material, ignore some of it, and modify the rest. The thing to keep in mind is that this is a commercial product. As a company, ICE has to appeal to a large audience and provide material that can be used by most of the customers that use our systems.

Players should keep the above discussion in mind when reading ***RMCIII***; some of this material may not be appropriate for your Gamemaster's game. The GM must decide which parts of this material will be used in his world — not the players. The GM should always be the authority in any role playing session that involves his world. The manner in which a GM interprets, modifies, excludes, or includes rules and guidelines is entirely up to him (or her). This is true for the standard rules as well as a set of optional rules, such as ***RMCIII***. A Gamemaster should never feel that the rules are an etched-in-concrete, unbreakable, unbendable, absolutely fixed system; they are provided to help the GM develop, manage, and run his world.

On the other hand, the Gamemaster has an obligation to his players to make clear what the physical laws of his world entail (i.e., the game mechanics). As efficiently as possible, the GM should indicate what rules and guidelines are being used and which ones have been modified or changed. In addition, a GM must strive to be consistent in his decisions and in his interpretations of the rules. Without consistency, the players will eventually lose trust and confidence in the GM's decisions and his game. When this happens a FRP game loses much of its pleasure and appeal. Both GM and players must cooperate to have a successful FRP game.

NOTE: *For readability purposes, these rules use the standard masculine pronouns when referring to persons of uncertain gender. In such cases, these pronouns are intended to convey the meanings: he/she, her/him, etc.*

1.1 DESIGNER NOTES

Rolemaster (***ChL&CaL***, ***AL***, ***SL***, and ***C&T***) is a system that provides a tight set of core rules for experienced role players. It is a system that was designed to allow easy modification and expansion by individual GMs so that it would be more appropriate for each GM's campaign. Our design philosophy here at ICE is to keep the core rules as the base system and to present any "improvements" and expansions in the form of Optional Rules. This means that GMs who find the core rules sufficient can ignore the Optional Rules, while other GMs have a wide selection of variants and interesting options for their worlds.

Character Law & Campaign Law has a set of these Optional Rules that were developed between the publication of the original ***Character Law*** and the publication of ***ChL&CaL***. ***Rolemaster Companion*** (I) is a set of Optional Rules developed after ***ChL&CaL***; most of this material was designed by Mark Colborn for his own game and then developed and published by ICE. Similarly, ***RMCII*** was primarily designed by Mike Carlyle, Singh Khanna, and Art Ridley, and then developed by ICE.

Rolemaster Companion III is collection of optional rules, professions, and spell lists from a wider variety of sources, primarily by ICE and the following designers:

CKR — Mike Carlyle, Singh Khanna, and Art Ridley
CS — Chris Stone
DA — Darrin Anderson
DC — Don Coatar
HP — Hywel Phillips
MC — Mark Colborn
MV — Michael Veach
TT — Tim Taylor

The initials given above are used in the Table of Contents to indicate which authors designed which sections.

1.2 NOTATION

The material in ***RMCIII*** uses the standard notation from the ***Rolemaster*** products: ***Arms Law & Claw Law (AL&CL)***, ***Spell Law (SL)***, ***Character Law & Campaign Law (ChL&CaL)***, and ***Creatures & Treasures (C&T)***. Those products should be consulted for specific references; for example, the spell lists all use ***SL*** abbreviations and notation in the spell descriptions.

Two type of notation for dice rolls are used in this product:

1) The range notation, #-#, where the first # is the beginning range and the second # is the end of the range; for example, 1-100 is a roll resulting in a number between 1 and 100 (00).

2) The die type notation, #D#, where the first # is the number of dice to roll (and sum the results) and the second # is the 'type' (number of sides or possible results from 1 to #) of dice to roll. For example, 2D6 = roll two six-sided dice and sum the results; 1D8 = roll one 8-sided die; 3D10 = roll three 10-sided dice and sum the results.

2.0 OPTIONAL PROFESSION "LAWS"

In addition to several new professions, this section presents a number of *variant professions*. A variant profession is a profession that is very similar to one of the professions in **ChL&CaL**, **RMC I**, or **RMC II**, with skill development costs differing only for a relatively small set of skills. Some of the variant professions have their own unique rules and spell lists.

The professions presented in **RMC III** are:

NON-SPELL USERS (Section 2.1):
  Bounty Hunter — a variant profession of Ranger & Fighter
  Assassin — a variant profession of Rogue
  Bashkar — a variant profession of High Warrior Monk
  Farmer — a variant profession of "No Profession" & Fighter
  Duelist — a variant profession of Fighter
  Craftsman — a variant profession of "No Profession"
  Cavalier — a variant profession of Fighter
  Gypsy — a variant profession of Trader
  Sailor — a variant profession of Rogue
  Warrior — a variant profession of Fighter

SEMI-SPELL USERS (Section 2.2):
  Crafter — a variant profession of "No Profession"
  Noble Warrior — a variant profession of Paladin
  Chaotic Lord — a variant profession of Ranger
  Macabre — a variant profession of Necromancer
  Montebanc — a variant profession of Rogue & Bard
  Moon Mage — a variant profession of Dervish
  Sleuth — a variant profession of Bard

OTHER SPELL USERS (Section 2.3):
  Professional — a variant profession of "No Profession"
  Crystal Mage — a hybrid spell user of Essence and Channeling
  Magus — a pure Channeling spell user **or** a pure Essence spell user **or** a hybrid Channeling & Essence spell user
  Dream Lord — a hybrid spell user that is a variant profession of Illusionist (Ess. and Ment.) **or** Shaman (Chan. and Ment.)

2.1 NON-SPELL USERS

2.11 BOUNTY HUNTER

The Bounty Hunter is a non-spell user who specializes in tracking down a person, animal, or object. Bounty Hunters normally operate outdoors and are well versed in survival and combat skills. The Bounty Hunter is a non-spell user variant profession of *Fighter* and *Ranger*.

Weapon Skills: 2/5, 2/7, 3/8, 4, 6, 8	
Maneuvering in Armor:	**Magical Skills:**
Soft Leather 1/*	Spell Lists 15
Rigid Leather 1/*	Runes 8
Chain 3/*	Staves & Wands 6
Plate 4/*	Channeling 25
	Directed Spells 20
Special Skills:	**General Skills:**
Ambush 2/6	Climbing 3/6
Linguistics 3/*	Swimming 2/6
Adrenal Moves 2/6	Riding 2/6
Adrenal Defense 20	Disarming Traps 2/5
Martial Arts 3/7	Picking Locks 3/6
Body Development 1/5	Stalk & Hide 1/4
	Perception 1/3

Other Skills: Refer to Development Point Costs given below for those skills unique to the Bounty Hunter Profession. All other skill costs are identical to the Ranger's DP cost.
Prime Requisites: AG/CO

Academic Skills:	**Athletic Skills:**
Dragon Lore 3	All as a Fighter .... varies
Lock Lore 3/7	
Combat Skills:	**Deadly Skills:**
Subduing 1/4	All as a Fighter .... varies
Rest as a Fighter ...... varies	
General Skills:	**Gymnastic Skills:**
Rope Mastery 1/3	Jumping 1/3
Skinning 1/3	Tumbling 1/5
Magical Skills:	**Medical Skills:**
All as a Fighter .... varies	All as a Fighter .... varies
Perception Skills:	**Social Skills:**
Lie Perception 2/6	Interrogation 1/3
Poison Perception 1/5	Leadership 3/6
Surveillance 1/3	
Tracking 1/2	
Subterfuge Skills:	**Survival Skills:**
Set Traps 1/3	Scrounge 1/5
Trap-Building 1/3	Streetwise 1/4
Level Bonuses:	
Arms Law Combat ...... +1	Athletic Skills .... +1
Body Development ..... +1	Outdoor Skills .... +3
Subterfuge Skills .... +1	Perception .... +3

2.12 ASSASSIN

An Assassin is a non-spell user who concentrates in infiltration and deadly skills. Assassins are usually loners who are hired to eliminate a specific enemy. An Assassin generally does not wear armor unless he is posing as a Fighter. In some cultures Assassins are called Spies.

The Assassin is a variant profession of *Rogue*.

Weapon Skills: 2/5, 3/7, 3/9, 4, 6, 9	
Maneuvering in Armor: Soft Leather .... 1/* Rigid Leather .... 1/* Chain .... 4/* Plate 7/*	**Magical Skills:** Spell Lists .... 15 Runes .... 7 Staves & Wands .... 9 Channeling .... 20 Directed Spells 20
Special Skills: Ambush .... 1/2 Linguistics .... 1/* Adrenal Moves .... 3/8 Adrenal Defense .... 15 Martial Arts .... 3/7 Body Development 2/7	**General Skills:** Climbing .... 1/5 Swimming .... 2/5 Riding .... 3 Disarming Traps .... 2/5 Picking Locks .... 2/5 Stalk & Hide .... 1/3 Perception 1/3
Other Skills: Refer to Development Point Costs given below for those skills unique to the Assassin Profession. All other skill costs are identical to the Rogue's development point cost. **Prime Requisites:** QU/AG	
Academic Skills: Poison Lore .... 1/2 Lock Lore .... 2/4 Tactics 2/5	**Athletic Skills:** Diving .... 1/3 Rappelling .... 1/3 Rowing 2/5
Animal Skills: All Animal Skills 3	**Combat Skills:** Brawling 2/7
Concentration Skills: All Meditation Skills ... 2/4	**Deadly Skills:** Use/Remove Poison 1/3
Gymnastic Skills: Contortions .... 1/3 Tightrope Walking 2/4	**Magical Skills:** All as a Fighter .... varies
Social Skills: Diplomacy .... 1/3 Gambling 2/5	**Subterfuge Skills:** Disguise .... 1/3 Bribery 1/4
Medical Skills: Drug Tolerance 1/4	
Level Bonuses: Arms Law Combat ...... +2 Body Development ..... +1 Subterfuge Skills .... +3	Athletic Skills .... +1 Deadly Skills .... +3

2.13 BASHKAR

A Bashkar is a non-spell user who concentrates in mindless, all-out attacks. Bashkars are berserkers who have no regard for their own personal safety. They never carry shields and only wear light armor. Bashkars concentrate in frenzy and running skills. Most sane people shudder at the sight of an upset Bashkar.

The Bashkar is a variant profession of *Fighter* and *High Warrior Monk*.

Weapon Skills: 1/5, 1/5, 2/5, 2/5, 2/7, 3/8	
Maneuvering in Armor: Soft Leather .... 1/* Rigid Leather .... 1/* Chain .... 6/* Plate 10	**Magical Skills:** Spell Lists .... 20 Runes .... 9 Staves & Wands .... 10 Channeling .... 20 Directed Spells 20
Special Skills: Ambush .... 3/8 Linguistics .... 3/* Adrenal Moves .... 2/4 Adrenal Defense .... 15 Martial Arts .... 3/7 Body Development 1/3	**General Skills:** Climbing .... 2/6 Swimming .... 2/5 Riding .... 2/6 Disarming Traps .... 3/8 Picking Locks .... 3/8 Stalk & Hide .... 3/8 Perception 2/5
Other Skills: Refer to Development Point Costs given below for those skills unique to the Bashkar Profession. All other skill costs are identical to the High Warrior Monk's DP cost. **Prime Requisites:** ST/CO	
Academic Skills: Philosophy/Religious ..... 3 Tactics 5	**Athletic Skills:** Distance Running .... 1/2 Diving .... 1/5 Sprinting 1/2
Animal Skills: All Animal Skills 4	**Combat Skills:** Brawling .... 1/4 Disarm Foe .... 3/6 Iai, Subduing, & Yado .... 5 Tumbling, Evasion 5
Evaluation Skills: All Evaluation Skills ... 3/6	
Concentration Skills: Frenzy .... 1/2 All Other 2/6	**General Skills:** Painting 4
Gymnastic Skills: Pole Vaulting .... 2/5 Tightrope Walking 3/6	**Perception Skills:** All Perception Skills ... 2/6
Level Bonuses: Arms Law Combat ...... +3 Body Development ..... +3	Athletic Skills .... +2 Concentration Skills ..... +2

2.14 FARMER

The Farmer is often the most common NPC type in a society. Farmers are non-spell users who devote their lives to growing food that the rest of society consumes.

The Farmer is a variant profession of *"No Profession"* and *Fighter*.

Weapon Skills: 3/8, 4, 6, 15, 20, 20	
Maneuvering in Armor: Soft Leather .... 2/* Rigid Leather .... 3/* Chain .... 6/* Plate 7/*	**Magical Skills:** Spell Lists .... 20 Runes .... 10 Staves & Wands .... 10 Channeling .... 20 Directed Spells 20
Special Skills: Ambush .... 3/8 Linguistics .... 3/* Adrenal Moves .... 5 Adrenal Defense .... 20 Martial Arts .... 3/8 Body Development 1/4	**General Skills:** Climbing .... 2/5 Swimming .... 1/5 Riding .... 1/5 Disarming Traps .... 6 Picking Locks .... 5 Stalk & Hide .... 2/7 Perception 2/6

Other Skills: Refer to Development Point Costs given below for those skills unique to the Farmer Profession. All other skill costs are identical to the No Profession's DP cost.
Prime Requisites: ST/SD

Academic Skills: Flora Lore & Fauna Lore 1/4 Herb Lore & Stone Lore . 1/5 Trading Lore .... 1/5 Weather Watching 1/3	**Animal Skills:** All Animal Skills .... 1/3 **Combat Skills:** All Combat Skills 3/8
Deadly Skills: All Deadly Skills 3/8	**Magical Skills:** All as a Fighter .... varies
General Skills: Cookery .... 1/4 Crafting .... 1/5 Horticulture .... 1/2 Skinning .... 1/5 Wood-Crafts 1/5	**Subterfuge Skills:** Set Traps .... 1/5 **Survival Skills:** Region Lore 1/4
Level Bonuses: Animal Skills .... +3 Body Development ...... +2	General Skills .... +2 Outdoor Skills .... +3

2.15 DUELIST

The Duelist is a non-spell user who is a master of formal melee combat. They are rare individuals who possess a strange code of honor. The Duelist's code forces him to fight fair, one-on-one melee combats. Any Duelist that breaks the code will be hunted and fought (to the death) by other Duelists who learn of his crime. Sometimes rich individuals employ Duelists to settle arguments. A Duelist usually specializes heavily into one area of melee weapons (one-handed edged, one-handed concussion, or two-handed).

The Duelist is a variant profession of *Fighter*.

Weapon Skills: 1/3, 6, 8, 8, 20, 20 (the 20 costs must be assigned to Bows and Thrown)	
Maneuvering in Armor: Soft Leather .... 2/* Rigid Leather .... 3/* Chain .... 5/* Plate 7/*	**Magical Skills:** Spell Lists .... 20 Runes .... 7 Staves & Wands .... 12 Channeling .... 25 Directed Spells 20
Special Skills: Ambush .... 7 Linguistics .... 3/* Adrenal Moves .... 1/4 Adrenal Defense .... 6 Martial Arts .... 3/7 Body Development 1/5	**General Skills:** Climbing .... 3/7 Swimming .... 2/6 Riding .... 2/6 Disarming Traps .... 4 Picking Locks .... 4 Stalk & Hide .... 3/9 Perception 2/5

Other Skills: Refer to Development Point Costs given below for those skills unique to the Duelist Profession. All other skill costs are identical to the Fighter's development point cost.
Prime Requisites: ST/QU

Combat Skills: Disarm Foe, Armed ..... 1/3 Grappling Hook .... 4 Iai .... 1/3 Lancing .... 4 Missile Artillery .... 20 Reverse Stroke .... 20 Stunned Maneuver ..... 1/4 Tumbling 1/5	**Concentration Skills:** Body Dam. Stabilize ... 1/4 Frenzy .... 4 **Deadly Skills:** All Deadly Skills .... 7 **Social Skills:** Gambling .... 1/5 Leadership 3/6
Level Bonuses: Arms Law Combat .... +3 Body Development ..... +3	Athletic Skills .... +2 Concentration Skills ..... +2

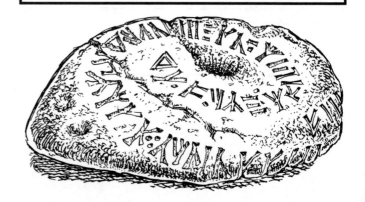

Profession "Laws": Craftsman & Cavalier

2.17 CAVALIER

The Cavalier is a non-spell user who follows a strict code of ethics and conduct. Cavaliers serve a Lord, Noble, or King of some kind; their goal in life is to uphold chivalry. Cavaliers would rather die than be dishonored. In many societies they wear distinctive orange and blue clothing.

The Cavalier is a variant profession of *Fighter*.

Weapon Skills: 1/5, 2/5, 2/7, 2/8, 4, 6	
Maneuvering in Armor: Soft Leather .... 1/* Rigid Leather .... 1/* Chain .... 2/* Plate 2/*	**Magical Skills:** Spell Lists .... 20 Runes .... 7 Staves & Wands .... 9 Channeling .... 25 Directed Spells 20
Special Skills: Ambush .... 9 Linguistics .... 2/* Adrenal Moves .... 3/8 Adrenal Defense .... 20 Martial Arts .... 4 Body Development 1/4	**General Skills:** Climbing .... 5 Swimming .... 3 Riding .... 2/5 Disarming Traps .... 6 Picking Locks .... 6 Stalk & Hide .... 6 Perception 2/5

Other Skills: Refer to Development Point Costs given below for those skills unique to the Cavalier Profession. All other skill costs are identical to the Fighter's development point cost.
Prime Requisites: ST/CO

Academic Skills: All Lore .... 1/5 Heraldry 1/3	**Combat Skills:** Brawling & Yado .... 3/7 Tumbling, Att. & Eva. .. 3/6
Concentration Skills: Body Dam. Stabilize ... 1/4	**Deadly Skills:** Silent Kill 5
Evaluation Skills: All Evaluation Skills ... 1/5	**Deadly Skills:** Silent Kill 5
General Skills: Smithing .... 2/5 Tactical Games 1/4	**Gymnastic Skills:** All Gymnastic Skills ... 2/7
Linguistic Skills: Public Speaking 1/5	**Magical Skills:** As a Rogue .... varies
Social Skills: Interrogation .... 1/5 Leadership 1/3	**Subterfuge Skills:** As a Paladin .... varies
Level Bonuses: Arms Law Combat ..... +3 Body Development ..... +3	Athletic Skills .... +3 Social Skills .... +1

2.16 CRAFTSMAN

The Craftsman is a non-spell user who concentrates in building/making objects/items. Most Craftsmen never adventure, being content with the "boring" life of working. Each Craftsman must chose one area of "concentration": e.g., woodworker, stone mason, blacksmith, baker, architect, etc.

The Craftsman is a variant profession of *"No Profession"*.

Weapon Skills: 4, 8, 9, 9, 9, 20	
Maneuvering in Armor: Soft Leather .... 2/* Rigid Leather .... 3/* Chain .... 6/* Plate 9/*	**Magical Skills:** Spell Lists .... 15 Runes .... 10 Staves & Wands .... 10 Channeling .... 20 Directed Spells 20
Special Skills: Ambush .... 3/9 Linguistics .... 2/* Adrenal Moves .... 5 Adrenal Defense .... 20 Martial Arts .... 4 Body Development 4	**General Skills:** Climbing .... 3/7 Swimming .... 3 Riding .... 2/6 Disarming Traps .... 3/9 Picking Locks .... 3/9 Stalk & Hide .... 3/9 Perception 2/6

Other Skills:

All Skills and Lore directly related to the Craftsman specific area of concentration have a 1/2 Development Point Cost (e.g., for a blacksmith this would include: Lock Lore, Mechanition, Metal Lore, all Evaluation skills applied to metal items, Crafting, Gimmickry, and Smithing).

All Skills and Lore indirectly related to the Craftsman specific area of concentration have a 1/5 Development Point Cost (e.g., for a blacksmith this would include: Drafting, Engineering, Mining, Physics, Siege Engineering, all Evaluation skills, Sculpting, and Trap-Building)

All other skill costs are identical to the No Profession's development point cost.

Prime Requisites: AG/SD or AG/RE

2.18 GYPSY

The Gypsy is a non-spell user who specializes in divinations, outdoor skills, animal handling, and some subterfuge abilities. The Gypsy normally comes from nomadic family clans with the eldest male being the clan leader.

The Gypsy is a variant profession of *Trader*.

Weapon Skills: 2/7, 3/8, 3/9, 4, 5, 6	
Maneuvering in Armor: Soft Leather .... 2/* Rigid Leather .... 2/* Chain .... 4/* Plate 15	**Magical Skills:** Spell Lists .... 8 Runes .... 6 Staves & Wands .... 4/7 Channeling .... 15 Directed Spells 15
Special Skills: Ambush .... 4 Linguistics .... 1/* Adrenal Moves .... 3/6 Adrenal Defense .... 20 Martial Arts .... 3/7 Body Development 3/5	**General Skills:** Climbing .... 4 Swimming .... 2/5 Riding .... 1/4 Disarming Traps .... 2/5 Picking Locks .... 2/6 Stalk & Hide .... 2/5 Perception 1/3

Other Skills: Refer to Development Point Costs given below for those skills unique to the Gypsy Profession. All other skill costs are identical to the Trader's development point cost.
Prime Requisites: AG/IN

Academic Skills: Demon/Devil Lore ...... 3/6 Military Organization 4	**Athletic Skills:** Athletic Games .... 4 Dancing 1/4
Evaluation Skills: Appraisal .... 2/4 Armor Evaluation .... 3/7 Metal Evaluation .... 2/4 Stone Evaluation .... 2/4 Weapon Evaluation 3/7	**Magical Skills:** Divinations .... 1/4 Magical Rituals .... 3/8 Power Perception 3/8
Medical Skills: Midwifery .... 2/6 Surgery 4	
Level Bonuses: General Skills .... +2 Magical Skills .... +1 Outdoor Skills .... +1 Social Skills .... +1	Linguistic Skills .... +2 Medical Skills .... +1 Perception Skills .... +1 Subterfuge Skills .... +1

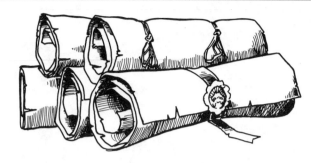

2.19 SAILOR

The following skills have been modified to reflect the Sailors special background and way of live around sea coast, water ways and ship living. The Sailor is a non-spell user that is also known as a pirate, seaman, fisherman, merchant marine, etc.

The Sailor is a variant profession of *Rogue*.

Weapon Skills: 2/5, 3/8, 3/9, 3/9, 3/9, 6	
Maneuvering in Armor: Soft Leather .... 1/* Rigid Leather .... 1/* Chain .... 4/* Plate 7	**Magical Skills:** Spell Lists .... 8 Runes .... 6 Staves & Wands .... 8 Channeling .... 20 Directed Spells 20
Special Skills: Ambush .... 2/5 Linguistics .... 3/* Adrenal Moves .... 2/6 Adrenal Defense .... 20 Martial Arts .... 3/7 Body Development 2/5	**General Skills:** Climbing .... 1/4 Swimming .... 1/2 Riding .... 3/7 Disarming Traps .... 2/6 Picking Locks .... 2/6 Stalk & Hide .... 2/4 Perception 1/3

Other Skills: Refer to Development Point Costs given below for those skills unique to the Sailor Profession. All other skill costs are identical to the Rogue's development point cost.
Prime Requisites: ST/AG

Academic Skills: Boat Pilot .... 1/4 Navigation .... 2/4 Ship Lore .... 2/4 Star-Gazing .... 1/4 Water Fauna Lore .... 2 Weather-Watching 2/4	**Animal Skills:** Animal Handling .... 2/4 Animal Training .... 4 Driving .... 2/6 Herding .... 2/4 Loading 2/4
Athletic Skills: Sailing 1/3	**Concentration Skills:** Balance 1/4
General Skills: Sail Repair .... 1/5 Skinning 2/6	**Perception Skills:** Read Tracks .... 3/7 Tracking 2/5
Level Bonuses: Arms Law Combat .... +3 Body Development ...... +1 Subterfuge Skills .... +2	Athletic Skills .... +2 General Skills .... +2

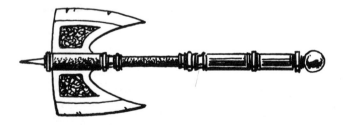

2.1.10 WARRIOR

The Warrior is a non-spell user who only concentrates in the basic fighting skills. Warriors prefer heavy armor and weapons. Warriors usually are very one dimensional, lacking development in all areas not directly related to combat. The members of many of the cruder, militant races may be primarily Warriors (i.e., Orcs, Trolls, Giants, etc.). The Warrior is a variant profession of *Fighter*.

Weapon Skills: 1/4, 1/5, 2/5, 2/7, 2/7, 5		
Maneuvering in Armor:		**Magical Skills:**
Soft Leather 1/*		Spell Lists 25
Rigid Leather 1/*		Runes 25
Chain 1/*		Staves & Wands 25
Plate 1/*		Channeling 25
		Directed Spells 25
Special Skills:		**General Skills:**
Ambush 4		Climbing 6
Linguistics 3/*		Swimming 5
Adrenal Moves 5		Riding 3
Adrenal Defense 20		Disarming Traps 6
Martial Arts 3/6		Picking Locks 6
Body Development 1/3		Stalk & Hide 6
		Perception 4

Other Skills: Combat skill costs are identical to the Fighter's development point costs. The development point cost for each other skill is 6 **or** the cost for a Fighter, whichever is greater.
Prime Requisites: ST/CO

Level Bonuses:	
Arms Law Combat .... +3	Athletic Skills .... +3
Body Development ...... +3	Deadly Skills .... +1

2.2 SEMI-SPELL USERS

2.21 CRAFTER

The Crafter is a semi-spell user who concentrates in building/making objects/items. Crafters differ from Craftsmen in that they can use spells related to their craft. Most Crafters never adventure, being content with the "boring" life of working.

The Crafter is a variant profession of *"No Profession"*, and he may choose any one of the three Realms as his Realm of Power (i.e., Channeling, Essence, or Mentalism).

CRAFTER BASE SPELL LISTS

Metal Lore (Arcane)   *Stone Lore* (Arcane)
Wood Shaping (Arcane)   *Constructing Ways* (Delver Base)
Delving Law (Delver Base)   *Mannish Ways* (Delver Base)

Weapon Skills: 3/9, 4, 6, 6, 6, 9		
Maneuvering in Armor:		**Magical Skills:**
Soft Leather 1/*		Spell Lists 4/*
Rigid Leather 2/*		Runes 3/6
Chain 4/*		Staves & Wands 3/6
Plate 5/*		Channeling 4
		Directed Spells 4
Special Skills:		**General Skills:**
Ambush 3/9		Climbing 3/6
Linguistics 2/*		Swimming 3/6
Adrenal Moves 2/7		Riding 3/6
Adrenal Defense 15		Disarming Traps 2/5
Martial Arts 3/7		Picking Locks 2/5
Body Development 2/7		Stalk & Hide 3/6
		Perception 1/5

Other Skills: Refer to Development Point Costs given below for those skills unique to the Crafter Profession. All other skill costs are identical to the No Profession's DP cost.
Prime Requisites: AG/IN, AG/EM, AG/PR (based on Realm of Power chosen).

General Skills:		**Academic Skills:**
Crafting 1/2		Drafting 1/4
Fletching 1/2		Engineering 1/4
Gimmickry 1/2		Lock Lore 1/3
Leather-Working 1/2		Mechanition 1/3
Rope Mastery 1/4		Metal Lore 1/2
Sculpting 1/5		Siege Engineering 1/5
Skinning 1/5		Stone Lore 1/2
Smithing 1/2		
Stone-Crafts 1/2		**Evaluation Skills:**
Wood-Crafts 1/2		All Evaluation Skills ... 1/2
Subterfuge Skills:		
Set Traps 1/5		
Trap-Building 1/3		

Level Bonuses:	
General Skills .... +3	Academic Skills .... +3
Evaluation Skills .... +3	Subterfuge Skills .... +1

2.22 NOBLE WARRIOR

The Noble Warrior is a class of warriors that have sworn complete allegiance to their Lord. They are the Lord's vassals and will, if necessary, sacrifice their live in his service. A Noble Warrior is the mirror image of a Paladin without the religious connections. This strict Code Of Honor is never broken lightly; for once broken, they are forever banned from the Noble Order. Each prospective member of a Noble Warrior order must successfully pass an entrance test. This test normally takes place in several areas: Weapon Skills, Riding Skill, and Athletic Skills.

The Noble Warrior is a variant profession of *Paladin*, but he is a semi-spell user of Mentalism instead of Channeling.

NOBLE WARRIOR BASE SPELL LISTS

Noble Armor — Protective spells.
Noble Weapon — Magical weapons and magical strikes.
Three Additional Base Lists: Normally three additional base spell lists may be chosen from the lists below:

Arm's Way (Paladin Base)   *Monk's Bridge* (Monk Base)
Evasions (Monk Base)   *Body Reins* (Monk Base)
Monk's Sense (Monk Base)   *Body Renewal* (Monk Base)
Combat Enhancement (Beastmaster Base)
Movement Enhancement (Beastmaster Base)

Weapon Skills: 2/5, 3/8, 4, 4, 4, 6	
Maneuvering in Armor:	**Magical Skills:**
Soft Leather 1/*	Spell Lists 4/*
Rigid Leather 1/*	Runes 7
Chain 2/*	Staves & Wands 5
Plate 3/*	Channeling 20
	Directed Spells 6
Special Skills:	**General Skills:**
Ambush .... 3 -	Climbing 5
Linguistics 3/*	Swimming 3
Adrenal Moves 2/7	Riding 2/4
Adrenal Defense 20	Disarming Traps 6
Martial Arts 3/7	Picking Locks 4
Body Development 2/5	Stalk & Hide 4
	Perception 3/7

Other Skills: Refer to Development Point Costs given below for those skills unique to the Noble Warrior Profession. All other skill costs are identical to the Paladin's DP cost.
Prime Requisites: ST/PR

Concentration Skills:	**Medical Skills:**
Cleansing 2/4	Diagnostics 3
Death 3/7	Hypnosis 4
Healing 3/7	Midwifery 4
Ki 3/8	Surgery 7
Sleep 3/7	
Trance 3/7	

Level Bonuses:	
Arms Law Combat .... +3	Athletic Skills .... +2
Body Development ...... +2	General Skills .... +1
Outdoor Skills .... +1	Social Skills .... +1

EXAMPLE: *The Order of Brightblade*
The Noble Warrior Order of Brightblade's entrance test consists of the following requirements:

1) 5 mile run in 40 minutes. (This is a hard static maneuver or the GM may elect to have the novice expend exhaustion points)

2) Mount a horse which is sprinting (This is a hard maneuver)

3) From the horse that is sprinting, without stopping or turning back, pick up two (2) flags that are on the ground (This is a very hard maneuver)

4) With the horse still at a sprint, ready a bow, fire at a set of dummy targets, one (1) target on the left, one (1) target on the right and the last target in front (Adjust OB by using mounted combat rules, dummy targets are man size)

5) At this point the novice must leap over to a fresh horse with out stopping (This is a medium maneuver)

6) Continuing on with the horse at a sprint, ready a sword, chop at a set of dummy targets, only one swing per target is allowed, targets will be placed with one (1) to the left, one (1) to the right, one (1) in front and the last one on a mount coming towards you (This is a hard maneuver and the mounted target has an DB based on the mount's speed)

7) The last test is a series of triple jumps. (The jumps have a difficulty of medium, hard, and very hard, respectively. If a jump is unsuccessful, it is not possible to make the next jump)

8) If the novice is successful in all of the test, he enters a probational period until first blood. Probational Noble Warriors are treated with all the rights as a proven Noble Warrior. If the Noble Warrior breaks the Code of Honor he has three options:

1) Demand trial by combat: Same as the above test except all dummy targets are manned by Noble Warriors. The Noble Warriors are armed the same way the Honor Breaker is.

2) Banishment & Branding: Considered the coward's way out. If a Noble Warrior spots a branded Honor Breaker, he will engage with the intent to maim, death is too good.

3) In extreme cases: Takes one's own life. This could be death or it could be selling oneself into slavery.

Profession "Laws": Chaotic Lord & Macabre

2.23 CHAOTIC LORD

The Chaotic Lord is a semi-spell user of the Realms of Arms and Channeling who specializes in the manipulation of chaos. The Chaotic Lord serve only one "master"; they live and die for the honor of the "master" and the master's house. The few Chaotic Lords that have betrayed their masters are rumored to have suffered slow and painful deaths. The Chaotic Lord by choice is deformed and mutilated as an expression of their total loyalty to their "master". No two Chaotic Lords are the same; a Chaotic Lord is a power to be feared.

A Chaotic Lord must accept a geas when taking on his *Chaotic Armor* (see the Chaotic Armor spell list); this is another instance of complete obedience to their "master". When a Chaotic Lord dies attempting to control or master Chaotic Armor, other Chaotic Lords only acknowledge the deed by announcing that the other was unworthy scum that tried to pass as one of the chosen.

The Chaotic Lord is a variant of *Ranger* profession.

Chaotic Lord Base Spell Lists

Chaotic Armor   Chaotic Mastery   Chaotic Weapon

Two Additional Base Lists: Normally two additional base spell lists may be chosen from the lists below:

Dark Law (Necromancer Base)   *Darkness* (Evil Magician Base)

Dark Lore (Evil Cleric Base)   *Dark Channels* (Evil Cleric Base)

Dark Contacts (Evil Magician Base)

Dark Summons (Evil Magician Base)

Weapon Skills: 3/7, 4, 6, 6, 6, 9	
Maneuvering in Armor:	**Magical Skills:**
Soft Leather 9	Spell Lists 4/*
Rigid Leather 9	Runes 3/7
Chain 10	Staves & Wands 3/7
Plate 10	Channeling 4
	Directed Spells 4/7
Special Skills:	**General Skills:**
Ambush 3	Climbing 5
Linguistics 3/*	Swimming 3
Adrenal Moves 2/7	Riding 6
Adrenal Defense 20	Disarming Traps 6
Martial Arts 3/7	Picking Locks 8
Body Development 3/5	Stalk & Hide 4
	Perception 2/7

Other Skills: Refer to Development Point Costs given below for those skills unique to the Chaotic Lord Profession. All other skill costs are identical to the Ranger's DP cost.

Prime Requisites: ST/IN

Academic Skills:	**Animal Skills:**
Boat Pilot 3,6	Animal Handling 6
Demon/Devil Lore 1/3	Animal Training 9
Dragon Lore 2/5	Beast Master 6
Fauna Lore 3/6	Driving 4/7
Flora Lore 3/6	Herding 5
Lock Lore 2/5	Loading 4/7

Level Bonuses:	
Arms Law Combat ....+2	Athletic Skills ....+1
Base Spell Casting ....+1	Body Development ......+2
Deadly Skills ....+1	Directed Spells ....+1
Magical Skills ....+1	Social Skills ....+1

2.24 MACABRE

NOTE: *Hybrid semi-spell users are treated exactly as Semi-Spell users, except they may learn spell lists from the Open lists of two realms, but they may not learn any closed lists.*

The Macabre is a hybrid semi-spell user of the realms of Arms, Essence, and Channeling. Macabres concentrate on: Death, Necromancy, and the weakening/sickening of the body. Macabres must be Evil, and thus are usually NPCs or "encounters."

Generally, a Macabre haunts the outskirts of civilization, whether that is the badlands, the dense forest, the ruined castle on the hill, the graveyard, etc. The Macabre seeks and hunts a victim who is usually an upstanding pillar of the community. After observing the victim's habits, the fiend then uses his bizarre spells to wreck the victim's health, standing in the community, marriage, sanity, etc.; hopefully causing society to ostracize the victim. Once the victim is separated from civilization's protections, the fiend slays him (for experience and pleasure). Then he often turns the corpse into some form of created Undead, adding to his retinue of abominations.

NOTE: *On Player Characters: Any player wanting to play this class should have some strange background:*

1. Madness in the family past

2. Great Evil in the family past

3. The family is outlandish, eccentric, etc.

4. PC is an orphan reared by a madman, etc.

The Macabre is a variant profession of *Necromancer*.

Macabre Base Spell Lists

Necromancy (Evil Cleric Base)   *Disease* (Evil Cleric Base)

Physical Erosion (Evil Magician Base)

Soul Destruction (Sorcerer Base)

Mind Subversion (Evil Mentalist Base)

Weapon Skills: 5, 7, 9, 9, 9, 15	
Maneuvering in Armor:	**Magical Skills:**
Soft Leather 2/*	Spell Lists 4/*
Rigid Leather 3/*	Runes 4
Chain 4/*	Staves & Wands 4
Plate 5/*	Channeling 4
	Directed Spells 8
Special Skills:	**General Skills:**
Ambush 6	Climbing 4
Linguistics 2/*	Swimming 3
Adrenal Moves 4	Riding 6
Adrenal Defense 20	Disarming Traps 5
Martial Arts 5	Picking Locks 5
Body Development 3/7	Stalk & Hide 2/5
	Perception 3

Other Skills: All other skill costs are identical to the Necromancer's development point cost.

Prime Requisites: EM/IN

Level Bonuses:	
Academic Skills ....+1	Base Spell Casting ....+2
Arms Law Combat ....+1	Body Development ......+1
Directed Spell Skills .....+1	Item Skills ....+1
Magical Skills ....+2	Subterfuge Skills ....+1

2.25 MONTEBANC

The Montebanc is a semi-spell user of the realms of Arms and Mentalism who combines minor magic with larceny to act as a "con man". The combination of subterfuge skills with Mentalism spells allows a Montebanc to create illusions, to disguise himself, and to do some minor detecting and appraisal. The Montebanc fights and maneuvers as well as most semi-spell users.

The Montebanc is a variant profession of *Rogue* and *Bard*.

MONTEBANC BASE SPELL LISTS

Mystic Escapes	*Appraisals*	*Beguiling Ways*
Lesser Illusions (Open Essence)		*Disguise Mastery*

Weapon Skills: 3/9, 4, 6, 6, 6, 9

Maneuvering in Armor:		Magical Skills:	
Soft Leather	2/*	Spell Lists	4/*
Rigid Leather	3/*	Runes	5
Chain	4/*	Staves & Wands	6
Plate	5/*	Channeling	13
		Directed Spells	10

Special Skills:		General Skills:	
Ambush	4	Climbing	3/9
Linguistics	3/*	Swimming	2/5
Adrenal Moves	2/7	Riding	2/6
Adrenal Defense	15	Disarming Traps	2/6
Martial Arts	3	Picking Locks	2/6
Body Development	3/8	Stalk & Hide	2/5
		Perception	2/4

Other Skills: Refer to Development Point Costs given below for those skills unique to the Montebanc Profession. All other skill costs are identical to the Rogue's development point cost.
Prime Requisites: PR/AG

Combat Skills:		Athletic Skills:	
All as a Bard	varies	All as a Bard	varies

Gymnastic Skills:		Social Skills:	
All as a Bard	varies	All as a Bard	varies

Magical Skills:		Subterfuge Skills:	
All as a Bard	varies	Acting	1/2
		Disguise	1/3

Level Bonuses:			
Arms Law Combat	+1	Base Spell Casting	+1
Body Development	+1	Linguistic Skills	+1
Perception Skills	+1	Social Skills	+2
Subterfuge Skills	+3		

2.26 MOON MAGE

The Moon Mage is a semi-spell user of the Realms of Arms and Channeling who specializes in the manipulation of *moon magic*. Moon magic emphasizes changing states: A Moon Mage's power ebbs and flows with the phases of the moon. During a full moon phase, light based Moon Mages are at full power while the dark based Moon Mages are at their weakest point. During new moon phases, the opposite is true. The Moon Mages also have a grey based cult which is at full power during half moons and is weakest during the full moon and new moon phases.

The Moon Mages are a variant profession of *Dervish*.

MOON MAGE BASE SPELL LISTS

Metamorphose — Ability to change appearance, mental condition, spiritual side and/or internal power matrix of themselves or others.

Moon Madness — Control over changing moods allowing them to influence, change and set them as they wish. They also have limited control over suicidal tendencies.

Moon Mastery — Magic which is related to the moon and it phases.

Two Additional Base Lists: Normally 2 additional base lists may be chosen based on the type of Moon Mage: Light, Grey, or Dark.

Additional Light based Moon Mage Spell Lists:

Light Law (Magician Base)	*Light Molding* (Illusionist Base)
Brilliance (Open Mentalist)	*Light's Way* (Open Channeling)
Starlights (Astrologer Base)	*Brilliance Magic* (Crystal Mage Base)

Additional Grey based Moon Mage Spell Lists:

Cloaking (Open Mentalist)	*Shifting* (Closed Mentalist)
Nature's Guises (Ranger Base)	*Mystical Change* (Mystic Base)
Hiding (Mystic Base)	*Confusing Ways* (Mystic Base)
Guises (Illusionist Base)	*Lesser Illusions* (Open Essence)
Ethereal Mastery (Arcane)	*Shapechanging Ways* (Arcane)
Glamours (Witch Base)	*Nature's Forms* (Druid Base)
Distractions (Nightblade Base)	*Phantom's Face* (Nightblade Base)

Additional Dark based Moon Mage Spell Lists:

Dark Lore (Evil Cleric Base)	*Dark Summons* (Evil Magician Base)
Dark Law (Necromancer Base)	*Dark Channels* (Evil Cleric Base)
Dark Contacts (Evil Magician Base)	*Darkness* (Evil Magician Base)

Weapon Skills: 3/9, 5, 6, 6, 9, 15

Maneuvering in Armor:		Magical Skills:	
Soft Leather	5/*	Spell Lists	4/*
Rigid Leather	7/*	Runes	3/7
Chain	9/*	Staves & Wands	3/7
Plate	20	Channeling	2/4
		Directed Spells	3/7

Special Skills:		General Skills:	
Ambush	6	Climbing	5
Linguistics	2/*	Swimming	3
Adrenal Moves	3/7	Riding	3
Adrenal Defense	20	Disarming Traps	6
Martial Arts	2/5	Picking Locks	8
Body Development	3/5	Stalk & Hide	4
		Perception	2/5

Other Skills: Refer to Development Point Costs given below for those skills unique to the Moon Mage Profession. All other skill costs are identical to the Dervish's DP cost.
Prime Requisites: IN/SD

Animal Skills:		Concentration Skills:	
Animal Handling	2/7	Body Damage Stabilize	2/6
Animal Training	3	Dowsing	2/7
Beast Master	3/5		
Driving	2/7	Evaluation Skills:	
Herding	2/5	Appraisal	2/5
Loading	2/6	Metal Evaluation	3/6
		Stone Evaluation	3/6

Level Bonuses:			
Arms Law Combat	+1	Athletic Skills	+1
Base Spell Casting	+1	Body Development	+1
Concentration Skills	+1	Directed Spells	+1
Linguistic Skills	+1	Magical Skills	+2
Social Skills	+1		

Profession "Laws": Sleuth 13

2.27 SLEUTH

The Sleuth is a semi-spell user of the realms of Arms and Channeling whose capabilities deal with detecting, analyzing, measuring, escaping, and sensing past and future events.

NOTE: *In worlds in which Delvers and Nightblades do not fit in, the Sleuth profession assumes some of their potential abilities. Thus the Sleuth need not fit our conception of a detective/gumshoe. A Sleuth is merely a character who detects, analyzes, and draws conclusions.*

NOTE: *The "alignment" of a Sleuth will usually dictate his mode of operation. Sleuths who are "lawful" will work with the local constabulary in solving crimes. "Lawful & good" Sleuths are more interested in helping people, even criminals! "Lawful & neutral" (neither good nor evil) Sleuths serve (blind) Justice, indiscriminately seeking law-breakers. "Lawful & Evil" Sleuths believe the Ends justify the Means and tend to be corrupt (e.g., bribes, hush-money, drug-dealing by selective busting, etc.; in fact all potential abuses of power). "Non-lawful but good" Sleuths are usually Consulting Detectives or Private Eyes, working for individual clients. "Neutral (with respect to law and chaos) & good" Sleuths may sometimes operate outside the law, in a "good" cause. "Chaotic & good" Sleuths usually operate outside the law, if that is the easiest way to protect an individual's rights/interests (their client); they may even seem to be a criminal to the local constabulary!).*

The Sleuth is a variant profession of *Bard*.

SLEUTH BASE SPELL LISTS

Analyses   *Sleuth's Senses*
Escaping Ways   *Time's Sense*

Mannish Ways: As the Delver Base List, except that there is no third level spell and the fifth level spell is *Spell Signature Feel* (from Delving Law, **RMCI**).

Optional Additional Base Lists: If the GM allows it, a Sleuth may choose 5 lists from the 5 above and the three optional lists below. The two lists not chosen are treated as Open lists for the Sleuth:

Distractions (Nightblade Base)
Phantom's Face (Nightblade Base)
Phantom Movement (Nightblade Base)

Weapon Skills: 3/7, 5, 7, 7, 7, 10	
Maneuvering in Armor:	**Magical Skills:**
Soft Leather 1/*	Spell Lists 4/*
Rigid Leather 2/*	Runes 4
Chain 4/*	Staves & Wands 6
Plate 8	Channeling 3
	Directed Spells 10
Special Skills:	**General Skills:**
Ambush 3	Climbing 3/9
Linguistics 2/*	Swimming 2/6
Adrenal Moves 2/7	Riding 2/6
Adrenal Defense 20	Disarming Traps 3/6
Martial Arts 4	Picking Locks 3/6
Body Development 3/8	Stalk & Hide 2/5
	Perception 1/3

Other Skills: Refer to Development Point Costs given below for those skills unique to the Sleuth Profession. All other skill costs are identical to the Bard's development point cost.
Prime Requisites: IN/RE

Academic Skills:	**Athletic Skills:**
Heraldry 2/5	Dance 1/5
Philosophy/Religious .. 2/6	
Racial History 2/6	**Combat Skills:**
	Subduing 1/5
Concentration Skills:	**Evaluation Skills:**
Mnemonics 1/5	Appraisal 2/5
Perception Skills:	**General Skills:**
Poison Perception 1/5	Advertising 2/5
Read Tracks 1/3	Painting 2/6
Surveillance 1/2	Play Instrument, all 3/6
Tracking 1/5	
Social Skills:	**Subterfuge Skills:**
Gambling 1/5	Falsification 1/5
Interrogation 1/2	Streetwise 1/3
Linguistic Skills:	
All Linguistic Skills 2/6	
Level Bonuses:	
Arms Law Combat .... +1	Base Spell Casting .... +1
Perception .... +3	Social Skills .... +3
Subterfuge Skills .... +2	

2.3 THE "PROFESSIONAL"

The "Professional" represents those characters with jobs and callings, as well as amateurs and professionals in some trade. This class is a powerful tool to represent various NPCs (sailors, inventors, blacksmiths, etc.). The "Professional" Profession is a variant of the "No Profession" Profession. The development costs are the same except for the following:

Primary Magical Skills — Increased as shown below

Any one skill or group of skills (GM discretion) — 2/* (may not include Primary, Combat, or Magical Skills).

Thus, the character may excel at any one (or more) ability: that is, his *Professional skill(s)*. Some of the variant professions presented in this product can also be easily represented using the "Professional" profession. For example, a "sailor" Professional might have a "sailing" Development point cost of 2/* (perhaps also, "rowing," "navigation," "rope mastery," etc. would cost 2/*). Similarly, an "Acrobat" professional might have 2/* for Acrobatics, Contortions, Diving and Tumbling; perhaps also for Adrenal Moves.

> **NOTE:** *If the skill group chosen is "Linguistics" (i.e., languages), the GM may choose to lower the cost to 1/* or even .5/*.*

> **NOTE:** *The "Professional" Profession could also be called the "Specialist," since this class specializes in one skill.*

> **NOTE:** *The "No-Profession" Profession is altered for the Professional in order to represent people who are relatively low-level and yet are very good at one activity. In order to balance the power of the 2/* cost skill, the Spell List Chance cost is 8/*. This greater cost means that there will be far fewer "Professional" characters with spells than "No-Profession" characters.*

> **NOTE:** *It is very important that one remembers that the 2/* cost skill(s) cannot be Primary, Combat, or Magical Skill(s).*

The Professional is a variant profession of the *"No Profession"* profession.

Weapon Skills: 3/6, 3/6, 4, 5, 6, 7

Maneuvering in Armor:		Magical Skills:	
Soft Leather	1/*	Spell Lists	8/*
Rigid Leather	2/*	Runes	4
Chain	3/*	Staves & Wands	4
Plate	4/*	Channeling	4
		Directed Spells	4

Special Skills:		General Skills:	
Ambush	3/6	Climbing	3/6
Linguistics	2/*	Swimming	2/6
Adrenal Moves	2/6	Riding	2/6
Adrenal Defense	15	Disarming Traps	3/6
Martial Arts	3/6	Picking Locks	3/6
Body Development	2/6	Stalk & Hide	2/6
		Perception	2/6

Other Skills: All skill costs other than the Professional skill(s) are identical to the No Profession's development point cost.
Prime Requisites: The stats that are used for stat bonuses for the Professional skill are the Prime Requisites; if there are a group of Professional skills, choose the 2 most common stats.

Level Bonuses: If Level Bonuses are used, Professionals use the No Profession Bonuses with the following exceptions:

• Allocate a +3/lvl bonus to their Professional skills

• Reduce three of the normal No Profession +1 bonuses to 0.

Thus, an "Acrobat" professional might have +3/Lvl for Acrobatics, Contortions, Diving and Tumbling; perhaps also for Adrenal Moves. However, he would have to reduce his Level Bonus in three areas from +1 to 0.

2.4 CRYSTAL MAGE

The Crystal Mage is a hybrid spell user of the Realms of Essence and Channeling. His ability to manipulate the deep earth elementals and mastery of diamonds makes the Crystal Mage well suited for volcanic areas and deep underground adventures.

CRYSTAL MAGE BASE SPELL LISTS

Crystal Mastery	*Deep Earth Healing* (Channeling Based)
Crystal Runestone	*Deep Earth Commune* (Channeling Based)
Crystal Magic	*Earthblood's Ways* (As the Arcane List)
Crystal Power	*Brilliance Magic* (Essence Based)
Fiery Ways	

The Crystal Mage will not under normal circumstances learn or master all of Crystal Mage Base Spell Lists. GMs should assign each Crystal Mage his own unique set of base lists.

Option 1: The Crystal Mage is the most common version of those Mages that rely on a focus to channel their powers. Depending upon the GMs world scheme, they are also known as Ruby Enchanters, Diamond Mages, Jewelled Sorcerers, Emerald Master, Sapphire Lord, etc. The Crystal Mage should be limited to one type of focus (i.e., rock crystal, quartz, sapphires, etc.) The GM should be warned that the more exotic gems and stones can quickly unbalance his world's economic system. It is recommended that if a diamond, ruby, sapphire, or emerald is allowed to be the mage's focus, the focus either is so common as to be almost worthless or completely undesired so that it's not wanted by anyone in the community but the Mage. The focus should also be of a special color, specific size and perhaps within a specific purity range in order for it to be allowed as a focus.

Option 2: If the GM allows a Crystal Mage to use more than one type of gem or stone as a focus, they should be ranked in order of importance. The least important focus should be the "work horse". This focus would be used for day to day magical chores. Normally it would not be used with any spell over 10th level. The next least important focus should be used with the spells of 11th level to 20th level. The most important focus should be for 25th, or higher, spells. It would also be used for holy duties, very special occasions, etc.

Weapon Skills: 9; 12; 15; 20; 20; 20

Maneuvering in Armor:		Magical Skills:	
Soft Leather	10	Spell Lists	1/*
Rigid Leather	12	Runes	2/6
Chain	15	Staves & Wands	2/5
Plate	20	Channeling	8
		Directed Spells	3/8

Special Skills:		General Skills:	
Ambush	9	Climbing	5
Linguistics	2/*	Swimming	3
Adrenal Moves	5	Riding	4
Adrenal Defense	20	Disarming Traps	6
Martial Arts	9	Picking Locks	4
Body Development	8	Stalk & Hide	5
		Perception	2

Other Skills: see *the Master Development Point Cost Table in Rolemaster Companion II.*
Prime Requisites: EM/IN.

2.5 MAGUS (Cabbalist)

The Magus is a spell user who studies and utilizes magical words, names, and runes (i.e. individual letters or symbols). Thus the Magus is also referred to as a Rune Master, Cabbalist, or Power Word Mage. The foundation of this art is the fact that a name or word often contains something of the Essence of the thing or person it represents. Someone who knows the *Truename* of a being may exercise great control or even domination over the unfortunate being (assuming the controller knows how). Even individual letters, or runes, are can be tied to the general forces of nature, fate, and emotion (e.g., harvest, grief, ice, doom, etc.) or can be infused with significant magical power of their own (i.e., spells).

So, the Magus is a specialist in crafting spells, power words, and items which utilize the magic of the written and engraved word. Additionally, and obviously, the Magus also becomes a master of languages: human, cryptic, and magical.

As a spell user, the Magus is somewhat unusual. Because he is so interested in the alchemy of permanently enruned items (which are greater but more costly than the temporary runes of the Bladerunes Arcane spell list), he is much more effective in the use of a limited number of weapons than other mages, while sacrificing proficiency in directed spells, channeling, and some other magical crafts. In terms of combat, the Magus is much more dangerous if he is prepared ahead to receive his enemies than if he must act quickly.

There are several different types of Magi based upon their realms of power. The most common are hybrid spell users of the realms of Essence and Channeling. However, some Magi are pure spell users of Essence or pure spell users of Channeling.

NOTE: *Because of the difficulty of playing a Magus and the potential power inherent in this profession, GMs and players should carefully confer before starting a character with this profession.*

Magus Base Spell Lists

Runes & Symbols *Linguistics*
Signs of Power *Command Words*
Power Words *Spirit Runes*

NOTE: *See Sections 4.1 for a description of the Great Commands referred to on the Command Words spell list. See Section 4.2 for a description of the Spirit Runes referred to on the Spirit Runes list.*

Weapon Skills: 4/10; 8; 8; 8; 15; 15	
Maneuvering in Armor: Soft Leather .... 7 (4/*) Rigid Leather .... 7 (5/*) Chain .... 8 (6/*) Plate 10 (7/*)	**Magical Skills:** Spell Lists .... 1/* Runes .... 1/2 Staves & Wands . 1/4 (2/5) Channeling .... 13 (5) Directed Spells 3/8
Special Skills: Ambush .... 9 Linguistics .... 1/* Adrenal Moves .... 6 Adrenal Defense .... 20 Martial Arts .... 9 Body Development 6	**General Skills:** Climbing .... 7 Swimming .... 3 Riding .... 3 Disarming Traps .... 8 Picking Locks .... 8 Stalk & Hide .... 6 Perception 3

Note: *Parenthetical values are for Pure Channeling Magi. All other values are for Pure Essence or Hybrid Essence/Channeling Magi.*

Other Skills: As a Bard
Prime Requisites: EM/IN (Hybrid), EM/RE (Pure Essence), IN/RE (Pure Channeling).

Level Bonuses:	
Academic Skills .... +2	Base Spell Casting .... +1
Directed Spells .... +1	Linguistic Skills .... +2
Magical Skills .... +3	Perception .... +1

2.4 DREAM LORD

The Dream Lord hybrid spell user who specializes in the manipulation of dreams, dream worlds, dream states, and other mind bending Realms. Dream Lords are often mistaken for Illusionists or Shamans. Many Dream Lords are loners (who wants to hang around someone who sleeps most of the time).

Option 1: The Dream Lord is a variant profession of *Illusionist*, but combines the Realms of Essence and Mentalism.

Option 2: The Dream Lord is a variant profession of *Shaman*, but combines the Realms of Channeling and Mentalism.

DREAM LORD BASE SPELL LISTS

Dream Guard — The spells on this list serve the Dream Lord in protecting his dream worlds from unwanted tampering, observation, or intrusion.

Dream Law — The spells on this list give a Dream Lord his base power in the "real" world. They allow him to use dreams to divine the future/past, to cause nightmares, to cause sleep, or to call forth a dream warrior for attack or protection.

Dream Lore — The spells on this list allow a Dream Lord to access the "dream plane".

Dream State — The spells on this list give a Dream Lord the ability to summon non-intelligent and intelligent helpers. They also provide the ability to produce dream state items for protection, basic needs, and comfort.

Illusionist variant: Normally two additional base spell lists may be chosen from the Illusionist Base Spell Lists or from the Mentalist Base Spell Lists.

Shaman variant: Normally two additional base spell lists may be chosen from the Shaman Base Spell List or the Mentalist Base Spell List.

ILLUSIONIST VARIANT

Weapon Skills: 9, 20, 20, 20, 20, 20

Maneuvering in Armor:	Magical Skills:
Soft Leather 9	Spell Lists 1/*
Rigid Leather 9	Runes 2/5
Chain 10	Staves & Wands 2/4
Plate 11	Channeling 8
	Directed Spells 3/7

Special Skills:	General Skills:
Ambush 6	Climbing 8
Linguistics 2/*	Swimming 3
Adrenal Moves 3/6	Riding 4
Adrenal Defense 20	Disarming Traps 8
Martial Arts 9	Picking Locks 8
Body Development 8	Stalk & Hide 5
	Perception 3

Other Skills: Refer to Development Point Costs given below for those skills unique to the Dream Lord Profession. All other skill costs are identical to the Illusionist's development point cost.

Prime Requisites: EM/PR

SHAMAN VARIANT

Weapon Skills: 6, 7, 9, 9, 9, 20

Maneuvering in Armor:	Magical Skills:
Soft Leather 2/*	Spell Lists 1/*
Rigid Leather 4/*	Runes 2/5
Chain 10	Staves & Wands 2/4
Plate 11	Channeling 2/4
	Directed Spells 3/7

Special Skills:	General Skills:
Ambush 6	Climbing 6
Linguistics 2/*	Swimming 3
Adrenal Moves 3/6	Riding 4
Adrenal Defense 20	Disarming Traps 8
Martial Arts 6	Picking Locks 8
Body Development 4	Stalk & Hide 4
	Perception 3

Other Skills: Refer to Development Point Costs given below for those skills unique to the Dream Lord Profession. All other skill costs are identical to the Shaman's development point cost.

Prime Requisites: IN/PR

OTHER SKILL COSTS

Academic Skills:	Animal Skills:
Mapping 3/6	Animal Handling 4
Planetology 2/4	Beast Master 4
Xeno-Lores 2/6	Herding 4

Perception Skills:	Linguistic Skills:
Detecting Traps 3/7	Lip Reading 3/6
Lie Perception 2/5	Mimicry 2/4
Poison Perception 4	Propaganda 3
Sense Ambush/Assassin .4	Tale Tells 3/6
Surveillance 3	Trading 3/6
Tracking 4	

Social Skills:	Subterfuge Skills:
Diplomacy 3/9	Acting 3/6
Leadership 3/7	Disguise 3/7
Seduction 3/6	Mimery 3/5
	Pick Pockets 3/7

Deadly Skills:
Trickery 3/5
Silent Kill 4
Use/Remove Poison 4

Level Bonuses:	
Academic Skills .... +1	Base Spell Casting .... +1
Concentration Skills ..... +2	Directed Spells .... +1
General Skills .... +2	Magical Skills .... +2
Medical Skills .... +1	

3.0 OPTIONAL ARMS "LAWS"

3.1 SIMPLIFIED INITIATIVE

As an alternative to the present initiative system, a GM can incorporate the following rules into his campaign:

1. Every PC and NPC should calculate his initiative bonus (**IB**). This is done by dividing the combatant's Quickness Bonus by five, and rounding to the nearest whole number. This can be a positive or negative number.
2. When combat occurs, each round each combatant involved must roll 1D10 and add their IB. The total is the combatant's Initiative roll (**IR**). If the IR is less than one, then treat it as one. If the IR is greater than ten, then make it ten.
3. After the IRs have been determined, the GM begins the combat round with the combatants who have the highest rolls. Characters who have the same initiative roll act at the same time.
4. Spell Casting, Missile fire, Maneuvers, and Melee attacks occur when one's IR is reached.
5. Any spells that take multiple rounds to cast will go off on the appropriate round as indicated by the IR rolled for the round during which the spell preparation started.
6. Any combatant is allowed to delay his action and act after his IR would normally allow him to act; he may chose to act when ever the GM calls for actions from combatants with an IR less than his. For example, character who has an IR of 8 may choose to hold an attack in order to wait to see what someone else is doing; later attacking as if his IR were 7, 6, 5, 4, 3, 2, or 1.
7. Spell casters who take physical damage during the current round, before they are allowed to act, may not cast spells.

Option: To speed up combat, the GM may decide to lump together a group of NPCs into one IR roll if every NPC has the same initiative bonus.

EXAMPLE: *Marcus, a powerful Magician, and Nirrad, a mean Barbarian, encounter a group of four Orcs while exploring a cave. The GM has each combatant roll initiative. Marcus has a +20 Quickness bonus, which gives him an initiative bonus of +4. Neither Nirrad nor the Orcs have quickness bonuses, and therefore they don't have an IB. Marcus rolls an 8 which is modified to a 12 because of his initiative bonus. Because 10 is the highest number allowed, Marcus has a modified initiative roll of 10. Nirrad rolls a three for initiative, and the Orcs get: 9,7,3,1. Marcus acts first this round, and decides to cast a spell. The spell will take him one round to cast, and therefore it will have effect with an IR of 10 during the next round. The Orcs who rolled a 9 and 7 act next. They both throw daggers at Marcus, hoping to cancel his spell. Nirrad and one Orc act on phase 3, and both attack one another with swords. Finally the last Orc who rolled a one acts, and takes a jab at Nirrad with his spear.*

3.2 SURPRISE

One major area that the standard *Rolemaster* rules neglect is surprise. Surprise can occur in almost any situation, from an ambush to a situation where two groups stumble blindly upon one another. It is therefore important that the GM has a method of determining if one side surprises the other.

When using these guidelines to determine surprise, the GM should have the character with the highest Perception skill (be it hearing, sight or smell) from each side roll 1D100 (open ended) and add their Perception skill. If there is a difference of 30 or more, then the side with the advantage gets one entire round to act without the other side being able to react. See the chart below for the various modifiers.

NOTE: *For a character to apply his Perception bonus he must be unstunned and conscious.*

Option 1: The GM may decide that one side cannot be surprised because they are aware of the other. In this case, if the other side wins the surprise roll, treat the result as if neither side has surprise.

Option 2: The GM can require each member of each group to make a Perception roll **and** average each group's rolls. If a group member's roll is 30 less than the opposing group's average, that group member is surprised and may not take any action on the first round of combat.

| SURPRISE CHART ||
Situation	Modifier
Ambush is set	+50
Aware of opponent	+30
Everyone is quiet	+10
Someone is in metal armor	-10
Someone is talking loudly	-30
Everyone asleep	-50
Note: *All modifiers are cumulative.*	

3.3 SELF-RELOADING WEAPONS

A self-reloading weapon reloads itself and is ready for another shot almost immediately after being fired. Most guns fall into this category: revolvers, automatic rifles, multiple-shot shotguns, automatic pistols, etc. In *Space Master*, self-reloading weapons may usually fire twice per round.

The standard *Rolemaster* combat system assumes that missile weapons are not self-reloading and thus have only one Missile Phase per round. If a GM introduces self-reloading weapons into his game, he may want to modify the standard Battle Round Sequence and insert a second Missile Phase and a second Missile Result Phase after the Movement/Maneuver Phase.

If a GM has *Space Master* available, he may use the Battle Round Sequence rules in Player Book Section 13.1; otherwise, he can use the following guidelines.

If a character fires a self-reloading weapon in the *First Missile Phase*, he may later in the same round:
- Melee with a -50 Mod to OB; **or**
- Move/Maneuver at 50% of normal; **or**
- Fire normally in the Second Missile Phase.

A character may **not** fire in the *Second Missile Phase* if during the round he has:
- Used a weapon that is **not** self-reloading; **or**
- Cast a spell; **or**
- Moved/maneuvered more than 50% of normal; **or**
- Fired in the First Missile Phase and moved/maneuvered; **or**
- Been incapacitated and/or failed an orientation or maneuver roll.

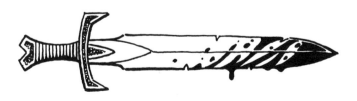

3.4 NEW WEAPONS TABLE

Weapon Name	Type	WT	LGN	F	Range Mod. (distance)				Table Used	20-17	16-13	12-9	8-5	4-1	Special
Cazingal	TH	2.5	2	3	-0(25')	-10(50')	-20(50')	-30(100')	Handaxe	-10	-10	-5	-5	-5	Dwarven.
Bulbova	2H	4.5	3	6	-5(10')	-25(25')	-50(50')	—	Battle Axe	-10	-5	0	+5	+5	Dwarven.
	1HE									-15	-10	-5	0	0	
Katari	1HE/TH	1	1.5	4	-10(25')	-25(40')	-50(100')	—	Dagger	-10	+5	+5	+10	+10	Used by Easterners and Desert Folk.
Jambiva	1HE/TH	1.7	1	3	-15(10')	-25(25')	-50(50')	—	Dagger	+5	+5	+5	0	0	Used by Desert Folk.
Naginate	PA	5	7	6	—	—	—	—	Polearm	-5	0	+5	+10	+10	Used by Easterners.
Runk	PA	6	7	7	—	—	—	—	Polearm	+10	+10	+5	+5	0	Used by Desert Folk.
Dalwal	2H	4	5.5	7	—	—	—	—	2H Sword	0	0	+5	+10	+15	Used by Desert Folk.
Goodar	1HE	3	3	4	—	—	—	—	Falchion	+5	+5	0	0	-5	Used by Desert Folk.
Killaj	1HE	5.5	3.5	6	—	—	—	—	Scimitar	+10	+5	0	0	+5	Used by Desert Folk.
Sultari	1HE	3.5	5	5	—	—	—	—	Broadsword	-5	-5	0	+5	+5	Used by Desert Folk.
Slan Mahrr	1HE/TH	2.5	3.5	5	-15(20')	-30(30')	-50(50')	—	Broadsword	-10	0	+5	+10	+20	Weapon of Honor.
Slan Orr	1HE	2.5	1.5	2	—	—	—	—	Shortsword	-20	-15	0	+15	+30	Weapon of Honor, Slash Criticals only.
Slan Shyrr	1HE/TH	2.5	2.5	6	-15(10')	-30(20')	-50(30')	—	Rapier	0	+5	+5	+10	+20	Weapon of Honor.
Correlledge	1HE	4	4	5	—	—	—	—	Broadsword	+10	+5	0	+5	+10	Elvish Longsword.
Dragonblade	1HE	4	3.5	4	—	—	—	—	Broadsword	+5	0	0	+5	+5	Used by Easterners.
Zharenzak	2H	10	4	5	—	—	—	—	Battle Axe	+5	+10	+5	0	0	Dwarven. An "E" critical Destroys part of any armor/shield struck for a +15 next strike.
Klhaizail	1HC	6	3	5	-10(10')	-20(20')	-40(30')	-80(40')	War Hammer	0	+10	+5	+5	+5	Dwarven. If desired, can be used to cause an unbalancing critical in addition to the regular critical (equal severity). However, this drops the users initiative next round by 75 points.
Khazorzim	1HC	7	3	10	—	—	—	—	Morning Star	-10	+10	-5	0	+5	Dwarven. Give double criticals (roll each critical twice). Also called Twin Star.

3.5 MOUNTED COMBAT

Some of the rules for mounted combat in *Rolemaster* are vague and left up to the individual GM. The rules state that a mounted rider receives a +20 bonus for the charge, but never specify as to what is considered a charge. The rules do not specify how much a horse can accelerate or decelerate in a round and as to what kind of attack a horse can make while it has a rider on its back. The most detail on these issues is found in *Creatures and Treasures* in the section on Riding and Draft Animals which sets standards for the mount's combat abilities.

In order to clarify the process of mounted combat, let us study the following situation:

EXAMPLE: *A mounted human is on a lesser warhorse, in full plate armor, and has a lance. There is a single Orc with a spear standing next to a large boulder. There is 500 feet of distance between them and neither are moving.*

The man will charge the Orc, but what happens if the Orc moves to where the boulder is behind him so that the rider will not be able to stop before he hits it? What happens if the Orc sets his spear for the charge and attacks the horse? How much distance does a rider need to accelerate and decelerate for the combat? How fast must the horse be moving to get the charge bonus? Does the horse get to attack? To answer these questions let's set up some guidelines.

ACCELERATION & DECELERATION

Acceleration: 2 "pace categories" a round

Deceleration: 3 "pace categories" a round

First let's look at acceleration/deceleration. *C&T* states that a lesser warhorse can walk at a rate of 90 feet per round. Its maximum pace is a dash. This means it can run at 450 feet per round or about 30 mph. The question is how long will it take to make that horse go from a dead stop to a full run? A horse can probably build up to its full speed in three rounds or thirty seconds. Using this as a base, let's say that a horse can accelerate 2 "pace categories" a round. This means that from a dead stop, a horse can go to a fast walk/jog the first round, a sprint/fast run the second round, and a full speed dash on the third round. A horse can slow down a little faster than it can accelerate, so allow a horse to slow down 3 pace categories at a time, coming to a dead stop from a full run in two rounds.

THE CHARGE BONUS

Thrusting Weapons: +1 bonus for each 10 ft/round of speed

Other Weapons: +1 bonus for each 20 ft/round of speed

The next question should be where in this course of acceleration does the +20 charge bonus kick in? A charge uses the horses momentum to add power to the attack, so even a little momentum will aid the attack. As a charge bonus, give a +1 bonus for each 10 feet per round of speed the horse is moving. This allows a lesser warhorse to have a bonus from 1 to 45.

PROBLEMS: *This only takes into account velocity, not mass. This means the faster the charge, the more devastating the attack.*

- On the other side of this, a spear set against a charge should have the same bonus against the charger. The spear should most likely attack the horse instead of the rider.

- A horse unable to stop before hitting something (the horse will probably attempt to avoid this) should be attacked with a fall/crush attack using the charge bonus as if it were feet fallen as an attack modifier.

- In order to charge, the rider must be using a weapon adapted for thrusting to get the charge bonus. These are weapons such as lance, spear, sabre, and rapier. These are just a few but the weapon must have a sharp point for thrusting. Other weapons should be given a bonus but not as great of a bonus as these weapons. After all, getting hit with a mace wielded by a man on a horse running 30 mph is going to hurt more than a man on foot winging his mace at you, but this attack is not as devastating as the lance attack. A non-thrusting weapon bonus for the charge should be half of the bonus of a thrusting weapons attack bonus, or a +1 for every 20 feet per round of speed the horse is moving.

- The horse should be allowed to attack with its trample attack, with the charge bonus being added to its attack bonus. All other horse attacks should follow the rules in *Creatures and Treasures*.

THE CHARGE RIDING MANEUVER

In order to make a charge, a rider must make a riding maneuver to determine his total OB. A rider's OB should be figured with the speed bonus added to the OB, then a roll should be made on the moving maneuver chart to get the final attack bonus. An example of this would be a rider with a +55 OB with lance. Charging a medium warhorse at full speed for an additional +45 OB, he would have a +100 OB. If his riding skill check resulted in a 50% action, then his OB would be only a +50. This rider obviously had trouble of some kind in the charge. If the rider had a riding skill check of 120%, then his bonus would be +120. This rider is having a good day!

THE DIFFICULTY OF THE CHARGE

How hard of a maneuver is charging the horse? Warhorses already have an easier time than most horses because of the riding bonus for the horse. This means that the difficulty should be based on how hard it is to get a horse to charge. To simply charge a horse against a single person should be an easy maneuver. This could be made more difficult by other factors. Charging a horse into a fire or against a natural enemy such as a lion should make for harder maneuvers.

CONCLUSION

Hopefully, these guidelines have answered many questions about mounted combat. The mounted soldier is an important part of any fantasy campaign and there will be many situations that call for judgement calls on the part of the campaign's master. These rules as all rules should be used only as the campaign's designer sees fit.

3.6 A SUPER-FAST COMBAT SYSTEM

The standard *Rolemaster* combat system is designed for role playing situations with a small to medium sized group. With large groups combat can slow play, and "dungeon" adventures can seem to take forever. This section presents a "Super-fast System" that is based on a hit dice system and more infrequent criticals. For fast play, this system does require different "sized" dice (i.e., D4, D6, D8, D10, D12, and D20).

NOTE: *This system only approximates normal* **RM** *combat; so, before using it in his game, a GM should examine it very carefully and play a few rounds of combat.*

EXPLANATORY NOTES

The values for this system were derived from the combat charts in **Arms Law**, **Claw Law**, *and* **Spell Law**. *Since there are no less than 1000 numbers in the table cross-indexing armor with weapon types, it is likely that there are inconsistencies. If a value appears which seems way out of line, either consult the* **Rolemaster** *charts directly, or the charts presented in* **RMCI** *(pages 67 and 69).*

Yes, all those numbers in the hit dice column designate the hit dice to be rolled on a successful hit, with each number corresponding to one hit die of the type indicated. Therefore, the first line, "broadsword," indicates the rolling of five twelve-sided dice on a successful hit, and a falchion is four twelve-siders and two ten-siders.

Explanatory Note: *Most of the members of our gaming crew are long term FRP addicts who have zillions of polyhedrons left over from "other FRP systems." If your crew is not like ours, go ahead, help that nice game-store owner buy his next car!*

Although the points generated by the hit dice look extreme at first, please: (1) remember that several dice statistically tend toward median rather than polar values; (2) this system will most often kill on hit points rather than on criticals (contrary to the tendency of the normal **RM** *structure); and (3) the weapon/armor mods were based on the value of the first* **Critical** *value on the Rolemaster charts, not the first hit (i.e., it was supposed to be dangerous at that level). So, go ahead and give it a try! This really has been extensively play-tested! You may very much enjoy the increased tempo of combat, and getting to roll all those dice!*

Why the **Space Master** *"Power Sword"??? Well, we used it for things like giants' clubs, huge bows (like ballistae), dragon breath (from* **big** *dragons), kicks from demi-gods, fall-crush attacks involving skyscrapers, you know ...*

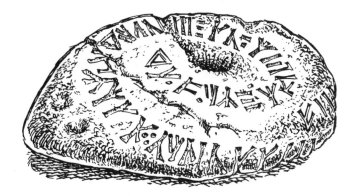

RESOLVING A SUPER-FAST COMBAT ATTACK

Italicized Factors may be found on the *Super-Fast Attack Chart*.

The Attack Roll:

1. Make a 1-100 open-ended high roll:
   a. If the result is in the *Fumble Range* for the attacker's weapon, the attack fails and this process stops immediately.
   b. If the original 1-100 roll was high enough the attacker rolls a Critical Success (see below); and the rest of this attack procedure proceeds normally.
2. Add the attacker's OB (offensive bonus).
3. Add attacker's *weapon modifier* for the target's armor type.
4. Subtract the target's DB (defensive bonus).
5. This total is the attack's "attack roll" and determines the success/failure of the attack.

The Hit-Dice Result:

1. If the final value is 75 or higher the attacker rolls and totals the *Hit-Dice* for his weapon.
2. The target's Armor Type (1-20) is subtracted from the Hit-Dice total to give the "Hits Delivered".
3. If the final value is 125 or higher the "Hits Delivered" is increased as indicated by the *Super-fast Hits Multiplier Chart*.
4. The target takes concussion hits equal to this "Hits Delivered" total.

CRITICAL SUCCESSES

Critical Successes are handled very differently from normal ***Rolemaster*** Critical Strikes, emphasizing speed in play:

1. Most attacks will not generate criticals at all in the normal ***Rolemaster*** sense. Instead, a very effective attack delivers more concussion hits. Effectively, this changes *RM* from a death-by-crit system to a death by concussion hit system.
2. All combatants still have an opportunity for an extremely effective attack if their percentile roll is high enough. The chance for a critical success is equal to the combatant's OB/10 (round down). This chance is figured on the "high end" of the die roll. For example, if a fighter has an OB of 123, his chance for a critical success is 12%, and he would be successful on any 1-100 attack roll which came up higher than 88 (88+). This chance can be increased by a successful ambush.
   A. The chance for a critical success against a large creature is half normal. In our example, only 6% (94+).
   B. Critical success against a super large creature is one-quarter normal. In our example, only 3% (97+).
   C. The actual crit roll is made on the new *Super-fast Critical Chart*. The critical die roll is modified by the critical success number (OB/10) and by ambush. In our example, the crit roll would be increased by 12 against a normal creature, 6 for a large, or 3 for a super-large.
   D. Generally, the exact details concerning the damage done to a target are figured after combat, and only then for PCs or other important beings to determine the appropriate healing measures, unless healing will be attempted during combat.
   E. A character may influence his critical towards a particular body area (aim) by 1 point after the GM determines the body area struck by the attacker.

ADDITIONAL NOTES

For Martial Arts and Claw Law type attacks limited by rank and size, when subtracting dice, always begin with the largest types.
   A. For Rank III / Large attacks roll 1 less hit die.
   B. For Rank II / Medium attacks roll 2 less hit dice.
   C. For Rank I / Small attacks roll 3 less hit dice.

Spells Which Only Generate Elemental Criticals: such as *Vacuums*, *Stun Clouds*, and *Death Clouds* can be rolled on the normal tables.

Creatures with special critical classes (see C&T) should be treated in the following manner:

Type I Creatures: increase basic hit capacity by 1/3.

Type II Creatures: increase basic hit capacity by 2/3.

Large Creatures: double basic hit capacity.

Super Large: triple basic hit capacity.

SUPER-FAST HITS MULTIPLIER CHART

01-74	Attack does no damage.
75-124	Attack does normal damage.
125-174	Hit dice value is x2.
175-224	Hit dice value is x3.
225-274	Hit dice value is x4.
275-324	Hit dice value is x5.
325-374	Hit dice value is x6.
etc.	etc.

SUPER-FAST CRITICAL SUCCESS CHART

01-44 Stagger — target is inactive for one round. This affects even those creatures not affected by stuns. A staggered creature is reduced to 25% activity for the round it is staggered or it may parry at 50%.

45-74 Injury — target suffers the following effects:
   1. 1 round of *stagger* (simple inactivity)
   2. 1-6 rounds of *stun* (if applicable).
   3. (10-60%) reduced ability.

75-94 Severe Injury — target suffers the following effects:
   1. 1 round of *stagger* (simple inactivity)
   2. (2-5)* x 2 rounds of *stun* (if applicable).
   3. (20-50%)* x 2 reduced ability.

95-98 Mortal Injury/Prolonged Death — soul-departure countdown begins after 2-12 rounds. In addition, make a roll for rounds of stun and percentage of activity reduction in the same way as for a *Severe Injury*.

99-00 Mortal Injury/Instant Death — soul-departure count-down begins next round.

* Use averaging dice to determine these values; i.e., roll D6: 1 results in 2, 2 results in 3, 3 results in 3, 4 results in 4, 5 results in 4, and 6 results in 5.

SPECIFIC DAMAGE DETERMINATION CHART

1D20 Roll	Body Area	Damage Type
1-3	Head	1. Bone (Cartilage 25%)
4	Neck	2. Muscle (Tendon 25%)
5-8	Upper Torso	3. Organ (Heart*)
9-11	Belly	4. Nerve (CNS**)
12	Groin	5. Blood (multiple vessels 25%)
13-14	R Arm	6. Multiple (1D4 rolls)
15-16	L Arm	
17-18	R Leg	* 50% of upper torso.
19-20	L Leg	** Refers to Central Nervous System. 80% of body areas 1-8.

Effects of Critical Successes	Bleeding
Instant Death: region Body Part destroyed.	20-50 per rnd.
Prolonged Death: region Shattered/Severed/etc.	11-20 per rnd.
Severe Injury: major damage.	5-10 per rnd.
Injury: minor damage.	1-4 per rnd.

Arms "Laws": Super-fast Attack Chart

SUPER-FAST ATTACK CHART
WEAPON MODIFIER BASED ON ARMOR TYPE

Attack/ Weapon	Armor Types																				Fumble Range	Hit-Dice
	1	2	3	4	5	6	7	8	9	10	11	12	13	14	15	16	17	18	19	20		
1-Handed Edged Weapons:																						
Dagger	5	15	0	-5	20	15	10	5	5	-5	-10	-15	-10	-20	-25	-30	-20	-30	-40	-45	1-1	3D12
Falchion	15	25	10	5	29	25	20	15	29	19	14	9	14	4	-01	-6	4	-6	-16	-21	1-5	4D12 & 2D10
Handaxe	10	20	5	0	25	20	15	10	28	18	13	8	15	5	0	-5	5	-15	-15	-20	1-4	4D10 & 2D8
Main Gauche	7	17	2	-3	22	17	12	7	10	0	-5	-10	-5	-15	-20	-25	-15	-25	-35	-40	1-2	1D20 & 2D10
Rapier	25	35	20	15	34	29	24	19	21	11	6	01	10	0	-5	-10	-5	-15	-25	-30	1-4	1D20 & 2D12
Scimitar	10	20	5	0	25	20	15	10	20	10	5	0	5	-5	-10	-15	0	-10	-20	-25	1-4	5D12
Broadsword	15	25	10	5	30	25	20	15	25	15	10	5	10	0	-5	-10	0	-10	-20	-25	1-3	5D12
Short Sword	20	30	15	10	30	25	20	15	20	10	5	0	0	-10	-15	-20	-10	-20	-30	-35	1-2	2D20 & D12
1-Handed Concussion Weapons:																						
Bare Fist	-10	0	-15	-20	-5	-10	-15	-20	-10	-20	-25	-30	-25	-35	-40	-45	-35	-45	-50	-50	1-1	1D20
Club	0	10	-5	-10	15	10	5	0	15	5	0	-5	0	-10	-15	-20	-5	-15	-25	-30	1-4	1D12 & 4D8
Mace	10	20	5	0	25	20	15	10	25	15	10	5	15	5	0	-5	5	-5	-15	-20	1-2	5D8 & 1D6
Morning Star	15	25	10	5	30	25	20	15	30	20	15	10	20	10	5	0	10	0	-10	-15	1-8	5D12 & 1D10
Warhammer	10	20	5	0	30	25	20	15	25	10	5	20	10	10	5	0	10	0	-10	-15	1-4	2D10 & 4D8
Whip	6	16	01	-4	20	15	10	5	15	0	-5	-10	-15	-25	-30	-35	-25	-35	-45	-50	1-6	2D12 & 2D10
Missile Weapons:																						
Bola	5	15	0	-5	20	15	10	5	15	5	0	-5	0	-10	-15	-20	-16	-26	-36	-41	1-7	5D8
Comp. Bow	6	18	5	0	28	28	25	20	20	15	10	5	20	10	5	0	5	-5	-15	-20	1-4	3D10 & 3D8
Hvy X-Bow	13	23	10	5	33	33	30	25	25	20	15	10	25	15	10	5	10	0	-10	-15	1-5	3D12 & 3D10
Lt X-Bow	8	18	5	0	25	25	20	15	20	15	10	5	13	5	0	-5	0	-10	-20	-25	1-5	2D10 & 4D8
Long Bow	10	20	7	7	28	28	28	23	20	18	13	8	23	13	8	3	8	-2	-12	-17	1-5	4D10 & 2D8
Short Bow	3	13	0	-5	23	23	20	15	13	5	0	-5	10	0	-5	-10	0	-10	-20	-25	1-4	3D10 & 2D8
Sling	3	13	-2	-7	15	10	5	0	19	10	5	0	5	-5	-10	-15	0	-10	-20	-25	1-6	5D8 & 1D6
Two-Handed Weapons:																						
Battleaxe	13	23	10	10	30	30	26	21	27	23	18	13	23	13	8	3	13	3	-7	-12	1-5	6D12 & 2D10
Flail	19	29	17	13	34	33	28	23	33	26	21	16	23	13	8	3	13	3	-7	-12	1-8	4D12 & 4D10
War Mattock	13	23	10	10	28	28	28	23	25	22	17	15	25	15	10	5	18	8	-2	-7	1-6	2D12 & 6D10
Quarterstaff	0	10	-5	-10	18	13	8	3	13	3	-2	-7	-2	-12	-17	-22	-15	-25	-35	-40	1-3	1D20 & 4D12
2 Handed sword	18	28	15	15	33	33	30	25	28	25	20	15	20	10	5	0	10	0	-10	-15	1-5	8D12
Pole Arms:																						
Javelin	9	-19	5	0	24	20	15	10	19	10	5	0	3	-7	-12	-17	-10	-20	-30	-35	1-4	1D12 & 4D10
Lance	13	23	10	10	28	28	28	28	23	20	15	18	20	18	15	10	18	10	0	-5	1-7	2D20 & 5D12
Polearm	12	22	10	5	27	25	20	15	22	15	10	5	10	0	-5	-10	0	-10	-20	-25	1-7	8D10
Spear	11	21	6	01	24	19	14	9	25	15	10	5	13	3	-2	-7	-4	-14	-24	-29	1-5	1D20 & 4D10
Animal / Natural Attacks:																						
Beak Pinch	39	36	21	12	27	21	15	12	18	9	3	0	18	6	3	3	15	6	0	-3	1-2	6D10
Bite	45	39	24	15	33	30	24	27	21	18	9	6	18	15	12	12	15	12	6	3	1-2	5D12 & 3D10
Claw-Talon	48	45	27	15	33	27	21	18	24	15	6	0	21	12	3	3	18	9	6	-3	1-2	6D8
Fall-Crush	66	63	57	51	63	60	57	54	48	42	33	24	51	45	42	39	39	33	27	18	1-2	5D20
Gr-Grasp-Swal	-3	18	6	12	3	15	27	30	18	21	27	33	21	24	33	36	24	27	33	39	1-2	6D6
Horn-Tusk	45	39	27	21	36	30	21	18	27	18	15	9	21	15	6	6	12	12	9	0	1-2	5D12 & 1D10
Ram-But-Bash	6	15	9	12	9	12	18	24	15	18	24	27	18	21	27	30	24	27	30	33	1-2	2D8 & 4D6
Stinger	45	42	33	21	27	21	15	12	21	15	12	0	21	12	3	3	18	9	3	-3	1-2	6D4
Tiny Animal	54	51	33	21	36	30	24	21	27	18	9	3	24	18	6	6	21	12	9	0	1-2	3D6 & 3D4
Trample-Stomp	60	60	45	39	51	42	39	36	36	27	18	12	39	30	21	18	30	21	18	9	1-2	2D20 & 4D10
Spell Attacks:																						
Cold Ball	87	79	71	67	71	63	59	59	71	67	59	51	71	67	59	55	71	67	59	51	1-4	4D8 & 2D6
Fire Ball	87	87	79	75	83	79	75	71	83	79	71	67	79	75	67	63	79	75	67	59	1-4	4D10 & 2D8
Fire Bolt	54	59	49	44	49	34	24	29	44	34	24	14	49	39	24	29	54	44	29	19	1-20	6D10 & 2D8
Ice Bolt	34	44	34	29	34	39	39	44	34	29	29	34	24	29	39	39	29	34	44	49	1-20	6D12
Lighten. Bolt	44	59	39	34	39	44	49	49	34	29	29	34	44	49	49	54	4	49	54	59	1-20	8D10
Shock Bolt	29	34	19	9	19	14	9	9	14	9	4	4	19	24	29	34	24	29	34	39	1-20	2D6 & 4D4
Water Bolt	24	34	24	9	14	19	19	24	14	9	9	14	9	14	19	19	9	14	14	19	1-20	2D10 & 4D8
Misc. Attacks:																						
MA-Strikes	45	42	36	30	42	51	36	33	27	21	12	3	30	24	21	18	18	12	6	-3	1-2	6D8
MA-Sw&Thr	0	9	3	6	18	21	27	33	21	24	30	33	27	30	36	39	36	39	42	45	1-2	6D4
Powersword	69	81	54	45	81	81	69	63	54	33	27	24	42	30	27	21	27	21	18	15	1-10	6D20 & 2D12

4.0 OPTIONAL SPELL "LAWS"

4.1 GREAT COMMANDS

The *Great Commands* are the legendary spells of the Magi (Cabbalists); these spells are included on the Magus Base list, Command Words. When a Magus learns the Command Words list to a level which permits the acquisition of a *Great Command*, the GM will permit him to gain one *Great Command* of the appropriate type. The specific spell acquired may be one selected by the GM based on his world and local culture, or the GM may permit the player to select one.

Option: A Magus may acquire additional *Great Commands* of the appropriate type by spending 1 "primary" development point (per spell gained) or 3 "secondary" development points (per spell gained).

> **NOTE:** *The availability of the spells, the requisites for obtaining them, etc. are all left to the discretion of the GM. Not all Great Commands need be available at all. And, of course, if the GM desires to alter the effects of the ones presented, or would like to design entirely new ones, he is encouraged to do so.*

> **NOTE:** *Each command has the Range, the Duration, and a RR modification in parentheses after the command name. "c" stands for concentration and "lvl" refers to the caster's level unless stated otherwise.*

COMMANDS OF THE OUTER CIRCLE (I)

1) Choke (100', Concentration, —) Target cumulatively takes 10% of his hits each round that the caster concentrates. After 10 rds (-100%) target becomes unconscious.

2) Sense (50', Concentration, -10) As long as he concentrates the caster may receive sensory data from the target; 1 sense/5 levels of the caster.

3) Compassion (25', 1 hr/lvl, -20) Target is overwhelmed with compassion for a person/place/thing specified by the caster.

4) Lose (300', 1 hr/lvl, —) Target either loses an item or loses his sense and memory of direction as specified by the caster.

5) Command (20', —, -30) Target will obey a command of up to 5 words in length from the caster. Command cannot be completely alien to target (e.g., suicide, blinding himself, etc.).

COMMANDS OF THE SECOND CIRCLE (II)

1) Choke (100', —, —) As *Choke* above except caster need not concentrate. But if the caster does concentrate for ten rounds after the target is unconscious, target dies.

2) Steal (25', —, -20) The target will attempt to steal one item specified by the caster.

3) Fear (20', varies, -30) Target flees in total fear from the caster (duration is 1 min/5% failure), or from one subject which the caster specifies (duration is 1 week/lvl).

4) Revert (100', 1 day/5% failure, -20) Permanently returns a domesticated target to a natural wild state. (GM may wish to make this duration permanent).

5) Ignore (50', 1 min/lvl, -10) Causes the target to ignore (not be aware of) one subject in sensory range.

6) Abandon (100', 1 day/lvl, —) Target loses sense of purpose and direction.

7) Summon (500'R, —, -20) Caster summons spirits (Faerie, rural, household, etc.), benign underground creatures, or enchanted creatures determined by the GM, within the radius. The beings are not controlled but are "drawn." Any malicious intent by the caster toward the beings may spoil the spell.

8) Thought (50', —, -10) Caster is able to plant one single concept thought in the target's mind.

9) Quarrel (25', 10 min/lvl, 30) Target is prone to argue and nitpick at his associates.

COMMANDS OF THE THIRD CIRCLE (III)

1) Reanimate (10', 1 rnd/lvl, —) Caster may temporarily revive the body (or the spirit if the body is ruined) of a dead target for the purpose of communication.

2) Exact (25', —, -30) Caster may exact an act of obedience from a being of the same alignment. Treat as a *Geas* (Ment. Mind Control list, Lvl 15).

3) Convert (25', 1 day/5% failure, +10) Permanently alters the target's "alignment" to one specified by the caster. Some beings may get additional RR mods (e.g., very evil beings such as Orcs might get +20-50). (GM may wish to make this duration permanent).

4) Remember (50', —, -10) Target remembers an event planted by the caster until presented with irrefutable evidence to the contrary.

5) Hold (50', Concentration, -10) Target is paralyzed and can do nothing as long as the caster concentrates.

6) Stun (100', 1 rnd/10% failure, -20) Target is numb, stunned, and -75 for all actions.

7) Mute (50', 1 hr/lvl, -20) Target loses the ability to talk and loses 1 sense/ 20% failure as specified by caster.

8) Stagger (100', 1 rnd/10% failure, —) Target takes a "D" Unbalancing crit each round.

COMMANDS OF THE STONE CIRCLE (IV)

1) Sleep (100', 1 min/10% failure, -20) Target is unconscious and unwakable.

2) Terror of the Abyss (100', for 1 day/10% failure, —) Target instantly experiences the horrors of hell. He is incapacitated with fear.

3) Unmind (100', 1 rnd/lvl, —) Target forgets every skill he knows (all skill rank bonuses are reduced to -25), but does not realize that a skill is forgotten until he attempts to use it.

4) Murder (20', —, —) Target will attempt to murder a being specified by the caster. Very lawful and good beings might get a RR bonus (e.g., up to +10-50).

5) Wereweird (25', —, 1 week/5% failure) Target contracts lycanthropy. Details determined by the GM.

6) Peace (Touch, 1 day/10% failure, —) Target eased from the effects of mind disease, grief, lycanthropy, hate, etc. There is a 1%/level chance that the effect will be permanent.

7) Burn (100', —, 1 rnd/10% fail.) Target takes a "D" heat crit each round.

COMMANDS OF THE ANCIENT CIRCLE (V)

1) Slumber (50', —, —) Target sleeps permanently and without aging until effect successfully dispelled or a condition specified is fulfilled (e.g., kissed by a prince).

2) Rot (50', Concentration, -10) Instantly rots organic nonmagic nonliving object or plant. Living targets receive a -10 penalty and lose 10% hit points per round of concentration. At 15 rounds (-150%) the target becomes a dead dried husk. If the caster ceases concentration before the effect is complete the target keeps hits and penalty. Heals at a rate of 10%/ day or immediately by a successful *Cure Disease* spell.

3) Repent (25', 1 day/5% failure, +10) As *Convert* above but also changes target's perspective on his friends and will probably alter his personality. (The GM may wish to make this duration permanent)

4) Changeshape (25', 1 day/5% failure, —) Target's form is altered to another living organism (must be appropriate to current environment) but the target retains his mental faculties; (e.g., the frog prince). (The GM may wish to make this duration permanent.)

5) Psychopathy (50', 1 day/5% failure, —) Target gains a psychopathic mental disorder. Severity depends on die roll failure with 01 = mild (e.g., lying) and 50+ = very severe (e.g., crazy murderer). Certain individuals may obtain an RR bonus (e.g., clerics, Mentalists, etc). (The GM may wish to make this duration permanent.)

6) Give (50', —, -10) Target gives an object he presently has in his possession to the caster.

7) Consume (100', 1 rnd/10% failure, —) Target takes a "C" heat critical and a "C" electricity critical every round.

8) Wrath (100', —, —) Deliver a Slaying crit to any being.

Commands of the Primitive Circle (VI)

1) **Truename** (300', —, —) Caster learns target's Truename. With this data the target is treated as suffering the effects of a *Mind Control True* (Mentalist Mind Control list, level 30).

2) **Invert** (10', —, —) Turns target's body inside-out making physical restoration nearly impossible. Caster must concentrate and the process takes 10 rounds and can be halted, saving the target, any time before round 5.

3) **Insane** (50', until dispelled, -20) Target is effected by a different mental disease each day until the effect is successfully dispelled. The caster may specify which the target is currently suffering from is he is within range and concentrating.

4) **Suicide** (25', —, -30) Target will immediately leave the immediate area and attempt suicide.

5) **Lycanthropy** (25', until dispelled, —) Target contracts permanent psychopathic lycanthropy. Details to be determined by the GM.

6) **Offer** (50', varies, -10) If the target fails an initial RR, target offers himself to the caster as metaphysical food. Caster may concentrate and take 2 hit points **or** 1 power point per round from the target until the target's totals are halved (round off). These points are added to the caster's totals and subtracted from the target's totals. The target may roll another RR each week to break the effect, if successful both target's and caster's totals revert to normal. The target will not necessarily obey the caster while the caster is absent, but submits whenever the caster is in sight or whenever the target hears his voice. Each spell user may only have these "offered" hit points (or power points) from one target at any one time.

7) **Heal** (Touch, 1 week/lvl, —) Cures lycanthropy, mind disease, grief, hate, etc. There is a chance equal to 2%/lvl that the condition is permanently cured.

8) **Killing Light** (50', —, -20) Instantly gives an evil target three Slaying Criticals.

Commands of the Circle of Night

1) **Be Not** (25', —, -20) The target ceases to physically exist. All items on the target's person remain while the target's body is uncreated and his tie to this world is severed.

2) **Slave** (50', varies, -10) As *Offer* above except the target is the caster's unquestioning slave at all times.

3) **Possess** (25', —, -20) The target dies (i.e., his soul is driven from his body and can only be returned through *Lifegiving*) and the soul of the caster enters and controls the body of the target. The caster's hit points and physical stat modifiers will be those of his new body.

4) **Shape-melt** (25', 1 week/5% failure, -20) The target thenceforth will change from one "shape" to another without control or cause. His physical attributes, gender, and modifiers will be those of the current "shape". The target will change on an average of once every four hours. (The GM may wish to make this duration permanent.)

5) **Slaying Light** (25', —, -20) Instantly gives an evil target one Slaying Critical (modified by +20) per 10% failure.

4.2 SPIRIT RUNES

Spirit Runes (see Spirit Runes, Magus Base list) involve not only the enchanting of combat items, but also the binding or imprisoning of a spiritual being within the item. This binding may or may not be with the consent of the bound being. In the case of supernatural beings, especially renegade deity types, the binding may require some of the caster's own life essence. Such "enruned" items may make up a large portion of existing magic items, with powers ranging from minor to legendary.

Spell Spirit Runes

A Magus may imbed a spell which normally occurs within the magic system into an item. He must either be able to cast the spell himself **or** he must have an item which casts the spell **or** he must have an associate willing to cast the spell **or** some other source for the spell. The principles of this sort of rune imbedding are fairly simple.

1. Each item is Tempered (see the *Temper* spell on the Spirit Runes spell list) for:

    "Spirit Rune Level" or *just "Rune Level"*
    (the maximum Level of Spirit Rune that can be imbedded)

    "Spirit Rune Capacity Level" or *just "Capacity Level"*
    (the total number of Spirit Runes that can be imbedded)

2. As the level of spell which the Magus is attempting to imbed increases, so also does the item's required "Spirit Rune Level" **and** the *Spirit Rune* spell required to imbed the spell. The following chart contains the progression:

Level of the Spell to be Imbedded	*Spell Rune* Required / the Item's Required "Rune Level"
1-5	Minor Spirit Rune / 10
6-10	Major Spirit Rune / 15
11-15	Lord Spirit Rune / 20
16-20	Spirit Rune of Might / 25
21-25	Spirit Rune of the Pale / 30
26-30	Spirit Rune of Power / 50
31-50	special circumstance only / 75

3. Each spell imbedded in the item requires the use of 1 unit of the "Spirit Rune Capacity" of the item. If a spell is imbedded once on an item, the item may cast the spell once per week (by using "Runes" skill). A spell may be imbedded more than once times if the Magus wants to be able to cast the imbedded spell more frequently (see the chart below). Alternately, at the time of creation, the Magus imbed a spell into the item so that it performs as a limited charge item (e.g., wand, rod, or staff). The number of charges will depend upon the number of times that the spell is imbedded (see the chart below). When all the charges are expended, the item will recharge itself in one year **or** the Magus may re-imbed the same or different runes. The relationship between the number of runes and casting frequency and number of charges is presented in the following chart:

# of times Rune Imbedded	Casting Frequency	Number of Charges
1	1 / week	5
2	1 / day	10
3	1 / 12 hr	20
4	1 / 8 hr	30
5	1 / 4 hr	50
6	1 / 2 hr	75
7	1 / 1 hr	100
8	1 / 30 min	100
9	1 / 10 min	100
10	1 / 1 min	100
11+	1 / 2 rnd	Constant (GM discretion)

NOTE: *A GM may wish to make the Casting Frequency correspond to the normal "Daily" items convention; in which case, the 1/12 hr is Daily II, the 1/8 hr is Daily III, the 1/4 hr is Daily VI, etc. Similarly, a GM may wish to restrict the Charge Items to: Wand (1-2 imbedded runes), Rod (3-5), and Staff (6-7); in this case, if 8 or more rune are imbedded, the item is "Constant".*

4. When imbedding an elemental spell, the Magus has the option of increasing the intensity or range of the elemental spell by imbedding the Spirit Rune of the appropriate level repeatedly. For each additional imbedding, intensity or range of the spell may be increased 100%. Note that if the Magus wants additional range and additional intensity he must imbed Spirit Runes for each. Also, if the Magus is purchasing increased frequency/charges for an item which throws **enhanced** elemental spells, he must multiply the total number of spells used to enhance the elemental spell by the total needed for the desired increase in frequency/charges. For example, a triple lightening bolt (3 imbeddings) castable "1 / 8 hr" (4 imbeddings) would require 12 units of an item's Rune Capacity (3 x 4).

EXAMPLE: *A Magus, being impressed with the Lightlaen sword, resolves to make one almost like it: a +25 broadsword, adds an additional heat critical of equal severity to any normally given, and may cast a x5 Firebolt (6th level spell) once every 4 hours. Using the preceding rules and spells from the Spirit Runes list:*

The +25 will require that the sword have a Rune Level of at least 25, and will require 5 units of the sword's Rune Capacity (i.e., one for each +5), see Rune of Striking on the Spirit Rune list.

The Firebolt is a 6th level spell, thus it normally requires a Major Spirit Rune (15 level spell), it uses 1 unit of the sword's Rune Capacity, and the sword must have a Rune Level of at least 15. For the Firebolt to do 5x damage (a 400% enhancement) requires 4 more units of the sword's Rune Capacity (5 total). The frequency of "1 / 4 hr" requires units of the sword's Rune Capacity, for a total Rune Capacity requirement for the Firebolt of 25 = (1 + 4) x 5.

The additional heat critical (a Lord Spirit Rune, level 20), the requires one more unit of the sword's Rune Capacity and requires that the sword have a Rune Level of at least 20.

So, the Lightlaen sword requires a Rune Level of 25 and a Rune Capacity of 31 = 5 + 25 + 1 and it will require that 31 Spirit Runes of the appropriate level be cast. The casting of the runes will not take long, but tempering the item will be a hassle.

According to the Temper chart in the Spirit Runes spell list: tempering the sword for a Rune Level of 25 will require at least 325 days, while a Rune Capacity of 31 will require 496 days. This is a total of 821 days, or two years and 91 days. However, since spell failures are very likely, as the Magus increases the sword's Tolerance Levels, the time is likely to be closer to 3 years (1000+ days).

NOTE: *No 25th level Alchemist could make the weapon in the preceding example although a 25th level Magus could. However, when an Alchemist did get high enough to make the item (about 30th level), it would only take him 130 weeks (910 days), regardless of non-lethal failures. The process requires the Weapon +25 (30th level), the firebolt x 5 (30th level), the Daily V (about 30th level), and the Flame Sword (20th level x 2 for the 2nd effect) for the Heat crits. In the final analysis, when dealing with items which may be created through the use of runes, the Magus is very close to the proficiency of the Alchemist, although he does not have the breadth of different creation abilities and it is possible to dispel his items' abilities since they are imbedded "Runes".*

NOTE: *If a GM wishes, he may make Spirit Runes permanent (i.e., do not allow normal "dispelling" and anti-magic to affect them). In this case, do not allow a Magus to change Spirit Runes once they are imbedded into a tempered item.*

Minor Spirit Runes (10)

1. Rune of Sharpness — for each *Rune of Sharpness*, the item will cause additional bleeding of 1 hit/rd on "A," "B," or "C" class criticals, and 2 hits/rd on "D" and "E" class criticals.

2. Rune of Cleaving — when striking a non-magic weapon, shield, item of armor, or wooden object no more than 1' diameter/thickness, the item must make a RR against a 10th level attack or be severed.

3. Rune of Flight — for each rune the caster may either: (1) increase the range of a ranged weapon by 100%, or (2) add 25' to the range of an unranged weapon.

4. Critical Negation — for each rune, the caster may reduce the chances for a critical effecting the protected area by 5%, to a maximum of 50%.

5. Fumble Modification — for each rune, the caster may reduce the chances of fumble with the item by 1 (minimum of 01).

6. Sense Evil — a wielder will sense the presence of evil within a 50' R. He must be wielding the item (e.g., have it out of scabbard) for the special ability to function. If the wielder concentrates, he may determine the source of the evil.

7. Empathic Contact — permits empathic contact between a wielder and his intelligent (any degree) enruned item within a radius of 10'.

8. Low Personality — instills a distinct sentient personality of low intelligence within the item.

Major Spirit Rune (15)

1. Free Hand — one *Free Hand* rune permits someone to wield a two-handed item with only one hand. Two *Free Hand* runes permits someone to wield a 1 handed item with "no hands". Three *Free Hands* runes permits someone to wield a 2 handed item with "no hands". "No hands" has a limit of 3' range between the wielder and the item.

2. Additional Lesser Criticals — the item inflicts an additional critical of the caster's choice (choose when imbedding rune) one level of severity less than the one normally given. To increase the number of criticals by imbedding additional runes, the caster must imbed a number of runes equal to: (the number of crits) squared (e.g., 3 additional criticals would require 9 runes).

3. Additional Unbalancing Criticals — as above except the item inflicts Unbalancing criticals equal in severity to the one given.

4. Limited Shifting — the item may take on an additional form for each rune embedded. Each additional rune also permits the item a 100% variation in mass (e.g., a five rune dagger of 1/2 pound might change to 2.5 pound broadsword).

5. Rune of Great Cleaving — as *Rune of Cleaving* above except that magic items may also be effected, and the spell attack is 15th level.

6. Unencumbering — each *Rune of Unencumbering* reduces the weight of an item by 10% per rune cast.

7. Bleeding — as *Sharpness* above except that the item inflicts 3 hits/rnd on "A," "B," or "C" class criticals, and 5 hits/rd on "D" and "E" class criticals.

8. Warning — if lying or worn near the owner, the item will telepathically alert him, even if owner is asleep, to unauthorized presences within 100'.

9. Medium Personality — instills a distinct sentient personality of medium intelligence within the item.

10. Goodness: Repulsions — Permits an additional slaying critical on Undead. Additionally, for each rune the wielder may cast 1 *Repulsions 10* per day.

11. Return by Flight — when called the item physically flies back to its owner at a rate of 500'/rnd. Range = number of runes x 500'.

Lord Spirit Rune (20)

1. Invulnerability — makes the item, for most purposes, invulnerable to destruction by a particular force: fire, lightning, etc). Please note that with physics considerations in mind, such invulnerability might do little to protect the wielder or wearer (e.g., a suit of armor invulnerable to impact will not prevent its wearer from being injured in a 100' fall).

2. Spirit Rune: Battle — the wielder may permit himself to be temporarily possessed by a battle spirit within the item and perform combat using the physical stats of the spirit: OB, number of attacks, ambush, size class, hit points, etc. Usually the type of spirit is appropriate to the level at which this rune is cast. Although the battle spirit will follow the instincts of the wielder, the wielder must make a successful SD roll (needs 101+ roll, adding SD mod) to completely recover his self-control. The spirit automatically relinquishes control at the cessation of combat. Please note: damage that might not incapacitate or kill the physical spirit might very well be maiming or fatal to the wielder. Also, **very** powerful spirits (e.g., Ordainers, etc) could alter the persona of the wielder over time.

3. Rune of White/Black — makes an item holy or unholy.

4. Spirit Rune: Vampire — when the wielder strikes an opponent, he saps 1 PP/lvl and 1 hit/lvl from his victim and adds them to himself (the level used is that at which the Vampire rune was cast). The power points are unaffected by Bonus PP items, but the wielder may temporarily (10 min/lvl) exceed his normal maximums.

5. Additional Equal Criticals — as *Additional Criticals* above except the criticals are equal in severity to those normally given.

6. Return by Long Door — as *Return by Flight* above except the movement is instantaneous and it occurs by Long Door.

7. RR Bonus — every rune adds 10% to the wearer's or wielder's Resistance rolls vs a particular realm of power **or** nasty thing (e.g., poison or disease).

8. Telempathy — as *Empathic Contact* above except the range is 100' per owner's level.

9. High Personality — instills a distinct sentient personality of high intelligence within the item.

10. Aligned — item is imbued with a particular alignment or purpose. Such items must have their strength of will determined (see ***RMCI*** pp. 52-54). Strength of will should be determined from the level of the item's intelligence. These items will contest owners of varying alignment or intent.

11. Invisible — the item is invisible. Note that this characteristic does not cause the wearer, wielder, or owner to become invisible.

Spirit Runes of Might (25)

1. Spirit Rune: Summons — summons the item to the owner from any distance on the same plane at a rate of 500'/rnd. The item moves by flight, and can be restrained.

2. Haste — item casts *Haste* at Will. Please note that every round of Haste after the 10th saps basic hits from the wielder at a rate of 2 hits per round.

3. Slaying — the item delivers slaying criticals against one particular kind of creature or being. The caster must have some sample of a portion of one of the creatures to engrave the rune. If a Caster desires an item to be able to slay more than one category of creature, the number of runes required for each additional kind increases: 2nd = 4 runes, 3rd = nine, etc.

Spirit Runes of the Pale (30)

1. Willshape — object may take any desired form desired by the wielder or owner subject to restrictions levied by the GM (e.g., no pistols, etc). The form may be as small as 1/10th the original mass, or up to 2x. Each additional rune may increase the mass's form by one category: 2x to 3x, 3x to 4x, etc.

2. Spirit Rune: Dance — as *Spirit Rune: Battle* above, except the item need not be wielded by the owner at all; i.e., it is treated as if it were being wielded by the spirit. If the spirit is ever killed, the Spirit Rune: Dance rune will be inactive for one year.

3. Spirit Rune: Magic — the item gains the spell casting ability of the spirit utilized (level of the spirit should be appropriate to the level at which this spell is cast). The GM may arbitrate some restrictions appropriate to his world.

4. Very High Personality — instills a distinct sentient personality of very high intelligence within the item.

5. Invisible Wielder — item may cast *Invisibility* at will on its wearer or wielder. However, if the wearer/wielder makes a violent move or attack, he will visible for at least 6 rounds following the action before the item may cast the spell again.

Spirit Runes of Power (50)

1. Spirit Rune: Doom — when presented in a defensive manner, the item casts a 30th level spell to reflect an attack of any type (e.g., magical, weapon, elemental, etc) back to its source.

2. Spirit Rune: Mastery — when presented in an upraised manner, the item casts the 30th level spell *Mind Control True* (Base Mentalist, Mind Control list, 30th level) on all viewing within 50'.

3. Artifact Personality — instills a distinct sentient personality of artifact intelligence within the item. If the Magus imbeds five of these runes in item, then the personality will be of legendary artifact intelligence.

4. Goodness: Lightblade — the item takes on the general characteristics of the "lightblades" (see ***Creatures & Treasures*** p. 73).

4.3 RITUAL MAGIC

Rolemaster's spell system lacks provision for the mighty magical rituals found in so many works of fiction. The system presented in this section is a set of guidelines that enable the GM to fit a ritual into a category and determine its chances for success.

Firstly, what is a ritual and why should it be used? In its simplest form, a ritual is a long magical preparation used to enable a caster to cast a higher level spell than he or she usually would be able to. In its most complex form, it would enable the caster to tailor-make his or her own spells without the lengthy research period required to learn how to cast it in the short space of time normally available during combat.

RITUAL CLASSES

We suggest that rituals be split up into *classes* for the purposes of developing skill ranks for performing the rituals. The suggested ritual classes are:

Alchemical: Covers the creation of items. This is usually done in conjunction with another type of ritual, as it is easier to invest an item with a ritual spell than to find a high enough level spellcaster to help.

Alteration: A catch-all type covering such things as transport spells, Telekinesis, magical locks, disintegrations, etc.

Auxiliary: Covers anything that will have an effect on another spell effect. This includes such things as Extension, Spell Store, Permanence, Ranging, etc.

Clerical: Covers direct acts of a cleric's faith such as raising the dead.

Druidical/Natural: Covers such things as herb enhancement, Weather control, Healing, and Purification.

Elemental: Covers manipulation of the elements through such spells as walls, balls, bolts, etc.

Influence: Covers such things as Charm, Quest, Sleep, etc.

Informational: Covers all forms of lore detects, etc.

Summoning/Possession: Covers the summoning of all forms of creatures, the possession of people by summoned beings, and the control of summoned beings.

DEVELOPING SKILL RANKS FOR RITUAL CLASSES

Skill must be developed separately for each Ritual Class, but the skill bonus will apply to any ritual that falls into that class. If a GM rules that a complex ritual might fall into two or more classes, average the bonuses. All rituals use Self Discipline as the bonus stat. A GM may use the development costs for "Magic Ritual" given in *RMCII* or the following development costs may be used:

Pure Essence or Channeling Spell Users	2/6
Pure Mentalism and Hybrid Spell Users	3/9
Semi-spell Users	9
Non-spell Users	20

There are several factors that may affect the success of a ritual. The following factors are suggestions; a GM should choose which are appropriate for his/her campaign.

Class of Conjuration. The ritual should have a base chance equal to the skill bonus of the caster for the class of ritual being performed.

Effect Level. The GM should consider how high level spells should be made available to the caster. We suggest that the chance of success should be lowered by 2.5 for every level the spell effect is higher than the caster. If there is more than one spell effect in the ritual, the level should be taken as the sum of: the highest level effect involved **plus** half of the sum of the levels of effect of the rest of the spells.

> **NOTE:** *It is this modification that is the major determining factor for the success or failure of rituals. The -2.5 per level modification is a suggestion. Any less than -2 per level would make ritual magic far too powerful. Any more than -3 per level would make the rituals nearly impossible to perform.*

Known List. If the spell effect is not a standard spell, or it is on a spell list that the caster cannot normally learn, then modify the chance by -20. If the spell effect is on a list that the caster could learn but doesn't yet know, the chance is modified by -5. If it is on a list that the caster does know but does not know to a high enough level, the chance is unaltered. If it is on a list that the caster knows to the appropriate level, but is above the caster's own level, the chance is at +10%. If there are several casters or several spells, find the overall average bonus and use that.

Foci. If the caster has a suitable focus, the chance of success is increased by the Base Spells bonus of the caster. Creating a focus is in itself usually an Alchemical ritual.

Time Spent. The minimum time required to perform any ritual is (spell level – caster's level) in hours. At the end of each eight hour block, the caster must either make an unmodified check on his or her ritual skill or hand the process over to another caster to continue the ritual. If the caster has to double up because of the length of the ritual then he or she must roll at the end of each eight hour period of casting . If the check is failed, the ritual will fail also. If multiple casters are used in the ritual, average the relevant stats for all of them (i.e., level, skill bonus, etc.) For every extra unit of time spent (i.e., spell level – caster's level) there is a +10% chance of success. If a ritual is disturbed by outsiders, the caster must make his or her Ritual Class skill roll to continue. The roll is at -20% for each round that the ritual has been disturbed. The only exception to this is Alchemy rituals. These may be left at will and restarted later so long as all of the ingredients are still intact. Casters may only change once every eight hours.

Spell "Laws": Ritual Magic

Power Invested. No ritual can succeed unless sufficient power points are invested. This investment is equal to the level of the ritual, as described under "Effect Level". More than one person may be used to provide points; the points from persons not actually performing the Ritual only count as half a point per point spent. Spell adders may be used and will provide a number of points equal to the level of their user. Spell multipliers will act as normal on PP invested. For every unit of the ritual's (Effect Level) points invested past the first unit, the chance of success is increased by +10%. At the end of any ritual, all participants will be drained to all spell points for the standard period (usually eight hours). Meditation will not help to bring these back: the participants must sleep.

Influences. This is a complex topic that adds both work and flavor to the system. The GM should determine a set of "ingredients" that will be used in the ritual. Some may be essential, others may just add to the chance of success. A table of sample influences is provided. We suggest that for each equivalent of 100gp (more if the scale of your campaign tends towards large amounts of money) the chance be increased by +10%.

Suggestions for Perverted Rituals

Alchemical. The item may break, or be flawed, or do something other than what was intended.

Alteration. The consequences of failure could be very nasty, such as disintegrating the wrong thing (the caster's focus is a good bet) or teleporting somewhere very unpleasant.

Auxiliary. The intended effects will not occur. For example, an Extension might shorten the spell, not prolong it.

Clerical. The god might become displeased with the Cleric and set a quest for him or her to "Atone". The Cleric might have inadvertently opened a gate for Demons to come through. The Cleric might have tried to use a ritual that would be in the sphere of influence of a different god.

Druidical/Natural. Healing might inflict wounds; growth or fertility might produce disease or withering. The Earth might reject the imposition of a different set of conditions and rebel against the caster.

Elemental. The normal consequence of this is a rebellion of the element by attacking the caster.

Influence. The spell might affect the caster, or the spell might be reversed so that a love ritual will engender hatred, etc.

Informational. The caster will be fed wrong information, or maybe he or she will become known to the person who they were trying to find out about.

Summoning/Possession. The caster may very well be possessed, or the summoned creature might be uncontrolled, or the caster may have called up something of much greater power than intended.

Resolution of the Ritual

At the end of all the procedures for the ritual, roll 1D100 open ended and add the total bonus to it. If the roll is above 100 then the ritual has succeeded. If not, there may be unwanted side effects. The table below indicates the effects of failure. If there is a * by a result, it means that the participants may choose to abort the ritual before completion, loosing all spell points, but taking no other ill effects. In this case, the ritual may not be attempted again by the same casters for at least as many days as the level of the spell.

Roll plus Bonus	Effects
100 – 90 *	The ritual succeeds, but all casters have no spell points for one whole day.
89 – 80 *	The ritual succeeds, but all participants have no spell points for one whole day.
79 – 70 *	The ritual succeeds, but the strain causes an "A" Cold critical on all casters. The other participants have no spell points for 1D10 days.
69 – 60 *	The ritual succeeds, but all participants are knocked out for 1D10 hours. They will be unable to cast spells for 1D10 days.
59 – 50 *	The ritual succeeds, but at great cost. All participants take a "C" Cold critical, are knocked out for 1D10 hours during which they may die of "frostbite," and lose all spell casting ability for a month.
49 – 40	The ritual fails, and all present are blown back 20 ft. All take an "A" impact critical and lose all spell points for a whole day.
39 – 30	The ritual fails, and the casters are badly hurt. They take an "E" impact, others a "C". All persons lose all spell points for 1D10 days.
29 – 20	The ritual fails. All participants take a "C" impact critical, lose spell points for 1D100 days, and are knocked out for 1D10 hours.
19 – 0	The ritual is perverted. The effects of this are up to the GM. Suggestions are given later in this section. In addition, all present take an "A" electricity critical and lose all spell points for a whole day.
(-01) – (-20)	The ritual is perverted, and all present take a "C" electricity and an "A" impact critical. All participants are unable to cast spells for 1D10 days.
(-21) – (-40)	The ritual is perverted. All present take an "E" electricity critical and a "C" impact critical. All are unconscious for 1D10 hours and lose spell points for 1D10 months.
(-41) – (-100)	The ritual is perverted. All present take an "E" electricity and an "E" impact critical and must make an RR vs. the level of the ritual of be deprived of all spell points permanently. All are unconscious for 1D10 days.
(-101) – (-200)	The ritual backfires in a spectacular manner, killing all involved instantly.
(-201) – (-300)	The ritual backfires in a blaze of arcane power. The spell effect will radiate out into a mile's radius, causing whatever effects the GM sees as necessary. The souls of all participants are ripped apart. They may be resurrected, but all mental stats will be halved.
(-301) – (-400)	The souls of all participants contribute their Essence to the power of the ritual. The spell effect will radiate out for several miles, with a total effective level equal to: (ritual level) + 0.5 x (sum of participants levels).
(-401) down.	The release of arcane power has caused a breach in reality that will call for a god to repair it. The souls of all participants are totally annihilated, along with the surrounding few acres of land. The magical repercussions will be felt by all spell casters within a thousand miles.

Foci

A focus is a magical device used to enhance the caster's chance of success with rituals. Its creation is an Alchemical ritual. The basic level of the ritual will be: the level of the caster **plus** one-half of his level for each Ritual Class that the focus will apply to.

Normally, the caster may only have one focus at a time. The caster's focus will normally be enchanted for him alone, and will give no bonus to another. If the focus is found by another person, they must also enchant it to be able to use it. In this case it will act for two people only: The last person to enchant it plus the original caster. Focus creation rituals may only have one caster, though there may be any number of other participants. The form of the focus will often be determined by the type(s) of ritual that it may be used for. Suggestions are as follows:

Alchemical. Typically a forge or a brewing cauldron.

Alteration. Commonly a wand.

Auxiliary. These are varied according to the caster's tastes. A familiar is commonly used for this type of focus.

Clerical. Usually a holy symbol of the god.

Druidical/Natural. Often a staff of living wood. Healers will often substitute a ring.

Elemental. Commonly a staff of iron tipped with gemstones.

Influence. Usually a piece of jewelry. As the caster gets a bonus for the ritual for the cost of the ingredients, the focus of a ritual Magician will often be very ornate and bejewelled. A common type of focus is a familiar, which normally has little actual value but is very convenient to have around. Spell casters thus may seek far and wide for a rare or especially fine animal to serve as their familiar. When used, foci have a chance of being destroyed. This chance is: (level of ritual) ÷ (level of caster).

Informational. Often a mirror, a telescope, a crystal ball, etc.

Summoning/Possession. Often a sacrificial knife or similar implement.

Multiple Classes: For rituals whose effects fall into more then one class, a focus may be used if there are more Effect Levels from the focus' class than than from the rest of the classes put together.

Influences

In addition to a focus, the GM may wish to allow bonuses for the use of rare and precious ingredients. The GM should give rare items a rough gp value for the purpose of the ritual. There is a list below of some influences that could be used for different classes of ritual. These are by no means rules, or really even guidelines; they are suggestions. The GM may wish to require at least one precious ingredient for the ritual to succeed. Another suggestion is to limit the total number of influences that can be used. The GM may well wish to adjust the 100 gp standard unit to take account of the general wealth level of his campaign.

Alchemical. All the usual bunk of bats' eyes, Black lotus, Dragon scale, etc., are commonly used to make items.

Alteration. These should be tailored to the spell by whatever the GM considers logical.

Auxiliary. Probably the most difficult to tailor things to fit. I would suggest using alchemical ideas. (See the *RMCI* for a list of substances that could be used.)

Clerical. Things holy to the god are a good bet; also sacrifices of rare and magical artifacts to the god.

Druidical/Natural. Rare herbs or spices; the juices of a rare plant, etc.

Elemental. The most common influences are gemstones; such as Sapphires for air, Emeralds for water, Rubies for fire, Diamonds for Earth, etc.

Influence. Rare perfumes, exotic spices, intoxicants and valuable gifts may all help.

Informational. Things such as gifts to informational Demons, precious spices burnt on the fire so that the caster can go into a trance, etc.

Summoning/Possession. The usual paraphernalia of magic circles of powdered gold, altars encrusted with gems, magical knives, old scrolls, etc, all have a place in these rituals. Sacrifices might also be called for.

It is suggested that the GM decide what will help a ritual; this will prevent players from "chucking in" unwanted items to create a better one. It should be noted that the presence of influences may seem to suggest that an Alchemical class ritual should be used. If the effects are "one-time use", like a love potion, the GM may wish to classify this as a straight Influence ritual, because the influences will be destroyed as the ritual takes effect (i.e., the potion is used). In general, if there is some permanent remnant of the influences used in the ritual, the ritual will involve an Alchemy class ritual. If all of the influences used are destroyed at the end of the ritual then the ritual will not involve an Alchemy class ritual.

EXAMPLES OF RITUAL MAGIC

EXAMPLE 1. Consider Fred the Foolish, a third level Mage. He wishes to cast a *fireball* to dispose of a small group of nasty Orcs. In addition to this, he must cast a *Spell Store*, so that he can cast the ritual in a safe place and then travel to the Orc hideout. He knows both Fire Law and Spell Reins to 10th.

Class: The class is a combination of *Elemental* and *Auxiliary*. He has six skill ranks in each but no SD bonus, so his basic Ritual skill bonus is +30.

Level: 8 for the fireball **plus** 8 x 0.5 for the spell store **equals** an Effect Level of 12. The difference is 9 levels (12 - the caster's level of 3), giving -23 (-2.5 x 9).

Known List: Since Freddy already has both spells on his known lists, he receives a +10 bonus.

Foci: With a lack of foresight, Freddy has not made a focus.

Time Spent: Freddy needs (9 - 3) = 6 hours. He decides that he is in a hurry and will not spend extra time.

Power Invested: Freddy has 6 PP and his friend Oddi the druid has another 6 PP. Between the two of them they just get the 9 PP required. (Freddy's 6 + 0.5 x Oddi's 6).

Influences: The GM rules that the ruby that Freddy and Oddi had obtained as a reward from their last escapade will work as an influence. It is worth 50gp, and the GM is generous enough to give then a +5 modification

The total modification is 22 = 30 - 23 + 10 + 5. The dice roll is 30. ... Oops... 30 + 22 = 52; not over 100. Reading the failure result, Oddi and Freddy rapidly abandon the ritual and decide to fight the Orcs instead.

EXAMPLE 2. Consider the powerful witch Morgan. She is a fifteenth level Sorcerer and she wants to cast *Quakes* to topple the castle of an opponent. This is a 50th level spell, but she only knows the list that *Quakes* is on to 20th.

Class: *Alteration.* She has 20 skill ranks for this Ritual Class and a +10 SD bonus. Modification: +80.

Level: (50 - 15) x 2.5 = -87.5 = -88.

Known List: Yes, but not to a high enough level. +0

Foci: Morgan has a black cat as an enchanted focus for Alteration, Information, and Influence rituals, so she gets her base spells bonus of +30.

Time Spent: (50 - 15) = 35 hours. 35 ÷ 8 = 4 checks based on 8 hour intervals. She has an 80% (her skill bonus for this Ritual Class) chance of doing these, and she succeeds on all of them.

Power Invested: Morgan has 30 PP naturally and a x3 multiplier and a +2 adder. This gives 90 PP + 30 PP = 120 PP. This is a bit over twice the points required (240%), giving a +14 bonus.

Influences: The GM rules that a Diamond is necessary to cast the spell. Nothing else that she has would help, although the GM notes that the eye of a Medusa would add another +15 to the chance. The only diamond Morgan has is worth 170 gps, and she reluctantly uses it. This gives her a +17 bonus.

The total modification is 53 = 80 - 88 + 30 + 14 + 17. The dice roll is 57. ... Success! ... 57 + 53 = 110; over 100. The walls of the castle come tumbling down.

EXAMPLE 3. A coven of witches wishes to summon and bind a Demon. The caster of the ritual is an eighth level Illusionist. Only five other witches have any spell points to contribute: a total of 20 extra. They decide to try for a Type III Demon. Thus, the spells required are *Lesser Demonic Gate* and *Demon Mastery III*.

Class: *Summoning*. The caster has nine skill ranks for this Ritual Class and a +5 SD bonus, Modification: +50.

Level: 13 (*Demon Mastery* spell) **plus** 0.5 x 5 (*Gate* spell) **equals** an Effect Level of 16. The modification is $(16 - 8) \times 2.5 = -20$.

Known List: The caster could know the list but doesn't, so the modification is -5.

Foci: The caster has a focus for Alterations, but that won't help him here.

Time Spent: $(16 - 8) = 8$ hours. The caster has a 50 chance (his skill bonus for this Ritual Class) of being able to keep it up. He just makes it.

Power Invested. The caster has 16 PP and a +1 adder. The coven add 10 PP = 20 ÷ 2. Total PP = 34 PP = 16 + 8 + 10. This is just over twice the points (≈ 210%), giving a modification of +11.

Influences: Since one member of the coven is a wealthy merchant, the coven can afford to inscribe a magical circle out of powdered gold worth 130gp. This gives a +13 modification.

The total modifiaction is $49 = 50 - 20 - 5 + 11 + 13$. The dice roll is 02; open-ended low! The 2nd roll is 53, so the final result is $-2 = 49 + 02 - 53$. This means that the ritual is perverted and the Demon escapes. The coven are badly hurt, taking "C" Electricity and "A" Impact crits. They are deprived of their spell points for 1D10 days each. They must now figure out what to do with that damn Demon!

EXAMPLE 4. Finally, consider an extreme case. What if Freddy from Example 1 wants to cast *Stone Fires*, a 30th level spell.

Class: *Elemental*, so the modification is +30.

Level: $(30 - 3) \times 2.5 = -68$.

Known List: Yes, but too high level so +0.

Foci: Nope.

Time Spent: $(30 - 3) = 27$ hours, so he must make three 30% checks. Let's assume he makes them.

Power Invested: Normally, Freddy couldn't pull together 30 PP. But say he has found a x3 spell multiplier and that Oddi has brought a couple of friends. He can just about scrape the points together; modification: +0.

Influences: In a fit of generosity, the GM decides that no influences are actually needed. This is good, since Freddy hasn't got any.

The total modification is $-38 = 30 - 68$, so there is a good chance that Freddy, Oddi and company will get comprehensively fried by the backlash. A shame after making all those rolls to concentrate, isn't it?

COMMENTS

It may seem from Example 2 that a spell caster could cast devastating spells at low levels. Remember, however, that Morgan would have had to have been defended for the 35 hours that the ritual took. Also, she had obviously spent a lot of time and effort in creating a powerful focus and she had used many development points in learning how to cast rituals. Finally, notice that there is one hell of a penalty for failure in the ritual system. The other thing that may seem odd is how come the caster can stand up for 35 hours, let alone cast a spell for that long. I suggest that the magical power set in motion by the casting of the ritual is sufficient to sustain the caster for as long as he or she can remain absolutely in concentration on the ritual, thus the need for a ritual roll every eight hours.

Finally, note that abandoned rituals are stopped just before the final invocation is said, and so require the full time of the ritual. At the GM's option, it may be necessary to make a ritual roll to be able to abandon the ritual. The possibility of ritual failure by failing concentration is suggested, but no penalties are suggested for this. One alternative would be a roll on the Spell Failure table, maybe with a chance to avoid it by making a second ritual roll.

4.4 DIRECTED SPELLS

Option 1: The GM may feel that the skills of *Directed Spells* are in fact quite similar to each other and so fall under the precedent of similar skill treatment (e.g., casting fire bolts are similar to casting ice bolts). Be warned, however, that this allowance will result in spell users being better than perhaps is normal in the casting of directed spells. At the very least they will have more development points freed up for the development of other skills. In order to show the difficulty of mastering the directed skill as a similar skill, we strongly suggest that this Option only be open to pure spell users, those who use the directed spells much more often and have to rely more upon them.

Option 2: The GM may decide allow *Directed Spell* skill for the elemental "Ball" spells. When using this Option, no +30 for "center of effect" is allowed, and the *Directed Spell* skill bonus is applicable to the "center of effect" target only.

4.5 INDIVIDUAL SPELL DEVELOPMENT

These optional rules presents a new system of spell acquisition based upon a spell by spell (rather than a list by list) theory.

NOTE: *The concept of paying Development Points for a chance at receiving a whole block of spells may seem incongruous to some GMs. Some GMs have referred to it as: "being like having a Thief pay 1 development point (DP) in order to get a 5% chance of receiving Stalk and Hide to level 10!" In addition, for low level campaigns when level advancement is slow, Magicians must have more versatility in order to survive, especially when considering the lack of power of* **Rolemaster***'s 1st level magic users.*

A big advantage that this system offers is increased flexibility. For players, the flexibility is obvious as magic using characters have a more varied selection of spells. Since they pay only for the spells they will use, there are fewer wasted DPs. GMs will also appreciate the new system: as always, new lists can be introduced, but now GMs have the option of introducing singular "non-list" spells into their campaigns.

The mechanics of the system are not complex:

- Spells are purchased individually at costs determined by the Spell Development Cost Chart. Any number of spells may be acquired at one level.
- Spells must be purchased in order of level, so to learn a 50th level spell, the rest of the list must be learned first.
- At 1st level, a pure or hybrid spell used may select spells from up to 4 different lists; a semi-user from 2, and a non-user from only one. At each later character level, the character may select from one additional new list.
- If a spell list has no spell for a particular level, that "slot" must still be purchased. The cost to buy a blank slot is 1 DP for all classes. The cost is cumulative though with consecutive "slots" purchased for that character level. Buying 2 slots in a row without a spell would cost 3: 1 + (1 + 1). Buying 3 would cost 6, etc. A character never pays more for an empty slot than he would for a spell of the same level, so actually most pure and hybrid users will pay only 2 DPs for "empty slots" of levels 1-10.

NOTE: *A GM can easily tinker with the details of this system to make magic users weaker or more powerful in his or her campaign.*

NOTE: *It is strongly suggested that GMs restrict and/or monitor new spell acquisitions by PCs. Since this system is so flexible and open, it does have a loophole or two in terms of game balance. In a group of good role players, this should not be much of a problem.*

NOTE: *Low-level (1 to 3) magic using characters (pure, hybrid, and semi) become much more powerful than they were under the "old system." They are still in line with the power of low level Fighters, Thieves, etc. Second, high level (10+) magic using characters tend to be a bit weaker than they used to be, though not overly so.*

All point costs are per individual spells, not for the entire list.

No level may be skipped when selecting spells, i.e., to buy a third level spell in list *x*, you must have the first and second level spells from list *x*.

SPELL DEVELOPMENT COST CHART

Pick Type	Pure	Hybrid	Semi	Non
BASE LISTS (Own)				
A	—	—	—	—
B	2*	2*	8*	—
C	—	—	—	—
D	4*	4*	15*	—
E	8/16/32	8/16/32	20/32/50	—
OPEN LISTS (Own Realm)				
A	—	—	8*	2x
B	2*	2*	—	—
C	—	—	16*	3x
D	4*	4*	32*	—
E	8/16/32	8/16/32	—	—
CLOSED LISTS (Own Realm)				
A	—	2*	16*	4x
B	2*	—	—	—
C	—	4*	32*	—
D	4*	4*	32*	—
E	10/18/36	25/-/-	—	—
BASE LISTS (Not own, but same Realm)				
A	6*	8*	40*	—
B	—	—	—	—
C	12*	16*	—	—
D	20*	30*	—	—
E	40/50/-	—	—	—
OPEN LISTS (Different Realm)				
A	8*	10*	24*	5x
B	—	—	—	—
C	16*	20*	—	—
D	32*	—	—	—
E	—	—	—	—
CLOSED LISTS (Different Realm)				
A	16*	32*	—	—
B	—	—	—	—
C	32*	—	—	—
D	—	—	—	—
E	—	—	—	—
BASE LISTS (Different Realm)				
A	32*	—	—	—
B	—	—	—	—
C	—	—	—	—
›D	—	—	—	—
E	—	—	—	—

Pick	Spell Levels
A	1-5
B	1-10
C	6-10
D	11-20
E	25,30,35,40/50

* These costs applies to as many spells as the character wishes to develop / learn.

5.0 OPTIONAL SKILLS/STATS "LAWS"

5.1 QUICKIE STAT GENERATION

For some reason, one of the most consistently difficult processes for new *Rolemaster* players to grasp in the character generation process is the generation of Potential Stats from Temporary Stats (Table 15.11 *ChL&CaL*). When the process is understood it still takes some time, and even experienced players are tempted sometimes to read the table backwards. If the GM offers the players the option of varying which Potential Rolls go with which Temporaries, the time problem and confusion can become intense. If a GM decides to eliminate the whole Temps/Pots rule, and just run with Pots only, they may use the following table. The whole process of Temps to Pots is removed by summarizing the results in one table which uses a 3 ten sided dice to generate numbers from 1-1000 (D1000).

Die Roll	Stat	Die Roll	Stat
001-012	25	507-519	64
013-025	26	520-532	65
026-038	27	533-545	66
039-051	28	546-558	67
052-064	29	559-571	68
065-077	30	572-584	69
078-090	31	585-597	70
091-103	32	598-610	71
104-116	33	611-623	72
117-129	34	624-636	73
130-142	35	637-649	74
143-155	36	650-662	75
156-168	37	663-675	76
169-181	38	676-688	77
182-194	39	689-701	78
195-207	40	702-714	79
208-220	41	715-727	80
221-233	42	728-740	81
234-246	43	741-753	82
247-259	44	754-766	83
260-272	45	767-779	84
273-285	46	780-792	85
286-298	47	793-805	86
299-311	48	806-818	87
312-324	49	819-831	88
325-337	50	832-844	89
338-350	51	845-857	90
351-363	52	858-870	91
364-376	53	871-883	92
377-389	54	884-896	93
390-402	55	897-909	94
403-415	56	910-922	95
416-428	57	923-935	96
429-441	58	936-948	97
442-454	59	949-961	98
455-467	60	962-974	99
468-480	61	975-987	100
481-493	62	988-999	101
494-506	63	000	102

5.2 "MODS ONLY" DEVELOPMENT

With a view to making things quick and easy, a GM may decide to forget all about Pots and Temps, and just use straight "Stat Mods" on the chart in this section. If there are a couple of stats that you need percentile values for (such as CO for determining Death due to Hits, or QU for an initiative system) those can be derived from the mods generated by this chart. The following chart may prove to be an extremely quick and easy way to develop characters.

> **NOTE:** *For those who like to play super-charged heroes, or like to play against super-charged opponents, a line has been added for extra high character mods: "Super Mods". Characters generated in this way will resemble our favorite story-book, fantasy novel, and movie super heroes.*

BONUSES FOR UNUSUAL STATS

1-1000 roll	Bonus Mod	Dev. Points	Power Points	Super Mods
000	+35	11	4	+55
988-999	+30	10	3	+50
975-987	+25	10	3	+45
949-974	+20	9	2	+40
910-948	+15	9	2	+35
845-909	+10	8	1	+30
780-844	+5	8	1	+25
650-779	+5	7	1	+20
455-649	0	6	0	+15
338-454	0	5	0	+10
195-337	0	5	0	+5
001-194	-5	4	0	0

5.3 INNATE STAT ABILITIES

The special abilities enumerated below detail the powers gained when character statistics reach values greater than 101. For each of the ten stats, the abilities are in three groupings:

Group A (modest or initial abilities for a stat range of 102-104)
Group B (strong abilities for a stat range of 105-109)
Group C (powerful abilities for a stat range of 110-120)

NOTE: *A GM who decides to use these guidelines should examine these ranges and adapt them to fit the scale of his/her game. GMs should also feel free to add to or modify the abilities listed to retain play balance in their campaigns.*

For each stat that attains a value of 102-104, a special ability from group A may be chosen from the special abilities for that stat. If a stat reaches a value in the range 105-109, a group B pick **or** two A picks may be chosen. Finally, if a stat becomes 110 or greater, one of the following may also be chosen: one C pick **or** one B pick and two A picks. Picks chosen are cumulative; thus, a character with a 112 Quickness may have 5 A picks **or** 1 A, 1 B, and 1 C pick from the Quickness special abilities.

Note that all these abilities are innate. They may resemble spells but are not magical in that sense. No power points need be expended since no spell is actually being cast; other restrictions governing spellcasting are nonapplicable as well. Some of the abilities are identical to background options listed in *RCMI* while others are best treated by referring to a spell description; still others are completely unique. All spell-like abilities may be employed an unlimited number of times per day (unless stated otherwise), but only once per round.

CONSTITUTION

• **A Picks:**
1. *Unnatural Stamina* as the background option.
2. *Tolerance* as the background option.
3. Healing occurs at twice the normal rate.
4. Stat loss (due to stress) never occurs upon gaining a level; i.e., stat gain rolls of 01-04 are ignored.
5. *Clotting I* as the spell, once per round.

• **B Picks:**
1. *Natural Physique* as the background option.
2. *Pain Relief I* as the spell.
3. *Major Fracture/Cartilage Repair* as the Healer spell.
4. *Muscle/Tendon Repair* as the Healer spell.
5. *Preservation* as the Cleric spell, 1 hour per level duration.
6. *Cut Repair I* as the spell.
7. Healing occurs at three times the normal rate (not cumulative with 3. above).
8. Skin toughens to AT 3 permanently.
9. *Poison/Disease Resistance I* as the Open Channeling spell.
10. Stuns accumulated from each blow taken are reduced by one round.

• **C Picks:**
1. *Undisease/Unpoison* as the Open Channeling spell, usable 5 times per day.
2. *Cancel True* as the Closed Essence spell, usable 5 times per day. Alternatively, only one realm may be cancelled but this ability may be used once per round an unlimited number of times per day.
3. *Major Vessel Repair I* as the Healer spell.
4. *Major Fracture Repair True* as the Healer spell.
5. *Muscle/Tendon Repair True* as the Healer spell.
6. All criticals taken are reduced one level in severity.

AGILITY

• **A Picks:**
1. *Natural Facility with Armor* as the background option.
2. *Body Control* as the Nightblade spell.
3. *Landing* (10' per level) as the Closed Mentalism spell.
4. *Edgerunning* as the Monk spell.
5. All fumble ranges are halved (round down).

• **B Picks:**
1. *Ambidextrous:* All one-handed melee weapons that character has proficiency in may be used in either or both hands; no cost for this two-weapon combination.
2. Weapon Kata penalties are eliminated.
3. Directed elemental attack spells may be parried using melee OBs and a weapon/shield.
4. Agile parrying ability causes opponents to resist vs. character's level or be disarmed if the character uses at least half of his OB to parry.

• **C Picks:**
1. *Scope Skill* (choose directed or nondirected spells); otherwise as the background option.
2. Penalties for engaging in multiple melee attacks are reduced by 50%.
3. *Pinpoint Accuracy:* All missile, directed spell, or melee criticals delivered increase one level in severity.
4. *Deftness:* Open-ended high (OEH) roll range for rolls involving skills that receive an AG bonus becomes 91-100.
5. *Sureness:* Open-ended low (OEL) range for rolls involving skills that receive an AG bonus becomes 01-02.

SELF-DISCIPLINE

• **A Picks:**
1. *Courage* as the Paladin spell.
2. *Levitation* as the Closed Essence spell.
3. *Meditation III* as the Shaman spell.
4. *Unpain 50%* as the Open Mentalism spell.

Skills/Stats "Laws": Innate Stat Abilities

- **B Picks:**
1. *Improved Frenzy:* when frenzied, defense is normal and crits are reduced one level. A total roll of 116 is needed to achieve this state.
2. *Iron Will:* Adds +50 to RRs versus any mind-influencing spells.
3. Stuns accumulated from each blow taken are reduced by one round.
4. *Concentration II* as the Monk spell.
5. *Unpain 100%* as the Open Mentalism spell.

- **C Picks:**
1. *Unpresence* as the Mystic spell.
2. *Hyperfrenzy:* as Improved Frenzy above, but instantaneous spells may be cast while frenzied, crits are reduced two levels, and a roll of 131 must be attained.
3. *Mountain Heart I* as the Nightblade spell, usable 3 times per day.
4. *Temporal Skill* as the background option.
5. Additional +15 bonus to all RRs that can be actively resisted (i.e., nonsubtle attacks).
6. *Self-Keeping* as the Monk spell.

MEMORY

- **A Picks:**
1. *Total Recall* as the Closed Mentalism spell.
2. All Languages are learned at half-cost (and time).
3. *Study I* as the Bard spell.
4. Permanent 5% bonus to all earned experience.
5. Procedural Memory allows two chosen skills to be developed at half cost, subject to GM approval. Skills must be specific; examples: martial arts striking, a certain spell list, or acrobatics.

- **B Picks:**
1. *Subconscious Discipline* as the background option.
2. *Spell Store* as the Closed Essence spell, except one other spell may be cast before the stored spell.
3. Permanent 10% bonus to earned experience (noncumulative with 4. above).

- **C Picks:**
1. Permanent 15% bonus to earned experience (noncumulative with experience bonuses above).
2. Permanent +10 bonus to all actions (must have been previously seen or attempted).

REASONING

- **A Picks:**
1. *Tactician* as the background option (substitute reasoning for intuition).
2. *Judge of Weaponry* as the background option.
3. Detect Lie (50% chance per lie).
4. *Observation* as the Closed Mentalism spell.
5. *Calculate II* as the Sage spell.
6. *Awareness* as the Mentalist spell.

- **B Picks:**
1. Clever attacking strategies increase effectiveness of martial art ranks used by one factor.
2. *Correlate* as the Closed Mentalism spell.
3. *Detect Illusion* as the Monk spell.
4. *Calculate III* as the Sage spell.

- **C Picks:**
1. *Weigh Decision* (45% bias) as the Sage spells.
2. Ambush skill rank increases 50% and is one-half cost thereafter.
3. *Awareness True* as the Mentalist spell.
4. Complete understanding of one race allows crits against the race to be 'Slaying'.

STRENGTH

- **A Picks:**
1. Armor minimum maneuver penalties are halved.
2. *Hammerhand* as the background option.
3. All missile ranges increase 50%.
4. Crits delivered also yield Unbalancing crits (2 degrees less severity).
5. Firm Grip allows 2-handed weapons to be wielded in one hand at a -25 penalty. Two-weapon combo is unusable when employing this ability.

- **B Picks:**
1. Death Grip yields Krush crits the following round after grappling a target.
2. *Shocking Blows:* All melee strikes yield double concussion damage.
3. *Bow Tester:* All missile strikes yield double concussion damage.
4. *Heave-Ho:* May throw objects as a giant would, with a 200' range. Skill must be developed.

- **C Picks:**
1. *Bone Breaker:* 50% of all strikes made with blunt weapons are 'Shattering'.
2. Hulking Frame yields ability to throw weight into blows, inflicting additional Impact crits in melee.
3. Items as strong as Mithril may be bent/broken if the item fails an RR.
4. *Ginsu Master:* 50% of all strikes made with edged weapons are 'Cleaving'.

QUICKNESS

- **A Picks:**
1. *Fluidity* adds +5 to all OBs and non-rear DBs (includes DB versus elemental attack spells).
2. *Lightning Reactions* allow negation of 1 surprise or disorientation round.
3. Ability to roll with blows subtracts 5 from all crits taken (if aware of the attack).
4. *Efficiency* gives an additional 10% activity each round.
5. Ability to change facing in melee prevents character from being flanked/attacked from rear by less than 3 opponents (if aware of these opponents).

- **B Picks:**
1. *Fluidity:* as above (noncumulative) except bonus is +10.
2. Opponent's Quickness and/or adrenal defense may be negated 50% of the time (if opponent possesses quickness below 102).
3. *Preemptive Striking:* Character may act one combat phase earlier (i.e. he could fire a missile in the spell phase); a penalty of -30 to first swing points (FSP) is applied when this ability is used.
4. *Efficiency:* As above except additional activity is 20% (noncumulative).

- **C Picks:**
1. *Fluidity:* as above (noncumulative) except bonus is +15.
2. *Dodging III* as the Monk spell.
3. *Spell Dodge II* as the Nightblade spell.
4. *Efficiency:* as above (noncumulative) except additional activity is 40%.

PRESENCE

• A Picks:

1. *Look of Eagles* as the background option.
2. *Suggestion* as the Closed Essence spell; targets gain a +30 to resist.
3. *Mind Merge* as the Mentalist spell.
4. *Mind Shield* as the Open Mentalism spell.
5. *Inner Thoughts* as the Mentalist spell.
6. *Mind Voice 100′* as the Mentalist spell.

• B Picks:

1. *Look of Terror I* as the Warlock spell.
2. *Aggression* as the background option, except applies to all attack rolls.
3. *Inner Wall V* as the Closed Mentalism spell.
4. *Aura* as the background option.
5. *Lifekeeping* (1 hour per level) as the Cleric spell.
6. *Charm Kind* as the Mentalist spell; targets gain a +30 to RRs.
7. *Hold Kind* as the Mentalist spell.

• C Picks:

1. *Inspirations II* as the Paladin spell.
2. *Misfeel True* as the Mystic spell.
3. *Control Demon V* as the Evil Magician spell.
4. *Master of Kind* as the Mentalist spell; targets gain a +30 to RRs.
5. *Fist of Power:* Ability to externalize mind force allows the caster to simulate the effects of the Mentalist spell *Shock E* twice per day. Alternatively, 'Shattering' may be used.

INTUITION

• A Picks:

1. *Dream I* as the Cleric spell.
2. *Divination* as the secondary skill, 80% chance of success.
3. *Direction Sense* as the background option.
4. *Guess* as the Cleric spell.
5. +50 bonus to the skill Spatial Location Awareness.
6. Intuitive understanding of near future bestows a +10 bonus to all DBs (including rear DBs).

• B Picks:

1. *Awakening* as the Monk spell.
2. *Intuitions V* as the Cleric spell.
3. *Detect Ambush* as the Ranger spell.
4. *Channel Opening* (10 miles per level) as the Cleric spell.

• C Picks:

1. *Luck* as the background option.
2. *Destiny Sense* as the background option.
3. *Dangersense* as the background option.
4. *Fervor:* special tie to deity allows use of the Dervish spell Dance of Fervor once per week.
5. *Anticipate True* as the Open Mentalism spell.

EMPATHY

• A Picks:

1. *Animal Friendship* as the background option.
2. *Mind Typing* as the Mentalist spell.
3. *Emotions* as the Mentalist spell.
4. *Detect Realm:* as *Detect Channeling*, but applies to all realms.
5. *Mana Sensing* as the background option.
6. *Presence/Feel/Mind Store* as the Mentalist spells.
7. *Location 500′* as the Open Channeling spell.

• B Picks:

1. *Visions* as the background option.
2. *Mana Reading* as the background option, except 50% chance for each ability.
3. *Awareness* as the Mentalist spell.
4. *Neutralize Curse* (1 minute per level) as the Cleric spell.
5. *Analysis* as the Open Essence spell.

• C Picks:

1. *Transcendence* as the background option.
2. *Spatial Skill* as the background option.
3. *Detect True* as the Open Essence spell.
4. *Ensorcellment Cure* as the background option.
5. *Power Parasite:* Power may be leeched from an earthnode, item, or person imbued with Essence power; rate of drain is 10 PP per round and user must make a BAR vs unwilling targets, who then make an RR to attempt to resist the draining. Concentration must be maintained during each round of the drain.

5.4 LUCK

Luck is a relative measure of how well one is blessed by the gods. The Luck (LU) statistic is determined just like the 10 normal *RM* stats: roll for temporary and potential values. Use *ChL&CaL* Table 15.13 to determine the unusual statistic bonus. If a GM wants to, he may assign racial Luck bonuses for the races in his world (see the Luck Chart in this section for some suggestions).

Option 1: The luck bonus can be applied by the GM to many situations. If the GM deems that a situation is a completely random affair he may use the luck bonus to add to (or subtract from) the following: direction sense, divination, foraging, gambling, general perception, locate secret opening, mining, navigation, surprise rolls, tactical games, RRs, etc.

Option 2: Divide the luck statistic (not the bonus) by ten and round to the nearest whole number to determine a character's Lucky Break #. This number represents the percentage chance that a character will avoid a death blow. If an attack result indicates that a character is killed, roll 1D100 and add his Lucky Break #. If the result exceeds 100, then the character is not dead, but instead is unconscious at the brink of death but in a stable condition (not bleeding). Every time that process is used, the character's Lucky Break # is reduced by one. Note that cats have a Lucky Break # of nine.

Option 3: If a GM wants a less deadly game, use Option 2 above, but to obtain the Lucky Break # divide the Luck stat by 5 instead of 10.

Option 4: The GM can choose to use the luck statistic (not the Bonus) as a skill modifier. Whenever a situation occurs that involves pure luck (like gambling on the draw of a card, playing Russian Roulette, etc.). The player would roll 1D100, add his luck statistic and add the difficulty modifier (see Luck Chart); a 101+ result would then indicate success.

EXAMPLE: *Nirrad, an ugly Human Barbarian, rolls 99 for his luck statistic. This gives him a Luck Bonus of +20; he doesn't have a racial bonus. His Lucky Break # is 10 = 99 ÷ 10 (rounded off).*

LUCK CHART			
Difficulty	**Mod**	**Race**	**Luck Bonus**
Routine	+0	Halflings	+10
Easy	-10	Elves	+5
Light	-20	Humans, Half Elves	0
Medium	-30	Dwarves	-5
Hard	-40	Others	-10
Very Hard	-50		
Extremely Hard	-60		
Sheer Folly	-80		
Absurd	-100		

5.5 LEVEL INTENSIVE COMBAT

In *Rolemaster* a spell user continues to become significantly more effective as he builds up his experience levels. However, above fifth level, and especially above tenth, experience levels can make little difference to an arms user. Combat, as it now stands, is stat intensive; i.e. above tenth level a character's stat bonuses are going to make a lot more difference than, say, five or ten skill levels. The reason for this, of course, is the declining scale for skill ranks developed. By the present system (i.e. 5,2,1,1/2) a nineteenth level Fighter will only have a skill rank bonus 15 points better than a ninth level Fighter, assuming two combat skill ranks per level are developed. Naturally, in this range, the per level bonus will be the significant difference. Even this distinction disappears at very high levels when the per level bonus declines or disappears entirely (e.g., a 29th level Fighter will have a 10 point Skill bonus advantage over a 19th level Fighter). This does not even consider the problems a 36th level Ranger has when tackling a 19th level Fighter (who should be frightened to confront the Ranger even in melee).

For those who desire a skill intensive system, so that increasing experience levels does make a significant difference in one's combat abilities, the declining scale may be altered. The suggested scale is 5,4,3,2,1. This will insure that the Lord Fighter's skill bonus will be at least twenty points higher than the tenth level Fighter's.

Theoretically this scale could be used with all primary and secondary skills, but this would distort many of the system mechanics. Since combat is a skill against skill system (i.e. the wise defender may parry), such a scale can be appropriate for melee, missile, or thrown attack skill. The chart below presents the progression for skill ranks 1-50; the progression above 50 is +1 per skill rank.

NOTE: *If this system is used, the OBs for higher level creatures should be increased by 20-50% to compensate for the higher weapon OBs.*

Option: Let the minimum skill rank bonus be 2 per skill rank; i.e., the progression is 5,4,3,2.

Skill Rank	Bonus	Skill Rank	Bonus
1	5	26	108
2	10	27	111
3	15	28	114
4	20	29	117
5	25	30	120
6	30	31	122
7	35	32	124
8	40	33	126
9	45	34	128
10	50	35	130
11	54	36	132
12	58	37	134
13	62	38	136
14	66	39	138
15	70	40	139
16	74	41	140
17	78	42	141
18	82	43	142
19	86	44	143
20	90	45	144
21	93	46	145
22	96	47	146
23	99	48	147
24	102	49	148
25	105	50	149

5.6 ELOQUENCE (Mental Quickness)

The Memory stat in *Rolemaster* is, perhaps without question, the least used stat in the game; a GM must usually rely on the player's Memory and not the Character's. Very seldom, at least in our experience, are characters required to make "Memory" rolls. The use of Memory for Primary skill stat bonuses is non-existent, and for secondary skills it is rare. Some character classes have Memory as a prime requisite, but very seldom do those classes in an adventure have much reason to rely on that stat. Since Memory is a stat, a GM may decide to replace Memory with another stat: *Eloquence* (abbreviated EL), call it Mental Quickness (MQ) if you wish.

Eloquence is a measure of mental quickness and is suitable for such actions as orientation rolls, speed of spell casting, quickness of perception, changes of action, and obviously, quick decision making. Thus, the Agility stat would represent dexterity, gymnastic ability, and quickness of small body motions, such as the movements of the fingers playing an instrument. Quickness, is a measure of body-speed "flat-out," such as in running, or other kinds of track events.

Eloquence is the *Mental* capacity for making decisions quickly. It is the trademark of genius (or lack thereof): the admirable quality in leaders and executives. In our experience, we have seen those persons who are built for slow motion, but who think in rapid response. Likewise, there are those who are adept on the track but slow upstairs. Mental quickness, Eloquence, is a stat that will be used again and again whereas Memory always seems to lie dormant in game play. It also makes sense that Eloquence, speed of thought, could replace Memory as a development stat since, obviously, speed of mental processes relates directly to learning. It makes sense to derive development points from that stat. If this optional rule is used, whenever a Memory roll of some kind is required, use the Reasoning stat in place of Memory.

5.7 SIMPLE POTENTIAL GENERATION

Table 15.11 (Character Law) may be too cumbersome for some GMs to use to create a large number of PCs and NPCs. One method of avoiding this table is to use a Simple Potential Generation roll. If the GM desires, he should roll 1D100 and have that roll be the potential.

One exception to this rule is that if the Temporary roll is 100 and the Potential roll is 100, then the Potential should be 101.

EXAMPLE: *Nirrad, a Human Barbarian, has a temporary Strength of 92. If the player rolls a 96 for his potential, then the potential is a 96. If, however, one used* **ChL** *Table 15.11, then the potential would have been a 99.*

Using Simple Potential Determination will result in lower potential statistics, but will reduce the time needed to create a character.

6.0 OPTIONAL CREATURE & TREASURE "LAWS"

6.1 TREASURE GENERATION

This section presents a chart for quickly generating treasures after an encounter. The level of the defeated opponent determines the column used; roll once for each type of potential treasure. If there were multiple opponents, the GM may roll one set of potential treasures for each opponent **or** roll one set based upon the combined levels of the opponents.

The GM should use discretion if using this chart **or** the treasure may become much too rich. If the GM determines this to be the case, he may use a column based upon the square root of the opponents' levels.

CHART KEY

If there is a "—" for a treasure type, that indicates that there is no chance of such a treasure being present. A percentage, of course, indicates a percentage chance of finding the indicated number of items in that category. If there is just a number, then that number of items are found. If there is a die roll expression, players find the number indicated by the dice.

bp, sp, gp, pp, mp = coins: bronze pieces, silver, gold, platinum and Mithril. 1 pp = 10 gp and 1 mp = 100 gp.

Gems: various valuable stones. The GM may determine the values by any approved system. Suggested value is about 10-60 gp each with a possibility of extreme value (e.g., 10% = x10).

Jewels: various items formed with valuable stones, metals, etc. Suggested values are 100-600 gp each with a possibility for an extreme value (e.g., 10% = x10).

Combat: valuable items of a military nature (weapons, armor, shields, etc.). S, S+, and S++ are indications of great value. They may be of greater than +15 enchantment and may have GM-designed additional abilities. Or, these may be rolled for using *C&T*'s charts and the following bonuses: S = +100, S+ = +200, S++ = +250.

1 Use, Modest, Potent, Most Potent, Artifact = types of magical treasures found. *1 Use* = potion, rune, etc. *Modest* are worth less than 500 gp value. *Potent* are of 500-1000 gp value. *Most Potent* is a very broad category embracing all items from 1000-10,000 gp value. *Artifacts* are any magical items of over 10,000 gp value. GMs should probably never roll randomly for "legendary artifacts."

6.2 ARCANE ARTIFACTS AND ITEMS

POTENT ITEMS

Amulet of Soul Succor: Allows an additional +25 on RRs vs. stat draining or soul-damaging effects. Even if the RR fails, only half damage is taken.

Chain Shirt of Encumbrance: A cursed set of AT 16 which encumbers as AT 20. Remove Curse is necessary to ditch the unwanted item.

Circlet of Evasion: A headband that: adds +10 to DB and RR; allows 50% critical negation for head; casts Spell Dodge, Aim Untrue, and Bladeturn I twice/day each.

Heartbreaker Potent: A +20 throwing kynac that: inflicts an extra Puncture critical of 1 degree less severity; doubles bleeding hits delivered; and Longdoors (300') back to thrower after striking.

Helm of Taurus: This cursed +10 full helm negates 90% of head criticals and allows the wearer to develop a Butt attack using the helm. However, any time the wearer is in combat with a creature of lower level, he must resist a Lvl 15 Mentalism attack or charge the opponent, giving +30 to OB and double damage. The wearer will then continue to charge any and all opponents using his full Butt OB until all are down or have fled.

Mask of Many Faces: This thin, translucent mask casts a continual *Impersonation Facade* complete with all senses. The facade is immune to most magical detections, but spells over 20th level get to make RRs **and** a character that makes a successful Perception roll modified by -70 gets to make a RR.

Rune of Spellweaving: This powerful rune, when read, allows the wearer to cast any number of spells simultaneously (including concentration spells, which must, however, still be concentrated on after casting, 50% activity each). Two rounds of preparation are required, and one round is needed to read the rune. Any overcasting is still subject to ESF rolls, so difficult spells are best left for last — the spells are cast simultaneously but spell failures must be rolled in the order that the spells are listed. It is possible for the caster to expend all of his PPs using this rune. In any case, a D100 roll must be made, adding a quarter of the PPs expended and subtracting the caster's SD bonus and the average of his spellcasting stats. If the adjusted roll exceeds 100, the caster will take an electricity critical of 1 degree severity per 10 points over 100; i.e., a roll of 101-110 indicates a "A", 111-120 a "B", etc.

The Gemini Sword: A +20 green laen two-handed sword that is a x4 Essence multiplier. It may split itself into two other 2-hand swords; each +15 and x3 multipliers, one of yellow and one of blue laen

The Serpent Staff: A +20 quarterstaff; upon delivering a critical, the target must resist against a level 20 nerve poison or die in CO/10 rounds.

TREASURE GENERATION CHART

Treasure Type	\multicolumn{8}{c}{LEVELS}
	1 to 2	3 to 4	5 to 7	8 to 11	12 to 15	16 to 23	24 to 29	30+
bp	2D10	2D12	2D20	3D12	50%—4D20	50%—2D100	50%—2D1000	50%—5D1000
sp	20%—1D10	1D10	2D10	3D12	4D20	5D20	50%—5D100	50%—2D1000
gp	05%—1D6	20%—1D6	50%—2D6	3D6	4D10	4D20	2D100	1D1000
pp	0	05%—1D2	20%—1D6	50%—1D10	2D12	4D12	4D20	2D100
mp	0	0	05%—1D2	10%—1D3	20%—1D4	50%—1D6	50%—1D10	5D10
Gems	0	0	05%—1D4	20%—1D6	50%—1D10	1D20	2D20	4D10
Jewels	0	0	01%—1	05%—1D2	20%—1D3	50%—1D6	50%—1D10	2D10
Combat	05%—1	25%—1D2	50%—1D3	1D4	1D4S	1D4S+	2D3S+	2D4S++
1 Use Item	01%—1	05%—1	20%—1D2	25%—1D3	50%—1D4	1D4	1D6	2D6
Modest	0	01%—1	5%—1D2	20%—1D3	50%—1D3	1D4	1D6	2D6
Potent	0	0	01%—1	05%—1D2	20%—1D3	50%—1D4	1D4	1D6
Most Potent	0	0	0	01%—1	03%—1	05%—1D2	20%—1D3	50%—1D4
Artifact	0	0	0	0	.1%—1	01%—1	05%—1D2	20%—1D3

Creature & Treasure "Laws": Items 37

The Shieldarang: A +20 normal shield that: can be thrown (ranges as spear); will return (up to 300') via flight; and attacks on the war mattock table (Krush criticals).

White Eog Ring: Bestows a bonus of +15 versus Evil spells and an additional +30 versus Evil Channels.

MOST POTENT ITEMS

Amulet of Adrenal Frenzy: Adds +20 to frenzy skill; allows wearer to retain 50% of normal DB when frenzied; and allows casting of instantaneous spells when frenzied.

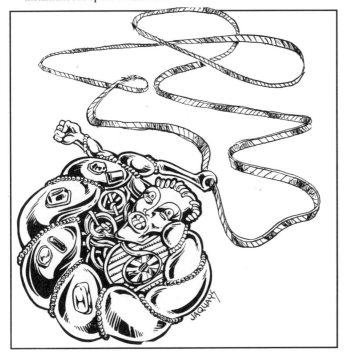

Bracers of the Blinding Strike: A x3 Essence multiplier that gives a +15 additional bonus to wearer's Quickness. It also allows a *Cobra Strike* 3 times/day, bracers inject target with a poison equal to the wearer's level upon striking. The poison causes lethargy: if target fails RR by 1-10 / 11-30 / 31+ then the result is -30 all actions / -75 all actions / total paralysis and -100 on static actions. Effects last 1-100 min.

Headband of Dharius: A x4 multiplier for any class that: adds +15 to perception; bestows subconscious discipline (as the **RMCI** background option) while worn; and adds +10 to mental attack and defense rolls.

Ring of Mind Mastery: When worn: concentration spells cost only 25% normal activity; wearer can concentrate on 2 spells simultaneously; and it adds 25 to RRs vs. mental attack

Ring of Sky-Blue: Adds +20 to outdoor skills; allows an additional +30 bonus and an extra x1 damage to *Lightning Bolts* cast by wielder; and casts *Fly 300'* and *Death Cloud 10'R* 2/day each.

Snakeskin Robes: Protect as AT 4 (-15); adds +15 to DB, RR, MR (Maneuver Roll); and sheds once/week to take on most common color in present terrain, acts as Camouflage in that terrain.

Spinetingler: A +20 Holy broadsword that: changes to a dagger or a two-handed sword instantly; delivers extra cold critical of equal severity; and, upon delivering a critical, target must resist a level 20 *Distraction* spell (-25 to OBs and maneuvers), spell has a duration of 20 minutes and the RR is at -30.

The Stomping Staff: Normally, the +15 staff does double damage. However, if an opponent has been flipped or is down, attacks with the staff as part of a weapon kata may be used to 'stomp' the opponent. The attack uses the kata OB but results are determined on the Fall/Krush Table (double damage). The secondary critical for the kata will be Impact instead of Unbalancing.

ARTIFACTS

Assassin's Armor: AT 14 (-15); encumbers as AT 5; constant *Silent Moves*, *Shadows*, and *Darkvision* (100'); and adds +4 to Ambush skill.

Bane: This medallion allows the wearer to choose a creature type that is the '*enemy*'.(e.g., a particular Mannish race, Grey Elves, evil spell user, etc.). If the wearer achieves a critical against an 'enemy', the critical will be 'slaying' if: if the creature is *super-large* and the crit severity is "E" **or** the creature is *large* and the crit severity is "C"–"E" **or** the creature is normal and the crit severity is "B"–"E". The 'enemy' type may be chosen up to twice per week. It takes the medallion 10 hours to attune itself for a new 'enemy'; during this time it confers no special powers. The wearer also gains the use of the special list Guardian Ways (must apply to the 'enemy') up to his level and a bonus of 20 PP for spellcasting on that list only. The wearer will never fear or obey an 'enemy' and gains +10 to RRs and DB versus the designated enemies. The wearer must roll 101+ (using SD bonus) whenever confronting an 'enemy' for the first time in each day **and/or** every round of combat when an enemy is within 50'. Failure means that he must attack the nearest enemy (if the 'enemy' happens to be a current ally, then +20 may be added to the SD roll).

Bracer of Contact: When worn, it adds +20 to Channeling skill; spells cast by wearer are *Ranged* by 100'; and it allows the wearer to channel to a target irregardless of whether target is concentrating on the realm or is otherwise ready to receive a spell or PPs.

Bracers of Fortune: A x4 Essence multiplier that gives wearer 'Luck' (as per background option in *RMCI*); if wearer already has the option, then the Luck power is increased to ±10. It also adds +15 to OB, DB, MR, and RR. Wearer's Open-Ended Low (OEL) range becomes 01-02 instead of 01-05.

Collar Majestic of Dwarvenkind: Allows non-Dwarven wearer to acquire the innate Dwarven attributes of spell and poison resistance: +40 vs. Essence and Mentalism and +20 vs. poison. However, if the wearer casts any spells from these realms, he must first make an ESF at +40 due to the very nature of the Collar making the caster resistant to these realms.

Gauntlet of the Vengeful Healer: Adds +30 to ESF rolls on the Healer Base lists. Healer spells can be reversed by wearer to harm a target; range is touch and recovery takes double the normal time. the gauntlet also casts *Disruption* upon touch.

Goldleaf's Wreath: A x3 Channeling multiplier that: adds 10 levels for spellcasting on Nature's Forms list; protects as helm / 50% critical negation for head; casts 50 PP/day from the Inner Walls list (up to level 30); cast *Green Channel II* 1/day: this spell turns the target into a Slowroot (has a 50' range, and a RR Mod of -50).

Grovestaff: A +40 Druidstaff that is a +7 Channeling Adder. In areas that are Holy for the wielder, the staff allows access to a special list called Soulfires; the list is identical to Mana Fires except a bonus of +30 to ESF is allowed for spellcasting on the list and all fire spells from the list will only harm fauna, not flora.

Retributor (or *Myshtahra*, "Halfling's Hope"): A +25 laen short sword that: uses the broadsword table for attacks; is 'Slaying' against 'Lunkies' (i.e., any creature taller than 6'0"); casts *Unpain 75%* and *Strength III* 2/day each; and wielder may *Defend* (as the rune) against 2 melee attacks per round in addition to normal action.

The Black Bow: A +20 Short Bow fashioned of enchanted black Shereth wood. Uses longbow table for range and damage. String and bow will not normally break. Normally fires 2 arrows per round (no rapid-fire penalty), which teleport back to wielder's quiver upon striking or missing. Fumbles only on '01' and all range penalties are halved.

The Redstone: A +5 Mentalism Adder. Allows possessor to act without hindrance when casting Mentalism spells that involve head coverings, metal or otherwise, on the target and/or the possessor. The 'General' column is used for attacks against helmed opponents and the possessor need make no ESFs due to any head coverings he wears.

The Zodiac Symbol: This evil item casts the following spells upon demand (1/rnd): *LBolt +80(3D), Teleport I, Misfeel True, Friend Speech, Protection V, Master of Kind, Dispel True, Displacement III*. Wielder's spells only fail on an '01'.

Wand of Loci: This wand absorbs elemental attacks directed against the wielder and redirects them back towards the attacker. The redirected attack uses the wielder's bonus with the spell but with an additional +10 and additional 1x damage bonus. The wand, unlike most, will perform this function an unlimited number of times up to 3 times per round. Attacking magic that resists against 40th level will be absorbed but not reflected. In this case the wand will bestow PPs upon the wielder equal to the PPs that the attacker put into the attack.

6.3 REPULSIONS

NOTE: *These optional rules are for GMs who feel that the Repulsions spell list is too powerful. The original list was intended to be a reflection of a **True** Cleric's power over the Undead; i.e., extremely effective. These guidelines make Undead much more powerful and deadly.*

Any GM who has reffed **Rolemaster** for very long, and has used Undead, has discovered that the Cleric's Repulsions list is very effective against the Undead. The following rules for the use of the Cleric's base Repulsions list make Clerics less effective and the Undead more powerful.

Simply put, the Cleric's base Repulsions list is to be used "as is" only for created Undead; i.e., those Undead which occur through the use of the evil Cleric's Necromancy *Create Undead* spells. These Undead can be effected fully by the normal Repulsion's list as it occurs in the rules. However, naturally occurring Undead, such as Barrow Wights, Vampires, Ghouls, are tougher and resist Repulsions according to different rules. GMs should modify these rules for game balance in their world.

1. All "naturally occurring" Undead (i.e., those not those created by Necromancy Create Undead spells) double the value of their Type number when resisting against the normal Repulsions lists. Thus, a type IV Undead is treated as a Type VIII.
2. Those Undead who are higher than Type III (unmodified) also get a bonus of +25 to their Resistance Rolls. So, a Type V natural Undead, is treated as a Type X (from rule 1) and gets a +25 RR bonus against the Cleric's Repulsions attempt. Therefore, if a high level Cleric can throw a Repulsions XV, he may effect one Type V (treats it as a Type X) and the five points remaining (XV – X) will exactly neutralize the V's RR bonus (V x 5), according to *Spell Law*'s Repulsions spell list.
3. Those Undead who must be dealt with in special ways, such as the Vampire's stakes and items of silver, cannot be destroyed through Repulsions, even should they fail their RR by more than 50. They are treated as simply having to flee normally. Thus, a high level Cleric may be able to make Dracula flee temporarily with a Repulsions spells, but he could not kill him outright till he tracked him down and hammered in that stake.
4. The Cleric's hefty *Repel Undead True* spell, level 20 Base Cleric Repulsions list, is to be treated as a Repulsions XX.

*The four 9th level adventurers, Fighter, Mentalist, Sorcerer, and Cleric, enter the crypts. Suddenly (says the GM), the door slams shut and a loud cracking sound comes from the dusty mausoleum shelves. Name-plates fall, breaking on the floor, and out of the shelves attack five Barrow Wights. The GM chuckles: the players should never have come in here — he warned them that they needed to be better prepared. These are type IV Wights, 10th level monsters. Round 1: the Fighter swings at a Wight and hits, getting a critical, but reduced two levels of severity. He rolls a good crit, but, Sorry (the GM says), Wights are immune to stunning and bleeding hits. The Wight returns the swing and the Fighter (who is not immune to stuns and bleeding) begins to lose Constitution as well. The Sorcerer throws a panic spell at one; and the GM says, Sorry, immune also to fear. The Mentalist begins to panic, he's having a hard time thinking of any spell in his arsenal that effects Undead. Sleep? No. Charm? No. Calm? Probably not. He's not high enough to throw a Shocks spell which could effect one, with the crits being lowered two levels. Maybe a Pain spell? Maybe not. But then the cleric fires his Repel Undead IX spell one round early (it's only 6th level) and the GM asks the Cleric whether we wants to aim the whole spell at one target or multiple targets. Now the Cleric chuckles. The most the Wights could be are type IV, he thinks. If I aim the spell at one he will have an additional RR penalty of at least -25 (see **Spell Law**, Base Cleric Repulsions list) and I can probably destroy it in one round. Or, I can aim for more (in this case, two) and send them both fleeing. The GM groans and covers his head. By the time the battle's over, in only three rounds, the Mentalist is wounded and frustrated; the Sorcerer broke up one Wight and it is now flopping on the floor; the Fighter finally killed one Wight on hit points (but has lost a lot of temp Constitution); and the cleric got the other **three**.*

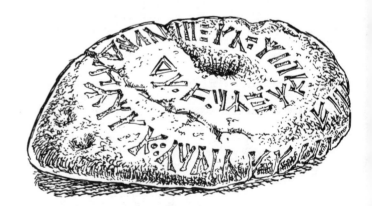

Creature & Treasure "Laws": Monster Mashing   39

6.2 MONSTER MASHING

Considerable effort went into *C&T* in evaluating all of a creature's abilities into its experience level. For example, Dragons have much lower offensive bonuses than you might expect because of their magic and multiple attacks. Similarly, the Tyrannosaurus, which has one of the highest OBs in *C&T,* is only rated at level 8 because it defines new standards for stupid. Even so, some **Rolemaster** players would like for creatures to have combat values very closely related to their experience value. GMs thus have an easier time figuring play balance and generating quickie creatures (and NPCs). The players have a better idea what they will be confronting at a particular difficulty level. The following chart suggests values for quickie generation of creatures and NPCs.

Explanation: *Three categories are offered, arms class, semi-arms class, and non-arms (spell user) class. Arms was calculated at purchasing 2 skill ranks per level, with a +3/lvl bonus, and a total miscellaneous factor which ranges from 20 at level 0 to 60 at level 100. This miscellaneous bonus is intended to represent all applicable bonuses (e.g. totals of Strength, weapon quality, etc). Semi-arms was calculated at 1 1/2 skill ranks per level, a +2/lvl bonus, and a miscellaneous add of 15 to 55. Non-arms was figured at 1 skill ranks per level, no level bonus, and a miscellaneous add of 10 to 50. Hit points are calculated by purchasing the same number of body development skill ranks as for weapons; but arms users 'roll' 12-sided dice, semi's are 10's, and the others roll 8's. Asterisks (*) mark where most human types should stop. The 12-sided hit points are useful for beasts and monsters, Ogres, Trolls, beefy humans, etc. Defensive bonus is quickly recognizable as the regular declining stat scale.*

LEVEL BASED COMBAT ABILITIES CHART

Lvl	DB	ARMS OB	ARMS Hits	SEMI-ARMS OB	SEMI-ARMS Hits	NON-ARMS OB	NON-ARMS Hits
0	5	30	14	25	12	15	5
1	10	43	28	32	18	20	10
2	15	56	42	44	30	25	15
3	20	69	56	51	36	30	20
4	25	87	70	68	48	40	25
5	30	94	84	75	54	45	30
6	35	101	98	86	66	50	35
7	40	108	112	96	72	55	40
8	45	115	126*	107	84	65	45
9	50	127	140	117	90	70	50
10	52	132	154*	123	102	72	55
11	54	137	168	133	108	74	60
12	56	142	182	139	120*	76	65
13	58	152	196	149	126	83	70
14	60	157	210*	154	138	85	75
15	62	161	224	159	144	87	80
16	64	165	238	164	150*	89	85
17	66	169	252	169	162	91	90
18	68	173	266	174	168	93	95
19	70	177	280	179	180	95	100
20	71	186	294	189	186	101	105
21	72	188	308	192	198	102	110
22	73	190	322	196	204*	103	115
23	74	192	336	198	216	104	120*
24	75	194	350	201	222	105	125
25	76	196	364	203	234	106	130
26	77	198	378	206	240	107	135
27	78	200	392	208	252	108	140
28	79	202	406	211	258	109	145
29	80	204	420	213	270	110	150*
30	80	211	434	221	276	115	155
35	83	221	504	233	324	118	180
40	85	231	574	245	366	120	205*
50	90	256	714	276	456	130	255
60	95	276	854	301	546	135	305
70	100	301	994	331	636	145	355
80	105	321	1134	356	726	150	405
90	110	346	1274	386	816	160	455
100	115	366	1414	411	906	165	505

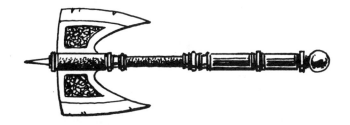

7.0 OPTIONAL MISCELLANEOUS "LAWS"

7.1 ARCANE SOCIETIES

There are no definite guidelines given in *RMCI* for the Arcane Societies which regulate the learning of Arcane spell lists, although mention is made of specialized groups in EarthBlood's Ways. These Arcane Societies keep alive the lore of the distant past, but only amongst the members of the society, of course. these societies may vary in power from slight (like Masons, Kiwanis, Scouting for boys or girls) to very powerful (like the Bavarian Illuminati or The Gnomes of Zurich). Arcane Societies also may vary in complexity from slight (e.g., all *RMC* character professions, Colleges, Librarians, adventuring parties), to very detailed and involved (e.g., the *Court of Ardor*, the *Cloud Lords of Tanara*, the Loremasters, or the *Iron Wind*). thus any guidelines must be vague enough to allow any type of organization the GM may wish to represent, and yet definite enough to be useful.

Since a great way to introduce Arcane spell lists into play is by the use of such organizations, here are some guidelines for Arcane Societies:

1) Arcane Societies are usually very old, with roots reaching back into the mists of time.
2) Arcane Societies are usually secret, although some may be openly known (such as Monastic Groups, Guilds, Navigators).
3) Arcane societies are usually limited in the scope of their power to one location (exceptions include Missionary Groups, Navigators, etc.) whose operations may be nearly anywhere and everywhere).
4) Money and the acquisition of it are not important to Arcane Societies, except insofar as money is a tool of power.
5) Arcane Societies almost always should have a goal towards which the whole organization strives (e.g., bring back to earth some long forgotten godling, save civilization, topple the government, transport everyone everywhere; control some aspect of the economy; World Domination; bring the word of god to the heathen; protect all knowledge gathered in the Great Library of Seezur).
6) Some minimum requirements should be determined in order to be initiates of the Arcane Society. These minimum requirements might be: minimum Stat requirements; minimum level requirements; certain outlook, religion, alignment, etc.; rigorous initiation rites; only a certain sex, profession, social class, race, or clan.
7) Arcane Societies usually have a hierarchical structure, with the more elevated members knowing more about the society and its innermost mysteries.
8) Usually, Arcane Societies have a Supreme Leader, although it may seem that there are several (puppet) leaders. Most Arcane Societies have a "hero," "patron saint," founder, demi-god, etc. who has died for the Arcane Society.
9) Each Arcane Society may be as simple or as convoluted as the GM desires, examples follow.

SIMPLEST

Tolkien's "Rangers of the North" is a very simple Arcane Society; in effect, just a profession.

VERY SIMPLE

"The Order of Librarians of Imperial Eldea"

About 300 years ago, the then Emperor Grimnir created an order by Imperial decree. This Order had the task of guarding and preserving Grimnir's magnificent Library. since the Emperor's death, the Order has expanded to encompass all the Libraries of the Empire of Eldea. Presently, the Order openly seeks to protect and preserve all books, especially the books of the Empire. Secretly, the Lord Librarian plans to one day control the dissemination of all knowledge (even the various Head Librarians do not realize this!).

Minimum Requirements to become an initiate are

1 — Must have a Memory of 90 or more;
2 — Must be at least first level;
3 — Must be either a Scholar or a Sage (see *RMCII*);
4 — Must have at least one skill rank in the following abilities:
    a: BookLore (Study);
    b: Book Binding (Craft);
    c: Materials Conservation — books (Craft);
    d: Administration; and
    e: One other Knowledge Skill or Xeno-Skill,
5 — Must Love and Respect books;
6 — Must be Lawful in alignment/outlook.

All Eldean Libraries charge 1 sp to use their facilities (no charge for Librarians!) for the operating costs of the Libraries and a small retinue of guards (entirely under the control of the Lord). Thus the Power of the Librarians is the wealth of Arcane knowledge they possess.

Miscellaneous "Laws": Arcane Societies

MODERATELY COMPLEX
The Navigators

Note: *This order of Navigators is used an example; it is not the absolute template for the Navigators in ICE's* **Loremaster** *and* **Shadow World** *modules.*

Throughout recorded history, The Navigators have been transporting people and goods by the sea for profit. The navigators openly advertise their transport service to such an extent that in some places theirs is the only service available. Thus, the Navigators are known far and wide.

No one questions who the Navigators are. No one wonders from whence they come. Everyone just uses the Navigators, but it is really the Navigators who use their clients.

Essentially, the Navigators transport anything anywhere (possible). However, they will take nothing without fair, prior payment. Naturally, with such control over the flow of commodities, the Navigators tend to exert near complete control over the economies they service.

This economic power rests in no one man's grasp, but among all of the Council of Elders. The Council of Elders meets but once a year, on Midsummer's Day, to discuss trade policies. It is every member's duty to know what policies the Council follows and abide by them.

There are three ranks within this Arcane Society: initiates, navigators, and Elders. Each of these has its own minimum requirements. One must first be an initiate to become a navigator and one must be a navigator to become an Elder.

Initiates travel with navigators in order to learn from them. Often, the captain of a vessel is a navigator, while the rest of the crew are composed of initiates and other "sailors". Elders control many vessels (even fleets).

Requirements Common to All Members of the Navigators

1 — All members must swear to deliver their cargo, even at the risk of their own lives, if necessary;

2 — All members must be completely Neutral in alignment/outlook. They never take sides in any dispute (except, of course, disputes involving their cargo);

3 — All members must be No-Profession or Sailor characters.

Minimum Requirements for Initiates

1 — Must have a CO, AG, IN, and EM of 75, or more;

2 — Must be at least first level;

3 — Must have at least one skill rank in Climbing, General Perception, Hostile Environments (Sea), and Shipwright;

4 — Must have at least two skill ranks in Boat Pilot, Direction Sense, Rope Mastery, and Weather Watching;

5 — Must have at least three skill ranks in Rowing and Star Gazing;

6 — Must have at least four skill ranks in Navigation and Sailing.

Minimum Requirements for Navigators

1 — Must have an IN and EM of 90 or more;

2 — Must be at least Fifth Level;

3 — Must have at least four skill ranks in Advertising and Diplomacy;

4 — Must have at least five skill ranks in appraisal, General Perception, Mapping, Signalling, Trading, and Trading Lore;

5 — Must have at least six skill ranks in Direction Sense, Rope Mastery, Rowing, and Shipwright;

6 — Must have at least seven skill ranks in Boat Pilot, Leadership, Hostile Environments (Sea), and Weather Watching;

7 — Must have at least eight skill ranks in Region Lore and Sailing;

8 — Must have at least nine skill ranks in Star Gazing;

9 — Must have at least ten skill ranks in Navigation; and

10 — Must have at least one of the Arcane Base Lists available to members of the Navigators (EarthBlood's Ways and Way of the Navigator).

Minimum Requirements for Elders

1 — Must have an IN and EM of 95 or more;

2 — Must be at least Tenth Level;

3 — Must have at least ten skill ranks in Administration, Advertising, Appraisal, Boat Pilot, Mapping and Hostile Environments (Sea);

4 — Must have at least fifteen skill ranks in Diplomacy, Direction Sense, Leadership, Shipwright, Trading, Trading Lore, and Weather Watching;

5 — Must have at least twenty skill ranks in Navigation, Region Lore, Sailing, and Star Gazing;

6 — Must know both of the Arcane Base Lists available to members of the Navigators (EarthBlood's Ways and Way of the Navigator).

Even an initiate may learn spell lists from a realm (as a normal No-Profession), since the Navigators are knowledgeable in magical lore gleaned from the whole world. Also members of the Navigators may learn two Arcane Base Lists (these Arcane Lists are treated as Base Lists), EarthBlood's Ways (***RMCI***, p.11) and Way of the Navigator (detailed in this product).

VERY COMPLEX
Covens

There have always been pagans who band together for protection from a usually hostile world. This hostility springs largely from ignorance and fear of the secretive group. The members tend to be nature-oriented, but still live near civilization, either in a group or separately. Because of the usually secret nature of a Coven, members often fit perfectly into society, seeming like respectable citizens.

Covens are Arcane Societies with their own set of Arcane Base Lists. These spells are unknown to the world outside the secret society because they are so carefully guarded. The most powerful "core" spell lists are even more jealously guarded. These High Secret Order Arcane Base Spell Lists are known only by the most powerful members of the coven.

An example of this type of Arcane Society is the Greenbriar Coven. In order to be a member of the Greenbriar, one must first be accepted by the most powerful members. Usually, only female members are accepted, since this group worships the Earth Mother. Non-spell users cannot join this Coven. Eligible initiates still must undergo an initiation into the Coven. This takes the form of a rite to find their "Totem Familiar" (see Shaman in ***RMCII***) after having fasted and remained awake at least one day. Upon finding the "Totem" the initiate becomes a member.

One woman, Dy-Cién, is the mutually acknowledged head of Greenbriar. The Coven as a whole shares her specific outlook/alignment, which might be called "chaotic good." Members not adhering to this outlook may either stay, or split away forming a scion Coven. The Greenbriar Coven itself was formed when Dy-Cién split from an evil, easterly Coven.

Near the mansion where the members live there is a Major Earthnode called Taurëgûl Celebfëo (Q. Celehfëo's Enchanted Wood). This Earthnode is where all rites of initiation are held.

SPELL LISTS: The following Arcane Coven Base Lists are available to all members of the Greenbriar Coven (cost to learn is double normal cost).

Earth Mother's Way (exactly like Earthblood's Ways)

Barrier Ways	*Allurement*
Household Magic	*Hearth Magic*
Brewing Lore	*Wax Magic*

Additionally, there is a High-Secret Order within the Greenbriar Coven composed of the most powerful member(s) of the Coven. These hand-picked member(s) know the innermost mysteries of the Coven. This includes additional Arcane Base Spell Lists and special individual spells detailed hereafter.

ADDITIONAL ARCANE COVEN BASE LISTS: Available only to members of the High-Secret Order.

Shapechanging Ways (***RMCI***)	*Midwifery* (***RMCI***)
Ceremonies (***RMCI***)	*Mending Ways* (Detailed in this product)
Familiar's Law (***RMCI***)	*Holy Vision* (Astrologer's Base list)

ADDITIONAL ARCANE COVEN BASE SPELLS: Only High-Secret Order members receive these additional spells.

I. ON THE BARRIER WAYS BASE LIST:
20—**Open Prison (F)** (*RMC I* p. 35)
25—**Mystical Cage (F)** (*RMC I* p. 34-35)
35—**Curtain Wall (F)**   **Realm:** Arcane   **Range:** 10'   **Duration:** varies   The caster causes a 10'x10' wall of mist to form. This is a gateway into an extra-dimensional space. Passing through this mist wall/gateway takes one into this extra-dimensional room that may be used as an abode. Once the caster is inside the room, the gateway may disappear from the location where it was summoned. This closes the gateway on anyone inside or outside. When this spell is cast from inside the room, the *Curtain Wall* may reappear in any location the caster has seen before. The dimensions of the room are roughly 20'x20'x20'. When not in use, the room still exists, allowing the caster to store goods or people there.
50—**Circle of Blindness (FM)**   **Realm:** Arcane   **Range:** 1'/Level radius   **Duration:** 1 minute/Level   When a being enters the circle and fails a RR, the being can no longer see as long as it remains in the Area of Effect.
60—**Sphere of Force (F)**   **Realm:** Arcane   **Range:** 1'/Level radius   **Duration:** 1 minute/Level   Creates a sphere of force about the caster through which nothing may pass.
75—**Mirror Wall (FM)**   **Realm:** Arcane   **Range:** 1'/Level   **Duration:** 1 minute/Level   Creates a 10'x10' wall of force which reflects all physical and magical attacks back on the perpetrator.

II. ON THE ALLUREMENT BASE LIST:
30—**Indictment (F)** (*RMCI*)

III. ON THE HOUSEHOLD MAGIC BASE LIST
1—**Muster (M)**   **Realm:** Arcane   **Range:** 10' radius   **Duration:** 10 minutes/Level   All beings in the Area of Effect who fail the RR must help the caster to clean a specified area.
19—**Gather True (F)** As *Gathering*, but with no restrictions as to Range and Area of Effect.

IV. ON THE BREWING LORE BASE LIST
60—**Lord Potion (F)** As *Brew Potion*, but up to a twentieth level spell may be imbedded in the potion.

V. ON THE WAX MAGIC BASE LIST
20—**Long Sleep Wax Fruit (F)** As *Lesser Wax Fruit*, except the sleep will last as long as the caster specified, coming to an end only after a specific triggering event has occurred.
40—**Golden Candle (F)** As *White Candle*, except with golden wax, the caster creates a candle in which up to a twentieth level spell may be imbedded.

Final Curse: Lastly, High-Secret Order Coven members may cast *Interpretation* or *Doom Interpretation* (*RMCI*) if the situation calls for a final curse.

7.2 SOCIAL STANDING

Social Standing represents the environment that a character grew up in. This rating allows a character's background to be more fully described. Social Standing will have a great impact upon characters who are novice adventurers, but after they set their own reputation, Social Standing will have little effect. A character's Social Standing also determines how much money he begins the game with.

A character's Social Standing can never be changed, even if his environment does. Even if a peasant were knighted, nobility would still view the knight as an ex-peasant.

To determine a character's Social Standing, roll a closed-ended 1D100. Then cross reference this result with the Social Standing Chart to determine one's Social Standing and beginning wealth.

In some societies, certain social classes may not exist. In these cases, the PC should be given the closest Social Standing possible.

If a GM decides to use these guidelines, he should examine this sample chart and modify it to more closely fit his own world and campaign.

Example: *Nirrad, a Human Barbarian, rolls a 01 for his social standing. Because Nirrad's tribe doesn't practice slavery, the GM has Nirrad be from the Lower-Lower Class, and gives him one copper piece as starting money.*

Option 1: Some GMs may wish to restrict their characters from becoming certain classes if their Social Standing is too low. For example, a GM may require Noble Warriors to be from an upper-class family.

SOCIAL STANDING CHART		
Result	Social Standing	Starting Money
01	Former Slave	none
02-09	Lower Lower Class (LLC)	1cp
10-35	Middle Lower Class (MLC)	5cp
36-45	Upper Lower Class (ULC)	1bp
46-56	Lower Middle Class (LMC)	3sp
57-70	Middle Middle Class (MMC)	8sp
71-80	Upper Middle Class (UMC)	2gp
81-90	Lower Upper Class (LUC)	10gp
91-96	Middle Upper Class (MUC)	35gp
97-99	Upper Upper Class (UUC)	50gp
100	Royalty	100gp

7.3 DEATH OPTIONS

Constitution is the stat used for determining how easily a character may survive a traumatic injury and how frequently he may be resurrected (i.e., soul returned by Lifegiving, raised from the dead, etc.). The following adds some control to the number of resurrections player characters may endure, (and thus cause them to be more cautious when they face dangerous enterprises).

1. A traumatic injury is a crit which specifies that an injury is deadly. Whether the blow is fatal immediately or not, (e.g. 12 rnds and then dies), the blow is still considered traumatic.

2. If a character receives a traumatic injury (as defined above) he must make a **trauma roll** to determine if resurrection measures will be necessary. This roll is necessary even if the injury is repaired within the allotted time before death (if an injury specifies that an organ is damaged and the character will die in 6 rounds, even if the organ is repaired or replaced before the 6 rounds are up, the character must make a trauma roll). Shock, temporary loss of arterial blood pressure, stroke, etc are all likely results of such an injury, and may cause a character to die even if the specific damage is quickly fixed.

3. The character attempting to make his trauma roll must roll less than or equal to his temporary Constitution stat to succeed. The roll is open-ended (e.g., a character with a 102 can still fail).

4. If the character makes his trauma roll, his temp CO stat is reduced by 1 point, but no *Lifegiving, Lifekeeping,* or *Restoration* measures will be required if the injury can be repaired in time (e.g., before soul departure). If the character fails his trauma roll the soul immediately departs necessitating normal *Lifegiving* measures and a resurrection roll (see below). Naturally the GM may want to keep this unfortunate situation secret until the players have opportunity to determine the injured party's status.

5. If a character; A) fails his trauma roll **or** B) suffers normal soul departure **or** C) requires *Lifegiving,* **or** D) requires *Lifekeeping,* he must make a **resurrection roll** before the soul can return or remain. This roll is like a trauma roll: the character must roll less than or equal to his temp CO stat to succeed. If the roll succeeds, the soul measures were effective but the character's temp CO is reduced by 5 points. If the character does not succeed with his resurrection roll, he is irrecoverably dead and out of the game. Because of their special nature, Elves must roll less than or equal to their temp CO – 10 (only for resurrection rolls).

6. The CO points lost by trauma and resurrection rolls are recoverable by normal means (e.g., level advancement, herbs, etc.). However, the reduced Constitution may not be recovered with respect to future trauma and resurrection rolls. This, obviously, sets a nearly absolute limit on the number of times a character may be resurrected, since his constitution will continue to irremediably decrease by 5 for every resurrection roll. A character will of necessity keep separate track of what value his CO is reduced to for the purpose of future trauma and resurrection rolls.

Example: *if a character with a 99 temp CO is resurrected, his temp CO stat drops to 94. At a later date the character goes up a level and gets 4 points back. However, he must keep track of the 94 as a separate number because the points are irrecoverable with respect to future trauma/resurrection rolls: his next chances of success for trauma and/or resurrection are only 94%*

7. Because of the dangers associated with receiving traumatic injuries, transferring Healers may choose to take more than the required amount of time casting transferral spells so that they need not suffer the effects of trauma themselves:

   A. If a transferring Healer is healing someone else using his transferral spells, and he spends (20 – his lvl) minutes (minimum of 1 minute) for his transferral spell, then the victim must make any necessary trauma or resurrection rolls.

   B. If the Healer is injured himself **or** if he cannot take the time specified above, he suffers the roll(s) himself.

Options: A GM may decide to use some, all, or none of the guidelines above; this decision will significantly affect the deadliness level of his campaign. For example, a GM may decide to use trauma rolls but not resurrection rolls.

BRAIN DAMAGE

A number of crits involve the head of the target and naturally there is good chance of some degree of damage to the brain itself. Most of the crits potentially injuring the brain do not specify the degree of damage suffered. Some are easy to guess (e.g., crushed skull probably means total jelly). Others are difficult (e.g., fatal injury through the cheek). The following system may be used to resolve the severity of brain injuries (if any) for crits which specify brain damage or **any** fatal injury to the head.

BASIC BRAIN DAMAGE CHART

01-15 Brain damage is not directly related to the injury. GM determines some other cause (e.g., shock, blood loss, etc) and repair measures needed.

16-30 Minor Brain Damage: 03-30% damaged; each *Minor Brain Repair* spell may repair 10% of the damage. Comparable percentage of experience is lost according to the percentage of damage done, but experience is automatically restored after healing.

31-55 Major Brain Damage: determine percentage of brain severely damaged by a straight percentage roll (01-100). See below.

56-80 Major Brain Damage + Irreversible Stat Loss (as Major Brain Damage above plus Normal Irreversible Stat Loss below).

81-00 Brain Destroyed: as Major above (but loss is automatically 91-100%) plus Severe Irreversible Stat loss below.

Major Brain Damage

1. If percentage of brain damaged is less than 50%, *Minor Brain Repair* spells are permitted reduced effectiveness for repairs: each mends 5% of the brain tissue damaged.

2. If the percentage of brain damaged is greater than 49%, the *Brain Regeneration* spell is required to replace the damaged tissue.

3. Experience point loss is based on percent damaged and the *Restoration* spell is required to restore lost experience.

Irreversible Stat Loss

Stats lost cannot be restored by level gains; only perhaps by special GM cases (e.g., wishes or special herbs like Lestagii).

1. **Normal Irreversible Stat Loss:** all mental stats (SD, ME, RE, PR, IN, EM) lose Temp and Pot according to rolls on the 15+ column of Table 15.12 in *ChL&CaL*.

2. **Severe Irreversible Stat Loss:** As Normal above except losses obtained from Table 15.12 are doubled in severity.

7.4 LINGUISTIC ADDENDUM

There are numerous languages already available for a GM to choose from for his world scheme, and most are already in place in a well designed world. Here we would like to set forth the general types of languages for GM consideration. In a complex and multi-faceted world these do deserve some attention.

RACIAL LANGUAGES: These are the languages generally used and recognized by the individual race. For example, Elven and Dwarvish.

CULTURAL LANGUAGES: These are the language variations in an area, usually related to some extent to the racial language(s). For example Easterner and Westron.

SOCIAL LANGUAGES: These are the language variations in a particular culture. For example, High Speech is used by the nobility in Eria, Common Erian is spoken by most others, while Street Talk is used by the lower classes. It is up to the individual GM to determine whether any such variants exist and what their relationship to each other is (knowing Erian High Speech allows 1/2 skill level in Common Erian and 1/4 skill level in Street Talk).

PROFESSIONAL LANGUAGES: These languages are the special languages spoken by a particular profession, and need not be related to any spoken language. For example, Sword Tongue is spoken by the members of the Brotherhood of the Blade and is a special manufactured language used for recognition and secrecy by the higher echelons, while Old Landalian is spoken by the members of the Elcaluva College (spell-users) for the same reasons plus the fact that it is the now dead language that many of the ancient Magi used (and wrote their texts in). The Thieves' Guild uses a hyper-slang language known as Thieves' Cant, for recognition, secrecy, and safety. Thieves' Cant can be spoken at 1/4 skill by the local populace.

RELIGIOUS LANGUAGES: These languages are the special languages spoken by the various religious orders, for reasons of tradition, ceremony, and recognition. They may or may not be related to any other spoken language. For example, the Priests of Kanorak speak Kanorakki in High Ceremony and for recognition (a god-given language for the followers of the True Faith), and Old Nakrin, an ancient form of the current language which can be spoken by laymembers at 1/2 skill level. Druid Tongue, however, has been preserved unchanged untold Eons and while spoken by the Inner Circle of Druidry, is now too far removed from current languages to be considered related.

MAGICAL LANGUAGES: These languages are rarely spoken except in conjunction with spell casting, where they aid the spell's potency. Added to the list of Magical languages is Elya, First Speech, the tongue of power which creates. This is the language of *Power Words*. Refer to 2.4 Magical Languages, *RMCI*.

7.5 USING THE RMCIII CRITICAL TABLES

There are six new crtical striketables and one *Space Master* critical strike table included in *RMCIII*, see Section 12.0. GMs may find a variety of uses for these tables; below find a few suggestions:

Physical Alteration: This table is used with the Chaotic Armor spells (see Section 8.23). It can also be used with the Changling spells (*RMCII* 8.21); when a "Type ß" option' is used on a target, then the target also takes a Physical Alteration crit of severity "ß" and the transformation is complete when a cummulative 100% is achieved (e.g., a "Type A" option gives a 'A' severity P.A. critcal, a "Type C" gives a 'C' P.A. crit, etc.). Similarly, a GM can use this table whenever a spell causes a physical alteration in a target (e.g., *Shrink Self*, *Change to Kind*, *Changing*, etc.).

Depression: This table is included to reflect the effects of Mental stress and illness; a GM should exercise discretion based upon the level of intense role playing that his players are capable of.

Stress: A GM may use this table whenever a character performs an action that places great physical stress on his body. A common example is the use of *Speed* or *Haste* spells or herbs; a GM may apply a Stress critical after an extended period of *Speed/Haste*.

Acid: The use of this table is pretty straightforward.

Shock: Use this table for spells and situations where a character may be stunned or dazed but does not have a significant chance of serious injury (e.g., for Stun Clouds, coming out of darkness into bright daylight, etc.).

Disruption (from *Space Master*): A very deadly table, used with the Nether Mastery list.

Plasma (from *Space Master*): A very deadly table, used with the Plasma Mastery list.

8.0 BASE SPELL LISTS FOR RMCIII PROFESSIONS

8.1 MONTEBANC BASE LISTS

8.11 MYSTIC ESCAPES (Montebanc Base)

	Area of Effect	Duration	Range
1—Blur	self	1 min/lvl	self
2—Balance c	self	V	self
3—Shadow	self	10 min/lvl	self
4—Invisibility (1')	self	24 hr or V	self
5—Silence	self	1 min/lvl	self
6—Leaving (100')	self	—	self
7—Fly (1 mph)	self	1 min/lvl	self
8—	self	1 min/lvl	self
9—Displacement I	self	1 min/lvl	self
10—Screens	1000 sq'	C	100'
11—Long Door (50')	self	—	self
12—Leaving (500')	self	—	self
13—	self	1 min/lvl	self
14—Displacement II	self	1 min/lvl	self
15—No Sense	self	24 hr or V	self
16—Long Door (100')	self	—	self
17—Merging	self	1 min/lvl	self
18—	self	1 min/lvl	self
19—	self	1 min/lvl	self
20—Long Door (500')	self	—	self
25—Displacement III	self	1 min/lvl	self
30—Fly (20 mph)	self	1 min/lvl	self
50—Leaving True	self	—	self

1,3,4,5,9,10,14,15,17,25—As the spells of the same names on the Mystic Base spell list, Cloaking.

2—As spell of the same name on the Closed Mentalism spell list, Shifting.

6,11,12,16,20,50—As the spells of the same names on the Closed Mentalism spell list, Mind's Door.

7,30—As spells of the same names on the Closed Mentalism spell list, Movement.

Montebanc Base Spell Lists

8.12 DISGUISE MASTERY (Montebanc Base)

	Area of Effect	Duration	Range
1—Study	1 being	—	300'
2—Face Shifting True	self	1 hr/lvl	self
3—			
4—Facades	self	1 hr/lvl	self
5—Misfeel Kind •	self	C	self
6—			
7—Misfeel Calling •	self	C	self
8—Facades II	self	1 hr/lvl	self
9—			
10—Change to Kind	self	10 min/lvl	self
11—Misfeel Power •	self	C	self
12—			
13—Camouflage	self	10 min/lvl	self
14—			
15—Change	self	10 min/lvl	self
16—			
17—			
18—Misfeel	self	C	self
19—			
20—Unpresence	self	C	self
25—Camouflage True	self	10 min/lvl	self
30—Misfeel True	self	10 min/lvl	self
50—Submerge Self	self	varies	self

1,2,5,7,10,11,15,18,20,30,50—As the spells of the same names on the Mystic Base spell list, Mystical Change.

4,8,13,25—As the spells of the same names on the Open Mentalism spell list, Cloaking.

8.13 BEGUILING WAYS (Montebanc Base)

	Area of Effect	Duration	Range
1—Question	1 target	—	10'
2—Sly Ears	1 target	10 min/lvl	100'
3—Empathy	1 target	1 rnd/lvl(C)	10'
4—Charm Kind	1 target	10 min/lvl	50'
5—Forget I	1 target	P	100'
6—Emotions	1 target	1 rnd/lvl(C)	50'
7—Suggestion	1 target	V	10'
8—Thoughts	1 target	1 rnd/lvl(C)	100'
9—Sleep	1 target	—	50'
10—Hold Kind	1 target	C	50'
11—Forget X	1 target	P	100'
12—			
13—			
14—True Charm	1 target	10 min/lvl	50'
15—Lord Forget	1 target	P	100'
16—			
17—			
18—True Hold	1 target	C	50'
19—			
20—Amnesia	1 target	1 day/5% fail.	100'
25—True Sleep	1 target	1 min/10% fail.	100'
30—Forget True	1 target	P	100'
50—Thought Steal	1 target	1 rnd/lvl	100'

1,4,7,9,10,14,18,25—As the spells of the same names on the Mentalist Base spell list, Mind Control.

2—As the spell of the same name on the Closed Mentalism spell list, Sense Mastery.

3,6,8,50—As the spells of the same names on the Mentalist Base spell list, Mind Merge.

5,11,15,30—As the spells of the same names on the Evil Mentalist Base spell list, Mind Death.

20—As the spell of the same name on the Mystic Base spell list, Confusing Ways.

8.14 APPRAISALS (Montebanc Base)

	Area of Effect	Duration	Range
1—Gem Appraisal	1 gem	—	touch
2—Detect Mentalism	5'R/rnd	1 min/lvl(C)	50'
3—Detect Power	1 item/rnd	1 rnd/lvl	touch
4—Detect Essence	5'R/rnd	1 min/lvl(C)	50'
5—Detect Channeling	5'R/rnd	1 min/lvl(C)	50'
6—Significance	1 item	—	touch
7—Detect Evil	5'R/rnd	1 min/lvl(C)	50'
8—Origins	1 item	—	touch
9—Past Vision	varies	varies	touch
10—Appraisal True	1 object	—	touch
11—Item Lore	1 item	—	touch
12—			
13—Past Visions (1 day/lvl)	varies	varies	touch
14—			
15—Past Hold	1 item	varies	touch
16—			
17—			
18—Past Visions (1 mo/lvl)	varies	varies	touch
19—			
20—Item Analysis	1 item	—	touch
25—Past Vision (1 yr/lvl)	varies	varies	touch
30—Past Vision (10 yr/lvl)	varies	varies	touch
50—Origins True	1 item	—	touch

1—Gem Appraisal (P) Allows caster to determine the value (within 10%) of a gem; he may calculate different values will be for the different cultures that he is familiar with.

3,6,8,50—As the spells of the same names on the Bard Base spell list, Item Lore.

2,4,5,7—As the spells of the same names on the Open Mentalism spell list, Detections.

9,11,13,15,18,20,25,30—As the spells of the same names on the Open Mentalism spell list, Delving.

10—Appraisal True (P) As *Gem Appraisal* except that any gem, piece of jewelry, or piece of art can be appraised.

8.2 CHAOTIC LORD BASE LISTS

8.21 CHAOTIC WEAPONS (Chaotic Lord Base)

NOTE 1: *A blade is a 1-Handed Edged weapon or a 2-Handed Edged weapon (e.g., 2-Handed sword, battle-axe, halberd, etc.); a GM may wish to extend this list to cover all weapons.*

NOTE 2: *Only one spell from this list may be active on a given blade.*

NOTE 3: *A GM may wish to restrict the use of certain spells on this list. He may also wish to allow these spells to be used only on non-magic weapons.*

	Area of Effect	Duration	Range
1—Chaotic Strike I	1 blade	1 rnd/lvl	touch
2—Lesser Skeletal Strike	1 blade	1 rnd/lvl	touch
3—Lesser Poison Strike	1 blade	1 rnd/lvl	touch
4—Chaotic Strike II	1 blade	1 rnd/lvl	touch
5—Vamperic Strike I	1 blade	1 rnd/lvl	touch
6—Skeletal Strike	1 blade	1 rnd/lvl	touch
7—Poison Strike	1 blade	1 rnd/lvl	touch
8—Vamperic Strike II	1 blade	1 rnd/lvl	touch
9—Chaotic Strike III	1 blade	1 rnd/lvl	touch
10—Greater Poison Strike	1 blade	1 rnd/lvl	touch
11—Vamperic Strike III	1 blade	1 rnd/lvl	touch
12—Greater Skeletal Strike	1 blade	1 rnd/lvl	touch
13—Chaotic Strike IV	1 blade	1 rnd/lvl	touch
14—Life Force Drain I	1 blade	1 rnd/lvl	touch
15—Lesser Serpents Strike	1 blade	1 rnd/lvl	touch
16—Life Force Drain II	1 blade	1 rnd/lvl	touch
17—Essence Strike	1 blade	1 rnd/lvl	touch
18—Mentalism Strike	1 blade	1 rnd/lvl	touch
19—Channeling Strike	1 blade	1 rnd/lvl	touch
20—Chaotic Strike V	1 blade	1 rnd/lvl	touch
25—Serpents Strike	1 blade	1 rnd/lvl	touch
30—Life Force Drain III	1 blade	1 rnd/lvl	touch
50—Greater Serpents Strike	1 blade	1 rnd/lvl	touch

1—Chaotic Strike I (F) This spell is cast on a blade; when the blade delivers its next critical strike, the target receives an "A" Physical Alteration critical in addition to the normal critical.

2—Lesser Skeletal Strike (F) As *Chaotic Strike I* except an additional "A" impact critical is delivered.

3—Lesser Poison Strike (F) Allows the caster to make a blade poisonous. When the blade delivers its next critical strike that gives "hits/rnd", the target must resist the poison. The poison affects one of the target's temporary stats; reducing that stat by 1 point/round until the total reduction reaches 1 point/1% failure **or** until the poison is neutralized. If the stat is reduced to zero, the target is dead. Roll 1D10 to determine which stat the poison affects: 1) CO, 2) SD, 3) AG, 4) ME, 5) RE, 6) ST, 7) QU, 8) PR, 9) IN, 10) EM.

4—Chaotic Strike II (F) As *Chaotic Strike I* except the critical is a "B" Physical Alteration critical.

5—Vamperic Strike I (F) As *Lesser Poison Strike* except the target takes 1D10 concussion hits each round as long as the target is within 100' of the blade In order to stay within this range the blade will drag itself towards the target at 10'/rnd. Any target killed by a *Vamperic Strike* weapon has a 1%/lvl chance of becoming a Vampire.

6—Skeletal Strike (F) As *Lesser Skeletal Strike* except the critical is a "C" impact critical.

7—Poison Strike (F) As *Lesser Poison Strike* except two temporary stats are reduced at the same time. If a stat is rolled twice, then that stat is reduced by 2 every round.

8—Vamperic Strike II (F) As *Vamperic Strike I* except that the "draining range" is 300' and the weapon's movement is increased to 25'/rnd. The chance of becoming a vampire increases to 2%/lvl.

9—Chaotic Strike III (F) As *Chaotic Strike I* except the critical is a "C" Physical Alteration critical.

10—Greater Poison Strike (F) As *Lesser Poison Strike* except 3 temporary stats are reduced at the same time. If a stat is rolled twice, then stat loses 2 points/rnd; and if the stat is rolled three times then stat loses 3 points/rnd; .

11—Vamperic Strike III (F) As *Vamperic Strike I* except the "draining range" is 500' and the weapon's movement is increased to 50'/lvl. The chance of becoming a vampire increases to 3%/lvl.

12—Greater Skeletal Strike (F) As *Lesser Skeletal Strike* except the critical is a "E" impact critical.

13—Chaotic Strike IV (F) As *Chaotic Strike I* except the critical is a "D" Physical Alteration critical.

14—Life Force Drain I (F) As *Vamperic Strike I* except that it drains "Life Essence" at a rate of 1 point/round. The chance of becoming a vampire increases to 4%/lvl.

15—Lesser Serpents Strike (F) When the blade delivers its next critical strike, the wounds may not be healed through normal means: bleeding will not stop, concussion hits will not heal, broken bones will not set and mend, etc. Herbs and magic will heal heal such a wound.

16—Life Force Drain II (F) As *Life Force Drain I* except the drain is 2 points/round. The chance of becoming a vampire increases to 5%/lvl.

17—Essence Strike (F) When the blade delivers its next critical strike, the target will lose all Essence PPs for 24 hours. Hybrid spell users with Essence as one of their realms, lose half of their PPs and may not cast Essence spells for 24 hours.

18—Mentalism Strike (F) When the blade delivers its next critical strike, the target will lose all Mentalism PPs for 24 hours. Hybrid spell users with Mentalism as one of their realms, lose half of their PPs and may not cast Mentalism spells for 24 hours.

19—Channeling Strike (F) When the blade delivers its next critical strike, the target will lose all Channeling PPs for 24 hours. Hybrid spell users with Channeling as one of their realms, lose half of their PPs and may not cast Channeling spells for 24 hours.

20—Chaotic Strike V (F) As *Chaotic Strike I* except the critical is a "D" Physical Alteration critical.

25—Serpents Strike (F) As *Lesser Serpents Strike* except only magic will cure this would. Herbs and normal healing have no effect.

30—Life Force Drain III (F) As *Life Force Drain I* except the drain is 3 points/round. The chance of becoming a vampire increases to 6%/lvl.

50—Greater Serpents Strike (F) As *Lesser Serpents Strike* except there is no known cure.

8.22 CHAOS MASTERY (Chaotic Lord Base)

This is perhaps one of the most dangerous spell lists ever devised. The act of "creating chaos" should only be attempted in a controlled environment or perhaps as a last resort in a hazardous situation. Created chaos grows by consuming everything in its path; everything it touches is dissolved and serves to make the chaos larger. Each round created chaos is capable of increasing it's size by a 1'R (i.e., an increase of an are of 1'R, **not** 1' to its total radius). There are several ways to halt and/or control this growth:

1) Let it run lose; once it has obtained sufficient size (GM discretion), it will melt/dissolve its way down into the magma zone of the planet. There the internal heat of the lava/magma will consume the chaos faster than the chaos can consume the magma; after the chaos is totally consumed, the magma rushes forth and fills crater created by the chaos, creating a magma lake. A new problem, but one that will slowly solidify in a couple of centuries.

   Chaos is heavier than water and sinks rapidly. Gravity does have an effect on chaos; so it tends to "flow" down hill, taking the path of least resistance (like a river or a tornado).

Chaotic Lord Base Spell Lists

2) There has been some success in stabilizing the chaos (i.e., it stops growing) by neutralizing all of its Essence, Channeling and Mentalism (e.g., by using Unessence, Unmentalism and Unchanneling). If it is stabilized, a successful Stone/Earth spell can substitute stone for 100 cu' of the chaos (GM may require the use of Spell Mastery skill). However, if the chaos successfully resists this spell, it immediately begins to grow again. Chaos resists at 10th level, with every 100 cu' of chaos giving it an additional +1 bonus. Sorcerers have had similar success with Solid Destruction True.

3) The creation of a "magical vortex" has also been successful in combating growing chaos; but this leaves another problem perhaps even greater then the chaos problem. A magical vortex is created by super-saturating an area with more Essence than the area can safely handle. The number of PPs required varies, but is on the order of 100,000 PPs discharged in an area varying in radius from 10' to 1 mile depending upon the local "strength of the fabric of space". A magic vortex acts as vacuum cleaner (i.e., tornado, hurricane, etc.) on all power within its area of effect.

4) The spells on this list are designed to control chaos.

NOTE 1: *Due to the potential damage of chaos, the mere presence of a Chaotic Lord is often enough to cause warring factions to make temporary peace in order to face the Chaotic Lord as a united front. There are safe havens for Chaotic Lords, but not many. It has been rumored that the Assassin's Guild have given these Lords top target priority.*

NOTE 2: *Chaos is raw elemental material, mixed with free floating Essence, Channeling and Mentalism power. It has no internal matrix, so giving it an actual internal structure (GM discretion) may serve to stop its growth.*

NOTE 3: *Some items do survive engulfment by chaos; these items are almost always artifacts.*

NOTE 4: *"•" denotes that this spell does not require the caster to spent power points to utilize this spell.*

	Area of Effect	Duration	Range
1—			
2—Chaos Presence * •	10'R/lvl	—	Self
3—			
4—			
5—Dissolve Chaos	1'R	1 min/lvl(C)	10'
6—			
7—			
8—			
9—			
10—Create Chaos	1'R	—	10'
11—			
12—Control Chaos	Chaos	1 min/lvl (C)	10'
13—			
14—			
15—Diminish Chaos	Chaos	P	10'
16—Master Chaos	Chaos	1 min/lvl	10'
17—			
18—			
19—			
20—Manipulate Chaos	Chaos	24 hours	10'
25—Master Chaos True	Chaos	1 hr/lvl	10'
30—Expel Chaos	Chaos	P	10'
50—Chaos Mastery	Chaos	24 hours	10'

2—Chaos Presence (U*•) Allows the caster to immediately become aware of all chaos within a 10'R/lvl.

5—Dissolve Chaos (F) Allows the caster to dissolve a 1'R area of chaos every round that he concentrates. The chaos continues to grow at a rate of a 1'R area per round, so basically this creates a stand off.

10—Create Chaos (FE) Allows the caster to create a 1'R sphere of chaos. Unless controlled immediately the begins growing at a rate of 1' R per round. It dissolves everything in it's path. The chaos does damage determined by plasma ball table, with all criticals being Acid criticals.

12—Control Chaos (F) Allows the caster to stop the growth of the chaos for 1 min/lvl as long as he maintains concentration.

15—Diminish Chaos (F) As *Dissolve Chaos* except chaos stops growing and thus is condensed back to nothingness at a 1'R area per round.

16—Master Chaos (F) As *Control Chaos* except caster does not need to concentrate.

20—Manipulate Chaos (F) Allows the caster to handle and manipulate chaos material, limiting damage to 1D10 hits a turn. Caster can shape chaos into an inanimate, non-intelligent, magical object. The chaos material is extremely difficult to work with. Its hardness is variable is (roll 1D10 + 1); its magical bonus is + [1D100 (open-ended) divided 5]; and it radiates the most prevalent emotion/mental state of the caster at the time the object is shaped. This spell will manipulate enough material to create a magical dagger of its equivalent in weight. A GM may wish to give powerful "dispelling" spells and fields a chance of causing a chaos object to revert to its base state of uncontrolled chaos. A chaos object also serves as a power stabilizer (i.e., the wielder of object never drops below his intrinsic power points). If the caster casts a spell that reduces his PPs below his intrinsic PPs, the chaos object draws power from the caster's concussion hits: the caster takes 1D10 hits and his PPs return to his intrinsic PP total (i.e., his PP total ignoring any spell multiplier). For example: Korwind, who wields a chaos object, has an intrinsic PP total of 9. Anytime Korwind's PP total drop below 9 points, he will take 1D10 concussion hits and his PP total will be restored to 9.

25—Master Chaos True (F) As *Master Chaos* except duration is 1 hr/lvl.

30—Expel Chaos (F) As *Diminish Chaos* except the rate of condensing is ten 1'R areas per round.

50—Chaos Mastery (F) As *Manipulate Chaos* except the chaos item acts as a power stabilizer for the wielder's PP total as increased by a spell multiplier.

8.23 CHAOTIC ARMOR (Chaotic Lord Base)

NOTE 1: *When a Chaotic Lord "learns" spells from this list, they are normally "taught" only the next higher Chaotic Armor #, Control Chaotic Armor #, and Master Chaotic Armor # spells. Thus, instead of learning the list with normal B, D, and E picks, a GM may wish to require separate picks for each set of "#" spells (e.g., 1st pick is for the spells at 1st, 2nd, and 7th level, 2nd pick is for 5th, 6th and 11th, 3rd pick is for 9th, 10th, and 15th, etc.).*

NOTE 2: *It is possible to use a Control Chaotic Armor # spell to control at range someone else's Chaotic Armor with a number less than "#" .(e.g., a Chaotic Lord who at taken utilization of Chaotic Armor II, can have his Chaotic Armor controlled by his "master" who would could use Control Chaotic Armor III., IV, V, or VI)*

NOTE 3: *When taking Physical Alteration Criticals, the Chaotic Lord continues to take them at a rate of 1 per round until the percentage of change equals or exceeds 100%.*

EXAMPLE: A Chaotic Lord begins the transformation rite, he rolls a 06 on the "A" severity column which yields nothing; next round he rolls a 67 which yields a neck strike, 90% change, target is stunned next round, fights at -10, +6 hits. The Chaotic Lord must roll again next round and rolls a 83 which yields a side wound, a 100% change, foe is stunned for 2 rounds, add +20 to your next action, +9 hits. The Chaotic Lord has successfully made the transformation 90% + 100% = 190% and may stop rolling "A" criticals. The Chaotic Lord is still stunned for two rounds; the Demon being bound has a +20 for it's next action; the Chaotic Lord has a neck wound of 6 hits and a side wound of 9 hits. Each round that the Chaotic Lord takes an "A" critical, he also suffers 1D10 hits (see spell #1 on this list) which in this example, yields 20 points. In addition, the Chaotic Lord was also required to take 1D10 damage for 4 additional rounds after taking "A" criticals yielding 23 hits; for a hit total of 58.

NOTE 4: *When a Chaotic Lord increases the number of his Chaotic Armor, they shed the old, lower numbered armor and "put on" the new, higher numbered armor. To shed the old armor, reverse the process of initially getting the armor. After optional rest and healing, the process of "putting on" the new armor can be started. This can be very dangerous! Once stripped of Chaotic Armor, all benefits from it are lost. Once the Demon has been released, it travels back to it's home plane where it must remain for 1 day for every day that it was on this plane.*

	Area of Effect	Duration	Range
1—Chaotic Armor I	1 target	P	10'
2—Control Chaotic Armor I *	C. Armor	24 hrs	10'
3—			
4—			
5—Chaotic Armor II	1 target	P	10'
6—Control Chaotic Armor II *	C. Armor	24 hrs	10'
7—Master Chaotic Armor I *	C. Armor	P	10'
8—			
9—Chaotic Armor III	1 target	P	10'
10—Control Chaotic Armor III *	C. Armor	24 hrs	10'
11—Master Chaotic Armor II *	C. Armor	P	10'
12—			
13—Chaotic Armor IV	1 target	P	10'
14—Control Chaotic Armor IV *	C. Armor	24 hrs	10'
15—Master Chaotic Armor III *	C. Armor	P	10'
16—			
17—Chaotic Armor V	1 target	P	10'
18—Control Chaotic Armor V *	C. Armor	24 hrs	10'
19—			
20—Master Chaotic Armor IV *	C. Armor	P	10'
25—Chaotic Armor VI	1 target	P	10'
30—Control Chaotic Armor VI *	C. Armor	24 hrs	10'
50—Master Chaotic Armor V *	C. Armor	P	10'
70—Master Chaotic Armor VI *	C. Armor	P	10'

1—Chaotic Armor I (FM) Allows the caster to bind a type 1 Demon into the target's skin and thus transform it into a suit of sentient armor. The armor is actually the type I Demon "bonded" to the outer skin of the target. The transformation requires that a cumulative 100% or better result be obtained by rolling on the "A" column of the *Physical Alteration Critical Strike Table* found in Section 12.0. Each round until a cumulative 100% change has been obtained, the target suffers the results of an "A" Physical Alteration critical **and** 1D10 concussion hits. He also receives 1D10 hits each round for 1D10 rounds after the transformation is completed. If the target survives this process, his skin is transformed into a harden, mobile, extremely flexible layer of living armor. The Demon gives the target to following benefits: AT 3, +20 to DB, an additional 35 hits, a +10 movement bonus or a base movement rate of 90', +20 to initiative determinants, and one random trait from the Chaotic Table that follows this spell list. If the Demon is not *Controlled* or *Mastered*; the wearer may make a 'hard' maneuver roll (modified level and by average bonuses for ST and SD) to control his own body each and every round. If the result (not the roll) is "70" or higher, the wearer may function normally. If the result is "40-60", the wearer is paralyzed. If the wearer does not attempt control or if his result is "30" or less, the Demon will attack the closest living creature. Demon has IQ of 7-25 (i.e., a ME and RE average for the GM to use for determining the "cleverness" of its actions).

2—Control Chaotic Armor I (FM*) Allows the caster to totally control a type 1 Demon (the chance of non-control is the 2%).

5—Chaotic Armor II (FM) As *Chaotic Armor I* except a type II Demon is bonded, and the target benefits are as follows; AT 4, +30 to DB, an additional 60 hits, a +10 movement bonus or a base movement rate of 110' (may not fast sprint or dash), +30 to initiative determinants, and one random trait from the random Chaotic Table. During the bonding process, the target uses the "B" column on the *Physical Alteration Critical Strike Table*; **and** takes 2D10 hits when required instead of 1D10 **and** takes the

hits for 2D10 rounds after bonding. It is a 'very hard' maneuver for the wearer to control his body if the Demon is not *Controlled* or *Mastered*. Demon has an IQ of 13-40 (ME and RE averaged).

6—Control Chaotic Armor II (FM*) As *Control Chaotic Armor I* except controls type II Demon and chance of non-control is 4%.

7—Master Chaotic Armor I (FM*) As *Control Chaotic Armor I* except control is permanent.

9—Chaotic Armor III (FM) As *Chaotic Armor I* except a type III Demon is bonded, and the target benefits are as follows: AT 4, +50 to DB, an additional 90 hits, a +20 movement bonus or a base movement rate of 130' (may not dash), +50 to initiative determinants, and one random trait from the random Chaotic Table. During the bonding process, the target uses the "C" column on the *Physical Alteration Critical Strike Table*; **and** takes 3D10 hits when required instead of 1D10 **and** takes the hits for 3D10 rounds after bonding. It is a 'extremely hard' maneuver for the wearer to control his body if the Demon is not *Controlled* or *Mastered*. Demon has an IQ of 23-50 (ME and RE averaged).

10—Control Chaotic Armor III (FM*) As *Control Chaotic Armor I* except controls type III Demon and chance of non-control is 6%.

11—Master Chaotic Armor II (FM*) As *Control Chaotic Armor II* except control is permanent.

13—Chaotic Armor IV (FM) As *Chaotic Armor I* except a type III Demon is bonded, and the target benefits are as follows: AT 4, +60 to DB, an additional 120 hits, a +40 movement bonus or a base movement rate of 160', +60 to initiative determinants, and one random trait from the random Chaotic Table. During the bonding process, the target uses the "D" column on the *Physical Alteration Critical Strike Table*; **and** takes 4D10 hits when required instead of 1D10 **and** take the hits for 4D10 rounds after bonding. It is a 'sheer folly' maneuver for the wearer to control his body if the Demon is not *Controlled* or *Mastered*. Demon has an IQ of 60-86 (ME and RE averaged).

14—Control Chaotic Armor IV (FM*) As *Control Chaotic Armor I* except controls type IV Demon and chance of non-control is 8%.

15—Master Chaotic Armor III (FM*) As *Control Chaotic Armor III* except control is permanent.

17—Chaotic Armor V (FM) As *Chaotic Armor I* except a type III Demon is bonded, and the target benefits are as follows: AT 11, +50 to DB, an additional 300 hits, a +20 movement bonus or a base movement rate of 100' (may not dash), +50 to initiative determinants, and one random trait from the random Chaotic Table. During the bonding process, the target uses the "E" column on the *Physical Alteration Critical Strike Table*; **and** takes 5D10 hits when required instead of 1D10 **and** take the hits for 5D10 rounds after bonding. It is a 'absurd' maneuver for the wearer to control his body if the Demon is not *Controlled* or *Mastered*. If the Demon wins control during a round, the Demon will attempt to dominate other living creatures until they comply with the Demons desire or they are destroyed. Demon has an IQ of 80-98 (ME and RE averaged).

18—Control Chaotic Armor V (FM*) As *Control Chaotic Armor I* except controls type V Demon and chance of non-control is 10%.

20—Master Chaotic Armor IV (FM*) As *Control Chaotic Armor IV* except control is permanent.

25—Chaotic Armor VI (FM) As *Chaotic Armor I* except a type III Demon is bonded, and the target benefits are as follows: AT 12, +60 to DB, an additional 250 hits, a +50 movement bonus or a base movement rate of 150', +60 to initiative determinants, and one random trait from the random Chaotic Table. During the bonding process, the target uses the "E" column on the *Physical Alteration Critical Strike Table* **and** takes 6D10 hits when required instead of 1D10 **and** take the hits for 6D10 rounds after bonding. It is a 'absurd' maneuver for the wearer to control his body if the Demon is not *Controlled* or *Mastered*. Demon has an IQ of 35-65 (ME and RE averaged).

30—Control Chaotic Armor VI (FM*) As *Control Chaotic Armor I* except controls type VI Demon and chance of non-control is 12%.

50—Master Chaotic Armor V (FM*) As *Control Chaotic Armor V* except control is permanent.

70—Master Chaotic Armor VI (FM*) As *Control Chaotic Armor VI* except control is permanent.

The Chaotic Table

8.24 THE CHAOTIC TABLE

ROLL 1D6 TO DETERMINE THE CHART
1) Stat/Resistance Bonuses Chart
2) Gift Chart
3) Geas Chart
4) Skill Determination Chart
5) Skill Category Determination Chart
6) Anatomy Chart

STAT/RESISTANCE BONUSES CHART

ROLL 1D20

(also roll on Plus/Minus Chart for each Stat/Resistance result)

1—Roll Again on this Chart	10—Intuition
2—Constitution	11—Empathy
3—Self Discipline	12—Power Points
4—Agility	13—Essence RR
5—Memory	14—Channeling RR
6—Reasoning	15—Mentalism RR
7—Strength	16—Poison RR
8—Quickness	17—Disease RR
9—Presence	18—Roll Again on this Chart
19—Roll Again on this Chart and once on the Geas Chart	
20—Roll Twice on this Chart and once on the Geas Chart	

PLUS/MINUS CHART

ROLL 1D20

1) -5/lvl	5) -1/lvl	9) -10	13) +15
2) -4/lvl	6) -25	10) -5	14) +20
3) -3/lvl	7) -20	11) +5	15) +25
4) -2/lvl	8) -15	12) +10	16) +1/lvl
17) +2/lvl			
18) +3/lvl and roll once on the Geas Chart			
19) +4/lvl and roll once on the Geas Chart			
20) +5/lvl and roll twice on the Geas Chart			

GIFT CHART

ROLL 1D100

1—**Accelerated Mending** (Character's injuries heal twice as quickly as normal.)

2—**Acute Hearing** (Character's acute hearing enables him to perceive, isolate and understand any sound; range is 100' for open areas or 25' when listening through solid objects.)

3—**Acute Smell** (Character's sense of smell enables him to perceive and distinguish odors up to 100' upwind, 2000' downwind, and 500' in still air. Should he track something based on experience with its odor, he has a +25 bonus.)

4—**Aggression** (+10 bonus on base attack or elemental spell rolls.)

5—**Archetype** (The character normally has 2x normal power points. If he is using a power point multiplier, the bonus increases 1 level; e.g., x2 to x3, etc..)

6—**Archmage Abilities** (Character has abilities similar to an Archmage; his spell list acquisition development point costs are now the same as any one hybrid spell users; his original base lists do not change, but he may now make spell picks as a hybrid, but for all three realms.)

7—**Armored Skin** (roll 2D10 for Armor Type.)

8—**Aura** (+1 power point per level.)

9—**Bane** (Character may select one creature type, subject to the GM approval, against which all his criticals will be "slaying".)

10—**Blessed** (Character enjoys the favor of a particular god, demi-god, angel, etc.; also he gets the disfavor of that beings enemies.)

11—**Breathe Weapon** (1 use per day—1'R—Range 20'.)

12—**Danger Sense** (GM may warn of general danger on a roll less than or equal to the character's IN mod.)

13—**Dark Temptation** (Character is tempted to the "Dark Side", he learns one evil spell list to 50th level. GM controls details.)

14—**Destiny Sense** (Character knows the direction which will lead to a desired objective.)

15—**Agility Focus** (Dev. Pts. Doubled for AG.)

16—**Constitution Focus** (Dev. Pts. Doubled for CO.)

17—**Memory Focus** (Dev. Pts. Doubled for ME.)

18—**Reasoning Focus** (Dev. Pts. Doubled for RE.)

19—**Self Discipline Focus** (Dev. Pts. Doubled for SD.)

20—**Differing Eyes** (Character's eyes are of different color. Character has the capability to close his eyes and concentrate for a round in order to reorient his vision so that he can see invisible objects, but not visible organic objects. To return to normal vision, he must reverse the process.)

21—**Directed Weapons Master** (One selected category of weapons yields 3 skill ranks for every 2 skill ranks developed. All other weapon development coats are increased by 50%.)

22—**Disarm Skill** (Character may intentionally attempt to disarm an opponent. Procedure—subtract enemy's OB from character's OB; add open-ended roll; if 101+, enemy must roll RR vs character's level or lose his weapon.)

23—**Eloquence** (Character requires one less round of preparation than normal to cast a spell. It still takes 1 round to cast the spell.)

24—**Enchanting Quality** (Character has an enchanted quality about himself and is naturally proficient with spells. Character start knowing one spell list up to the level equivalent to one pick by a character of his profession. If Character is a non-spell user or a semi-spell user, his spell list development costs are half of normal..)

25—**Enticing Eyes** (Character possesses a pair of enticing, sparkling eyes which provide him with a charismatic air. Adds +15 bonus for all actions involving leadership or influence: e.g., public speaking, seduction, "charm" spells, "hold" spells, etc.)

26—**Ethereal Sight** (Character may see invisible or ethereal items if he concentrates.)

27—**Exceptionally Enchanted** (Character is exceptionally enchanted. Character has a +50 RR bonus versus spells from one realm (roll: 01-40 = Essence; 41-70 = Channeling; 71-00 = Mentalism) and a +25 bonus when casting such spells or attempting to understand and use inscriptions and items whose power is based on that realm.)

28—**Eye of the Tiger** (Character may prepare as for the adrenal move "Strength" except that his chance of success is his level + (SD mod + EM mod)/2. If he succeeds, his OB and DB are modified by +15 for the next round..)

29—**Favored** (Liked by a very high ranking noble. May be a relative.)

30—**Hammerhand** (Hands hit as maces when using martial art strikes; treat as a "mace" weapon kata with no penalty.)

31—**Immovable Will** (Immune to fear and charm attacks. Sleep attacks are halved for attack level and duration.)

32—**Firewalker** (Immune to fire once per day for 10 min/lvl.)

33—**Power-taker** (Increase PPs by 1 each time a spell is cast with character as the target; total PPs may not exceed normal maximum.)

34—**Infravision** (Character possess ability to see sources of heat up to 100' away, so long as it is dark.)

35—**Innate Magician** (Character may designate 1 spell list on which he never needs to make an Extraordinary Spell Failure roll.)

36—**Invincible** (Character is unaffected by stun results.)

37—**Chaney** (Invisibility once per day.)

38—Beman (Leaping range doubled.)

39—Leg Spring (Character's legs have a tremendous "spring" and gains +10 bonus for all leaping maneuvers. A vertical jump of up to 4', a standing jump of up to 8', or a running jump of up to 20' is routine. Character's hand joints share this uniqueness and you receive the +10 bonus for actions involving picking locks, rowing, or pulling on things with their hands: i.e., tugging on a rope or firing a non-mechanical bow.)

40—Lightning Reactions (Character has lightning reactions which gives +5 DB, +5 OB, and +20 for determining imitative and +25 for quickdraw of weapons.)

41—Light Sleeper (Character may make perception rolls to wake and take action immediately from normal sleep.)

42—Lore (May learn Arcane spell lists as if they were his base list.)

43—Lucky (May add (+5 x 1D20) to any roll once per day; decide before making the roll.)

44—Lucky (Once per day you get to reroll one die roll.)

45—Lung Capacity (Character's tremendous lung capacity enables him to hold his breath for up to 5 minutes without damage. In addition, the Character has twice the endurance he normally would have.)

46—Mana Reading (10% chance of determining each ability of a magic item; roll each characteristic.)

47—Mana Sensing (Character's necks hairs prickle around a great power source, enchanted locations, etc.)

48—Martial Art Training (A non-monk character may train in martial arts, adrenal moves, and defense at monks cost. Monk and Warrior Monk characters have no penalty when using weapon kata.)

49—Master Tactician (Has open-ended chance equal to his IN mod to receive information directly from the GM concerning an immediate tactical situation.)

50—Mind Over Matter (Adrenal Moves skill bonuses modified by +5 x 1D20; roll each time one of the bonuses is used.)

51—Mind Over Matter (Adrenal Defense skill bonus modified by +5 x 1D10; roll each time bonus is used.)

52—Mover (Base movement rate is doubled.)

53—Multiple Limbs (Character has 1D4 extra limbs, character choice.)

54—Natural Archer (All negative range modifiers are halved.)

55—Natural Assassin (Ambush skill development cost are halved.)

56—Natural Facility with Armor (All armor development cost are halved.)

57—Natural Physique (Body development cost is halved and racial maximum is increased by 50%.)

58—Natural Weapons Master (Character may develop skill ranks in one similar weapons category; all weapons in that category may use that skill rank for their OBs.)

59—Neutral Body Odor (Character's body odor is a peculiar neutral odor which cannot be smelled and masks the odor of anything within 5')

60—Awareness (Never Surprised.)

61—Nimble Skeleton (Character nimble skeleton allows a +20 bonus when making moving maneuvers.)

62—Outdoorsman (Character gets +50 to all foraging, fire starting, and locate shelter rolls while outdoors. He receives +20 to all tracking, trapping and stalk/hide rolls while outdoors.)

63—Power (Character knows any 1 spell list to 50th level. May be from any realm or profession.)

64—Portage Skill (Encumbrance penalties are halved.)

65—Psionic (Character has an additional set of power points base on his PR stat to use with the lists in *Space Master* (if not available, reroll); the list may be developed as if the Character were a "Semi-telepath".)

66—Quick Concentration (Character's exceptional ability to quickly concentrate and focus on matters enables him to prepare actions [i.e., spells, bow attacks, etc.] one round quicker than normal.)

67—Quick Stride (Character has quick but quiet stride: gives +20 bonus when attempting to move silently [i.e., stalking]; **and** allows you to ambush anyone who you can strike from behind, with a +2 ambush skill rank bonus; **and** gives you a +20 bonus for balancing maneuvers.)

68—Regenerative Power (Heal 1 hit/round.)

69—Resiliency (Reduce hits taken from any attack by 1D10.)

70—Resiliency (Reduce hits taken from any attack by 1D20.)

71—Resiliency (Reduce any critical taken by one severity level.)

72—Resiliency (Reduce any critical taken by two severity levels.)

73—Resiliency (Reduce hits taken from any magical attack by 1D10.)

74—Resiliency (Reduce hits taken from any magical attack by 1D20.)

75—Resiliency (Reduce any physical critical taken by one severity level.)

76—Resiliency (Reduce any physical critical taken by two severity levels.)

69—Resiliency (Reduce hits taken from any physical attack by 1D10.)

70—Resiliency (Reduce hits taken from any physical attack by 1D20.)

71—Resiliency (Reduce any physical critical taken by one severity level.)

72—Resiliency (Reduce any physical critical taken by two severity levels.)

81—Resistance (+25 bonus for RRs for any 1 realm.)

82—Scope Skills (Radii and "number of targets" are doubled.)

83—Shape Change (Aerial and land animal shapes.)

84—Shape Change (Aerial animal shape.)

85—Shape Change (Land animal shape.)

86—Shape Change (Random.)

87—Spatial Skills (Range factors of all character's spells are doubled; "self" become "touch" and "touch" becomes 5'.)

88—Spell Invincibility (Not affected by 1st level spells.)

89—Spell Invincibility (Not affected by 1st-2nd level spells.)

90—Spits Contains Acid (1D100 potency; useable 1/day; delivers an "A" acid criticals.)

91—Subconscious Preparation (Readies weapons and bows 1 round quicker than normal.)

92—Survival Instinct (When using entire OB to parry, the OB is modified by an additional +25.)

93—Taste Bad (75% chance monster will spit you out; i.e., he may take one bite, but he won't eat you.)

94—Temporal Skills (Durations of all character's spells are doubled; concentration spell are not effected in any way.)

95—Tolerance (Character may take 150% of total hit points before becoming unconscious.)

96—Null Factor (Undetectable by Magic.)

97—Unnatural Stamina (May run at up to 3x normal movement rate and spend only 1 exhaustion point every 60 rounds.)

98—Unusually Strong (Character is unusually strong and has a +20 strength stat bonus [in addition to normal bonus]. This bonus is due to character's great stature: the maximum size for one of his race.

99—Withstand Pain (Character has an exceptional inner reserve which allows him to withstand pain and adds +3 to each body development skill rank roll.)

100—Wings (Character can use wings to fly; flying rate is equal to normal Base Movement Rate with the "Mod Due to Stride" subtracted instead of added.)

The Chaotic Table **51**

GEAS CHART
Roll 1D100

1—Abnormal sized body part (Roll on Plus/Minus Chart to get the percent of size change and roll on random Anatomy Chart to determine which part of the body is changed.)

2—Aged (-10 pts to 1 random potential and -5 to all others.)

3—Aged (-15 pts to 1 random potential and -5 to all others.)

4—Aged (-15 pts to 1 random potential and -10 to all others.)

5—Aged (-20 pts to 1 random potential and -5 to all others.)

6—Aged (-20 pts to 1 random potential and -10 to all others.)

7—Aged (-20 pts to 1 random potential and -15 to all others.)

8—Aged (-25 pts to 1 random potential and -5 to all others.)

9—Aged (-25 pts to 1 random potential and -10 to all others.)

10—Aged (-25 pts to 1 random potential and -15 to all others.)

11—Aged (-25 pts to 1 random potential and -20 to all others.)

12—Aged (-30 pts to 1 random potential and -5 to all others.)

13—Aged (-30 pts to 1 random potential and -10 to all others.)

14—Aged (-30 pts to 1 random potential and -15 to all others.)

15—Aged (-30 pts to 1 random potential and -20 to all others.)

16—Aged (-30 pts to 1 random potential and -25 to all others.)

17—Animal Hatred (One particular type of animal or beast has a hatred of the character and will attack him at first sight. Animal has +25 OB when attacking character due to the hatred.)

18—Attracts Elementals (Add +30 to elemental attacks against character.)

19—Aura of Power (Character is surrounded by a visible glow of magical energy. Even if the Character is invisible the "aura" is visible. The "aura" is bright red.)

20—Bad Reputation (People know you on sight; 1D100% chance.)

21—Battle Fatigue (After combat, must sleep 1D4 hours.)

22—Body damaged (Roll on Anatomy Chart.)

23—Cannibal.

24—Non-parry (Can't parry.)

25—Non-read (Can't read.)

26—Illiterate (Can't read or write.)

27—Stone-like One (Can't swim.)

28—Slasher (Can't use crushing weapons.)

29—Lead Feet (Can't use dash pace multiplier.)

30—Krusher (Can't use edged weapons.)

31—Lead Legs (Can't use fast sprint or dash pace multiplier.)

32—Pyrophobe (Can't use or handle fire.)

33—Meleer (Can't use ranged weapons.)

34—Non-defender (Can't use shields.)

35—Spaz (Can't use thrown weapons.)

36—Small Armsman (Can't use two handed weapons.)

37—Non-write (Can't write.)

38—Coward (50% chance of fleeing from danger.)

39—Deafness (1 ear -D100 to hearing perception rolls.)

40—Deafness (Both ears -D100 to hearing perception rolls.)

41—Chronic Disease (Character must roll once at the beginning of each week to see if the disease flares up: 01-10 indicates the disease has struck and the Character is at [-5 x 1D20] for 1 week. During this time, the Character Appearance and temporary Presence are at half value.)

42—Cold sensitivity ([-5 x 1D20] to all skills when "cold"; based upon standard climate of GM's world.)

43—Colorblindness (Roll 1D4: 1–blue-greens; 2–red-greens; 3–total; 4–yellow-orange.)

44—Colored hair (Bright blue, White and purple splotches, etc.)

45—Colored skin (Bright red, Yellow stripes.)

46—Darkblindness (Can't see in the dark.)

47—Dark sensitivity ([-5 x 1D20] to all skills while in "darkness".)

48—Overweight (Double average body weight for height.)

49—Dwarfism (Reduce size by [1D10 x 10%], reroll zero.)

50—Wimp (Exhaustion rates doubled.)

51—Farsighted (can't see things close up.)

52—Fear of Darkness (Character is inflicted with a peculiar fear of dark, enclosed spaces which occasionally flares up. Whenever he enters such a situation he must roll a RR [no bonus] versus a 1st level attack. If he fails, he will panic and pass into a coma for 1D10 hours. For example, he is fine outside on a dark night, but when he enters a dark cave complex he must roll. Say he succeeds, but someone lights a torch whose flame then goes out; he must roll again.)

53—Flashback (Character is plagued by a terrifying childhood experience that affects the character during combat. After the first round of each combat, the character rolls: 01-10 indicate the flashback strikes leaving the character curled up on the ground, sniveling and shivering for 1D10 rounds.)

54—Friend Slayer (Instead of following normal attack spell failure procedures, the attack spell is cast on the nearest friend or associate within range.)

55—Giantism (Increase size by 1D10 times 10%, reroll zero.)

56—Heat Sensitivity ([-5 x 1D20] to all skills when "hot"; based upon standard climate of GM's world.)

57—Heavy Sleeper (May not be awakened "even magically" during the first hour of slumber.)

58—Hemophilia (All bleeding, hits/round, is doubled.)

59—Hunted by (1D100% chance of involvement per week. Roll 1D6; 1–single person; 2–several people [2-20]; 3–small group [21-100]; 4–medium size group [101-1000]; 5–large size group [1001-5000]; 6–very large size group [5001+].)

60—Insensitivity to burns (No stun from burn [hot or cold] damage; but bleeding damage, hits/round, from all criticals is doubled.)

61—Insensitivity to cuts (No stun from slash criticals; but bleeding damage, hits/round, from all criticals is doubled.)

62—Insensitivity to pain (No stun from criticals; but bleeding damage, hits/round, from all criticals is doubled.)

63—Insensitivity to touch (No stun from slash criticals; but bleeding damage, hits/round, from all criticals is doubled.)

64—Lightblindness (Can't see in the light.)

65—Light sensitivity (-5 x 1D20 to all skills while in bright light.)

66—Lightning-phobe (Character is frighten of lightning and thunder and will be incapacitated if caught in a thunderstorm; in such a case, the character will be at -50 if under partial cover or will drop, freeze, and be immobile if outside and exposed to the elements.)

67—Nearsighted (Can't see things in the distance.)

68—Animal Hater (Never rides animals.)

69—Fearless (Never runs from a fight.)

70—Metalphobe (Never wears any metal items.)

71—Diseaseprone (No resistance to disease.)

72—Poisonprone (No resistance to poison.)

73—Overpowering Strength (Anytime character consciously applies his strength he must make a RR versus a 1st level attack (use SD stat bonus) or the Character will apply all of his strength involuntarily. For example, you should develop a consciously limp handshake, for any conscious application of your grip might crush the hand of the one you greet.)

74—Physical Investments (Any time the character casts a spell that is over 8th level the character takes 5 hits.)

75—Plagued by Random Pain (Whenever character rolls 66, he is at -30 for an hour.)

76—Plagued by Random Paralysis (Whenever the character rolls open-ended high or low, they suffer random paralysis which lasts for 1 hour. Determine location of paralysis from Anatomy Chart.)

77—Poor Control (Roll non-attack spell failures as attack spell failures. Add an additional +10 to all spell failure rolls.)

78—Poisonous Saliva (Roll 1D10 for level of poison.)

79—Poisonous Touch (Roll 1D10 for level of poison.)

80—Prejudice (Deep irrational hatred for members of one race.)

81—Psychotic Temper (Character has a (40 – SD mod)% chance of responding to an insult or an offense with a killing rage.)

82—Sleepiness (Your peculiar need for sleep requires 10 hours rest each day and you are at -5 for each hour short of that figure (e.g., Character is at -10 if they only get 8 hours sleep.)

83—Narcophile (Should Character walk more than 5 hours without resting for at least two hours the Character has problems staying awake. At the beginning of each hour and thereafter the Character must roll and any result of 01-25, causes both of the Character's arms to fall "asleep": the arms become useless for 1D10 hours.)

84—Spell ranges are halved (And 5' becomes touch and touch become self.)

85—Sterile (May not have children.)

86—Stoned Breath (Anyone that the character breathes on is turned to stone once per day; a RR is allowed; each target must roll only once per day..)

87—Stoned Looks (Anyone that looks at the character and fails their RR is turned to stone; each target must roll only once per day.)

88—Stoned Touch (Any person who touches the character and fails their RR is turned to stone; each target must roll only once per day.)

89—Superstitious (Morale is influenced by encountering a "bad omen": -10 x 1D10 for 1D10 days.)

90—Takes double crit damage (From [Roll 1D4]: **1**–animals attacks; **2**–elemental attacks; **3**–magical attacks; **4**–melee weapons.)

91—Takes double damage (From [roll 1D6]: **1**–crushing attacks; **2**–elemental attacks; **3**–falls; **4**–fire attacks; **5**–puncture attacks; **6**–slash attacks.)

92—Lightweight (Spells require double normal PPs.)

93—Terrible Fearlessness (Character has a [40-SD mod]% chance of charging heedless into any combat situation.)

94—Trophy (Takes ears, scalps, eyes, tongue, etc. from victims.)

95—Unlucky (Roll 1D10: **1**–open-ended range decreased to 97-00; **2**–open-ended range decreased to 98-00; **3**–open-ended range decreased to 99-00; **4**–open-ended range decreased to 00; **5**–fumble range increased by +1; **6**–fumble range increased by +2; **7**–fumble range increased by +3; **8**–fumble range increased by +4; **9**–fumble range increased by +5; **10**–roll again.)

96—Watched by (1D100% of involvement during a session [Roll 1D6]: **1**–single person; **2**–several people [2-20.]; **3**–small group [21-100.]; **4**–medium size group [101-1000.]; **5**–large size group [1001-5000.]; **6**–very large size group [5001+].)

97—Weakened Bones (1D50% chance of breakage when under stress.)

98—Wings (Character has a pair of wings but cannot fly or glide.)

99—Wraith (Character has the disfavor of a particular god, demi-god, Demon etc.)

100—Roll twice on this table.

SKILL DETERMINATION CHART
ROLL 1D4

1—Devoid of talent with one skill (skill ranks may never be developed for that skill).

2—Natural talent with one skill (skill ranks developed for that skill are doubled).

3—One skill bonus has a special modifier (roll on *Plus/Minus Chart* to determine the modifier).

4—Unnatural talent with one skill (skill ranks developed for that skill are halved, round up).

SKILL CATEGORY DETERMINATION CHART
ROLL 1D4

1—Devoid of talent with one skill category (skill ranks may never be developed for skills in that category).

2—Natural talent with one skill category (skill ranks developed for skills in that category are doubled).

3—The bonuses for the skills in one category have a special modifier (roll on *Plus/Minus Chart* to determine the modifier).

4—Unnatural talent with one skill category (skill ranks developed for skills in that category are halved, round up).

ANATOMY CHART
ROLL 1D100

01-02	Ankle		
03-04	Arm	51-52	Leg
05-06	Balance	53-54	Lips
07	Bladder	55	Liver
08	Body Hair	56-57	Lower Arm (elbow down)
09-10	Brain	58-59	Lower Leg (calf down)
11-12	Cheek	60-61	Lung
13-14	Collar Bone	62	Mammary Glands
15-16	Ear	63-64	Neck
17-18	Elbow	65-66	Nose
19-20	Eye	67-68	Rib
21-22	Facial Hair	69-70	Sight
23-24	Feeling	71-72	Shoulder Blade
25-26	Finger	73-74	Shoulder Joint
27-28	Foot	75-76	Skull
29	Gall Bladder	77-78	Olfactory Organ
30	Gonads	79	Spleen
31-32	Groin	80-81	Sternum
33-34	Hand	82-83	Stomach
35-36	Head Hair	84-85	Tail
37-38	Hearing	86-87	Tail Bone
39-40	Heart	88-89	Taste
41-42	Hip	90-91	Teeth
43	Intestine	92-93	Throat
44-45	Jaw	94-95	Toe
46	Kidneys	96-97	Tongue
47-48	Knee	98	Voice Box
49-50	Knee Cap	99-100	Wrist

8.3 MOON MAGE BASE LISTS

8.31 MOON MADNESS (Moon Mage Base)

NOTE: Mood Swing *and* Mood Setting *spells effects vary depending upon the exact type of "mood" being established. In most cases, this will yield a positive or negative modification for most given action, depending upon whether the action corresponds to the mood (+) or opposes it (–). It is recommended that the modification be +5/-5 for every 3 levels of the caster (round down). Hence a 7th level Moon Mage would adjust his target's overall performance with a +10 or -10 modifier. (e.g., the mood, "frightened", in a combat situation would give a target a -10 modification if he stays to fight and a +10 if he flees.)*

	Area of Effect	Duration	Range
1—Mood Swing I	1 target	1 rnd/lvl	50'
2—Mood Setting I	1 target	1 rnd/lvl	50'
3—Suicidal I	1 target	1 rnd	50'
4—Mood Swing II	2 targets	1 rnd/lvl	50'
5—Mood Setting II	2 targets	1 rnd/lvl	50'
6—Suicidal II	2 targets	1 rnd	50'
7—Mood Swing III	3 targets	1 rnd/lvl	50'
8—Mood Setting III	3 targets	1 rnd/lvl	50'
9—Suicidal III	3 targets	1 rnd	50'
10—Mood Swing IV	4 targets	1 rnd/lvl	50'
11—Mood Setting IV	4 targets	1 rnd/lvl	50'
12—Suicidal IV	4 targets	1 rnd	50'
13—Mood Swing V	5 targets	1 rnd/lvl	50'
14—Mood Setting V	5 targets	1 rnd/lvl	50'
15—Suicidal V	5 targets	1 rnd	50'
16—Mood Swing VI	6 targets	1 rnd/lvl	50'
17—Mood Setting VI	6 targets	1 rnd/lvl	50'
18—Suicidal VI	6 targets	1 rnd	50'
19—			
20—Mood Swing True	varies	1 rnd/lvl	50'
25—Mood Setting True	varies	1 rnd/lvl	50'
30—Suicidal True	varies	1 rnd	50'
50—Lunacy	varies	varies	100'

1—Mood Swing I (M) Reverse the "primary mood" of the target. For example: if the targets is filled with rage, he becomes very calm; if the target is overcomed with grief, he becomes overjoyed; hate reverses to love; fear reverse to courage; etc.

2—Mood Setting I (M) As *Mood Swing I* except caster can choose the mood. (e.g., grief, shame, bashfulness, dirty, sad, glad, hungry, thristy, joy, etc.).

3—Suicidal I (M) Influences the target to attempt suicide. To be affected the target must not only fail his normal RR, but he must fail an additional RR modified by SD. If affected, the target will usually make an critical roll against themselves; and this is normally only an "A" Puncture critical.

4—Mood Swing II (F) As *Mood Swing I* except 2 targets are affected.
5—Mood Setting II (F) As *Mood Setting I* except 2 targets are affected.
6—Suicidal II (F) As *Suicidal I* except 2 targets are affected.
7—Mood Swing III (F) As *Mood Swing I* except 3 targets are affected.
8—Mood Setting III (F) As *Mood Setting I* except 3 targets are affected.
9—Suicidal III (F) As *Suicidal I* except 3 targets are affected.
10—Mood Swing IV (F) As *Mood Swing I* except 4 targets are affected.
11—Mood Setting IV (F) As *Mood Setting I* except 4 targets are affected.
12—Suicidal IV (F) As *Suicidal I* except 4 targets are affected.
13—Mood Swing V (F) As *Mood Swing I* except 5 targets are affected.
14—Mood Setting V (F) As *Mood Setting I* except 5 targets are affected.
15—Suicidal V (F) As *Suicidal I* except 5 targets are affected.
16—Mood Swing VI (F) As *Mood Swing I* except 6 targets are affected.
17—Mood Setting VI (F) As *Mood Setting I* except 6 targets are affected.
18—Suicidal VI (F) As Suicidal I except 6 targets are affected.
20—Mood Swing True (F) As *Mood Swing I* except 1 target/3 lvls that the caster has obtained are affected.
25—Mood Setting True (F) As *Mood Setting I* except 1 target/3 lvls that the caster has obtained are affected.
30—Suicidal True (F) As *Suicidal I* except 1 target/3 lvls that the caster has obtained are affected.
50—Lunacy (F) At night during the proper power phase of the moon (full moon for light based Moon Mages; half moon for grey based Moon Mages; new moon for dark based Moon Mages), 1 target/lvl will "channel" all of their PPs (1PP/round each) to the caster (i.e., for the moon god/goddess). Any target failing his RR by 50 or more will experience a permanent 10% decrease in total PPs; this can be considered "burn out" **or** perhaps the god/goddess' direct intervention.

8.3 MOON MASTERY (Moon Mage Base)

NOTE 1: *This spell list is adverserly affected by the moon and it's phases. There are three basic type of Moon Mastery (each Moon Mage has one type of Moon Mastery) with modifiers based upon the phase of the moon:*

	Light	Grey	Dark
Full Moon	x1	x.25	x0
3/4 Moon	x.75	x.5	x.25
Half Moon	x.5	x1	x.5
1/4 Moon	x.25	x.5	x.75
New Moon	x0	x.25	x1

NOTE 2: *A spell user's "moon of power" is the phase of the moon during which the modification above is "x1": light based: full; grey based: half; dark based: new*

NOTE 3: *The duration, range, and effects of spells marked with "†" are modified based upon type of Moon Mastery and phase of the moon (see above). For example, Moon Glow, cast by a light based 10th level Moon Mage under a full moon (x.5), will give x2 power for 10 hours; but, the same spell cast cast by the same Moon Mage during a half moon will only yield x1 power for 5 hours.*

NOTE 4: *These spells only work when the caster is outside at night* **and** *the moon is "up"*

	Area of Effect	Duration	Range
1—Moon Shade †	1 target	10 min/lvl	touch
2—Moon Shine †	1 target	10 min/lvl	touch
3—Moon Lite †	10'R	10 min/lvl	touch
4—Moon Bath †	1 target	10 min/lvl	touch
5—Moon Wort †	1 target	1 min/lvl	touch
6—Moon Beam (100') †	1 target	—	100'
7—Moon Eye †	1 target	1 min/lvl	touch
8—Moon Drops †	10' R	1 rnd	100'
9—			
10—Moon Glow †	x2 power	1 hr/lvl	self
11—Moon Lightning †	1 target	—	100'
12—			
13—Moon Beam (300') †	1 target	—	300'
14—Moon Glade †	1 target	1 rnd	10'
15—Moon Struck †	1 target	P	100'
16—Moon Maddness †	1 target	1 min/lvl	100'
17—Moon Beam (500') †	1 target	—	500'
18—Moon Blind †	1 target	10 min/lvl	100'
19—Moon Lightning (300') †	1 target	—	100'
20—Moon Stone †	1 moon stone	24 hours	touch
25—Moon Child †	Newborn Child	P	touch
30—Moon Quake †	50'R/lvl	1 rnd	touch
50—Moon Maiden †	1 Moon Maiden	1 rnd/lvl	10'

1—Moon Shade (I†) Target can see in the dark as if it was daylight.

2—Moon Shine (U†) Allows the caster to enchant a beverage: 5 ounces per power point used in the spell (limited to 1PP/lvl). This spell does not create the beverage or container. For every ounce drunk, the drinker receives a +3 RR bonus (magical, poison, and disease) and a -3 OB bonus.

3—Moon Lite (F†) Illuminates a 10'R area with moon light. The enchantment may be placed on an object will move as the object moves.

4—Moon Bath (F†) Target heals 1 hit per minute if outside under the moon.

5—Moon Wort (FM†) Enchant 1 dose of a moon herb called Moon Wort. After enchantment, eating or drinking the herb makes the imbiber speak honestly.

6—Moon Beam (100') (E†) A bolt of "moon essence" is shot from the palm of the caster; attacks are resolved using the Shock Bolt Attack Table (*SL* 10.41), with criticals as follows: *light based:* fire criticals; *grey based:* impact criticals; *dark based:* cold criticals.

7—Moon Eye (FI†) Allows the target to see objects that are affected by moon essence. The object will appear to be surrounded by a magical field/aura as follows: *light based:* slivery; *grey based:* grey; *dark based:* black.

8—Moon Drops (F†) Allows the caster to create a small, sudden storm of "moon drops" (i.e., hail stones), giving each target in the area an "A" impact critical.

10—Moon Glow (F†) Gives the caster double normal intrinsic PPs for the duration of this spell. This modification is not cumulative with PP multipling items.

11—Moon Lightning (F†) As Moon Beam except that the Lightning Bolt Attack Table (*SL* 10.45) is used.

13—Moon Beam (300') (F†) As *Moon Beam (100')* except range is 300'.

14—Moon Glade (F†) Allows the target to travel along "moon glades" (slivery reflection of moon light on the surface of water); this spell is basically a limited teleport. In one round, target may move up to 1 mile/level in a straight line along a watery/icy surface. If the route encounters solid material (e.g., land, a boat, a bird, etc.) **or** an area not outside and under the moon, the target will stop 5' from that point.

15—Moon Struck (FM†) This spell may only be cast if the phase of the moon is the caster's "moon of power" (i.e., the modifier is "x1"). The target will go on an eating and drinking spree for several hours. When the moon reaches its highest point in the sky, the target will go running wildly into any open area under the moon. The target will continue to run about until totally exhausted, at which point he will fall into a deep sleep.

16—Moon Maddness (FM†) Target is enraged and becomes a berserker; use "frenzy" guidelines.

17—Moon Beam (500') (F†) As *Moon Beam (100')* except range is 500'.

18—Moon Blind (FM†) During the day **or** when the moon is "down" **or** if not outside, the target is totally blind. Otherwise, the target's sight and perception varies based upon the phase of the moon and the caster's type (i.e., at night when the moon is "up", using the modifiers in the "NOTE 1" for this list, the effect is: x0 = totally blind, x.25 = can see with a +20 perception bonus, x.5 = can see with a +40 perception bonus, x.75 = can see with a +60 perception bonus, or x1 = can see with a +80 perception bonus).

19—Moon Lightning (300') (F†) As *Moon Lightning (100')* except range is 300'.

20—Moon Stone (F†) This spell enchants an appropriate stone, rock, or gem (GM discretion); allowing it to act as a spell adder (+1/5 lvl of caster) and as a PP storer (1 PP/lvl of caster); this will vary depending upon the phase of the moon and the caster's type. For example, a moon stone enchanted under a half moon by a 20th level grey based spell caster is a +4 spell adder/20 PP storer; enchanted under a new or full moon, it is only a +1 spell adder/5 PP storer; and under a 1/4 or 3/4 moon, it is a +2 spell adder/10PP storer. A moon stone glows very slightly under the caster's moon of power. Each Moon Mage may only have one Moon Stone enchanted at any one time.

25—Moon Child (F†) Blesses and initiates a newborn child into the ranks of a moon society of spell casters (normally, the only way one can become a moon based spell caster). A child so blessed has a natural tendency to use this spell list and suffers no ESF when casting spells on this list. The child also has a +5 bonus for all magical, poison, and disease RRs.

30—Moon Quake (F†) Causes a very minor earthquake which could cause shoddy construction to collapse; this can be very terrifying. This is approximately 5.5 on the Richter scale.

50—Moon Maiden (F†) Allows the caster to summons a very minor moon goddess (base chance of summoning = .5%/lvl of caster); details are dependent on the GM's world system.

> **EXAMPLE:** *She will arrive driving two moon steeds (color is based on the caster's moon of power) pulling her chariot. Everyone of her alignment will gain a +30 bonus as long as they remain within view of her. She will fight for the caster (100OB, 25DB, 150 hits, AT 1). In addition to physically attacking, she will use one spell on this list each round. If she is killed during the duration of this spell, the caster will never be able to cast this spell again* **and** *all spells on this list will become ESF (+25)* **and** *all spells on this list will require twice normal PPs to cast.*

8.33 METAMORPHOSE (Moon Mage Base)

NOTE 1: *The spells on this list can duplicate physical, mental, spirit and power forms, but they cannot duplicate mannerism and memory.*

NOTE 2: *Full effect for each Metamorphosis spell above 9th level requires one hour per type of change desired (e.g., if a Metamorphosis involves Bio-Metamorphosis, Psi-Metamorphosis, and Spirit-Metamorphosis, the complete Metamorphosis would require three hours). During this period the target must remain is a state of meditation or sleep. If the target is distrubed and "awakened" before the required time is over, he will assume his natural form gradually within an hour **and** he takes a Physical Alteration critical whose degree of severity is based upon the number of hours of Metamorphosis not completed (i.e., the target of a Metamorphosis interrupted 1-60 minutes before completion would take an "A" Crit; 61-120 minutes would deliver a "B" Crit; etc.). Every 15 minutes after the intial critical due to interruption, the target takes another Physical Alteration critical one degree less severity than the previous critical; this process continues until an "A" critical is taken. For example, if a target is "awakened" during the 1st hr of a Metamorphosis which requires 3 hrs, the target takes a "C" P.A. Crit, 15 min. later he takes a "B" P.A. Crit, and 15 min. later he takes an "A" P.A. Crit.*

NOTE 3: *Any non-magical attempt to "awaken" a target out of Metamorphosis is an 'extremely hard' static maneuver. Magical attempts should treat the target as if he were in a coma.*

NOTE 4: *The Metamorphosis spells create a "cocoon" around the target. It takes a weapon or a 'hard' static maneuver (modified by ST bonus) to break it.*

NOTE 5: *When the Metamorphosis is complete, the target has no PPs, has no exhaustion points, is extremely hungry, and is thirsty. The target must make a 'hard' static maneuver (modified by SD bonus) to try to do any activity besides eating, drinking, and then sleeping.*

NOTE 6: *The Metamorphosis target will gain those abilities that are natural to the form they Metamorphose into. However, magical abilities are not gained. For example; if the target is Metamorphosed into a Dragon, he can fly (most likely not very well initially) and he will have the size and physical combat abilities of the Dragon; but the target will not have the Dragon's magical breathe weapon.*

NOTE 7: *All mass changes greater than x2 but less than x4 the target's mass require the target to take a "D" Physical Alteration crit. All mass changes greater than x4 the mass require an "E" Physical Alteration crit.*

NOTE 8: *All power changes greater than x2 but less than x4 the target's mass require the target to take a "D" Physical Alteration crit. All power changes greater than x4 the mass require an "E" Physical Alteration crit.*

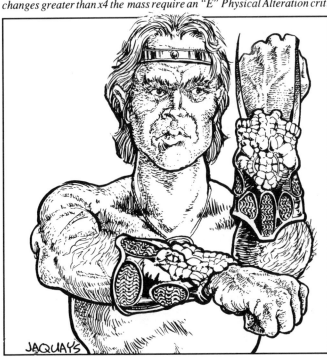

	Area of Effect	Duration	Range
1—Birth Sign	1 target	—	touch
2—			
3—Bio-Metamorphosis Typing	1 target	—	50'
4—			
5—Psi-Metamorphosis Typing	1 target	—	50'
6—Spirit-Metamorphosis Typing	1 target	—	50'
7—			
8—Power-Metamorphosis Typing	1 target	—	50'
9—			
10—Bio-Metamorphosis	1 target	1 day/lvl	touch
11—			
12—Psi-Metamorphosis	1 target	1 day/lvl	touch
13—			
14—Spirit-Metamorphosis	1 target	1 day/lvl	touch
15—			
16—Power-Metamorphosis	1 target	1 day/lvl	touch
17—			
18—Bio-Metamorphosis True	1 target	1 wk/lvl	touch
19—			
20—Psi-Metamorphosis True	1 target	1 wk/lvl	touch
25—Spirit-Metamorphosis True	1 target	1 wk/lvl	touch
30—Power-Metamorphosis True	1 target	1 wk/lvl	touch
50—Metamorphosis True	1 target	P	touch

1—Birth Sign (I) Allows the caster to learn if the target has favorable birth sign for Metamorphosis spell useage. Roll 1D100:

1-75	not a likely candidate.
76-90	can handle 1st—10th lvl Metamorphosis spells
91-95	can handle 1st—20th lvl Metamorphosis spells
96-97	can handle 1st—25th lvl Metamorphosis spells
98-99	can handle 1st—30th lvl Metamorphosis spells
100	can handle 1st—50th lvl Metamorphosis spells

3—Bio-Metamorphosis Typing (I) Allows the caster to analyze a physical form which he may use later when *Bio-Metamorphosing*.

5—Psi-Metamorphosis Typing (I) Allows the caster to analyze a mental form/pattern which he may use later when *Psi-Metamorphosing*.

6—Spirit-Metamorphosis Typing (I) Allows the caster to analyze a spiritual form (e.g., the life essence, vivacity or soul pattern of the target) which he may use later when *Spirit-Metamorphosing*.

8—Power-Metamorphosis Typing (I) Allows the caster to analyze a power form (e.g., how the target handles Essence, Channeling, Mentalism, etc.) which he may use later when *Power-Metamorphosing*.

10—Bio-Metamorphosis (F) Target's body is metamorphosed into a physical form which caster has previously *Bio-Metamorphosis Typed*.

12—Psi-Metamorphosis (F) Target's mental pattern is metamorphosed or changed into a mental pattern which caster has previously *Psi-Metamorphosis Typed*.

14—Spirit-Metamorphosis (F) Target's spiritual pattern is metamorphosed or changed into a spiritual pattern which caster has previously *Spirit-Metamorphosis Typed*.

16—Power-Metamorphosis (F) Target's power pattern is metamorphosed or changed into a power pattern which caster has previously *Power-Metamorphosis Typed*.

18—Bio-Metamorphosis True (F) As *Bio-Metamorphosis* except duration is 1 week/lvl.

20—Psi-Metamorphosis True (F) As *Psi-Metamorphosis* except duration is 1 week/lvl.

25—Spirit-Metamorphosis True (F) As *Spirit-Metamorphosis* except duration is 1 week/lvl.

30—Power-Metamorphosis True (F) As *Power-Metamorphosis* except duration is 1 week/lvl.

50—Metamorphosis True (F) The duration of a set of Metamorphosis spells (i.e., Bio-, Psi-, Spirit-, and Power-) is permanent.

8.4 NOBLE WARRIOR BASE LISTS

8.41 NOBLE ARMOR (Noble Warrior Base)

NOTE 1: *Only one spell from this list may be active on a given individual and his set of armor.*

NOTE 2: Shield Blow *spells are only useful against melee and missile attacks that the target is aware of. If the caster is ambushed or attacked from the rear or unable to get the shield in position to intercept the blow (e.g., shield wedged in a opening, an opponent has a hold of the shield, etc.), the* Shield Blow *spell is of no use.*

	Area of Effect	Duration	Range
1—Shield *	1 set of armor	1 min/lvl	self
2—Armoring Cloth	cloth	1 min/lvl	touch
3—			
4—Armoring Leather	1 set of armor	1 min/lvl	touch
5—Shield Blow I	1 shield	1 min/lvl	self
6—Armoring Chain	1 set of armor	1 min/lvl	touch
7—			
8—Armoring Plate	1 set of armor	1 min/lvl	touch
9—			
10—Shield Blow II	1 shield	1 min/lvl	self
11—Mystical Cloth	cloth	1 min/lvl	touch
12—Armoring Robes	cloth	1 min/lvl	touch
13—			
14—Mystical Leather	1 set of armor	1 min/lvl	touch
15—Shield Blow III	1 shield	1 min/lvl	self
16—			
17—Mystical Chain	1 set of armor	1 min/lvl	touch
18—			
19—Shield Blow IV	1 shield	1 min/lvl	self
20—Mystical Plate	1 set of armor	1 min/lvl	touch
25—Shield Blow True	1 shield	1 min/lvl	self
30—Mystical Armor	1 set of armor	1 min/lvl	touch
50—Mystical Armor True	1 set of armor	1 min/lvl	touch

1—Shield (F*) Creates an invisible force shield in front of the caster; it subtracts 25 from melee and missile attacks and functions as a normal shield.

2—Armoring Cloth (F) Allows the caster to increase the armor protection of AT 1 or AT 2 by +4 in armor type (i.e., AT 1 would become AT 5 and AT 2 would become AT 6). Armor/clothing so enchanted is treated as if it were the lower AT for determination of armor penalties.

4—Armoring Leather (F) As *Armoring Cloth* except that leather armor (ATs 5-12) may be improved by +4 or cloth armor (ATs 1-2) may be improved by +8 (i.e., AT 1 would become AT 9, AT 11 would become AT 15, etc.).

5—Shield Blow I (F) Allows the caster to use his shield to automatically intercept the next attack (melee or missile) that delivers a critical; the attack may not be from the rear. The critical strike will be changed to reflect this (e.g., a neck strike would be changed to a shield arm strike, etc.).

6—Armoring Chain (F) As *Armoring Cloth* except that chain armor (ATs 13-16) may be improved by +4 or leather armor may be improved by +8 (i.e., AT 7 would become AT 15, AT 11 would become AT 19, AT 14 would become AT 18, etc.).

8—Armoring Plate (F) As *Armoring Leather* except soft leather armor is improved by +12.

10—Shield Blow II (F) As *Shield Blow I* except critical is lowered one level in it's severity (i.e., "E" crit = "D" crit, "D" crit = "C" crit, "C" crit = "B" crit, "B" crit = "A" and "A" criticals are ignored).

11—Mystical Cloth (F) As *Armoring Cloth* except all critical strikes made against this armor are reduced one level in severity (i.e., "E" crit = "D" crit, "D" crit = "C" crit, "C" crit = "B" crit, "B" crit = "A" and "A" criticals are ignored).

12—Armoring Robes (F) Allows the caster to create armor out of ordinary cloth (e.g., robe, cloak, etc.). Gives the cloth +1 AT for every two levels of the caster.

14—Mystical Leather (F) As *Armoring Leather* except all critical strikes made against this armor are reduced one level in severity.

15—Shield Blow III (F) As *Shield Blow I* except critical is lowered two levels in it's severity (i.e., "E" crit = "C" crit, "D" crit = "B" crit, "C" crit = "A" crit and "B" and "A" criticals are ignored). This spell has no effect if the caster uses the large or super-large critical tables.

17—Mystical Chain (F) As *Armoring Chain* except all critical strikes made against this armor are reduced one level in severity.

19—Shield Blow IV (F) As *Shield Blow III* except critical is lowered three levels in it's severity (i.e., "E" crit = "B" crit, "D" crit = "A" crit and "C", "B" and "A" criticals are ignored).

20—Mystical Plate (F) As *Armoring Plate* except all critical strikes made against this armor are reduced one level in severity.

25—Shield Blow True (F) As *Shield Blow III* except critical is lowered four levels in it's severity (i.e., "E" crit = "A" crit, and "D", "C", "B" and "A" criticals are ignored).

30—Mystical Armor (F) As *Mystical Plate* except all melee and missile criticals are reduced two levels. This spell has no effect if the caster uses the large or super-large critical tables.

50—Mystical Armor True (F) As *Mystical Armor* except all melee and missile criticals are reduced three levels (i.e., "E" crit = "B" crit, "D" crit = "A" and "C", "B" and "A" criticals are ignored).

Noble Warrior Base Spell Lists 57

8.42 NOBLE WEAPONS (Noble Warrior Base)

NOTE 1: *Only one spell from this list may be active on a given weapon.*
NOTE 2: *A GM may wish to restrict the use of certain spells on this list. He may also wish to allow these spells to be used only on non-magic weapons.*

	Area of Effect	Duration	Range
1—Weapons Grace	1 weapon	1 rnd/lvl	touch
2—Parry Weapon	1 weapon	1 rnd/lvl	touch
3—Hidden Strike	1 weapon	1 rnd/lvl	touch
4—Singing Strike	1 weapon	1 rnd/lvl	touch
5—Multiple Strike II	1 weapon	1 rnd/lvl	touch
6—Lesser Strike	1 weapon	1 rnd/lvl	touch
7—Lesser Hammer Strike	1 weapon	1 rnd/lvl	touch
8—Lesser Elemental Weapon	1 weapon	1 rnd/lvl	touch
9—Multiple Strike III	1 weapon	1 rnd/lvl	touch
10—Lesser Noble Weapon	1 weapon	1 rnd/lvl	touch
11—Greater Hammer Strike	1 weapon	1 rnd/lvl	touch
12—Elemental Poison	1 weapon	1 rnd/lvl	touch
13—Greater Strike	1 weapon	1 rnd/lvl	touch
14—Multiple Strike IV	1 weapon	1 rnd/lvl	touch
15—Greater Elemental Weapon	1 weapon	1 rnd/lvl	touch
16—Dancing Weapon	1 weapon	1 rnd/lvl	touch
17—Fear Weapon	1 weapon	1 rnd/lvl	touch
18—First Strike Weapon *	1 weapon	1 rnd/lvl	touch
19—Multiple Strike True	1 weapon	1 rnd/lvl	touch
20—Greater Noble Weapon	1 weapon	1 rnd/lvl	touch
25—Shield Severer	1 weapon	1 rnd/lvl	touch
30—Elemental Weapon True	1 weapon	1 rnd/lvl	touch
50—Noble Weapon True	1 weapon	1 rnd/lvl	touch

1—Weapons Grace (F) Gives up to a +2/level bonus to wielder's OB; PP cost is 1 PP per +2 bonus.

2—Parry Weapon (F) Increases the portion of OB put into parrying by 50% (e.g., if wielder puts 30 from his 70 OB into parrying, his DB is actually increased by 45).

3—Hidden Strike (F) Weapon's next critical strike roll is modified by +5. Any result over 100 is treated as 100.

4—Singing Strike (F) This blade fills the air with song of courage and greater glory. Those "allies" within 10'R of the blade are immune to fear effects **and** those outside of the 10'R but within hearing range receive a +10 to all RRs versus fear effects.

5—Multiple Strike II (F) Allows the weapon two attacks each round; but the OB for each attack is decreased by 40% of the OB **or** by 30 (which ever is less).

6—Lesser Strike (F) For the next critical, this spell increases the severity by 1 level; a 'no crit' result is still a 'no crit', and an 'E' crit is still an 'E'. (i.e., "A" crit = "B" crit; "B" crit = "C" crit; etc.)

7—Lesser Hammer Strike (F) Doubles the amount of concussion damage the weapon does on its next strike that delivers concussion hits.

8—Lesser Elemental Weapon (E) When the weapon delivers its next critical strike, it will deliver an "A" elemental critical in addition to the normal critical; caster choses elemental type (e.g., fire elemental yields heat criticals; ice elemental yields cold criticals; water elemental yields impact critical; etc.).

9—Multiple Strike III (F) As *Multiple Strike II* except it allows the weapon three attacks each round; but the OB for each attack is decreased by 50% of the OB **or** by 40 (which ever is less).

10—Lesser Noble Weapon (F) Gives the wielder +25 to initiative, delivers double concussion damage, and all "E" criticals obtained have a 10% chance of severing a limb provided that the critical is a arm, leg, or neck strike.

11—Greater Hammer Strike (F) Triples the amount of concussion damage the weapon does.

12—Elemental Poison (F) If the next crit that is obtained causes "hits/rnd" and the victim fails his RR (modified by CO bonus), he is consumed by an elemental poison (caster chooses fire, ice, water, etc.) that slowly consumes his body. The victim takes 1D10 "elemental" hits per round for 1 rnd/1% failure. If the "elemental" hit total reaches the victim's *concussion hit total + Constitution*, the body is consumed by the elemental poison: e.g., fire elemental poison causes the body to literally go up in smoke; ice elemental poison turns the body into a living ice statue; water elemental poison turns the body into a pool of water; etc. The only know cures are: the caster may 'cancel' the poison **or** the "elemental" hits may be cured as they are taken at half normal rate (e.g., curing 10 normal hits would only cure 5 "elemental" hits) **or** an opposite "elemental" poison can be applied (GM discretion).

13—Greater Strike (F) As *Lesser Strike* except critical severity is increased two levels; and if the weapon does concussion damage but does not score a critical, an "A" crit is delivered.

14—Multiple Strike IV (F) As *Multiple Strike II* except it allows the weapon four attacks each round; but the OB for each attack is decreased by 60% of the OB **or** by 50 (which ever is less).

15—Greater Elemental Weapon (E) As *Lesser Elemental Weapon* except delivers "B" critical in addition to the normal critical obtained.

16—Dancing Weapon (F) Allows the weapon to leave the hand of its wielder and attack (on it's own) an opponent within 50' (it moves 50' per round). The dancing weapon has an +50 OB when attacking on it's own. The caster must be able to see the dancing weapon and its target in order for the weapon to attack.

17—Fear Weapon (F) Any one desiring to confront the wielder of this weapon must first overcome a 10'R sphere of 'fear' surrounding the wielder. All individuals must make RR each round they are within the 10'R. Those who fail their RR will flee from wielder of weapon for 1 min/5% failure.

18—First Strike Weapon (F*) Doubles the wielder's normal initiative number.

19—Multiple Strike True (F) As *Multiple Strike II* except it allows the weapon five attacks each round; but the OB for each attack is decreased by 70% of the OB **or** by 60 (which ever is less).

20—Greater Noble Weapon (F) As *Lesser Noble Weapon* except adds +50 to initiative, delivers 3x concussion damage, and severing chance is 30% for "E" criticals, 20% for "D" criticals and 10% for "C" criticals.

25—Shield Cleaver (F) Any shield strike has a 50% chance of immediately severing the shield into two parts; the target's shield arm is also severed, doing an additional 15 concussion hits and 6 hits/rnd. Magic shields may make RRs.

30—Elemental Weapon True (E) As *Lesser Elemental Weapon* except the elemental weapon delivers a "C" critical.

50—Noble Weapon True (F) As *Greater Noble Weapon* except initiative number is doubled, delivers 4x concussion damage, and the severing chance is 50% for "E" criticals, 40% for "D" criticals, 30% for "C" criticals, 20% for "B" criticals and 10% for "A" criticals.

8.5 SLEUTH BASE LISTS

8.51 ANALYSES (Sleuth Base)

	Area of Effect	Duration	Range
1—Food & Drink Analysis	1 portion	—	6"
2—Text Analysis I	self	1 min/lvl(C)	self
3—Drug/Poison Analysis	1 portion	—	1'
4—Speech Analysis I	self	1 min/lvl(C)	self
5—Text Analysis II	self	1 min/lvl(C)	self
6—Power Analysis	1 target	—	10'
7—Speech Analysis II	self	1 min/lvl(C)	self
8—Text Analysis III	self	1 min/lvl(C)	self
9—Metal Analysis	1 piece	—	10'
10—Delving	1 item	—	touch
11—Speech Analysis III	self	1 min/lvl(C)	self
12—Code Analysis	caster	1 min/lvl(C)	self
13—Liquid Analysis	1 liquid	—	10'
14—Solid Analysis	1 solid	—	10'
15—Gas Analysis	1 gas	—	10'
16—			
17—Channeling Analysis	1 spell	—	100'
18—			
19—Mentalism Analysis	1 spell	—	100'
20—Essence Analysis	1 spell	—	100'
25—Death Analysis	self	—	touch
30—Microscopic Analysis	self	1 min/lvl(C)	self
50—Analysis	self	1 rnd/lvl(C)	self

2,5,8,9,10,13,15,25,50—As the spells of the same names on the Open Essence spell list, Delving Ways.

1—Food & Drink Analysis (I) Allows caster to learn the origins, purity, and general worth of one portion of food or drink. Any impurity will be discovered; only its type (bacteria, poison, dirt, excrement, chemical, etc.) will be indicated.

3—Drug/Poison Analysis (I) As *Food and Drink Analysis* except one drug/poison (if any) in the portion is analyzed; caster will also learn the antidote (if any) as well as the drug/poison's potency (i.e., level).

4—Speech Analysis I (I) As *Text Analysis I* except caster can understand, but not speak, one spoken language.

6—Power Analysis (I) One item, person, or place may be examined to determine if it has power, which realm the power is from, and a basic idea of the power's origin and nature.

7—Speech Analysis II (I) As *Text Analysis II* except caster can understand, but not speak, one spoken language.

11—Speech Analysis III (I) As *Text Analysis III* except caster can understand, but not speak, one spoken language.

12—Code Analysis (I) As *Text Analysis III* except texts written in code are fully comprehended.

14—Solid Analysis (I) As *Metal Analysis* except a solid is examined.

17—Channeling Analysis (I) As *Spell Analysis* on the Open Essence spell list, Delving, except only a Channeling spell may be analyzed.

19—Mentalism Analysis (I) As *Spell Analysis* on the Open Essence spell list, Delving, except only a Mentalism spell may be analyzed.

20—Essence Analysis (I) As *Spell Analysis* on the Open Essence spell list, Delving, except only an Essence spell may be analyzed.

30—Microscopic Analysis (I,U) Allows caster's next spell to pick up information a "microscopic" scale. The GM must determine what information this is capable of determining in his world.

8.52 SLEUTH'S SENSES (Sleuth Base)

	Area of Effect	Duration	Range
1—Detect Drugs	10'R	—	self
2—Detect Crime	varies	—	self
3—Detect Evasions	1 being	1 min/lvl(C)	self
4—Detect Emotions	1 being	1 min/lvl(C)	self
5—Taste	self	1 min/lvl	self
6—Detect Poison	10'R	—	self
7—Detect Good	1 being/object	—	100'
8—Detect Motive	1 being	1 min/lvl(C)	self
9—Touch	self	1 min/lvl	self
10—Detect Evil	1 being/object	—	100'
11—Detect Disguise	1 being	—	10'
12—Detect Lie	1 being	1 min/lvl	self
13—Scent	self	1 min/lvl	self
14—Detect Law	1 being/object	—	100'
15—Slyears	self	1 min/lvl	self
16—Detect Chaos	1 being/object	—	100'
17—Side Vision	self	1 min/lvl	self
18—Night Vision	self	1 min/lvl	self
19—Detect Illusion	self	1 min/lvl(C)	100'
20—Detect Invisible	self	1 min/lvl(C)	100'
25—Detective's Ear	self	1 min/lvl(C)	100'/lvl
30—Detective's Eye	self	1 min/lvl(C)	100'/lvl
50—Sense True	self	1 rnd/lvl	self

1—Detect Drugs (P) Allows caster to perceive any drugs in a 10'R.

2—Detect Crime (P) Allows caster to determine if a "crime" is being committed within his field of vision/hearing.

3—Detect Evasions (P) Allows caster to sense if a person he is talking to is being evasive.

4—Detect Emotions (P) Allows caster to sense target's dominant emotion.

5—Taste (P) Caster gains an extremely acute sense of taste.

6—Detect Poison (P) Allows caster to detect any poison in a 10'R.

7—Detect Good (P) Caster can tell if a person or thing is "Good" in alignment.

8—Detect Motive (P) Allows caster to determine the target's motives.

9—Touch (U) Caster gains an extremely acute sense of touch.

10—Detect Evil (P) As *Detect Good* except detects "Evil".

11—Detect Disguise (P) Allows caster to sense if a target is "disguised".

12—Detect Lie (P) Allows caster to tell if a target is lying.

13—Scent (U) Caster gains an extremely acute sense of smell.

14—Detect Law (P) As *Detect Good* except detects "Lawful".

15—Slyears (U) Caster gains an extremely acute sense of hearing.

16—Detect Chaos (P) As *Detect Good* except detects "Chaotic".

17—Side Vision (U) Caster has a 300° field of vision.

18—Night Vision (U) Caster can see at night as if it were daylight.

19—Detect Illusion (P) Detects any illusion; caster can concentrate on a 5' radius area each round.

20—Detect Invisible (P) As *Detect Illusion* except detects invisible beings and objects; all attacks against something so detected are at -50.

25—Sleuth's Ear (U) As *Listen* on the Open Essence spell list, Essence's Perceptions, except range is 100'/lvl and the caster must have been at the point before.

30—Sleuth's Eye (U) As *Sleuth's Ear* except caster can see from the point.

50—Sense True (U) Allows caster to cast one of the lower level spells on this list each round.

Sleuth Base Spell Lists

8.53 ESCAPING WAYS (Sleuth Base)

	Area of Effect	Duration	Range
1—Locklore	1 lock	—	touch
2—Unlock I	1 lock	—	1'/lvl
3—Escaping I	self	1 rnd	self
4—Unlock II	1 lock	—	
5—Magic Lock	1 portal	1 min/lvl	touch
6—Escaping II	self	2 rnds	self
7—Traplore	1 trap	—	touch
8—Unlock III	1 lock	—	1'/lvl
9—Escaping III	self	3 rnds	self
10—Jamming	1 door	P	50'
11—Remove Blindfold	self	—	self
12—			
13—Unlock IV	1 lock	—	1'/lvl
14—Escaping IV	self	4 rounds	self
15—Ungag	self	—	self
16—			
17—Unlock V	1 lock	—	1'/lvl
18—Escaping V	self	1 minute	self
19—			
20—Escaping VI	self	2 minutes	self
25—Escaping VII	bonds	3 minutes	self
30—Unlock True	1 lock/rnd	1 rnd/lvl	10'/lvl
50—Escaping True	self	4 minutes	self

1,5,7,10—As the spells of the same names on the Open Essence spell list, Unbarring Ways.

1—Locklore (I) Gives the caster +20 on picking the lock analyzed, and +10 to anyone to whom he describes the lock.

2—Unlock I (F) Caster can cause any "mundane" complexity lock (e.g., sliding bolts) he can see (within range) to be unlocked or locked (lock is just normally unlocked/locked and can be locked/unlocked normally).

3—Escaping I (F) Allows caster to escape from cloth bindings in 1 rnd.

4—Unlock II (F) As *Lock I* except "Routine" to "Medium" complexity locks can be locked **and** there is a chance such a lock will unlock: Routine (50%), Easy (40%), Light (30%), Medium (20%).

6—Escaping II (f) Allows caster to escape from rope bindings in 2 rounds.

7—Traplore (I) As *Locklore* except applies to disarming traps.

8—Unlock III (F) As *Lock II* except "Routine" to "Extremely Hard" complexity locks can be unlocked/locked; locking is automatic and the chance of unlocking is: Routine (70%), Easy (60%), Light (50%), Medium (40%), Hard (30%), Very Hard (20%), Extremely Hard (10%).

9—Escaping III (F) Allows caster to escape from leather or wooden bindings in 3 rounds

11—Remove Blindfold (F) Removes any "eye covering" from caster's face.

13—Unlock IV (F) As *Lock II* except "Routine" to "Sheer Folly" complexity locks can be unlocked/locked; locking is automatic and the chance of unlocking is: Routine (80%), Easy (70%), Light (60%), Medium (50%), Hard (40%), Very Hard (30%), Extremely Hard (20%), Sheer Folly (10%).

14—Escaping IV (F) Allows caster to escape from chain bindings in 4 rounds.

15—Ungag (F) Removes any "mouth covering" from caster's face.

17—Unlock V (F) As *Lock II* except "Routine" to "Absurd" complexity locks can be unlocked/locked; locking is automatic and the chance of unlocking is: Routine (90%), Easy (80%), Light (70%), Medium (60%), Hard (50%), Very Hard (40%), Extremely Hard (30%), Sheer Folly (20%), Absurd (10%).

18—Escaping V (F) Allows caster to escape form reinforced chain bindings in 1 minute.

20—Escaping VI (F) Allows caster to escape from locked metal bands (shackles) in 2 minutes.

25—Escaping VII (F) Allows caster to escape from solid metal or stone bonds in 3 minutes.

30—Unlock True (F) As *Lock II* except "Routine" to "Absurd" complexity locks can be unlocked/locked; locking is automatic and the chance of unlocking is: Routine (95%), Easy (90%), Light (80%), Medium (70%), Hard (60%), Very Hard (50%), Extremely Hard (40%), Sheer Folly (30%), Absurd (20%).

50—Escaping True (F) Allows caster to escape any bonds in 4 minutes.

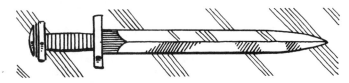

8.54 TIME'S SENSE (Sleuth Base)

	Area of Effect	Duration	Range
1—Origins	1 item	—	touch
2—Guess	self	—	self
3—Intuition I	self	—	self
4—Crime Lore: Object	1 item	—	touch
5—Vision Behind	self	C	self
6—Intuition III	self	—	self
7—Crime Lore: Person	1 being	—	10'
8—Anticipation *	1 being	—	100'
9—Intuition V	self	—	self
10—Vision Behind (1 hr/lvl)	self	C	self
11—Crime Lore: Place	1 locale	—	100'
12—Vision Guide	self	varies	self
13—Past Store *	1 person/place	—	self
14—Anticipation II *	2 beings	—	100'
15—Vision Behind (1 day/lvl)	self	C	self
16—Crime Lore: Time	self	—	self
17—Intuition X	self	—	self
18—Anticipation III *	3 beings	—	100'
19—Vision Location	self	—	self
20—Vision Behind (1 mo/lvl)	self	C	self
25—Vision Behind (1 yr/lvl)	self	C	self
30—Spell Anticipation *	1 being	—	100'
50. Crime Lore: True	self	1 rnd/lvl	self

5,10,12,13,15,19,20,25—As the spells of the same names on the Seer Base spell list, Past Visions.

1,3,6,8,9,14,17,18,30—As the spells of the same names on the Astrologer Base spell list, Time's Bridge.

4—Crime Lore: Object (I) Caster knows if item touched was used in a specified crime.

7—Crime Lore: Person (I) Caster knows whether or not target has been involved in a specified crime.

11—Crime Lore: Place (I) Caster knows if the target location was the "scene of a specified crime."

16—Crime Lore: Time (I) In conjunction with other "Crime Lore": spells, this spell allows caster to know the approximate time that a specified crime occurred.

50—Crime Lore: True (I) Allows caster to cast any one of the "Crime Lore" spells each round. This spell also enhances these other spells so that a specific crime need not be indicated.

8.6 MAGUS BASE LISTS

8.61 POWER WORDS (Magus Base)

This powerful and versatile spell list contains many of the words of power utilized in power word magic. As will be noted from the list, the spells are almost all concerned with power over the physical world.

	Area of Effect	Duration	Range
1—Shield*	1 target	1 min/lvl	10'
2—Repair	1 object	P	touch
3—Warp/Jam	1 wooden object	P	10'
4—Dust	1 stone/earth object	P	10'
5—Smoke	10'R/lvl	1 min/lvl	100'
6—Light/Ignite	5' (multiple)	P	5'R/lvl
7—Glamour	10 lb/lvl	1 day/lvl	10'/lvl
8—Bleed	1 target	V	100'
9—Disrupt	10 cu'	P	10'
10—Dance	1 obj/10 lvls	C	5'R/lvl
11—Animate	—	1 rd/lvl	10'/lvl
12—Shatter	1 object	—	100'
13—Bind	1 target	1 hr/lvl	5'/lvl
14—Wither	1 plant target	P	touch
15—Blast	1 target	—	100'
16—Solidify	100 cu'/lvl	1 min/lvl	100'
17—Unearth/Unstone	1000 cu'	P	100'
18—Lock	1 door or container	P	touch
19—Sail/Blow	1 ship	V	100'/lvl
20—Kill	1 target	—	touch
25—Petrify	1 organic target	V	1'/lvl
30—Create	1 object	V	10'
50—Stop	—	1 rnd	self

1—Shield (F*) Creates an invisible force shield in front of Caster which protects like a wall shield: it subtracts 30 from melee attacks and 40 from missile attacks and functions as a normal shield.

2—Repair (F) Caster may mend a single break in a metal object of 5 lbs or less, and multiple breaks, rips, or shatters in a larger (50 pounds or less) ceramic, wooden, stone, or cloth object. The object repaired cannot be magical and all component parts must be present (within a 10' radius).

3—Warp/Jam (F) This spell may be cast at two levels: 3 and 7. At third level the spell destroys the form, straightness, and strength of a piece of wood up to 1 lb/lvl. At level 7 the Caster may cause a wooden door or object (10 lb/lvl) to swell and jam (roll severity 1-100 ranging from slightly stuck to unopenable); or the Caster may reduce the inherent strength of the door or object by 50%.

4—Dust (F) The Caster may transform stone, earth, or wood to fine, dry, powder. The amount the Caster may transform depends on the level at which he casts the spell (4=10cu', 9=100cu', 14=1000cu', 25=100cu'/lvl).

5—Smoke (F) The Caster may create and manipulate smoke of a volume up to 10'R/lvl. The Caster may also manipulate the shape and movement of the smoke by concentrating. He may vary the density of the smoke from translucent to opaque, and may create any color of smoke.

6—Light/Ignite (F) The Caster may simultaneously ignite or extinguish every common light-giving implement (e.g., candles, torches, fireplaces, etc.) in the radius. The spell may effect any fire up to bonfire size (5'R). Caster may cast this spell at lower lvl (i.e., 3rd) to ignite one implement.

7—Glamour (E) This illusory spell effects one inanimate object of up to 10 lbs/lvl. The spell alters the look, feel, and shape of an object concealing its true nature. If the item is magical then the illusion may disguise the item's power level by 1 lvl/Caster's lvl. If a being makes a successful RR against the illusion he will know that the item is disguised but he will not discover the true nature of the item. If the being resists by 25+ he will know the true nature of the object. If the being resists by 50+ the illusion is dispelled if the being so desires.

8—Bleed (F) RR Mod: -20 The Caster may cause a living target to bleed (if applicable). The target begins to bleed through his skin at a rate of 1 hit point/5% failure each round. The duration of the effect depends on the degree to which the target failed: roll 1 ten-sided die/5% failure for the number of rounds the target suffers the loss. The Caster may will the process to stop prematurely. **Example:** *if a target fails by 33, he will lose 7 hits/rnd for a number of rnds equal to the total rolls of 7 ten-sided dice.*

9—Disrupt (F) Turns any 1 inorganic object to fine powder. The total volume of the item cannot exceed 10 cu'.

10—Dance (F) The Caster may cause a number of items equal to his level/10 to dance around in the area as if possessed with a life of its own. If cast on a melee weapon or on an object suitable for bashing, the item(s) may attack a target with a melee OB equal to (25 + 1/lvl). The items are considered to be wielded by a human wielder with AT 8(-20) and (1-10) hits/lvl. Most criticals, except for knock down results, will have no effect against a dancing weapon.

11—Animate (FE) The Caster may cause an amorphous mass of a suitable elemental (e.g., earth, stone, fire, water, wind, etc) material to act with a life of its own and obey simple commands. The creature's abilities are determined by the level of the spell used to create it: (11)=weak elemental; (18)=strong elemental.

12—Shatter (F) Can shatter an inorganic object explosively, up to 1 cu'. All within a 5'R take an "A" impact critical and holder takes a "C".

13—Bind (F) The target is wrapped in chains of energy. Any attempt to escape is usually resolved as a spell attack with the chains as the attacker (RR Mod: -20). If the target makes the difficult RR he escapes. If the target fails the RR he will suffer one impact critical of a severity determined by his failure: (1-10)=A; (11-20)=B; (21-30)=C; (31-40)=D; (41+)=E. If the attempt to escape is made utilizing magic (especially movement or transport spells, the target must resist three separate criticals (Impact, Electrical, and Heat) with their severities determined as above.

14—Wither (F) Caster may instantly kill and wither any one plant which he touches. Some plants may get an RR (e.g., magical, living, large, etc).

15—Blast (E) A bolt of lightning is shot from the palm of the caster; results are determined on the *Lightning Bolt* table.

16—Solidify (FE) The caster may cause fluids or solids to take desired shape (e.g., smoke staircases, warm water statues, etc) and solidify for the duration. The material will have a strength and consistency like wood.

17—Unearth/Unstone (F) Disintegrates 1000 cu' of earth, stone, sand, clay, etc.

18—Lock (F) A door (or container) can be magically "locked". The spell may be dispelled, or willed to cease by the original Caster, but the door (container) is unbreakable by normal means.

19—Sail/Blow (E) The Caster may either assist or impede a vessel's progress. The ship's speed is increased or decreased by 1 mph/lvl. If the Caster chooses he may instead treat this spell as a *Whirlwind* (Magician Base Wind Law level 14).

20—Kill (F) Shatters the heart and the nearby associated large blood vessels of the target. For almost all living creatures, unconsciousness occurs immediately after a very brief awareness of terrific pain, followed by physical death in 1 round. Interior bleeding occurs at the rate of 50 hit points/rnd.

25—Petrify (FE) Caster may cause a living or organic target to gradually turn to stone at the rate of 10%/rnd. The Caster may reverse the effect at any time if he is within range and concentrates. The effect may be simply dispelled. However, the petrified object receives a +20 RR bonus vs.any dispelling attempt, and failed attempts are treated as attack spell fumbles.

30—Create (F) The Caster may duplicate any non-magic object (e.g., broadsword, table, etc.) which he has seen or designed from a mass of inorganic component materials not to exceed 1 lb/lvl. The item created will be of the same polish, texture, and quality as the component materials utilized. The effect is permanent except the item may be normally dispelled, at which time it will resume the form of the original materials.

50—Stop (F) The Caster is propelled for one rnd into timelessness. To him it appears that the universe has stopped for the duration of the spell and he may take any action during that round which he might normally take. Please note: this spell may not be enhanced in length or range.

8.62 RUNES & SYMBOLS (Magus Base)

This list demonstrates the Magus' mastery of the common craft of magical calligraphy (runes) or iconography (symbols). The Magus' twin interest in both runes and symbols also explains why the majority of Magi are hybrid users in Essence and Channeling, since these are the normal realms for these arts. In these fields the Magus is the professional artist; all other magic-users who dabble in these forms are, compared to him, like folk craftsmen.

		Area of Effect	Duration	Range
1	Analysis (Realm)	1 rune or symbol	—	10'
2	Rune II	1 rune paper	V	touch
3	Symbol/Unsym. I	1 immobile stone	P	10'
4	Analysis (Danger)	1 rune or symbol	—	10'
5	Rune III	1 rune paper	V	touch
6	Analysis (Spell)	1 rune or symbol	—	10'
7	Rune V	1 rune paper	V	touch
8	Symbol/Unsym. III	1 immobile stone	P	10'
9	Rune VI	1 rune paper	V	touch
10	Symbol/Unsym. V	1 immobile stone	P	10'
11	Rune VII	1 rune paper	V	touch
12	Symbol/Unsym. VI	1 immobile stone	P	10'
13	Rune VIII	1 rune paper	V	touch
14	Symbol/Unsym. VII	1 immobile stone	P	10'
15	Rune X	1 rune paper	V	touch
16	Symbol/Unsym. VIII	1 immobile stone	P	10'
17	Analysis (Caster)	1 rune or symbol	—	10'
18	Rune XV	1 rune paper	V	touch
19	Symbol/Unsym. X	1 immobile stone	P	10'
20	Lord Rune	1 rune paper	V	touch
25	Lord Symbol	1 immobile stone	P	10'
30	Rune of Power	1 rune paper	V	touch
50	Image of Power	special	V,P	touch

1—Analysis (Realm) (I) The caster immediately determines the realm of any spell contained within either a rune or symbol.

2—Rune II (F) The caster may inscribe a *Rune I* or a *Rune II* as *Rune I* on the Open Essence Rune Mastery spell list.

3—Symbol/Unsymbol I (F) The caster may emplace or remove one *Symbol I* in any 1 given non-mobile stone as in *Symbol I* or *Unsymbol I* in the Closed Channeling Symbolic Ways spell list.

4—Analysis (Danger) (I) The caster immediately determines if any 1 given rune or symbol is inherently dangerous to read or trigger (e.g., a Rune of Disembowelment). Inherently dangerous is defined as that which, even when successfully and knowingly activated by a being, will perform any sort of attack on the being (e.g., elemental, physical, base attack, etc). This spell has a 1% chance per level of the "enruned" spell that the rune will be "set-off."

5—Rune III (F) As *Rune I*, except it can inscribe 1st-3rd level spells.

6—Analysis (Spell) (I) The caster may determine which spell is inscribed within a rune or emplaced within a symbol. He gains the capacity to cast the rune or activate the symbol as if he had completely succeeded with a Runes die roll. This spell has a 1% chance per level of the "enruned" spell that the rune will be "set-off."

7—Rune V (F) As *Rune I*, except it can inscribe 1st-5th level spells.

8—Symbol/Unsymbol III (F) As *Symbol/Unsymbol I*, except Caster can emplace or remove 1st-3rd level symbols.

9—Rune VI (F) As *Rune I*, except it can inscribe 1st-6th level spells.

10—Symbol/Unsymbol V (F) As *Symbol/Unsymbol I*, except Caster can emplace or remove 1st-3rd level symbols.

11—Rune VII (F) As *Rune I*, except it can inscribe 1st-7th level spells.

12—Symbol/Unsymbol VI (F) As *Symbol/Unsymbol I*, except Caster can emplace or remove 1st-6th level symbols.

13—Rune VIII (F) As *Rune I*, except it can inscribe 1st-8th lvl spells.

14—Symbol/Unsymbol VII (F) As *Symbol/Unsymbol I*, except caster can emplace or remove 1st-7th level symbols.

15—Rune X (F) As *Rune I*, except it can inscribe 1st-10th lvl spells.

16—Symbol/Unsymbol VIII (F) As *Symbol/Unsymbol I*, except caster can emplace or remove 1st-8th level symbols.

17—Analysis (Caster) (I) The caster may examine any 1 given rune or symbol. If the caster has met the original maker of the Rune or Symbol he will recognize the one who cast the rune or symbol spell and learn the age of the rune or symbol. If the caster has not met the maker of the rune or symbol, he will learn the Profession of the maker, the maker's level, and the age of the rune or symbol. This spell has a 1% chance per level of the "enruned" spell that the rune will be "set-off."

18—Rune XV (F) As *Rune I*, except it can inscribe 1st-15th lvl spells.

19—Symbol/Unsymbol X (F) As *Symbol/Unsymbol I*, except caster can emplace or remove 1st-10th level symbols.

20—Lord Rune (F) As *Rune I*, except it can inscribe 1st-20th lvl spells.

25—Lord Symbol (Lord Research) (FI) As *Symbol/Unsymbol I*, except caster can emplace or remove 1st-20th level symbols. If the GM wishes, this spell may be treated as a *Lord Research* spell as described in **Spell Law** optional rule 9.93.

30—Rune of Power (F) Duration: Until the rune is cast the caster may inscribe a rune which stores a number of power points equal to the level of this spell. The caster may opt to throw this spell at a higher level if he is capable of it and has a sheet of rune paper of sufficient level. Likewise, the caster, after acquiring this spell, may throw the spell at a lower level to store a smaller number of power points. The power points stored must be considered to be of the same realm as the caster, and they may not be multiplied in any way when the rune is eventually activated.

50—Image of Power (F) The caster may cast this spell in four different ways. The spell may serve as a *Rune True*, permitting the caster to inscribe a rune of any level less than or equal to his own level. Secondly, this spell may be treated as a *Symbol True*, permitting the caster to emplace a symbol of any level less than or equal to his own level. The Image may be treated as *Unsymbol True*, permitting the caster to remove any 1 given symbol of a level less than or equal to his own level. Finally, the caster may cast the Image as a *Symbol of Power*, which acts as a *Rune of Power*, except that the symbol (of course) is permanent and will recharge itself every 24 hours.

8.63 SIGNS OF POWER (Magus Base)

Every spell on this list, with the exceptions of the two *Signwatch* spells, inscribes a magical sign on any non-mobile surface as described in the spell *Sign of Stunning*, Level 11, of the Open Essence Rune Mastery spell list. Unless stated otherwise, a sign will vanish after one use. A Magus' magical calligraphy is an excellent tool for defending his demesne (or that of a friend or anyone who is sufficiently wealthy to afford his services).

	Area of Effect	Duration	Range
1—Observation	1 immobile surface	P	touch
2—			
3—Pain	1 immobile surface	V	touch
4—			
5—Weakness	1 immobile surface	V	touch
6—			
7—Stunning	1 immobile surface	V	touch
8—Fear	1 immobile surface	V	touch
9—Stumbling	1 immobile surface	V	touch
10—Transport	1 immobile surface	V	touch
11—Holding	1 immobile surface	V	touch
12—Signwatch	self	C	10 mi/lvl
13—Sleep	1 immobile surface	V	touch
14—Torment	1 immobile surface	V	touch
15—Blinding	1 immobile surface	V	touch
16—Ice	1 immobile surface	V	touch
17—Paralysis	1 immobile surface	V	touch
18—Flame	1 immobile surface	V	touch
19—Force	1 immobile surface	V	touch
20—Fatal Channels	1 immobile surface	V	touch
25—Signwatch	self	C	100 mi/lvl
30—Mass Sign	1 immobile surface	V	touch
50—Dragon's Eye	1 immobile surface	V	touch

1—Observation (F) With this spell the Caster may inscribe an *Observation* sign, the only permanent sign on this list. This sign's only function is to act as a point of reference and perception for the *Signwatch* spells on this list. The Caster may never have more of these Signs active at any one time than his level divided by two (round up). But he may cancel a previously inscribed *Observation* sign to permit a new one to be inscribed somewhere else.

3—Pain (F)   RR Mod:-20   This sign afflicts the target triggering the sign with Pain, and he takes 25% of his remaining concussion hits for 10 min/10% failure.

5—Weakness (F) As *Pain* except the target feels weak and drained, subtracting 20 from all maneuvers and melee for 10 min/10% failure.

7—Stunning (F) As *Pain* except the target is stunned for 10 min/10% failure.

8—Fear (F) As *Pain* except the target will flee the place of the sign for 1 min/5% failure.

9—Stumbling (F)   RR Mod:-20   The target takes an Unbalancing critical of a severity determined by the degree to which he fails his RR: (1-5)="A"; (6-10)="B"; (11-20)="C"; (21-30)="D"; (31+)="E"

10—Transport (F) Target is teleported to one of the Caster's designated *Observation* signs. Note that this spell does not carry an RR subtraction as do many of the others on this list.

11—Holding (F) As *Pain* except the target will be held to 25% of his normal physical action for 10 min/10% failure.

12—Signwatch (U) Caster's point of seeing and hearing may be moved to any of his *Observation* signs within range. The Caster's vision may rotate around the point of the *Observation* sign (except that he will not be able to look backwards through the surface the sign is on if it is opaque).

13—Sleep (F) As *Pain* except the target falls into sleep from which he cannot be awakened for 10 min/10% failure.

14—Torment (F) As *Pain* except the target takes 90% of his remaining hits for 10 min/10% failure. Thenceforth the target cannot usually be persuaded to approach the area of the sign ever again unless he succeeds in making a "Hard" static maneuver roll using Self-Discipline as a bonus modifier.

15—Blinding (F) As *Pain* except the target is blind for 1 hr/10% failure.

16—Ice (F) As *Pain* except the critical suffered is a cold critical.

17—Paralysis (F) As *Pain* except the target is paralyzed for 1 hr/10% failure.

18—Flame (F) As *Stumbling* except the critical suffered is a heat critical.

19—Force (F) As *Stumbling* except the critical suffered is an impact critical.

20—Fatal Channels (F)   RR Mod: -20   Target is treated as if he has just suffered the effects of an *Absolution Pure* (Cleric Channels Base Spell List level 20).

25—Signwatch (U) As *Signwatch* above (lvl 12) except the range is 100 miles/lvl.

30—Mass Sign (F) As *Pain* except any sign may be used; and it will not be canceled until it has been triggered (perhaps more than once) by targets whose combined levels exceed the caster's level.

50—Dragon's Eye (F) As *Fatal Channels* above except the body of the target also suffers three E class criticals of a type designated by the Caster.

8.64 LINGUISTICS (Magus Base)

The Magus' skill in linguistics in second to none, although the Bards come close. With his obsession with words and languages, Magi often serve as scholars in this field.

	Area of Effect	Duration	Range
1—Study I	—	C	self
2—Text Analysis I	—	1 min/lvl	self
3—Learn Language II	—	C	self
4—Linguistics III	—	P	self
5—Study II	—	C	self
6—Learn Language III	—	C	self
7—Text Analysis II	—	1 min/lvl	self
8—Linguistics V	—	P	self
9—History	—	-	touch
10—Study III	—	C	self
11—Passage Origin	—	C	self
12—Learn Language IV	—	C	self
13—History True	—	-	touch
14—Text Analysis III	—	1 min/lvl	self
15—Study V	—	C	self
16—Linguistics VII	—	P	self
17—Nature Speech	—	1 min/lvl	self
18—Text Analysis True	—	1 min/lvl	self
19—Study True	—	C	self
20—Linguistics IX	—	P	self
25—Cryptics True	—	1 min/lvl	self
30—Linguistics True	—	P	self
50—Language Master	—	P	self

Magus Base Spell Lists

1—Study I (P) Allows the Caster to retain anything he reads or learns as if he had a photographic memory with total recall.

2—Text Analysis I (PI) Caster can read text written in an unknown language, but only understands basic concepts from it. The Caster will know what language the work is written in, and the author if he was noteworthy or the Caster has seen his work.

3—Learn Language II (P) Doubles the rate at which the Caster can learn a language.

4—Linguistics III (PI) If the Caster has a book-length piece of written material, he may learn the written form of a language to rank 3 by concentrating on the written material for 24 hours. If the Caster has a speaker of the language available who knows the language to at least Skill Rank 3, the Caster can learn the language (spoken form) to Skill Rank 3 by touching the being and concentrating for 24 hrs. **Note:** *The GM may wish to limit this and the other Linguistic spells by requiring the caster allocate one development point (i.e., expend one DP when his next level is reached) every time this spell is successfully used.*

5—Study II (P) As *Study I*, except Caster can also read at 2x normal rate.

6—Learn Language III (P) As *Learn Language II*, except rate is 3x.

7—Text Analysis II (PI) As *Text Analysis I*, except gives a complete technical analysis (vocabulary & syntax) but not an understanding of idioms or jargons, implications, or cultural references.

8—Linguistics V (PI) As *Linguistics III* except the Caster may learn the language to Skill Rank 5.

9—History (I) Gives the area of origin of an item, the race of the being who made it, and when it was made (within 100 years). Also determines if the item has any cultural or historical significance but not exactly what those significances are.

10—Study III (P) As *Study II*, except Caster can read at 3x normal rate.

11—Passage Origin (P) Caster can read a piece and tell if it has been translated; and if so what the original language was and possibly the author if he was noteworthy or the Caster has seen his work.

12—Learn Language IV (P) As *Learn Language II*, except rate is 4x.

13—History True (I) As *History* except Caster also learns what the exact cultural or historical significances are.

14—Text Analysis III (I) As *Text Analysis I* except everything but implications are known (e.g., answers to riddles or codes are not known automatically).

15—Study V (P) As *Study II*, except Caster can read at 5x normal rate.

16—Linguistics VII (PI) As *Linguistics III* except the Caster may learn the language to Skill Rank 7.

17—Nature Speech (I) Caster can communicate and/or visualize the thoughts and emotions of any 1 animal, plant, stone, or dead organic object.

18—Text Analysis True (I) As *Text Analysis I* except all implications are known automatically (e.g., answers to riddles, cultural references, jargons, technical terms, etc). Coded sections may make a RR against the Caster at the level of the writer.

19—Study True (P) As *Study II*, except Caster can read as fast as he can glance at a page.

20—Linguistics IX (PI) As *Linguistics III* except the Caster may learn the language to Skill Rank 9.

25—Cryptics True (I) As *Text Analysis I* except all implications are known and all codes are automatically deciphered and explained.

30—Linguistics True (PI) As *Linguistics III* except the Caster is not limited in the Skill Rank he may attain. He may achieve whatever Skill Rank is represented in the text or the speaker he has available.

50—Language Master (PI) As *Linguistics III* except the Caster is able to learn any code or any magical language in this fashion and he may learn both spoken and written skills from either a text or a speaker of the language. The Caster has complete ability to communicate, write, or compose magical effects in the language (if applicable).

8.65 COMMAND WORDS (Magus Base)

Magi are perhaps best known, alongside their powers of writing magic, as the masters of will and command. This is the power maybe most awesome to the people around them, who whisper tales that a Magus can cause you to commit any act, no matter how vile. However, this superstitious regard is generally untrue (except for those who are very powerful), and simply assures the practitioners of the art a reputation which they do not refute. Magi vary considerably in specifically which words of command they master, especially the so-called Great Commands (see Section 4.1). A Magus of deep experience may know several of the Great Commands in each circle of his art.

	Area of Effect	Duration	Range
1—Calm	1 target	1 min/lvl	100'
2—Truth	1 target	C	10'
3—Confuse	1 target	1 rd/5% failure	100'
4—Fascinate	1 target	10 min/lvl	50'
5—Great Command I	1 target	V	V
6—Forget	1 min/lvl	P	50'
7—Dream	1 target	C	10'/lvl
8—Emote	1 target	1 min/lvl	100'
9—Like/Dislike	1 target	1 day/5% failure	100'
10—Great Command II	1 target	V	V
11—Doubt	1 target	P	100'
12—Love/Hate	1 target	1 day/5% failure	100'
13—Vengeance	1 target	V	100'
14—Invoke	1 being	C	self
15—Great Command III	1 target	V	V
16—Dismiss/Banish	1 entity	V	10'/lvl
17—Shout of Panic*	50' radius	1 rnd/5% failure	self
18—Shout of Command*	lvl in targets	V	V
19—Shout of Confusion*	50' radius	1 rnd/5% failure	self
20—Great Command IV	1 target	V	V
25—Great Command V	1 target	V	V
30—Great Command VI	1 target	V	V
50—Great Command VII	1 target	V	V

1—Calm (M) Target will take no aggressive/offensive action, and will fight only if attacked. If the caster casts this spell at an already "calmed" target, the target will fall asleep.

2—Truth (M) Target must answer single concept questions truthfully. He may roll RRs to break the spell again after every question.

3—Confuse (M) Target is incapable of making decisions or initiating action; he may continue to fight current foes or in self-defense.

4—Fascinate (M) Target believes that Caster is of the same alignment as himself, is influential, and is superior to himself in rank, power, and/or efficiency. Target will usually seek to ingratiate himself to the Caster.

5—Great Command I (M) One of the *Great Command I* Spells (Commands of the Outer Circle) that the caster "knows" may be used. The Gamemaster decides which ones are to be used on the basis of culture and world system. If the Caster knows more than one of the *Great Command I* spells, he may select which he desires to cast.

6—Forget (M) Target permanently forgets up to 1 min/lvl of specified memories as selected by the Caster.

7—Dream (MP) Caster may dictate the dreams of a specific sleeping target. If the target succeeds in his RR by 25+, he wakens (unless somehow prevented) and knows what was attempted. If he succeeds by 50+ he knows also who attempted it. This spell may be cast through intervening obstacles such as floors, ceilings, etc. Magical obstacles get an RR.

8—Emote (M) Caster causes the target to experience any 1 specified emotion.

9—Like/Dislike (M) The target likes or dislikes a person, place, or thing as specified by the Caster. If the target has very strong feelings about the subject previously, the GM may indicate that the target may attempt a second RR if he fails the first one.

10—Great Command II (M) As *Great Command I,* except a *Great Command II* (Command of the Second Circle) is cast.

11—Doubt (M) Target develops a very serious and troublesome doubt concerning a previously accepted fact, action, or idea.

12—Love/Hate (M) RR Mod: -20 As *Like/Dislike* above except the target experiences either devoted love or repulsive hatred toward the subject. For the duration the intensity of the emotion will be such that the target will have a difficult time focusing on anything else other than his love or hate. At the end of the duration, the target must make an additional RR (with a +20 instead of a -20 RR mod) or the effect will become permanent.

13—Vengeance (M) Target will seek to enact some sort of vengeance against a person, place, or thing as specified by the Caster. There must be in the target's mind some concept of the subject having wronged the target for the spell to be effective. The exact form of the vengeance sought depends on the character of the target, and the severity of his RR failure (1 = mild; 50+ = very severe).

14—Invoke (FM) The Caster may summon to himself by name any entity regardless of range, even to the ethereal and other planes. Each round there is a 35% chance that the specified entity would hear the summons, and a 15% chance that a random being may hear. This spell does not command the entity though the being will be heavily motivated (RR mod: -20) to come to the Caster. This spell is especially designed for, and the GM may restrict it to, supernatural spiritual entities (e.g., spirits, demons, elementals, deities, etc).

15—Great Command III (M) As *Great Command I,* except a *Great Command III* (Command of the Third Circle) is cast.

16—Dismiss/Banish (F) RR Mod: -20 Dismisses a spiritual being (e.g., demon, elemental, appropriate spirits, etc) from the Caster's present plane for 200-1200 years. In addition the Caster may force the entity to answer one single concept question truthfully before he is dismissed. If the demon resists or the spell fumbles, the Caster may be commanded by the entity. The Caster may attempt a new RR each day to break the effect of his spell failure.

17—Shout of Panic (M*) Targets flee in total panic from the Caster.

18—Shout of Command (M*) Caster may effect a number of targets up to his level with a *Great Command I*.

19—Shout of Confusion (M*) As *Confuse* above except effects all within the radius.

20—Great Command IV (M) As *Great Command I,* except a *Great Command IV* (Command of the Stone Circle) is cast.

25—Great Command V (M) As *Great Command I,* except a *Great Command V* (Command of the Ancient Circle) is cast.

30-Great Command VI (M) As *Great Command I,* except a *Great Command VI* (Command of the Primitive Circle) is cast.

50-Great Command VII (M) As *Great Command I,* except a *Great Command VII* (Command of the Circle of Night) is cast.

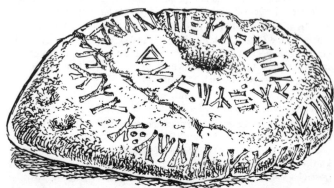

8.66 SPIRIT RUNES (Magus Base)

Perhaps the most peculiar aspect of the Magi is their interest in more mundane weaponry and armor. The Magi are willing to be less adept in some magical skills so that they can be more adept in some physical skills. But then again, perhaps this is not so odd when it is realized that the Magi have an interest in weapons and other combat items precisely because they can write on them. It is the Magi who have, through the ages, designed the great enruned items of power: runeswords and runestaves, enruned armors and shields. These all obviously bear the marks of the Magi' particular art: the magical word and the magical sign.

While the *Spirit Runes* of the Magi appear very similar to the Arcane *Bladerunes,* they are, in fact, more permanent and powerful (see Section 4.2). However, the making of them requires a much longer grueling process than common Alchemy. Although a Magus at a particular level, through his special abilities, will be able to make more powerful items than an Alchemist of comparable level, the Magus will need to take more time to do so. For example, an Alchemist can make a +20 sword in only 20 weeks (see Alchemy Base Enchanting Ways level 20) and for him it is a Lord level (20th) process. A Magus using the process described below may create the same sword at 16th level, but even with the lower level, the process requires a minimum of 21 weeks (146 days) and a maximum of nearly 40 weeks (272 days). In addition, the Magus will average 3 failures/fumbles during the process, adding anywhere from 6 days to over 60.

	Area of Effect	Duration	Range
1—Temper	1 item	P	touch
2—Rune of Striking	1 item	P	touch
3—Rune of Shielding	1 item	P	touch
4—Calibrate Bonuses/Temper	1 item	—	touch
5—Hand Rune	1 item	P	touch
6—Identify Spirit Runes	1 item	—	touch
7—			
8—Rune of Parry	1 item	P	touch
9—			
10-Minor Spirit Rune	1 item	P	touch
11-			
12-			
13-			
14-Erase Rune	1 Spirit Rune	P	10'
15-Major Spirit Rune	1 item	P	touch
16-			
17-			
18-Dismiss Spirit Rune	1 Spirit Rune	P	10'
19-			
20-Lord Spirit Rune	1 item	P	touch
25-Spirit Rune of Might	1 item	P	touch
30-Spirit Rune of the Pale	1 item	P	touch
50-Spirit Rune of Power	1 item	P	touch

1—Temper (F) This spell prepares an item to receive Spirit Runes: there are two "Tolerance Levels" (TL) that may be affected by this spell are:

"Spirit Rune Level" or just *"Rune Level"*
(the maximum Level of Spirit Rune that can be imbedded)

"Spirit Rune Capacity Level" or just *"Capacity Level"*
(the total number of Spirit Runes that can be imbedded)

- If an item has one of its Tolerance Levels equal to "ß", then casting *Temper* once a day for "ß+1" days will increase that Tolerance Level (**not** both TLs) to "ß+1" and requires "ß+1" power points per day.

- If the caster fails/fumbles the *Temper* spell on any of the "ß+1" days, the caster must restart the Tempering process from day 1 (e.g., if on the 19th day for a Tolerance Level increase from 19 to 20 the Caster fails/fumbles his spell roll, the item reverts to a TL of 19, and the Caster must cast the *Temper* spell each day for 20 days to obtain the TL of 20).

Magus Base Spell Lists

- Both Tolerance Levels for an item that has not already been tempered starts at 0.
- The level of the *Temper* spell is considered to be equal to the Tolerance Level being increased to (e.g., all *Temper* spells cast for to raise an item to a Tolerance Level of 20 are considered to be 20th level spells for purposes of power points and spell failure/fumble).
- The caster may freely alternate between Tempering an item for Capacity Level or for Rune Level: he need not devote himself to only one Tolerance Level at a time.
- The days of Tempering need not be consecutive.
- The caster may Temper more than one item each day; however a given item may only have one Temper spell cast on it each day.
- To actually imbed an individual rune on a Tempered item require only one minute per level of the rune; however, the Tempering process may require years.

EXAMPLE: *A 10th level Caster is beginning to Temper a untempered item. On one day he casts a Temper spell to raise the Rune Capacity to one. On another day he casts a second Temper spell to raise the Rune Level to one. His eventual goal is to make the item as powerful as possible for his level (i.e., being able to hold ten Spirit Runes of up to tenth level each). To raise the Capacity Level to two, he must cast a Temper spell on the item on two additional different days. The same is true if he wished to raise the Rune Level to two. This progression holds true up to the maximum Tolerance Levels of 10 each. If the Caster has succeeded in increasing both the item's Tolerance Levels to 9 without ever failing/fumbling a Temper spell, he must cast the Temper spell ten more times (on ten more days) to increase the Rune Capacity to ten, and an additional ten spells and days to increase the Rune Level to 10. The whole process would require 55 days for each Tolerance Level (110 days in all) as follows: 1 + 2 + 3 + 4 + 5 + 6 + 7 + 8 + 9 + 10 = 55. Thus, a Lord level item of Rune Capacity 10 and Rune Level 10 would take 420 days to Temper (i.e., 210 days for Rune Capacity and 210 days for Rune Level: 1 + 2 + 3 + ... 18 + 19 + 20 = 210). The following chart summarizes the number of days required to Temper an item for one of the two Tolerance levels. Obviously, you must double the values on this chart to find the number of days required to raise both Tolerance Levels (not counting additional days require because of spell failures/fumbles).*

\multicolumn{6}{c}{DAYS OF TEMPER PER TOLERANCE LEVEL}
lvl	Days	lvl	Days	lvl	Days
1	1	2	3	3	6
4	10	5	15	6	21
7	28	8	36	9	45
10	55	11	66	12	78
13	91	14	105	15	120
16	136	17	153	18	171
19	190	20	210	21	231
22	253	23	276	24	300
25	325	26	351	27	378
28	406	29	435	30	465
31	496	32	528	33	561
34	595	35	630	36	666
37	703	38	741	39	780
40	820	41	861	42	903
43	946	44	990	45	1035
46	1081	47	1128	48	1176
49	1225	50	1275	51	1326
52	1378	53	1431	54	1485
55	1540	56	1596	57	1653
58	1711	59	1770	60	1830

2—Rune of Striking (F) Each one of these that a Caster places on a properly tempered weapon raises it's OB by +5. However, as each additional (i.e., the Nth) *Rune of Striking* is engraved on the weapon, the level of the *Striking Rune* which the Caster must engrave increases according to the following formula: (N x N), so that the first such rune is only 1st level, the 2nd such rune is 4th, the 3rd is 9th, the 4th is 16, the 5th is 25, and the 6th is 36, etc. This requires not only the requisite Rune Capacity in the *Temper* of the item and the requisite levels from the Caster; but also requires the item to be *Tempered* to a Rune Level sufficient to hold the levels of runes required.

3—Rune of Shielding (F) As *Runes of Striking* above except the Caster raises an item's DB by +5 for each rune engraved. However, if the Caster is attempting to give a nondefensive item a DB bonus (e.g., a sword), the level required of the *Shielding Runes* increases 50%.

4—Calibrate Bonuses/Temper (I) The Caster may determine the plusses on a weapon or defensive item. He also may determine, if the item is an enruned item, what its current *Tolerance* and *Temper* levels are. However, the Caster acquires no further information.

5—Hand Rune (F) An item with this engraved rune may be summoned to either hand of someone who is wearing or wielding the item. This effect is so quick that the item may be used in the round the item is summoned to hand. The wearer or wielder must know that the item has this characteristic. Naturally, the item may not be such an item that is currently worn around the wearer's body, such as a breastplate.

6—Identify Spirit Runes (I) Caster learns the types and effects of all runes on an enruned item.

8—Rune of Parry (F) A being wielding an item with this rune may add +50 to his DB in any round in which he performs only defensive actions (e.g., no attacks, spells, maneuvers, etc).

10-Minor Spirit Rune (F) Caster may implant a *Minor Spirit Rune* that he "knows" into a properly Tempered enruned item. The Gamemaster decides which ones are to be used on the basis of his culture and world system, and how additional ones are acquired by players (if permitted). If the Caster knows more than one of the *Minor Spirit Rune* spells, he may select which he desires to cast.

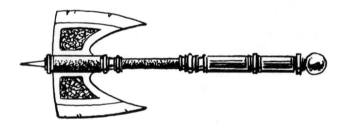

14-Erase Rune (F) Caster may attempt to permanently erase any rune on an item which is not a Spirit Rune of any type. If the Caster did not originally engrave the Rune on the item he is currently attempting to erase, the item receives a +30 RR bonus against the Casters attempt.

15-Major Spirit Rune (F) As *Minor Spirit Rune* above except Caster may engrave a *Major Spirit Rune*.

18-Dismiss Spirit Rune (F) As *Erase Rune* above except Caster may attempt to (dismiss) remove a Spirit Rune of any type. However the item receives an RR bonus as in *Erase Rune* above. If the item succeeds the Caster suffers the effects of an Attack spell failure, adding not only the level of this spell, but also the amount by which the item saved against his dismissal attempt.

20-Lord Spirit Rune (F) As *Minor Spirit Rune* above except Caster may engrave a *Lord Spirit Rune*.

25-Spirit Rune of Might (F) As *Minor Spirit Rune* above except Caster may engrave a *Spirit Rune of Might*.

30-Spirit Rune of the Pale (F) As *Minor Spirit Rune* above except Caster may engrave a *Spirit Rune of the Pale*.

50-Spirit Rune of Power (F) As *Minor Spirit Rune* above except Caster may engrave a *Spirit Rune of Power*.

8.7 CRYSTAL MAGE BASE LISTS

8.71 CRYSTAL POWER (Crystal Mage Base)

NOTE: *Use of 11th level or higher spells requires the caster to be speaking crystal tongue. Spells on this list are non-cumulative.*

	Area of Effect	Duration	Range
1—			
2—Crystal Adder I	crystal	24 hrs	touch
3—Crystal Store I	crystal	24 hrs	touch
4—Locate Minor Cry. Locality	50' R	C	10'/lvl
5—Crystal Matrix I	crystal	24 hrs	touch
6—Crystal Adder II	crystal	24 hrs	touch
7—Crystal Store II	crystal	24 hrs	touch
8—Locate Major Cry. Locality	100' R	C	100'/lvl
9—Crystal Matrix II	crystal	24 hrs	touch
10—Crystal Tongue	self	24 hrs	self
11—Crystal Store III	crystal	24 hrs	touch
12—			
13—Crystal Adder III	crystal	24 hrs	touch
14—			
15—Crystal Matrix III	crystal	24 hrs	touch
16—Crystal Store IV	crystal	24 hrs	touch
17—Crystal Heart	heart	24 hrs	self
18—			
19—Crystal Adder IV	crystal	24 hrs	touch
20—Crystal Matrix IV	crystal	24 hrs	touch
25—Crystal Store V	crystal	24 hrs	touch
30—Crystal Heart True	heart	24 hrs	self
50—Crystal Matrix V	crystal	24 hrs	touch

2—Crystal Adder (F) Allows a crystal of the caster's crystal color alignment to serve as a spell adder (+1). Once the crystal adder has been used once it turns to dust.

3—Crystal Store I (F) Allows caster to store power points in a crystal that has been treated with *Crystal Matrix I*. The caster charges the crystal and this spell stops power leakage.

4—Locate Minor Crystal Locality (I) Allows caster to locate a minor crystal locality. Minor crystal locality is an area which serves as a x2 power point multiplier for the caster as long as he is in the locality. Area is normally loaded with crystal's of the caster's crystal color alignment.

5—Crystal Matrix I (F) Allows the caster to create a power matrix inside of a crystal. This power matrix allows the caster to store and withdraw the power from the crystal. Crystal Matrix I allows the crystal to hold up to its essence rating in power. Exceed it's Essence rating and the crystal cracks and falls to pieces.

6—Crystal Adder II (F) As *Crystal Adder I* except adder is +2.

7—Crystal Store II (F) As *Crystal Store I* except powers up a *Crystal Matrix II*.

8—Locate Major Crystal Locality (I) As *Locate Minor Crystal* Locality except it locates a major crystal locality which will serve as x3 power point multiplier for the caster as long as the caster is in the locality.

9—Crystal Matrix II (F) As *Crystal Matrix I* except allows 2 times the essence value of the crystal to be stored.

10—Crystal Tongue (U) Allows caster to speak and understand the language of magical crystals. All 11th level or higher crystal spells must be spoken in crystal tongue to work.

11—Crystal Store III (F) As *Crystal Store I* except powers up a *Crystal Matrix III*.

13—Crystal Adder III (F) As *Crystal Adder I* except adder is +3.

15—Crystal Matrix III (F) As *Crystal Matrix I* except allows 3 times the essence value of the crystal to be stored.

16—Crystal Store IV (F) As *Crystal Store I* except powers up a *Crystal Matrix IV*.

17—Crystal Heart (F) Allows caster to replace his heart with a crystal heart. It serves as a x2 spell multiplier and cannot be pierced without the aid of magic. If his original heart is harmed, the caster is harmed.

19—Crystal Adder IV (F) As *Crystal Adder I* except adder is +4.

20—Crystal Matrix IV (F) As *Crystal Matrix I* except allows 4 times the essence value of the crystal to be stored.

25—Crystal Store V (F) As *Crystal Store I* except powers up a *Crystal Matrix V*.

30—Crystal Heart True (F) As *Crystal Heart* except it is a x3 multiplier.

50—Crystal Matrix V (F) As *Crystal Matrix I* except allows 5 times the essence value of the crystal to be stored.

8.72 DEEP EARTH HEALING (Crystal Mage Base)

NOTE 1: *#—denotes that full healing is complete in 1-10 hrs.*

NOTE 2: *The GM should set a fixed period required to "enchant the earth" for the healing spells on this list. We suggest: D10 – caster's level + level of the spell (a minimum time of 1 minute).*

NOTE 3: *All enchanted earth spells require that the caster get his materials from deep within the earth. The following are the earthen ingredients that the caster will need:*

Deep Earth Dust: *Dust from cooled molten rock*
Deep Earth Clay: *Earth material that is plastic and malleable*
Deep Earth Oil: *Greasy, combustible, liquid earth substances*
Deep Earth Mud: *Wet, soft, sticky earth material*
Deep Earth Water: *Water made as by product from rock formation*
Deep Earth Loam: *Mix of clay, oil and dust*

NOTE 4: *All enchanted healing earths must be stored in earthen pots. If sealed with deep earth clay that is hardened then the enchantment on the deep earth materials will last until the seal is broken. The pot must be made of enchanted deep earth clay that is hardened. (Hardening of deep earth clay destroys all healing properties that it may have.)*

NOTE 5: *Deep Earth Clay is packed into a bleeding wound and thus is able to stop all bleeding.*

NOTE 6: *The Heal Earth, Heal Metal and Heal Stone spells do not replace materials lost. (So one cannot take a gold bar, remove a chunk out of it, then cast Heal Metal and get more gold than he started with. Example: Start with 1 cu' of gold, cast heal metal spell, end with 1 cu' of gold.)*

	Area of Effect	Duration	Range
1—Enchant Earth I	1 cu'	24 hrs	touch
2—Heal Earth I	10 cu'	P	touch
3—Enchant Earth II	1 cu'	24 hrs	touch
4—Heal Metal I	1 cu'	P	touch
5—Heal Stone I	1 cu'	P	touch
6—Enchant Earth III	1 cu'	24 hrs	touch
7—Heal Earth II	50 cu'	P	touch
8—Enchant Earth IV	1 cu'	24 hrs	touch
9—Heal Metal II	5 cu'	P	touch
10—Heal Stone II	5 cu'	P	touch
11—Heal Earth III	100 cu'	24 hrs	touch
12—Enchant Earth V	1 cu'	24 hrs	touch
13—Heal Metal III	10 cu'	P	touch
14—Heal Stone III	10 cu'	P	touch
15—Enchant Earth VI	1 cu'	24 hrs	touch
16—Heal Earth IV	200 cu'	P	touch
17—Enchant Earth VII	1 cu'	24 hrs	touch
18—Heal Metal IV	50 cu'	P	touch
19—Heal Stone IV	50 cu'	P	touch
20—Enchant Earth VIII	1 cu'	24 hrs	touch
25—Heal Earth V	10 cu'/lvl	P	touch
30—Heal Metal V	2 cu'/lvl	P	touch
50—Heal Stone V	2 cu'/lvl	P	touch

Crystal Mage Base Spell Lists

1—Enchant Earth I (HF) Allows caster make healing salves. The caster may enchanted one of the following:
Deep Earth Dust—Heals 1-10 concussion hits. .... 1 dose
Deep Earth Clay—Stops bleeding (#). .... 1 dose

2—Heal Earth I (H) Allows caster heal 10 cu' of wasted, blasted, or blighted earth.

3—Enchant Earth II (HF) Allows caster make healing salves. The caster may enchanted one of the following:
Deep Earth Dust—Heals 1-10 concussion hits .... 2 doses
Deep Earth Clay—Stops bleeding (#) .... 2 doses
    —Heals muscle damage .... 1 dose
Deep Earth Oil—Heals 1st deg. burn or frost damage .... 1 dose

4—Heal Metal I (H) Allows caster to heal 1 cu' of rusted, or corroded metal.

5—Heal Stone I (H) Allows caster to heal 1 cu' of broken, blemished or cracked stone.

6—Enchant Earth III (HF) Allows caster make healing salves. The caster may enchanted one of the following:
Deep Earth Dust—Heals 1-10 concussion hits .... 3 doses
Deep Earth Clay—Stops bleeding (#) .... 3 doses
    —Heals muscle damage .... 2 doses
Deep Earth Oil—Heals 1st deg. burn or frost damage .... 2 doses
    —Heals 2nd degree burn damage .... 1 dose
Deep Earth Mud —Heals minor fracture (#) .... 1 dose

7—Heal Earth II (H) Allows caster heal 50 cu' of wasted, blasted, or blighted earth.

8—Enchant Earth IV (HF) Allows caster make healing salves. The caster may enchanted one of the following:
Deep Earth Dust—Heals 1-10 concussion hits .... 4 doses
Deep Earth Clay—Stops bleeding (#) .... 4 doses
    —Heals muscle damage .... 3 doses
Deep Earth Oil—Heals 1st deg. burn or frost damage .... 3 doses
    —Heals 2nd degree burn damage .... 2 doses
    —Heals 3rd degree burn damage .... 1 dose
Deep Earth Mud —Heals minor fracture (#) .... 2 doses
    —Heals major fracture (#) .... 1 dose
Deep Earth Water—Doubles healing time. .... 1 dose

9—Heal Metal II (H) Allows caster to heal 5 cu' of rusted, or corroded metal.

10—Heal Stone II (H) Allows caster to heal 5 cu' of broken, blemished or cracked stone.

11—Heal Earth III (H) Allows caster heal 100 cu' of wasted, blasted, or blighted earth.

12—Enchant Earth V (HF) Allows caster make healing salves. The caster may enchanted one of the following:
Deep Earth Dust—Heals 1-10 concussion hits .... 5 doses
Deep Earth Clay—Stops bleeding (#) .... 5 doses
    —Heals muscle damage .... 4 doses
Deep Earth Oil—Heals 1st deg. burn or frost damage .... 4 doses
    —Heals 2nd degree burn damage .... 3 doses
    —Heals 3rd degree burn damage .... 2 doses
Deep Earth Mud —Heals minor fracture (#) .... 3 doses
    —Heals major fracture (#) .... 2 doses
    —Heals shattered bones (#) .... 1 dose
Deep Earth Water—Doubles healing time .... 2 doses
Deep Earth Loam—Heals minor nerve damage (#) .... 1 dose

13—Heal Metal III (H) Allows caster to heal 10 cu' of rusted, or corroded metal.

14—Heal Stone III (H) Allows caster to heal 10 cu' of broken, blemished or cracked stone.

15—Enchant Earth VI (HF) Allows caster make healing salves. The caster may enchanted one of the following:
Deep Earth Dust—Heals 1-10 concussion hits .... 6 doses
Deep Earth Clay—Stops bleeding (#) .... 6 doses
    —Heals muscle damage .... 5 doses
Deep Earth Oil—Heals 1st deg burn or frost damage .... 5 doses
    —Heals 2nd degree burn damage .... 4 doses
    —Heals 3rd degree burn damage .... 3 doses
Deep Earth Mud —Heals minor fracture (#) .... 4 doses
    —Heals major fracture (#) .... 3 doses
    —Heals shattered bones (#) .... 2 doses
Deep Earth Water—Doubles healing time .... 3 doses
Deep Earth Loam—Heals minor nerve damage (#) .... 2 doses
    —Heals major nerve damage (#) .... 1 dose

16—Heal Earth IV (H) Allows caster heal 200 cu' of wasted, blasted, or blighted earth.

17—Enchant Earth VII (HF) Allows caster make healing salves. The caster may enchanted one of the following:
Deep Earth Dust—Heals 1-10 concussion hits .... 7 doses
Deep Earth Clay—Stops bleeding (#) .... 7 doses
    —Heals muscle damage .... 6 doses
Deep Earth Oil—Heals 1st deg. burn or frost damage .... 6 doses
    —Heals 2nd degree burn damage .... 5 doses
    —Heals 3rd degree burn damage .... 4 doses
Deep Earth Mud —Heals minor fracture (#) .... 5 doses
    —Heals major fracture (#) .... 4 doses
    —Heals shattered bones (#) .... 3 doses
Deep Earth Water—Doubles healing time .... 4 doses
Deep Earth Loam—Heals minor nerve damage (#) .... 3 doses
    —Heals major nerve damage (#) .... 2 doses
    —Heals minor organ damage (#) .... 1 dose

18—Heal Metal IV (H) Allows caster to heal 50 cu' of rusted, or corroded metal.

19—Heal Stone IV (H) Allows caster to heal 50 cu' of broken, blemished or cracked stone.

20—Enchant Earth VIII (HF) Allows caster make healing salves. The caster may enchanted one of the following:
Deep Earth Dust—Heals 1-10 concussion hits .... 8 doses
Deep Earth Clay—Stops bleeding (#) .... 8 doses
    —Heals muscle damage .... 7 doses
Deep Earth Oil—Heals 1st deg. burn or frost damage .... 7 doses
    —Heals 2nd degree burn damage .... 6 doses
    —Heals 3rd degree burn damage .... 5 doses
Deep Earth Mud —Heals minor fracture (#) .... 6 doses
    —Heals major fracture (#) .... 5 doses
    —Heals shattered bones (#) .... 4 doses
Deep Earth Water—Doubles healing time .... 5 doses
Deep Earth Loam—Heals minor nerve damage (#) .... 4 doses
    —Heals major nerve damage (#) .... 3 doses
    —Heals minor organ damage (#) .... 2 doses
    —Heals major organ damage (#) .... 1 dose

25—Heal Earth V (H) Allows caster heal 10 cu'/lvl of wasted, blasted, or blighted earth.

30—Heal Metal V (H) Allows caster to heal 2 cu'/lvl of rusted, or corroded metal.

50—Heal Stone V (H) Allows caster to heal 2 cu'/lvl of broken, blemished or cracked stone.

8.73 CRYSTAL MAGIC (Crystal Mage Base)

NOTE 1: *When the crystal fruit is eaten it dissolves in the body. It is poisonous to all but the persons protected by Crystal Infusion. For those that have been protected from crystal poison the fruit purges the body of all poisons and heals 10-100 concussion hits. The crystal fruit is about the size of a cherry. The crystal fruit has one seed in the middle and that is a natural crystal of the caster's crystal color alignment of course. Each seed is of 1 gold piece value on the open market (the GM may vary this cost).* **NOTE 2:** *Use of 11th level or higher spells requires the caster to be speaking the crystal tongue.*

	Area of Effect	Duration	Range
1—Crystal Infusion	self	24 hrs	self
2—Crystal Detection	5' R	C	self
3—Crystal Analysis	1 crystal	—	touch
4—Crystal Portal I	varies	1 rnd/lvl	touch
5—Crystal Location	1 crystal	1 min/lvl	self
6—Crystal Portal II	varies	1 rnd/lvl	touch
7—Crystal Quest	self	varies	self
8—Crystal Portal III	varies	1 rnd/lvl	touch
9—Crystal Location True	1 crystal	1 min/lvl	self
10—Crystal Portal IV	varies	1 rnd/lvl	touch
11—Crystal Seed	1" R	1 rd	touch
12—Crystal Spawn	crystal dust	24 hrs	touch
13—Crystal Flower	1" R	1 rd	touch
14—Crystal Portal V	varies	1 rnd/lvl	touch
15—Crystal Vine	1" R	1 rd	touch
16—Crystal Portal VI	varies	1 rnd/lvl	touch
17—Crystal Bush	1" R	1 rd	touch
18—Crystal Portal VII	varies	1 rnd/lvl	touch
19—Crystal Nodules	1" R	1 rd	touch
20—Crystal Portal VIII	varies	1 rnd/lvl	touch
25—Crystal Tree	1" R	1 rd	touch
30—Crystal Portal True	varies	1 rnd/lvl	touch
40—Crystal Rift	d. portal	varies	self
50—Crystal Life	self	P	self

1—Crystal Infusion (F) Allows caster to prepare his body for the use of crystal essence/magic. Note that without this protection the use of the other higher level spells on this list can cause severe damage to the caster. The caster gets an RR vs the spell level at twice it's normal level. (i.e., 3rd level spell acts like a 6th level spell). If the caster fails their RR then the following damage is taken: 01–75: Coma (1 to 6 months); 76–90: Mind Death (Vegetable); 91–100: Death. The first time this spell is cast the crystal welder color is chosen, normally it will be the color of his teacher, however, it can be chosen at random by the GM.

2—Crystal Detection (P) Detects any crystal within a 5' R/rnd.

3—Crystal Analysis (I) Gives nature and origin of crystal, and when and how crystal was obtained and worked.

4—Crystal Portal I (F) Opens a portal between two crystals. Portal is 3' x 6' x 1', through which anyone can pass. Both crystals are blackened and crumble to dust are successful casting of spell.

5—Crystal Location (P) Gives direction and distance to a specific crystal within 100'/lvl that caster is familiar with **or** has had described in detail.

6—Crystal Portal II (F) Opens a portal between two crystals. Portal is 3' x 6' x 10', through which anyone can pass. Both crystals are blackened and crumble to dust are successful casting of spell.

7—Crystal Quest (I) Allows caster to receive a vision of a quest that needs to be performed before qualifying the caster for his place in the after-life. The mission is normal taken at the time that the caster can uses this spell normally (without ESF). The task is normally for a particular crystal, with failure resulting in the temporary lost of status for after-life (may try crystal quest once again next level) and some other penalty may be determined by the GM. Task must be within the capabilities of the caster.

8—Crystal Portal III (F) Opens a portal between two crystals. Portal is 3' x 6' x 100', through which anyone can pass. Both crystals are blackened and crumble to dust are successful casting of spell.

9—Crystal Location True (P) Gives the direction and distance to any specific crystal that the caster is familiar with **or** has had described in detail within 1 mi/lvl.

10—Crystal Portal IV (F) Opens a portal between two crystals. Portal is 3' x 6' x 1 mile, through which anyone can pass. Both crystals are blackened and crumble to dust are successful casting of spell.

11—Crystal Seed (U) Allows the caster to take crystal fragments, and crystal dust (of the caster's crystal color alignment) and 5 teardrops from the caster to create a crystal seed.

12—Crystal Spawn (E) This is a special familiar. The familiar is shaped as a multifaceted cut crystal of the same crystal color alignment of the caster. The crystal spawn is created from the 5 teardrops from the caster, crystal dust of the caster's crystal color alignment and this spell cast 7 times a day at equal intervals for 7 weeks. Any interruption of this tight scheduled destroys the spell and all previous work is lost (must start again from scratch). The crystal spawn is normally set in a piece of jewelry and is given to a person the caster wishes to spy upon, or protect. The caster may have 1 crystal spawn per level. The caster is in constant contact with the crystal spawn until it is destroyed, or the caster is killed/dies. The caster has a visual range of 1 mile/lvl, audio range of 10 miles/lvl with the crystal spawn. Any crystal spawn out of this range is felt and only it's direction is known. If the crystal spawn is destroyed the caster suffers a losses of 40% of his current concussion hits and is at -50 for all actions for 1 week. **Note:** *The crystal spawn is able to get up and move about, 1' per round, and has a visual range up to 50' and an audio range of 100' (whispers decrease range down to 10' while someone yelling increases the range to 200-300 feet depending upon the loudness of the yelling). Crystal spawn will not move unless directed by the caster.*

13—Crystal Flower (F) A crystal seed is planted and 1 teardrop from the caster and this spell is all that is needed to have the crystal seed begin to grow. The seed will grow into a mystical crystal flower. It takes one month for the seed to grow into a mature crystal flower and the crystal flower bears 1 tear shaped crystal fruit. Once the seed has been picked the flower withers and dies. Flower grows to a height of 8". See note on crystal fruit.

14—Crystal Portal V (F) Opens a portal between two crystals. Portal is 3' x 6' x 10 mi, through which anyone can pass. Both crystals are blackened and crumble to dust are successful casting of spell.

15—Crystal Vine (F) A crystal seed is planted and one teardrop from the caster and the casting of this spell is all that is needed to have the crystal seed begin to grow. The seed will grow up into a mystical crystal vine. It takes two months for the seed to grow into a mature crystal vine and it bears tear shaped crystal fruit (1D3/vine per month for the length of the growing season). At the end of the growing season the vine crumples and dies. Vine grows 4-8'/month; crystal fruit grow in clusters. See note on crystal fruit.

16—Crystal Portal VI (F) Opens a portal between two crystals. Portal is 3' x 6' x 50 mi, through which anyone can pass. Both crystals are blackened and crumble to dust are successful casting of spell.

17—Crystal Bush (F) A crystal seed is planted and one teardrop from the caster and the casting of this spell is all that is needed to have the crystal seed begin to grow. The seed will grow up into a mystical crystal bush. It takes six months for the seed to grow into a mature crystal bush and another six months for the bush to bear it tear shaped crystal fruit (1D6/bush per month for the length of the growing season). Grows to height of 2-4 feet. If the bush is not cut down at the end of the growing season then there is 50% chance that the bush will sprout a new bush off of the root system. Crystal fruit hang singularly on the bush. See note on crystal fruit.

18—Crystal Portal VII (F) Opens a portal between two crystals. Portal is 3' x 6' x 100 mi, through which anyone can pass. Both crystals are blackened and crumble to dust are successful casting of spell.

19—Crystal Nodules (F) A crystal seed is planted and one teardrop from the caster and the casting of this spell is all that is needed to have the crystal seed begin to grow. The seed will grow up into a mystical crystal bush which does not bear crystal fruit but has 1D6 crystal nodules on its roots (similar to potatoes). It takes the crystal nodules bush six months to grow and six months to mature and bear the crystal nodules. The crystal nodule

Crystal Mage Base Spell Lists

has 1D6 crystals inside of it but otherwise, the nodule is identical to crystal fruit. Once the nodules are dug up, the crystal nodule bush dies.

20—Crystal Portal VIII (F) Opens a portal between two crystals. Portal is 3' x 6' x 200 mi, through which anyone can pass. Both crystals are blackened and crumble to dust are successful casting of spell.

25—Crystal Tree (F) A crystal seed is planted and one teardrop from the caster and the casting of this spell is all that is needed to have the crystal seed begin to grow. The seed will grow up into a mystical crystal tree. It takes one year for the seed to grow into a mature crystal tree and another year for the tree to bear it tear shaped crystal fruit (1D6/age of the tree). Tree grows 1-3 feet in height and 1/4 to 1/2 diameter each year. Crystal fruit hand singularly. See note on crystal fruit.

30—Crystal Portal True (F) Opens a portal between two crystals. Portal is 3' x 6' x 300 mi, through which anyone can pass. Both crystals are blackened and crumble to dust are successful casting of spell.

40—Crystal Rift (U) Causes the caster's next crystal portal spell cast within 3 rnds to open up to 1 yr/lvl in the past or future. This is random (roll D100, on an even die roll crystal portal opens up in the past and on an odd die roll crystal portal opens up in the future. Crystals used to form the portal are burnt out and crumble to blackened dust which is of no use.

50—Crystal Life (U) Allows the caster to stop the aging effect. Caster no longer ages. Note that if the caster fails to cast Crystal Infusion even for just one day, the caster will immediately begin aging and all the days, weeks, months, and/or years that the caster has cheated nature out of will consume the caster's body. For example, one particular 75th level spell user has all spell casting abilities cancelled for 1 week (spell failure). Because the caster is not able to cast the simple 1st level spell Crystal Infusion on the next day as this spell must be cast each and every day for users of crystal magic, the 30 years and 7 months and 12 days that the caster has not aged are suddenly thrust upon the spell user's body. The spell user has aged 367 months and will most likely die from the severe strain or extreme age. GMs are encouraged to have the victim's body roll an RR against heart failure vs his constitution applying a -1 for each month aged. In this case the spell caster has a negative 367.

8.74 DEEP EARTH COMMUNE (Crystal Mage Base)

NOTE: MDE — Minor Deep Earth spirit; LDE — Lesser Deep Earth spirit; DE — Deep Earth spirit; GDE — Greater Deep Earth spirit; GRDE— Guardian Deep Earth spirit.

	Area of Effect	Duration	Range
1—Guess*	1 question	—	self
2—Intuitions I	self	—	self
3—Dream I	1 topic	sleep	self
4—Summons MDE Spirit	1 spirit	1 rnd/lvl	self
5—Intuitions III	self	—	self
6—Speak With MDE Spirit	1 spirit	1 rnd/lvl	self
7—Intuitions V	self	—	self
8—Dream II	2 topics	sleep	self
9—Summons LDE Spirit	1 spirit	1 rnd/lvl	self
10—Deep Earth Empathy	self	1 rnd/lvl	touch
11—Speak With LDE Spirit	1 spirit	1 rnd/lvl	self
12—Intuitions VII	self	—	self
13—Dream III	3 topics	sleep	self
14—Summons DE Spirit	1 spirit	1 rnd/lvl	self
15—Intuitions X	self	—	self
16—Speak With DE Spirit	1 spirit	1 rnd/lvl	self
17—Dream IV	4 topics	sleep	self
18—Summons GDE Spirit	1 spirit	1 rnd/lvl	self
19—Intuitions True	self	—	self
20—Speak With GDE Spirit	1 spirit	1 rnd/lvl	self
25—Dream True	5 topics	sleep	self
30—Summons GRDE Spirit	1 spirit	1 rnd/lvl	self
50—Speak With GRDE Spirit	1 spirit	1 rnd/lvl	self

1—Guess (I*) When faced with a choice about which he has little or no information (i.e., which corridor leads outside the quickest); the caster may throw this spell and the GM will determine which way he goes, biasing the choice by 25%.

2—Intuitions I (I) Gains vision of what probably will happen if he takes a specified action, within the next minute.

3—Dream I (I) Caster has a dream relating to a topic decided upon just before retiring.

4—Summons MDE Spirit (FM) Caster may summon 1 Minor Deep Earth (MDE) spirit. As long as caster concentrates the minor deep earth spirit must remain with the spell affect area.

5—Intuitions III (I) As *Intuitions I* except effects next three minutes.

6—Speak With MDE Spirit (FI) Caster is able to communicate with a minor deep earth spirit. The minor deep earth spirit will answer all questions put to it during the duration of the spell. It will know the right or correct answer only 10% of the time. The answer will always be in the form of a riddle and never in a straight forth manner.

7—Intuitions V (I) As *Intuitions I* except affects next five minutes.

8—Dream II (I) As *Dream I* except limits is 2 dreams/night on different topics.

9—Summons LDE Spirit (I) Caster may summon 1 Lesser Deep Earth (LDE) spirit. As long as caster concentrates the lesser deep earth spirit must remain within the spell affect area.

10—Deep Earth Empathy (I) Caster can understand and/or visualize the thoughts and emotions of deep earth.

11—Speak With LDE Spirit (FI) Caster is able to communicate with a lesser deep earth spirit. The lesser deep earth spirit will answer all questions put to it during the duration of the spell. It will know the right or correct answer only 25% of the time. The answer will always be in the form of a riddle and never in a straight forth manner.

12—Intuitions VII (I) As *Intuitions I* except affects next seven minutes.

13—Dream III (I) As *Dream I* except limits is 3 dreams/night on different topics.

14—Summons DE Spirit (I) Caster may summon 1 Deep Earth (DE) spirit. As long as caster concentrates the deep earth spirit must remain within the spell affect area.

15—Intuitions X (I) As *Intuitions I* except affects next ten minutes.

16—Speak With DE Spirit (FI) Caster is able to communicate with a deep earth spirit. The deep earth spirit will answer all questions put to it during the duration of the spell. It will know the right or correct answer only 40% of the time. The answer will always be in the form of a riddle and never in a straight forth manner.

17—Dream IV (I) As *Dream I* except limits is 4 dreams/night on different topics.

18—Summons GDE Spirit (I) Caster may summon 1 Greater Deep Earth (GDE) spirit. As long as caster concentrates the greater deep earth spirit must remain within the spell affect area.

19—Intuitions True (I) As *Intuitions I* except caster can predict what will happen up to one minute/lvl into the future.

20—Speak With GDE Spirit (FI) Caster is able to communicate with a greater deep earth spirit. The greater deep earth spirit will answer all questions put to it during the duration of the spell. It will know the right or correct answer only 65% of the time. The answer will always be in the form of a riddle and never in a straight forth manner.

25—Dream True (I) As *Dream I* except limits is 5 dreams/night on different topics.

30—Summons GRDE Spirit (I) Caster may summon 1 Guardian Deep Earth (GRDE) spirit. As long as caster concentrates the guardian deep earth spirit must remain within the spell affect area.

50—Speak With GRDE Spirit (FI) Caster is able to communicate with a guardian deep earth spirit. The guardian deep earth spirit will answer all questions put to it during the duration of the spell. It will know the right or correct answer only 80% of the time. The answer will always be in the form of a riddle and never in a straight forth manner.

8.75 CRYSTAL MASTERY (Crystal Mage Base)

NOTE 1: *To use 11th level or higher spells require the caster be speaking crystal tongue.*
NOTE 2: Crystal Strength *and* Crystal Might *spells are non-cumulative.*
NOTE 3: Crystal Blade *spells are non-cumulative.*

	Area of Effect	Duration	Range
1—Crystal Ears	self	1 min/lvl	self
2—Crystal Strength I	self	1 min/lvl	self
3—Crystal Eyes	self	1 min/lvl	self
4—Crystal Scales	self	1 min/lvl	self
5—Crystal Strength II	self	1 min/lvl	self
6—Crystal Shot	target	—	50'
7—Crystal Skin	self	1 min/lvl	self
8—Crystal Strength True	self	1 min/lvl	self
9—Crystal Shot True	target	—	100'
10—Crystal Plate	self	1 min/lvl	self
11—Crystal Sight	self	1 min/lvl	self
12—Crystal Bolt	target	—	100'
13—Crystal Might I	self	1 min/lvl	self
14—Crystal Repercussion	target	—	100'
15—Crystal Blade	metal blade	1 min/lvl	touch
16—Crystal Might II	self	1 min/lvl	self
17—Crystal Bolt True	target	—	300'
18—Crystal Blade II	metal blade	1 min/lvl	touch
19—Crystal Repercussion True	target	—	300'
20—Crystal Might True	self	1 min/lvl	self
25—Crystal Charge Bolt	target	—	100'
30—Crystal Blade True	metal blade	1 min/lvl	touch
50—Crystal Charge Bolt True	target	—	300'

1—Crystal Ears (U) Caster is attuned to the vibrations of all the crystals within 100', thus the caster is able to listen in at the crystal remote location as if he was there.

2—Crystal Strength (U) Gives the caster +5 strength and +5 constitution bonuses.

3—Crystal Eyes (U) As *Crystal Ears* except caster gets a visual image.

4—Crystal Scale (U) Part of the caster's skin becomes as hard as a crystal. Acts as AT 9, +5 heat resistances, -10 to cold resistances.

5—Crystal Strength II (U) Gives the caster +10 strength and +10 constitution bonuses.

6—Crystal Shot (E) A small crystal (size of a "BB") is shot from the palm of the caster. Use the Shock Bolt chart and Impact criticals. Downgrade all criticals 1 level ("A" crit = no crit, "B" crit = "A" crit, "C" crit = "B" crit, etc.) The crystal shot is half of the size of a crystal seed and is worth 1 half gold piece.

7—Crystal Skin (U) Part of the caster's skin becomes as hard as a crystal. Acts as AT 13, +5 heat resistances, -10 to cold resistances.

8—Crystal Strength True (U) Gives the caster +15 strength and +15 constitution bonuses.

9—Crystal Shot True (E) As *Crystal Shot* except range is 100'.

10—Crystal Plate (U) Part of the caster's skin becomes as hard as a crystal. Acts as AT 17, +5 heat resistances, -10 to cold resistances.

11—Crystal Sight (U) Caster's eyes become faceted and caster views the world through many levels. Invisible objects are now visible, illusions are shapes of power, power levels oscillate, and the caster can see all this energy/power levels at night as well as in the day. Caster can not see beyond 50' range, but has 270 degree vision.

12—Crystal Bolt (E) A crystal fragment (size of pellet) is shot from the palm of the caster (use Shock Bolt table). Gives Impact and Stun criticals of equal severity.

13—Crystal Might I (U) Gives the caster +20 strength and +20 constitution bonuses.

14—Crystal Repercussion (F) When the caster snaps his fingers, he causes his body to vibrate with high pitch sound energy. The caster then focuses this energy into a beam of sound and directs it at a target. Any glass in the path will shatter, delivering a "A" Impact critical to anyone within the path of the flying glass (about 5' R). The sound beam causes the target to take a "C" Impact critical and everyone within 10'R must make a very hard orientation roll or they become stunned for 1 rnd due to the sudden discharge of noise.

15—Crystal Blade I (F) Allows the caster to enchant a metal blade. The blade has crystal strength, is transparent and is indestructible without the aid of magic. The blade has an OB of +35.

16—Crystal Might II (U) Gives the caster +25 strength and +25 constitution bonuses.

17—Crystal Bolt True (E) As *Crystal Bolt* except range is 300'.

18—Crystal Blade II (F) Allows the caster to magically enchant a metal blade. The blade has crystal strength, is transparent and is indestructible without the aid of magic. This blade will cut through anything that does not have a magical aura. Thus all non-magical armor types are treated as armor type 4.

19—Crystal Repercussion True (F) As *Crystal Repercussion* except the sound beam can attack a target at a range of 300' and anyone with 30' of the caster must make a sheer folly orientation or become stunned for 1 round.

20—Crystal Might True (U) Gives the caster +30 strength and +30 constitution bonuses.

25—Crystal Charged Bolt (E) As *Crystal Bolt* except adds a heat and electric crit of one lower level than the impact and stun criticals. (i.e., an "A" impact and stun crit = no heat and electric crit, a "B" impact and stun crit = a "A" heat and electric crit, etc.)

30—Crystal Blade True (F) Allows the caster to magically enchant a metal blade. The blade has crystal strength, is transparent and is indestructible without the aid of magic. This blade will cut through anything. Thus all non magical armor and magical armor that fails it's RR vs this 30th lvl spell are treated as armor type 4.

50—Crystal Charged Bolt True (E) As *Crystal Bolt* except adds a heat and electricity critical of equal severity as the impact and stun criticals.

Crystal Mage Base Spell Lists

8.76 FIERY WAYS (Crystal Mage Base)

NOTE: *Heat Armor and Fire Armor spells are non-cumulative.*

	Area of Effect	Duration	Range
1—Resist Heat	target	1 min/lvl	10'
2—Boil Liquid	1 cu'	C	10'
3—Warm Solid	varies	24 hrs	10'
4—Wood Fires	1'R	—	1'
5—Resist Heat (10')	target	1 min/lvl	10'
6—Heat Solid	varies	24 hrs	10'
7—Fire Bolt (100')	target	—	100'
8—Heat Armor	target	1 min/lvl	10'
9—Fire Ball (10')	10'R	—	100'
10—Control Fires	1 fire	1 min/lvl	10'
11—Fire Ball (20')	20' R	—	100'
12—Heat Armor (10')	target	1 min/lvl	10'
13—Fire Bolt (300')	target	—	300'
14—Circle Flame	10'Rx10'x6"	1 rnd/lvl	100'
15—Waiting Flame	10'x10'x10'	varies	100'
16—Metal Fires	target	1 rnd/lvl	100'
17—Fire Armor	target	1 min/lvl	10'
18—Fire Bolt (500')	target	—	500'
19—Immolation	5' R	1 rnd/lvl	self
20—Fire Armor True	target	1 min/lvl	10'
25—Fire Bolt V	varies	5 rds(C)	100'
30—Stone Fires	target	1 rnd/lvl	100'
50—Fire Armor Mastery	target	1 min/lvl	10'

1—Resist Heat (D) Target is totally protected from all natural heat (not fire), and adds +10 to RRs vs heat and -10 to elemental fire attacks.

2—Boil Liquid (F) 1 cu' of liquid/lvl can be heated to boiling at a rate of 1 cu'/rd.

3—Warm Solid (F) Any solid inanimate, non-metal material (1 cu'/lvl) can be warmed to 100°F at a rate of 1 cu'/rd.

4—Wood Fires (F) Causes any wood to ignite and burn. All wood ignited must be within 1' of caster's palm.

5—Resist Heat (10') As *Resist Heat* except all beings within 10' of target are protected.

6—Heat Solid (F) Any solid inanimate, non-metal material (1 cu'/lvl) can be warmed to 500°F at a rate of 100 degree/rd.

7—Fire Bolt (100') (E) A bolt of fire is shot from the palm of the caster; results are determined on the Fire Bolt Table.

8—Heat Armor As *Resist Heat* except protects against all natural heat and modifies spells involving heat by 20.

9—Fire Ball (10') (E) A 1' ball of fire is shot from the palm of the caster, it explodes to affect a 10'R area; results are determined on the Fire Ball Table.

10—Control Fires (F) Caster can control the temperature range of a fire (i.e., extinguish a fire, flare it up, etc).

11—Fire Ball (20') (E) As *Fireball (10')* except it affects a 20' R area.

12—Heat Armor (10') As *Heat Armor* except all beings within 10' of target are protected.

13—Fire Bolt (300') As *Fire Bolt (100')* except range is 300'.

14—Circle Flame (E) Creates an opaque circled wall of fire (10'Rx10'x6". Anyone through it takes an "A" heat critical (No RR). The circle of flame is centered around the caster and is immobile.

15—Waiting Flame (E) Creates a cube of flame (10'x10'x10'), it takes 1 complete round for the cube to form and be effective. An "A" critical is dealt for each round passing through (or in). Cube of flame will burn for 1 rnd/lvl and the effect can be delayed up to 24 hrs; triggered by time, sound, violent action, etc.

16—Metal Fires (F) Causes a metal object to burst into flames, the object can be up to 1 lb/lvl in mass. If the object is on a being, it gets a RR and if it fails the being takes a heat critical of a severity to be determined by tis location on the being's body.

17—Fire Armor (E) As *Resist Heat* except fire spells are affected (fire bolt and fireball). Fire/heat criticals are decreased by one level (i.e., "E"s become "D"s, "D"s become "C"s, "C"s become "B"s, "B"s become "A"s and "A"s are ignored) and all fire/heat concussion hits are reduced by 1/2.

18—Fire Bolt (500') (E) As *Fire Bolt (100')* except range is 500'.

19—Immolation (E) Caster's body is covered with powerful flames. He is immune to all forms of fire. Anyone within 5' suffers an "A" heat critical (No RR). Anyone in physical contact suffers a "C" heat critical. Physical attacks from the caster that deliver a critical also deliver an "A" heat critical. All items on the caster's person are immune to Fire for the duration of this spell, but any materials he touches (or walks on, etc) after he immolates must make a RR or be ignited.

20—Fire Armor True As *Fire Armor* except fire/heat criticals are decreased by two level ("E"s become "C"s, "D"s become "B"s, "C"s become "A"s and "B" and "A" criticals are ignored) and all fire/heat based concussion hits are reduced by 3/4.

25—Fire Bolt V As *Fire Bolt (100')* except five bolts of fire are shot from the palm of the caster, at a rate of 1 per round.

30—Stone Fires (F) As *Metal Fires* except a 300 sq' surface as affected and a "C" critical is given each round passing through (or in) the 3' flames.

50—Fire Armor Mastery As *Fire Armor True* except target cannot be harmed by fire based attacks.

8.77 BRILLIANCE MAGIC (Crystal Mage Base)

NOTE 1: *Self Aura and Aura spell are non-cumulative.*

NOTE 2: *GM may wish to allow the caster to use the Stun Critical Chart, for the Sudden Light spells. "E" crit to those within 1' R of the center, "C" crit to those within 5' R and and "A" crit to everyone else.*

	Area of Effect	Duration	Range
1—Blur	target	1 min/lvl	10'
2—Projected Light	50'	10 min/lvl	25'
3—Self Aura I	self	10 min/lvl	self
4—Light I	10' R	10 min/lvl	touch
5—Self Aura II	self	10 min/lvl	self
6—Lesser Sudden Light	10' R	—	100'
7—Self Aura III	self	10 min/lvl	self
8—Light V	50' R	10 min/lvl	touch
9—Aura I	5' R	10 min/lvl	self
10—Greater Sudden Light	20' R	—	100'
11—Light X	100' R	10 min/lvl	touch
12—Waiting Light	varies	varies	100'
13—Aura III	15' R	10 min/lvl	self
14—Beacon V	5 miles	1 min/lvl	touch
15—Light XX	200' R	10 min/lvl	touch
16—Sudden Light True	50' R	—	100'
17—Aura IV	20' R	10 min/lvl	self
18—Light Storm	varies	1 min/lvl	1 mi R/lvl
19—Aura True	25' R	10 min/lvl	self
20—Utter Light	100' R	1 min/lvl	touch
25—Beacon X	10 miles	1 min/lvl	touch
30—Light True	10' R/lvl	10 min/lvl	touch
50—Light Storm Mastery	varies	1 min/lvl	1 mi R/lvl

1—Blur (F) Causes target to appear Blurred to attackers, subtracting 10 from all attacks.

2—Projected Light (F) Beam of light (like a flashlight) springs from the caster's palm; 50' effective range.

3—Self Aura I (F) Causes a bright aura about the caster, making him appear more powerful and subtracting 5 from all attacks.

4—Light I (F) Lights a 10' R area about the point touched.

5—Self Aura II (F) Causes a bright aura about the caster, making him appear more powerful and subtracting 10 from all attacks.

6—Lesser Sudden Light (F) Causes a 10' R burst of intense light; all those inside the are stunned 1 rnd/5% failure.

7—Self Aura III (F) Causes a bright aura about the caster, making him appear more powerful and subtracting 15 from all attacks.

8—Light V (F) Lights a 50' R area about the point touched.

9—Aura I (F) Causes a bright aura about the caster 5' R, making him and all beings within the aura to appear more powerful and subtracting 5 from all attacks.

10—Greater Sudden Light (F) Causes a 20' R burst of intense light; all those inside the are stunned 1 rnd/5% failure.

11—Light X (F) Lights a 100' R area about the point touched.

12—Waiting Light (F) In conjunction with any light spell can delay the action of that spell until up to 24 hrs passes OR a being passes OR a certain word is spoken, etc.

13—Aura III (F) Causes a bright aura about the caster 15' R, making him and all beings within the aura to appear more powerful and subtracting 5 from all attacks.

14—Beacon V (F) Ray of light of any color springs from area touched; can be up to 5 miles long.

15—Light XX (F) Lights a 200' R area about the point touched.

16—Sudden Light True (F) Causes a 50' R burst of intense light; all those inside the are stunned 1 rnd/5% failure.

17—Aura IV (F) Causes a bright aura about the caster 20' R, making him and all beings within the aura to appear more powerful and subtracting 5 from all attacks.

18—Light Storm (F) Summons forces of nature in a fierce lightning with random lightning strikes. Can be delayed up to 1 hr/lvl after cast.

19—Aura True (F) Causes a bright aura about the caster 25' R, making him and all beings within the aura to appear more powerful and subtracting 5 from all attacks.

20—Utter Light (F) Lights a 100' R area about the point touched and the light nullifies all magically created darkness.

25—Beacon X (F) Ray of light of any color springs from area touched; can be up to 10 miles long.

30—Light True (F) Lights a 10' R/lvl area about the point touched.

50—Light Storm Mastery (F) Summons forces of nature in a fierce lightning and the caster has 50% chance of controlling lightning strikes. Can be delayed up to 1 hr/lvl after cast.

8.78 CRYSTAL RUNESTONE (Crystal Mage Base)

NOTE 1: Preparation of Crystal Runestones: *There are eight basic steps in preparing a Crystal Runestone for it's duties as a magical instrument.*

1—Pick a suitable Crystal Runestone. It should have some bearing on the individual that will be using it. This could be as simple as using birth stones or one specific type of Crystal Runestone. In the case of the Crystal Mage, the determinants for their Crystal Runestone are color, size, shape and crystal composition of the stone. Crystal Runestone can be made from a jewel, gem or any other precious stone/material.

2—If the Crystal Runestone has already been cut then this step is optional. This step is to provide any number of polished surfaces (facets) on the Crystal Runestone for the sole purpose of giving the crystal rune an unblemished surface in which to be inscribed on.

3—Once a cut stone has been obtained, it must have all residual energies removed from the surface of the stone. This is accomplished either by the use of the *Cleanse* spell on the Crystal Runestone spell list or by a very hard skill roll using the meditation skill, cleanse. This keeps outside factors from corrupting the Crystal Runestone and limiting it's usefulness to it's primary user.

4—The next step in preparing the Crystal Runestone is providing it with a containment matrix. This is done with the *Prime* spell off of the Crystal Runestone spell list. Priming of the Crystal Runestone allows the placement of many crystal runes without the interference of overlapping magics/energies. If the Crystal Runestone is not primed the use of any crystal runes on it will result in the attempted user being in gulfed in a Fire Ball with a OB of 10 per crystal rune on the Crystal Runestone. The Crystal Runestone is completely destroyed in the process.

5— Once the Crystal Runestone has been chosen, cut, cleansed and primed, it is ready to receive crystal runes with spell inscribed in them. Pick one of the faceted surfaces of the Crystal Runestone which is going to be the recipient of the crystal rune. Now select the desired Crystal Rune spell from the Crystal Runestone spell list and cast it. Then pick the spell which going to be inscribed within the crystal rune and cast it. The crystal rune will appear on the chosen facet of the Crystal Runestone.

6—There is a chance that the Crystal Runestone will reject the crystal rune. The modifiers for this rejection are +1/lvl of crystal rune spell and +1 for each crystal rune already inscribed upon the Crystal Runestone. A open-ended roll is added to the rejection modifiers and a roll of +101 indicates that the Crystal Runestone has rejected the crystal rune. **Note:** *GMs may wish to use the Alchemical Inertia Factors (AIFs) guidelines described in **RMCI**, section 3.54 and section 5.2.*

Crystal Mage Base Spell Lists

7—The Crystal Runestone can now be used as if it was rune paper. The spell inscribed within the Crystal Runestone can be released by a successful runes skill roll ('medium' difficulty rune skill roll for it's creator and 'hard' difficulty rune skill roll for someone who has received detailed instructions on the specific crystal rune and very hard difficulty rune skill roll for everyone else). These are general guidelines and the GM may feel free to assign their own modifiers to suit the individual game situations.

8—Once the spell on the Crystal Runestone has been successfully cast or released, the crystal rune fades from the faceted surface of the Crystal Runestone.

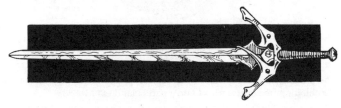

SUMMARY FOR PREPARING AND USING CRYSTAL RUNESTONES
1—Pick suitable Crystal Runestone.
2—Have Crystal Runestone cut (optional).
3—Cleanse the Crystal Runestone to remove unwanted energies.
4—Prime the Crystal Runestone for inscribing of crystal runes.
5—Inscribe crystal runes with desired spell
6—Check for crystal rune rejections.
7—Use of rune skill to cast inscribed spells.
8—Crystal rune fades.

NOTE 2: *To use 11th level or higher spells requires the caster to be speaking in crystal tongue.*

	Area of Effect	Duration	Range
1—Cleanse	crystal	1 min/lvl	touch
2—Prime	crystal	—	touch
3—Decipher Crystal Rune	crystal rune	1 rnd/lvl	touch
4—Crystal Rune I	crystal facet	until cast	touch
5—Crystal Rune Empathy	crystal rune	24 hrs	touch
6—Crystal Rune II	crystal facet	until cast	touch
7—Crystal Rune Link II	crystal rune	24 hrs	touch
8—Crystal Rune III	crystal facet	until cast	touch
9—Deep Inscription I	crystal rune	24 hrs	touch
10—Crystal Rune IV	crystal facet	until cast	touch
11—Crystal Rune Will	crystal rune	24 hrs	touch
12—Crystal Rune V	crystal facet	until cast	touch
13—Crystal Rune Link III	crystal rune	24 hrs	touch
14—Crystal Rune VI	crystal facet	until cast	touch
15—Crystal Rune Mind	crystal rune	24 hrs	touch
16—Crystal Rune VII	crystal facet	until cast	touch
17—Crystal Rune Link IV	crystal rune	24 hrs	touch
18—Crystal Rune VIII	crystal facet	until cast	touch
19—Deep Inscription II	crystal rune	24 hrs	touch
20—Crystal Rune IX	crystal facet	until cast	touch
25—Crystal Rune X	crystal facet	until cast	touch
30—Deep Inscription III	crystal rune	24 hrs	touch
50—Lord Crystal Rune	crystal facet	until cast	touch

1—Cleanse (F) Crystal rune stone is cleaned of all residual energies. (i.e., evil/good taints, old spell patterns that still linger, etc.)

2—Prime (F) Prepares the Crystal Runestone for reception of crystal runes and other related spells. Priming of the Crystal Runestone allows the placement of many crystal runes without the interference of overlapping magics/energies.

3—Decipher Crystal Rune (I) Gives the caster detailed information on crystal runes, thus allowing the crystal rune to be used. This spell will decipher 1 crystal rune per round.

4—Crystal Rune I (F) This spell inscribes a spell on a top surface facet of a crystal rune stone; the crystal rune can then be used to cast the inscribed spell once (depending upon the rules being used for casting runes). The caster expends the power points to cast the inscribed spell and the power points to cast the crystal rune spell. *Crystal Rune I* can only inscribe 1st level spells. The crystal rune stone can be reused. The crystal rune can be set to affect reader. Once the spell within the crystal rune has been released the crystal rune "mark" on the faceted face of the Crystal Runestone fades.

5—Crystal Rune Empathy (F) Gives the Crystal Runestone empathy, allowing anyone who has attuned themselves to it to use the crystal rune on it. This does not give any information on the crystal runes or the spells inscribe within the crystal runes, thus if the crystal runes are used they are used blindly without deciphering of the crystal runes. Note that it will be left up to the GM to decide if the spell has any effect, what the spell has effected, if the crystal rune has been "mis-read", or if there should be any effect to the user, etc.

6—Crystal Rune II (F) As *Crystal Rune I*, except caster can inscribe 1st-2nd level spells.

7—Crystal Rune Link II (F) Causes the caster's next two crystal rune spells cast to be linked to one and another. The first crystal rune cast after the crystal rune link spell is considered the primary crystal rune within the link and the second crystal rune spell is considered the linked crystal rune. When the primary crystal rune is released/used the linked crystal rune is immediately released/used (treat it as if it was an instantaneous spell). (e.g., the caster has cast *Crystal Rune Link II* on his Crystal Runestone. He then cast *Crystal Rune II* (primary rune) and inscribes *Crystal Strength I* and then cast the second crystal rune, *Crystal Rune I* (linked crystal rune) with *Crystal Ears* inscribed within it. When the caster makes a successful rune skill roll on the primary crystal rune the spell inscribed within is released and then the linked crystal rune is released.)

8—Crystal Rune III (F) As *Crystal Rune I*, except caster can inscribe 1st-3rd level spells.

9—Deep Inscription I (F) Causes the caster's next Crystal Rune spell to have multiple uses (two) before the crystal rune fades.

10—Crystal Rune IV (F) As *Crystal Rune I*, except caster can inscribe 1st-4th level spells.

11—Crystal Rune Will (F) Causes the caster's next Crystal Rune to be voice activated. To voice activate the crystal rune it's name must be spoken in the crystal magical tongue.

12—Crystal Rune V (F) As *Crystal Rune I*, except caster can inscribe 1st-5th level spells.

13—Crystal Rune Link III (F) As *Crystal Rune Link II*, except two crystal runes are linked sequentially to the primary crystal rune.

14—Crystal Rune VI (F) As *Crystal Rune I*, except caster can inscribe 1st-6th level spells.

15—Crystal Rune Mind (F) As *Crystal Rune Empathy*, except the crystal rune stone will inform the attuner what spells are inscribed in each of the crystal runes.

16—Crystal Rune VII (F) As *Crystal Rune I*, except caster can inscribe 1st-7th level spells.

17—Crystal Rune Link IV (F) As *Crystal Rune Link II*, except three crystal runes are link sequentially to the primary crystal rune.

18—Crystal Rune VIII (F) As *Crystal Rune I*, except caster can inscribe 1st-8th level spells.

19—Deep Inscription II (F) As *Deep Inscription I*, except the crystal rune may be used three times before the crystal rune fades.

20—Crystal Rune IX (F) As *Crystal Rune I*, except caster can inscribe 1st-9th level spells.

25—Crystal Rune X (F) As *Crystal Rune I*, except caster can inscribe 1st-10th level spells.

30—Deep Inscription III (F) As *Deep Inscription I*, except the crystal rune may be used four times before the crystal rune fades.

50—Lord Crystal Rune (F) As *Crystal Rune I*, except caster can inscribe 1st-20th level spells.

8.8 DREAM LORD BASE LISTS

8.81 DREAM GUARD (Dream Lord Base)

NOTE 1: *Dream Guards are type I through type VI demons. They each have the additional ability of dream state as described on Dream State spell list.*

NOTE 2: *Dream Guards block the entrance ways of dream worlds for the duration of the spell, caster releases it, it dies defending the entrance, or the caster dies, which ever comes first.*

NOTE 3: *Dream Guards has 5% chances per type of demon of taking over the caster's body in the event the dream guard was released from this magical pact due to the caster's death.*

NOTE 4: *Dream Guards are basically inside the caster's mind, the true path to dream worlds; so the caster is always aware of the status of the dream world entrance.*

NOTE 5: *Dream Unlock spells must overcome the resistance of the Dream Lock spells (at the level Dream Lock spell was cast) to succeed. Dream Unlock spells must be of equal or greater value to override the Dream Lock spell (e.g., A Dream Unlock II spell could unlock a Dream Lock I or II spell but not a Dream Lock III or higher spell.) Any attempt to unlock a higher level dream lock will alert the original caster of the dream lock that someone or something is amiss at the entrance to that particular dream world.*

NOTE 6: *Dream Unlock spells higher in level than the Dream Lock spell which are being utilized lower the chance of the alerting the monitoring dream guard by 10% per level above the dream lock spell. (e.g., a Dream Unlock IV being used to unlock a Dream Lock I would lower the chance of being detected by 30% (VI-I=3*10%) or 30%.)*

	Area of Effect	Duration	Range
1—			
2—			
3—			
4—			
5—Dream Unlock I	Dream Lock	1 rnd/lvl	self
6—Dream Lock I	Dream Travel	1 day/lvl	self
7—Dream Guard I	Dream Travel	1 day/lvl	self
8—			
9—Dream Unlock II	Dream Lock	1 rnd/lvl	self
10—Dream Lock II	Dream Travel	1 day/lvl	self
11—Dream Guard II	Dream Travel	1 day/lvl	self
12—			
13—Dream Unlock III	Dream Lock	1 rnd/lvl	self
14—Dream Lock III	Dream Travel	1 wk/lvl	self
15—Dream Guard III	Dream Travel	1 wk/lvl	self
16—Dream Unlock IV	Dream Lock	1 rnd/lvl	self
17—Dream Lock IV	Dream Travel	1 wk/lvl	self
18—Dream Guard IV	Dream Travel	1 wk/lvl	self
19—			
20—Dream Unlock True	Dream Lock	1 rnd/lvl	self
25—Dream Guard V	Dream Travel	1 month/lvl	self
30—Dream Lock True	Dream Travel	P	self
50—Dream Guard True	Dream Travel	1 month/lvl	self

5—Dream Unlock I (U) Allows the caster to unlock a level one dream lock for 1 round. If dream lock spell is overcome by 50% then the dream unlock will go unnoticed.

6—Dream Lock I (FD) Allows the caster to place a level 1 magical barrier prohibiting free dream travel into a particular dream world.

7—Dream Guard I (FD) Allows the caster to bind a type I demon to guard a particular dream world entrance. The dream traveller wishing to enter the dream world has one round in which to decide to confront the dream guard or leave. The Dream Guard will not let any pass save he who set him there. Combat with the Dream Guard is conducted normally.

9—Dream Unlock II (U) As *Dream Unlock I* except overcomes type I dream lock with 40% chance of being detected or type II dream lock with 50% chance of being detected.

10—Dream Lock II (FD) As Dream Lock I except level two magical lock.

11—Dream Guard II (FD) As *Dream Guard I* except binds a type II demon.

13—Dream Unlock III (U) As *Dream Unlock I* except overcomes type I dream lock with 30% chance of being detected or type II dream lock with 40% chance of being detected or type III dream lock with 50% chance of being detected.

14—Dream Lock III (FD) As Dream Lock I except 3rd level magical lock.

15—Dream Guard III (FD) As *Dream Guard I* except binds a type III demon.

16—Dream Unlock IV (U) As *Dream Unlock I* except overcomes type I dream lock with 20% chance of being detected or type II dream lock with 30% chance of being detected or type III dream lock with 40% chance of being detected or type VI dream lock with 50% chance of being detected.

17—Dream Lock IV (FD) As Dream Lock I except 4th level magical lock.

18—Dream Guard IV (FD) As *Dream Guard I* except binds a type IV demon.

20—Dream Unlock True (FD) As *Dream Unlock I* except may overcome a dream lock level of +1/every 5 levels of caster and chance of detection is -10% per level of dream Unlock over the Dream Lock spell.(e.g., a *Dream Unlock IV* being used to unlock a *Dream Lock I* would lower the chance of being detected by 30% (IV-I=3*10%) or 30%.)

25—Dream Guard V (FD) As *Dream Guard I* except binds a type V demon.

30—Dream Lock True (FD) As *Dream Lock I* except magical lock level is +1/every 5 levels of caster.

50—Dream Guard True (FD) As *Dream Guard I* except binds a type VI demon.

Dream Lord Base Spell Lists

8.82 DREAM LAW (Dream Lord Base)

	Area of Effect	Duration	Range
1—Daydream	1 target	varies	100'
2—Dream I	1 target	varies	100'
3—Sleep	1 target	1 rnd/lvl	50'
4—			
5—Nightmare I	1 target	varies	100'
6—Dream II	1 target	varies	100'
7—Sleepwalking	1 target	1 day/lvl	100'
8—Dream III	1 target	varies	100'
9—Nightmare II	1 target	varies	100'
10—Undream	1 target	1 day/lvl	100'
11—Sleep True	1 target/lvl	1 rnd/lvl	50'
12—Dream IV	1 target	varies	100'
13—Dream Killer I	1 target	varies	100'
14—Nightmare III	1 target	varies	100'
15—Dream Death	1 target	P	100'
16—Dream V	1 target	varies	100'
17—Dream Killer III	1 target	varies	100'
18—Dream Field	1'R/lvl	10 min/10% fail.	50'
19—Nightmare IV	1 target	varies	100'
20—Dream Shifting	1 target	varies	100'
25—Dream Killer True	1 target	varies	100'
30—Nightmare True	1 target	varies	100'
50—Dream Field True	1'R/lvl	P	100'

1—Daydream (FM) Target has a daydream relating to a topic decided upon by the caster at the time the spell was casted. Target is totally unaware of what is going on around them (-50 to orientation rolls). The daydream will not be horrifying, if that result is desired use a *Nightmare* spell.

2—Dream I (FM) Target has a dream relating to one topic decided upon by the caster at the time the spell was casted. The Dream occurs during the target's next sleep/meditation period. The dream will not be horrifying; if that result is desired use a *Nightmare* spell.

3—Sleep (FM) Target is placed into a magical sleep for the duration of the spell, after which he reverts into normal, non-magical sleep. During the magical sleep, he may only be "awakened" by appropriate magic, herb, or extreme pain.

5—Nightmare I (I) The target dreams of important situations/events involving him that may occur in the near future. Since every potential situation has many possible outcomes, the target will only see one outcome, the worst possible one. Thus the name "Doom Sayer" has been attached to an individual that has been exposed to this spell. These dreams manifest themselves as nightmares during the target's next sleep/meditation period.

6—Dream II (FM) As *Dream I* except the dream may involve two topics.

7—Sleepwalking (FM) The target has a 30% chance of getting up and wandering off during each of his sleep/meditation periods. If "awakened" during his jaunt he will not remember anything and will be completely confused.

8—Dream III (FM) As *Dream I* except the dream may involve three topics.

9—Nightmare II (I) As *Nightmare I* except the target has "nightmares" during his next two sleep/meditation periods.

10—Undream (FD) Target does not dream and may not utilize any "Dream" spells for the duration of this spell.

11—Sleep True (FM) As *Sleep* except affects 1 target/lvl.

12—Dream IV (FM) As *Dream I* except the dream may involve four topics.

13—Dream Killer I (FM) During the target's next sleep/meditation period, he will encounter and fight to the death a type I Demon in his dream. Any damage taken during the dream is actually taken by the target physical body. Note that, unless target has the Dream State spell list, he will be naked and unarmed against this foe. Target may use any material at hand and has his PPs and spells available. Any wounds taken during the dream will appear on the target's body as they occur; the target's body will toss and turn. Until the death duel is concluded one way or another, the target may only be "awakened" by spells or herbs. If "awakened" before the duel is concluded, the duel will start over again during the target's next sleep/meditation period. **Option 1:** The GM may wish to allow the target to have one of his items during the duel. **Option 2:** The GM may wish to conclude the duel upon unconsciousness rather than death.

14—Nightmare III (I) As *Nightmare I* except the target has "nightmares" during his next three sleep/meditation periods.

15—Dream Death (FM) Target is cursed and may never dream again until curse is removed, the caster dies, or the caster cancels the curse.

16—Dream V (FM) As *Dream I* except the dream may involve five topics.

17—Dream Killer III (FM) As *Killer Dream I* except the target must fight a type II Demon or a type III Demon. Roll 1D100: 1-70 = type II; 71-100 = type III.

18—Dream Field (F) Each round that a target (except caster) is in the area of effect, he must make a RR; if he fails, he will fall asleep and dream continuously. He may be awakened by appropriate magic, herbs, or extreme pain.

19—Nightmare IV (I) As *Nightmare I* except the target has "nightmares" during his next four sleep/meditation periods.

20—Dream Shifting (FM) During the target's next sleep/meditation period, the target's dreams are influenced by all the dreams of all beings within 10'R/(lvl of caster). The dreams are intermingled and very difficult for the target to comprehend. The GM may wish to make real certain effects/injuries that result in these types of dreams.

25—Dream Killer True (FM) As *Killer Dream* except the target must fight a type III-VI Demon. Roll 1D100: 1-40 = type III; 41-70 = type IV; 71-90 = type V; 91-100 = type VI.

30—Nightmare True (I) As *Nightmare I* except the target has "nightmares" for a number of sleep/meditation periods equal to the caster's level divided by 2 (round down).

50—Dream Field True (FM) As *Dream Field* except the duration is Permanent.

8.83 DREAM LORE (Dream Lord Base)

	Area of Effect	Duration	Range
1—Awaken *	1 target	P	touch
2—Dream Lore I	1 target	varies	touch
3—Dream Travel I	1 target	1 day/lvl	touch
4—			
5—Dream Path	Dream Travel	3 rnds	self
6—Dream Share I	Dream Travel	3 rnds	self
7—			
8—Substances I	1 target	1 day/lvl	touch
9—			
10—Dream Gate	6'x3'x1"	1 min	10'
11—Dream Lore II	1 target	varies	touch
12—Dream Travel II	1 target	1 wk/lvl	touch
13—			
14—			
15—Dream Share V	Dream Travel	3 rnds	self
16—Substances II	1 target	1 wk/lvl	touch
17—			
18—			
19—Dream Lore True	1 target	varies	touch
20—Dream Travel True	1 target	1 month/lvl	touch
25—Dream Share True	Dream Travel	3 rnds	self
30—Substances True	1 target	1 month/lvl	touch
50—Dream Gate True	10'x6'x1"	10 minutes	10'

1—Awaken (US*) Target is immediately awaken from a dream state. This spell will not revive someone in a coma unless the coma is the direct cause of dream world travel.

2—Dream Lore I (I) Caster learns general nature and history of 1 dream as well as being provided with the dreams parameters for future use. (e.g., dream is recurring nightmare of your adventure into the catacombs of Sirearlliff. I've never been to those catacombs. Ah, but you will go, your inner-self already knows.)

3—Dream Travel I (MF) Allows the target to enter into their dreams via mental transference. Your character is there in a pseudo-physical form. You come into the world with only your pseudo-body and your mental capabilities. Nothing else may be brought into this world by means of this spell. This form can be killed causing the target to lose 1 life level in their physical form. Lose enough life levels and you can die for real. The biggest threat to dream world adventuring is the lack of attention to your real body (left alone long enough it will die from starvation), outside forces still affect the body (nature forces such as heat, rain, snow, etc), and of course the threat of predators (animals, monsters, man, etc). If your real body dies while you are in a dream world you are stuck there and may never return to the physical world. Awaken from a dream travel session and subsequent return to the same dream world may or may not put you back in the same position you started in, left in or never have been in. Dreams are strange and who really knows how they operate.

5—Dream Path (I) Allows caster to locate the dream path to any dream world that has been previously dream lored.

6—Dream Share I (U) When Dream Travel is cast within 3 rounds it allows the caster to put two targets into the dream world.

8—Substances I (U) Allows the caster to slow down the metabolism of the target's body for the duration of the spell. Target's body does not require nourishment for the duration of the spell at which time normal aging process once again takes over. This spell by it's vary nature only works while the target is in the dream world (the source of nourishment that keeps the body alive) and consciousness voids this spell.

10—Dream Gate (F) Allows the physical entry into a dream world via a magical gateway. Physical items may be transferred into the dream worlds provided the following restrictions are applied: **1)** High Tech items convert to either magical oriented items of the same type in magical worlds or vice versus. (e.g., a flamethrower is brought through a dream gate into a magical oriented world. The flamethrower would be converted into a staff of fireballs with the same number of charges as the flamethrower has and vice versa for a magical item entering into a technical world.) **2)** Lower tech items may always be brought over as is. **3)** Lower magical items may always be brought over as is.

11—Dream Lore II (I) As *Dream Lore I* except caster also learns general enchantments/magics of the dream world. For example: no magic, limited magic (only up to 10th level), normal magic (no restrictions), etc.

12—Dream Travel II (MF) As *Dream Travel I* except duration is increased to 1 week/level of caster.

15—Dream Share V (U) As *Dream Share I* except allows five targets to enter into the dream world.

16—Substances II (U) As *Substances I* except duration is increased to 1 week/level of caster.

19—Dream Lore True (I) As *Dream Lore I* except also learns specific details of dream worlds magical/technical base. (names of spell lists and spells, names of tech weapons, etc.)

20—Dream Travel True (MF) As *Dream Travel I* except duration is increased to 1 month/level of caster.

25—Dream Share True (U) As *Dream Share I* except allows 1 targets/level of the caster to enter into the dream world.

30—Substances True (U) As *Substances I* except duration is increased to 1 month/level of caster.

50—Dream Gate True (F) As *Dream Gate* except duration is increased to 10 minutes and the size of the gate is increased to 10'x6'x1".

Dream Lord Base Spell Lists

8.84 DREAM STATE (Dream Lord Base)

NOTE 1: *Items of the dream state that are moved from their place of creation have a ever shifting form. Non-intelligent items remain non-intelligent, non-living remain non-living, intelligent beings remain intelligent, living remain living, etc.*

NOTE 2: *Items of one dream state that are moved from the place of their creation will not have bonuses in any other dream world or normal worlds of physical reality. These items will just appear to be shifting masses of matter. Living beings/beasts which are subject to this will indeed feel the forces of nature pulling at them to put them back in to their natural state (the state which exists only on the dream world of their creation). The beings/beasts will be in agony, being torn apart but not dying. Such an item/being/beast will fade 1 round after the spell which was affecting it has expired.*

NOTE 3: *"Created" Dream State items/objects are basically random. Normally the caster does not understand the physical laws that are operating in the dream world. GMs should allow the caster to make spell mastery attempts to obtain those items they wish to create. However, the items form and the method of using it can be familiar or very unfamiliar.*

	Area of Effect	Duration	Range
1—Detect Dream State I*	1 target	—	20'
2—			
3—Dream State I	varies	10 min/lvl	20'
4—Dream Pattern	DS item/object	P	touch
5—Dream Beast I	type I beast	10 min/lvl	100'
6—Dream Vision	target	10 min/lvl	touch
7—Dream Familiar I	type I beast	2 hours	100'
8—Dream State II	varies	10 min/lvl	20'
9—Dream Adaptation I	DS item/object	10 min/lvl	touch
10—Dream Companion I	1 being	10 min/lvl	100'
11—Dream Beast II	type II beast	10 min/lvl	100'
12—Dream Pattern True	DS being/beast	P	20'
13—Dream Familiar II	type II beast	2 hours	100'
14—Dream State III	varies	10 min/lvl	20'
15—Dream Adaptation II	DS item/object	10 min/lvl	touch
16—Dream Companion II	1 being	10 min/lvl	100'
17—Dream Beast III	type III beast	10 min/lvl	100'
18—			
19—Dream Familiar III	type III beast	2 hours	100'
20—Dream State True	varies	10 min/lvl	20'
25—Dream Beast True	varies	10 min/lvl	100'
30—Dream Adaptation True	DS item	10 min/lvl	touch
50—Dream Mastery True	varies	P	varies

1—Detect Dream State I (I*) Allows the caster to detect if an item is composed of dream state reality.

3—Dream State I (F) Allows the caster to create an item or object (non-living) which has +5 bonus. Bonus is only useable in the dream world in which the item was created. This spell allows the caster, who has entered a dream world through non-physical means, to create items that will function normally within the dream world.

4—Dream Pattern (I) Allows the caster to store patterns of items or objects made in a dream world. This allows the caster to recreate the item or object in another dream world or in the physical world. Note that the object may be duplicated but it may not work as it did in the dream world, this it totally up to the GM and his world scheme.

5—Dream Beast I (FM) Allows the caster to summon a type 1 dream beast. The dream beast will be loyal to caster and obey his commands. The dream beast is non-intelligent. If the dream beast is killed while under the influence of this spell the caster suffers an "A" stun crit and operates at -30 for 1 day.

6—Dream Vision (U) Allows the caster to see all dream state items clearly and in their true form. Everything else that is not of the dream state will appear blurry and will operate with negative modifier based upon the percentage of items that are blurry. (e.g., if only one item is of the dream state and the rest are of the normal world then the negative mod could be -90 to -99 or if the reverse is true than the negative mod could be -01 to -10.)

7—Dream Familiar I (M) Allows the caster to attune himself to a dream beast that he has summoned (called his dream familiar). The caster must cast this spell on the dream beast once/day for 1 week (concentrating for 2 hour per day). The caster can then control the familiar and view the world through its senses by concentrating on it (must be within 50'/lvl). If the dream familiar is killed the caster will be at -25 on all actions for 2 weeks. When the caster leaves the dream world where he has attuned to a familiar, the bond between the two is severed, the caster and familiar feel an emptiness and both operate at -10 for 1 day. If the caster returns to a dream world where he has had a familiar and the familiar sees the caster, the bond between the two must be reestablished but any rolls are modified by +30.

8—Dream State II (F) As *Dream State I* except the bonus is +10.

9—Dream Adaptation I (F) Allows the caster to create *Dream State I* items or objects whose patterns have been stored a *Dream Pattern* spell. Such an item receives a +5 bonus in the non-dream world or any other dream world. The dream item will have the same appearance in this world as it did in the dream world of its creation. This spell may also be used to allow a summoned type I dreambeast / familiar to remain alive outside of it's own dream world.

10—Dream Companion I (FM) Allows the caster to summons a 1st level dream world companion (NPC). This companion is under the influence of a "quest" type spell. The dream world companion may or may not like the idea of being your companion. He will assist and help the caster in all endeavors for the duration of the spell provided he is not endangered. A dream world companion who is endangered by the caster may make a RR at +30 to resist the caster's commands. If the dream world companion is successful, the spell's influence is broken.

11—Dream Beast II (FM) As *Dream Beast I* except a type II dream beast is summoned.

12—Dream Pattern True (I) As *Dream Pattern* except works on living dream state beings and beast.

13—Dream Familiar II (FM) As *Dream Familiar I* except a type II dream beast is attuned to the caster.

14—Dream State III (F) As *Dream State I* except the bonus is +15.

15—Dream Adaptation II (F) As *Dream Adaptation I* except Dream State II items, objects, type II dream beasts/familiars or 1st level dream world companions are affected.

16—Dream Companion II (FM) As *Dream Companion I* except 2nd level dream being is summoned.

17—Dream Beast III (FM) As *Dream Beast I* except a type III dream beast is summoned.

19—Dream Familiar III (FM) As *Dream Familiar I* except a type III dream beast is attuned to.

20—Dream State True (F) As *Dream State I* except the bonus is +5 per every 4 levels of the caster.

25—Dream Beast True (FM) As *Dream Beast I* except a type IV or type V or type VI beast may be summoned.

        01-50 type VI dream beast

        51-85 type V dream beast

        86+   type VI dream beast

30—Dream Adaptation True (F) As *Dream Adaptation I* except may affect any level dream state item, object, beast or companion.

50—Dream Mastery True (F) As *Dream Companion I* except the level of the dream world companion is +1 lvl for every 3 levels of the caster **and** the companion is under "True Quest" restrictions and will always be loyal to the caster until released. Once released the companion may react as the GM see fits.

9.0 ARCANE NAVIGATORS' BASE SPELL LIST

WAY OF THE NAVIGATOR

	Area of Effect	Duration	Range
1—Star Paths	self	C	self
2—Rain Prediction	self	—	10 miles/lvl
3—Water Finding	self	—	1000'/lvl
4—Resist Elements	self	10 min/lvl	self
5—Storm Prediction	self	—	10 miles/lvl
6—Path-Finding	self	C	1000'/lvl
7—Food Finding	self	—	1000'/lvl
8—Weather Prediction	self	—	10 miles/lvl
9—Star Lights	10'/lvl R	10 min/lvl	touch
10—Wind Call	one ship	10 min/lvl(C)	touch
11—Shelter Finding	self	—	1000'/lvl
12—Weather Pred. (3 days)	self	—	10 miles/lvl
13—Unfog	10'/lvl R	10 min/lvl(C)	touch
14—Calm Water	10'/lvl R	10 min/lvl(C)	touch
15—Current Command	varies	1 hr/lvl(C)	100'/lvl
16—Weather Pred. (5 days)	self	—	10 miles/lvl
17—Wind Mastery	50'/lvl R	10 min/lvl(C)	self
18—Whirlwind	10'R	C	self
19—Clear Skies	1 mile R	10 min/lvl(C)	self
20—Destination Sail	1 vessel	varies(C)	touch
25—Weather Pred. (30 days)	self	—	10 miles/lvl
30—Locating	varies	10 min/lvl(C)	1 mi/lvl
50—Crystal Ship	1 vessel	varies(C)	100'

2,5,8,12,16,17,19,25—As the spells of the same names on the Open Channeling spell list, Weather Ways.

1—Star Paths (I) Caster (on a clear night, when stars are visible) gains perfect directional and distance sense; he cannot be lost.

3—Water Finding (I) Caster can locate any natural source of running water, exposed groundwater, etc. (must exceed 1 gallon); caster also learns approximate size and quantity of the source.

4—Resist Elements (D) Protects caster from natural heat up to 200°F., natural cold down to -20°F., and gives a plus 10 to RR vs. heat and cold.

6—Path-finding (I) Caster learns the location(s) of any path(s), river(s), current(s), Gulf Stream(s), etc., within area of effect. Must be used outdoors.

7—Food Finding (I) Caster learns location, type, and approximate quantity of edible food — either dead animal matter, or any plant(s); food source must exceed 1 pound.

9—Star Lights (E) Caster causes the area within the radius to glow with a soft light from the stars. Indoors or out, the full starry sky will be visible to those within the radius. If the area outside the spell effect is more brightly lit than the area within the radius, the affected area will appear to be immersed in shadow or fog from the outside.

10—Wind Call (F) Caster causes a breeze to come forth which will fill the sails of a ship. Once set, the direction of the breeze will not change.

11—Shelter Finding (I) Caster learns location, type, and approximate size of any water-proof, covered space exceeding 125 cu'; shelter must have an entryway exceeding 2' radius bordering on open air.

13—Unfog (F) Completely dissipates all fog within the Area of Effect for the duration of the spell, then natural conditions take over.

14—Calm Water (F) Water within the area of effect is calmed; waves are cut by 30' in the center and less towards the perimeter.

15—Current Command (E) This spell creates a current in a body of water that can either propel a ship faster or impede a ship's progress. The ship's speed is increased or decreased by 1 MPH/Level of the caster (to a maximum of 25 MPH).

18—Whirlwind (E) Creates a whirlwind about the caster; it moves with the caster and is 10' in radius. No missile attacks can penetrate it and any movement or melee is cut by 80%.

20—Destination Sail (E) The caster may command the body of water to carry the target vessel to a specified known destination. the caster will be entranced for the duration of the journey. The vessel's speed is increased by 1 mph/level of the caster. The destination must be a place which is in contact with the water (a bank, coast, etc.).

30—Locating (P) Gives the direction and distance to any specific place or object with which the caster is familiar or that the caster has had described in detail to him.

50—Crystal Ship (F) As *Destination Sail*, except that the caster also causes any type of naval vessel (of up to 100 tons displacement) to form from the minerals in the sea and be bound together by magic so that the ship's hull is rated Strong. This Crystal Ship will function as if fully crewed, even if only the caster is aboard.

Coven Base Spell Lists

10.0 ARCANE COVEN BASE SPELL LISTS

10.1 ALLUREMENT (Arcane Coven Base)

	Area of Effect	Duration	Range
1—Presence	self	10 min/lvl	self
2—Charm Opp. Sex I	1 target	1 hr/lvl	100'
3—Self-Aura	self	10 min/lvl	self
4—Charm Plant	1 target	1 hr/lvl	100'
5—Seduction	1 target	V	10'
6—Charm Opp. Sex II	3 targets	1 hr/lvl	100'
7—Suggestion	1 target	V	10'
8—Charm Animal	1 target	1 hr/lvl	100'
9—Charm Same Sex	1 target	1 hr/lvl	100'
10—Charm Opp. Sex V	5 targets	1 hr/lvl	100'
11—Presence	self	10 min/lvl	self
12—Charm True	1 target	1 hr/lvl	100'
13—Great Aura	self	10 min/lvl	100'
14—Charm Opp. Sex VII	7 targets	1 hr/lvl	100'
15—Geas	1 target	V	10'
20—Charm Opp. Sex X	10 targets	1 hr/lvl	100'
25—True Geas	1 target	V	10'
30—Alkar	self	10 min/lvl	self
50—Charming Mastery	self	1 rnd/lvl	self

1—Presence (U) Adds 10 to the Presence stat (not the bonus) and 20 to the Appearance of the caster (to a maximum of 100). The stat increase will not affect the caster's PPs.

2—Charm Opposite Sex I (M) One humanoid target of the opposite sex believes the caster is a good friend.

3—Self-Aura (F) Causes a bright aura about the caster, making him appear more powerful and subtracting 10 from all attacks.

4—Charm Plant (M) As *Charm Opposite Sex I*, but 1 sentient plant is affected.

5—Seduction (M) Caster emotionally, sensually, and/or sexually manipulates one humanoid target (emotional attachment may result).

6—Charm Opposite Sex III (M) As *Charm Opposite Sex I* except up to 3 targets affected.

7—Suggestion (M) Target will follow a single suggested act that is not completely alien (e.g., suicide, etc.).

8—Charm Animal (M) As *Charm Opposite Sex I* except 1 animal is affected.

9—Charm Same Sex (M) As above, but affects humanoid of same sex.

10—Charm Opposite Sex V (M) As *Charm Opposite Sex I* except 5 targets may be affected.

11—Presence (U) As above, but 20 is added to Presence and 40 is added to Appearance (to a maximum of 101).

12—Charm True (M) As *Charm Opposite Sex I* except affects any sentient being.

13—Great Aura (F) As *Self-Aura* except 20 is subtracted from all attacks.

14—Charm Opposite Sex VII (M) As *Charm Opposite Sex I* except up to 7 targets affected.

15—Geas (M) Target is given one task, failure results in a penalty determined by the Gamemaster.

20—Charm Opposite Sex X (M) As *Charm Opposite Sex I* except but affects up to 10 targets.

25—True Geas (M) As *Geas*, but failure results in death.

30—Alkar (F) As *Self-Aura*, except caster seems like a demi-god and the subtraction is 30 (-30 from all attacks).

50—Charming Mastery (M) Caster can use one spell/rnd from this list.

10.2 HOUSEHOLD MAGIC (Arcane Coven Base)

	Area of Effect	Duration	Range
1—Cleansing	1 object	—	50'
2—Airing	10'x10'x10'	—	50'
3—Dusting	10'x10'x10'	—	50'
4—Polishing	10'x10'x10'	—	10'
5—Straightening	10'x10'x10'	—	50'
6—Cleaning I	10'x10'x10'	—	100'
7—Repel Small Vermin	10'x10'x10'	—	10'
8—Cleaning II	20'x10'x10'	—	200'
9—Gathering	100'R	—	50'
10—Cleaning II	30'x10'x10'	—	300'
11—Sterilize	10'x10'x10'	—	10'
12—Repair	1 small item	P	touch
13—Cleaning IV	40'x10'x10'	—	400'
14—Repel Large Vermin	10'x10'x10'	—	10'
15—Cleaning V	50'x10'x10'	—	500'
20—Cleaning X	100'x10'x10'	—	1000'
25—Exterminate	10'x10'x10'	—	10'
30—Cleaning True	10'x10'x10'/lvl	—	100'/lvl
50—Cleaning Mastery	self	1 rnd/lvl	self

1—Cleansing (F) Completely cleans one object of the caster's choice.

2—Airing (F) A gentle breeze freshens the air in area of effect, drying up moisture and getting rid of all bad smells. Works only if fresh air is available.

3—Dusting (F) Causes dust and grit to swirl together and fly outside.

4—Polishing (F) Polishes all items in area of effect, also removes corrosion.

5—Straightening (F) All items in area of effect are "put in their proper places." Caster determines proper place within area of effect. No item more than 50 lbs.

6—Cleaning I (F) As any or all above spells simultaneously, plus all walls, floors, dishes, clothes, windows, etc. are completely cleaned. Molds, mildew, micro-organisms and vermin remain unaffected.

7—Repel Small Vermin (M) All zero and first level creatures, determined by the caster to be pests, leave the area of effect. First level vermin get a RR; zero level vermin do not.

8—Cleaning II (F) As *Cleaning I* except for area of effect and Range.

9—Gathering (F) All pieces of a specific item within area of effect are gathered together in a pile. The pile must be in area of effect.

10—Cleaning III (F) As *Cleaning I* except for area of effect and Range.

11—Sterilize (M) All zero level creatures (except sentient beings) and things (including molds and micro-organisms) in area of effect are instantly dead; no RR. Does not act as a "Cure Disease."

12—Repair (F) Caster may mend a single break in a small (dagger-sized or less) metal object, and multiple breaks, rips, or shatters in a larger (10 lbs. or less) ceramic, wooden, stone, cloth, or leather object. The object repaired cannot be magical and all component parts must be present (within 10'R).

13—Cleaning IV (F) As *Cleaning I* except for area of effect and Range.

14—Repel Large Vermin (M) All pests of 3rd Lvl or less must leave area of effect. Zero level things do not get a RR.

15—Cleaning V (F) As *Cleaning I* except for area of effect and Range.

20—Cleaning X (F) As *Cleaning I* except for area of effect and Range.

25—Exterminate (M) As *Sterilize* except first level creatures may also be affected. First level creatures do get a RR, zero level do not.

30—Cleaning True (F) As *Cleaning I* except for area of effect and Range.

50—Cleaning Mastery (F) Caster can use one spell/rnd from this list.

10.3 BARRIER WAYS (Arcane Coven Base)

	Area of Effect	Duration	Range
1—Knock	1 lock	—	touch
2—Lock	1 lock	—	50'
3—Detect Traps	5'R	C	50'
4—Wall of Air	10'x10'x3'	1 min/lvl(C)	50'
5—Traplore	1 trap	—	touch
6—Detect Portals	5'R	C	50'
7—Spring Trap	1 trap	—	10'
8—Wall of Water	10'x10'x1'	1 min/lvl(C)	50'
9—Jamming	1 door	P	10'
10—Weakening	1 door	P	10'
11—Wall of Wood	10'x20'x2"	1 min/lvl(C)	50'
12—Magic Lock	1 door	1 min/lvl	10'
13—Wall of Earth	10'x10'x(3'-1')	1 min/lvl(C)	50'
14—Undoor	10'x10'x6"	P	10'
15—Wall of Ice	10'x10'x(2'-1')	1 min/lvl(C)	50'
20—Wall of Stone	10'x10'x1'	1 min/lvl(C)	50'
25—Portal	3'x6'x(3"/lvl)	P	10'
30—Spell Wall	10'x10'; plane	1 rnd/lvl(C)	10'
50—Wall of Force	10'x20'x1'	1 rnd/lvl(C)	10'

1—Knock (F) Caster unlocks (80% chance) a non-magically locked door, lid, etc. by loudly knocking on the locked item's surface. A GM may wish to assign the normal difficulty modifiers from the Static Maneuver Table.

2—Lock (F) Caster causes one lock to become locked (the lock is just normally locked and can be opened normally).

3—Detect Traps (P) Caster has a 75% chance of detecting any active traps; caster can concentrate on a 5'R area each round. This may be modified by certain traps (difficulty, accessibility, magical, etc.)

4—Wall of Air (E) Creates a wall of dense churning air; cuts all movements and attacks through it by 50%.

5—Traplore (I) Gives caster +20 on disarming the trap analyzed, and +10 to anyone to whom he describes the trap.

6—Detect Portals (P) As *Detect Traps*, but doors, openings, passages, etc. are revealed 75% of the time.

7—Spring Trap (F) Caster causes one trap to go off.

8—Wall of Water (E) Creates a wall of water; cuts movement and attacks through it by 80%.

9—Jamming (F) Causes a door to expand and jam into its frame (roll 1-100 for severity, ranging from slightly stuck to unopenable).

10—Weakening (F) Reduces the inherent strength of a door by 50%.

11—Wall of Wood (E) Creates a wall of wood; it must rest on a solid surface. It can be burned through (50 hits for a 2'R hole), chopped through (20 man-rounds), or toppled if one end is not against a wall or buttress of some kind.

12—Magic Lock (F) A door (or container) can be magically "locked"; the door can be broken normally or the spell can be dispelled, but otherwise the door cannot be opened.

13—Wall of Earth (E) As *Wall of Wood*, except wall is up to 10'x10'x(3' at base, 1' at top) of packed earth; and it can only be dug through (10 man-rounds at top, 30 man-rounds at base).

14—Undoor (F) Will vaporize a non-magic door up to 10'x10'x6" (if the door is thicker than 6" it will vaporize the closest 6").

15—Wall of Ice (E) As *Wall of Wood*, except wall is up to 10'x10'x(2' at base, 1' at top); it can be melted through (100 hits), chipped through (50 man-rounds), or toppled if not supported.

20—Wall of Stone (E) As *Wall of Wood*, but it is of stone and can be chipped through in 200 man-rounds (1'R hole).

25—Portal (F) Creates an opening up to 3'x6', with a depth of 3"/lvl, through any inanimate material.

30—Spell Wall (D) Creates a shimmering 10'x10' plane. Any spell passing through this plane must first make a RR successfully in order to resolve the spell effect. The attack level of the RR is the level of the caster of the Spell Wall and the defender level is the level of caster of the spell passing through the Spell Wall. If this RR is successful, then the spell procedure proceeds normally.

50—Wall of Force (E) Creates transparent barrier that is absolutely impassable by anyone or anything (GM discretion).

10.4 BREWING LORE (Arcane Coven Base)

NOTE: *All of these Brewing Spells require that the appropriate equipment be available for the entire duration.*

	Area of Effect	Duration	Range
1—Work Liquids	self	24 hours	self
2—Identify Drug	1 sample	—	1'
3—Brew Alcohol	1 cu'/lvl	1 week	10'
4—Identify Poison	1 sample	—	1'
5—Brew Stimulants	self	1 hour	self
6—Brew Potion I	1 dose	24 hours	self
7—Brew Minor Poison	self	1 hr/lvl	self
8—Brew Euphorics/Narcotics	self	1 hour	self
9—Brew Healing Drugs	self	1 hour	self
10—Brew Potion III	1 dose	24 hours	self
11—Brew Hallucinogens	self	1 hour	self
12—Brew Acids	self	1 hr/lvl	self
13—Brew Major Poison	self	1 hr/lvl	self
14—Brew Potion V	1 dose	24 hours	self
15—Brew Truth Drug	self	1 hour	self
16—Magic Cauldron I	cauldron	1 hr/lvl	touch
17—Brew Potion VII	1 dose	24 hours	self
18—Brew Antidote	self	1 hour	self
19—Magic Cauldron II	cauldron	1 hr/lvl	touch
20—Brew Potion X	1 dose	24 hours	self
25—True Brewing	self	1 hour	self
30—Poisons True	self	1 hr/lvl	self
50—Brewing Mastery	self	1 rnd/level	self

1—Work Liquids (F) Allows caster to work with non-magic liquids.

2—Identify Drug (I) Caster knows the origins, purity, and general worth of one drug sample. Any impurity will be known.

3—Brew Alcohol (F) Caster causes some base to rapidly ferment into an alcoholic beverage (beer, wine, etc.). This spell can also be used to distill whiskey, brandy, etc .

4—Identify Poisons (I) As *Identify Drug* except a poison is known.

5—Brew Stimulants (U) Allows caster to extract the stimulant essence from an herb (e.g., Pekoe Tea, Elben's Basket, Zulsendura, etc.).

6—Brew Potion I (F) Allows caster to brew one dose of a potion that can have a first level spell imbedded in it.

7—Brew Minor Poison (U) Allows caster to prepare, handle, and contain a known poison of up to tenth level potency (attack level).

8—Brew Euphoric/Narcotics (U) As *Brew Stimulants* except caster may extract the essence of a euphoric or narcotic herb (e.g., Rumareth, Breldiar, Grapeleaf, Arunya, Brorkwilb, Galenas, etc.).

9—Brew Healing Drug (U) As *Brew Stimulants*, except caster may extract the essence of an herb that heals hit points or analgesics, decongestants, and anaesthetics (e.g., Aloe, Thurl, Arkasu, Silraen, Margath, Maiana, Caranan, etc.).

10—Brew Potion III (F) As *Brew Potion I* except a third level spell or less may be imbedded in the potion.

Coven Base Spell Lists

11—Brew Hallucinogens (U) As *Brew Stimulants* except caster may extract the essence from an hallucinogenic herb (e.g., Gort, Hoak-Foerr, Magic Mushrooms, etc.)

12—Brew Acids (U) As *Brew Minor Poison*, but caster may work with acids.

13—Brew Major Poison (U) As *Brew Minor Poison* except allows caster to work with poisons up to twentieth level potency.

14—Brew Potion V (F) As *Brew Potion I* except a fifth level spell or less may be imbedded in the potion.

15—Brew Truth Drug (U) As *Brew Stimulant*, but caster brews a drug which causes the imbiber to tell the whole, naked truth for one hour.

16—Magic Cauldron I (F) Caster may "brew" any spell on this list at a rate of 1/hour.

17—Brew Potion VII (F) As *Brew Potion I* except a seventh level spell or less may be imbedded in the potion.

18—Brew Antidote (U) As *Brew Stimulants* except caster may extract the Essence of an antidote (e.g., Argsbargies, Eldaana, Menelar, etc.).

19—Magic Cauldron II (F) As *Magic Cauldron I* except two doses/hour may be brewed.

20—Brew Potion X (F) As *Brew Potion I* except a tenth level spell or less may be imbedded in the potion.

25—True Brewing (U) As *Brew Stimulants* except the Essence of any herb may be extracted by the caster.

30—Poisons True (U) As *Brew Minor Poisons* except caster may work with any poison.

50—Brewing Mastery (F) Caster can use one spell/round from this list.

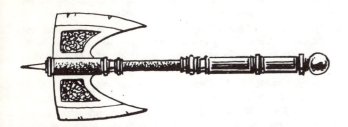

10.5 HEARTH MAGIC (Arcane Coven Base)

	Area of Effect	Duration	Range
1—Food Preparation	1 course	V	touch
2—Food Preservation	1 ration	1 week	touch
3—Food Dehydration	1 ration	V	touch
4—Sustenance Purification	1 ration	P	touch
5—Water Production I	1 ration	P	10'
6—Food Production I	1 ration	P	10'
7—Nutrient Conjures	1 ration	P	10'
8—Water Production II	2 rations	P	10'
9—Food Production II	2 rations	P	10'
10—Cookery	1 course	V	10"
11—Water Production III	3 rations	P	10'
12—Food Production III	3 rations	P	10'
13—Food Preserv. True	1 ration/lvl	1 week	10'
14—Food Dehydr. True	1 ration/lvl	V	10'
15—Water Production V	5 rations	P	10'
16—Food Production V	5 rations	P	10'
17—Sustenance Purif. True	1 ration/lvl	P	10'
18—Herb Mastery	1 herb	P	touch
19—Water Production True	1 ration/lvl	P	10'
20—Food Production True	1 ration/lvl	V	10'
25—True Cookery	1 course/lvl	V	10'
30—Banquet	varies	5 min/lvl	50'
50—Cooking Mastery	self	1 rnd./lvl	self

1—Food Preparation (F) Gives caster +20 to cooking (Cookery Roll) and +10 to anyone to whom she describes the preparation. Also chills or warms food to the proper serving temperature.

2—Food Preservation (F) This spell perfectly preserves one day's worth of food (1 ration) for one week. Also instantly "freshens" any slightly "turned" or spoiled food., e.g., wilted lettuce.

3—Food Dehydration (F) This spell removes most of the water from one day's worth of food, reducing the weight of the food by 80%-90%. The food will be edible only after water has been added to it (approximately 2 quarts for 1 ration). As long as the food is dry the food remains dehydrated and the normal spoilage rate (not preserved rate) is decreased by ten times.

4—Sustenance Purification (F) This spell neutralizes abnormal diseases, poisons, and other similar substances in one day's worth (1 ration) of food and/or water. It will not neutralize a poison or similar substance that is a natural part of the food (i.e. it will not neutralize the natural alkaloids in certain mushrooms). Special or magical poisons/diseases might be allowed a RR.

5—Water Production I (F) Caster can produce sufficient water in any available receptacle to supply any person for one day (1 ration).

6—Food Production I (F) Caster can produce sufficient food from the surrounding area to feed one hearty appetite for one day (1 ration). This food still needs to be prepared.

7—Nutrient Conjures (F) Caster can produce one loaf of waybread that weighs half of a pound and will support one being for one day; the loaf will lose potency in one month.

8—Water Production II (F) As *Water Production I* except produces 2 rations of water.

9—Food Production II (F) As *Food Production I* except produces 2 rations of food.

10—Cookery (F/I) Automatically successfully prepares one course of food, taking only half the normal preparation time. In addition to normal cooking, caster also detects spoiled or poisoned food, prepared and/or neutralized dangerous herbs and food ingredients, or may prepare minor poisons for insinuation in food.

11—Water Production III (F) As *Water Production I* except produces 3 rations of water.

12—Food Production III (F) As *Food Production I* except produces 3 rations of food.

13—Food Preservation True (F) As *Food Preservation I* except preserves 1 ration/level

14—Food Dehydration True (F) As *Food Dehydration* except dehydrates 1 ration/lvl

15—Water Production V (F) As *Water Production I* except produces 5 rations of water.

16—Food Production V (F) As *Food Production I* except produces 5 rations of food.

17—Sustenance Purification True (F) As *Sustenance Purification* except purifies 1 ration/lvl.

18—Herb Mastery (F) Caster can double the potency of any one herb/spice (growing or dead); spell may be employed but once per herb.

19—Water Production True (F) As *Water Production I* except produces 1 ration/lvl of food.

20—Food Production True (F) As *Food Production I* except produces 1 ration/lvl of food.

25—True Cookery (F/I) As *Cookery* except may prepare 1 course/lvl.

30—Banquet (F) Caster creates a banquet table complete with chairs, silver eatingware, crystal glasses, pitchers and bowls, and a wondrous dinner of wines, appetizers, gourmet foods, fruits, and desserts. The table will be initially set with beverages and introductory dishes in place, and then each course will be served by barely visible spirits as the previous course is finished. If a selection is refused, one different but comparable will be served. The serving spirits can be requested to bring special favorites. At the end of the duration, any leftovers disappear along with the spirits, table, chairs, cutlery, etc. This spell can serve up to one person per two levels of the spell caster.

50—Cooking Mastery (F) Caster can use one spell/round from this list.

10.6 WAX MAGIC (Arcane Coven Base)

NOTE: *A GM may wish to make the durations of these spells longer, so that the candles can be found/purchased and used by characters other than the creator (e.g., days or weeks instead of hours).*

	Area of Effect	Duration	Range
1—Wax Working	self	24 hours	self
2—Wax Lore	1 wax item	—	touch
3—Enchant Wax	wax or 1 item	V	self
4—White Candle (1st)	1 candle	1 hour	self
5—Lesser Wax Fruit (sleep)	1 wax fruit	1 hour	self
6—Grey Candle (smoke)	1 candle	2 hours	self
7—Brown Candle (2nd)	1 candle	2 hours	self
8—Burgundy Candle (intox.)	1 candle	3 hours	self
9—Red Candle (3rd)	1 candle	3 hours	self
10—Poison Wax Fruit	1 wax fruit	4 hours	self
11—Orange Candle (4th)	1 candle	4 hours	self
12—Dun Candle (sleep)	1 candle	5 hours	self
13—Yellow Candle (5th)	1 candle	5 hours	self
14—Wax Mask	1 wax mask	6 hours	self
15—Green Candle (6th)	1 candle	6 hours	self
16—Turquoise Candle (poison)	1 candle	7 hours	self
17—Blue Candle (7th)	1 candle	7 hours	self
18—Wax Doll	1 wax doll	8 hours	self
19—Purple Candle (8th)	1 candle	8 hours	self
20—Black Candle (curse)	1 candle	9 hours	self
25—Silver Candle (10th)	1 candle	10 hours	self
30—Wax-Shape	V	12 hours	self
50—Candle Mastery	1 candle	V	self

1—Wax Working (F) Allows caster to work with non-magical wax.

2—Wax Lore (I) Caster can ascertain the exact nature and origin of one wax item. This includes who made the item.

3—Enchant Wax (F) Allows caster to prepare wax sufficient to enchant one magical waxen item. In order to cast any Wax Magic spells listed below, this spell must first be cast on the item.

4—White Candle (F) After casting an *Enchant Wax* spell on an undyed candle, the caster may imbed a first level spell in the candle by casting *White Candle* (and the first level spell to be imbedded) on the candle. The duration is the time required to imbed the spell. The imbedded spell is released by the burning of the candle and affects all in the same room **or** within 50' if outside . In order to be affected by the magic of the candle, a target must be exposed to the burning candle (in the same room **or** within 50' if outside) for a full ten consecutive minutes The target should get a Perception roll every minute or so, to see if the effects of the candle magic are being felt. At the end of ten full minutes of exposure, the target(s) is affected by the magic in the candle; no RR! The casting of one *White Candle* spell allows the candle to "burn" for 10 minutes. Each additional casting of *White Candle* lengthens the burning time of the magic candle by an additional ten minutes. For example, a *White Candle* of "Question" which could burn 30 minutes would cause the caster to use 15 PP = 3 for *Enchant Wax* + (4 for White Candle x 3 for 30 minutes) not counting the casting of the imbedded *Question* spell. Similarly, a *Brown Candle* (7th level) of "Charm Kind" (3rd level) which could burn 60 minutes would cause the caster to use 45 PP = 3 for *Enchant Wax* + (7 for Brown Candle x 6 for 60 minutes) not counting the casting of the imbedded *Charm Kind* spell.

5—Lesser Wax Fruit (Sleep) (F) After casting an *Enchant Wax* spell, the caster creates a piece of waxen fruit which looks, tastes, and smells real. Consumption of the fruit causes the target to fall into a deep sleep if a RR (vs. caster's level) is not made.

6—Grey Candle (F) As *White Candle* except with grey wax; the caster creates a candle which will produce billowing clouds of thick, dense smoke when the candle is extinguished. The radius of the cloud will expand 10'/round until the room (or a 50'R) is filled. Winds will rapidly dissipate the cloud (1 rnd). The cloud completely obscures normal vision and smells bad.

7—Brown Candle (F) As *White Candle* except with brown wax; the caster creates a candle in which a second level spell may be imbedded.

8—Burgundy Candle (F) As *Grey Candle* except with burgundy wax; the caster creates a candle which will intoxicate all nearby beings (in the same room **or** within 50' if outdoors). This intoxication takes the form of a cumulative +1/rnd to RRs and a -1/rnd to all other activities for each round spent in the presence of the burning candle, wearing off after a few hours; the maximum modification is 50. Thus 50 rounds with a burning burgundy candle produces a +50 modifier to all RRs and a -50 modifier to all activities. This candle's effects are particularly insidious since the effects could easily be perceived as thoroughly enjoyable until the target is unable to safely move!

9—Red Candle (F) As *White Candle* except with red wax; the caster creates a candle in which a third level spell may be imbedded.

10—Poison Wax Fruit (F) As *Lesser Wax Fruit* except victim must make a RR vs. a poison of the caster's choice; determined upon the formation of the fruit and the casting of this spell.

11—Orange Candle (F) As *White Candle* except with orange wax; the caster creates a candle in which a fourth level spell may be imbedded.

12—Dun Candle (F) As *Grey Candle* except with dun wax; the caster creates a candle which will cause a deep sleep lasting one day.

13—Yellow Candle (F) As *White Candle* except with yellow wax; the caster creates a candle in which a fifth level spell may be imbedded.

14—Wax Mask (F) After casting an Enchant Wax spell, the caster may sculpt a wax mask which may or may not resemble someone else. When worn the wax mask looks very convincing, adding 50 to Disguising attempts.

15—Green Candle (F) As *White Candle* except with green wax; the caster creates a candle in which a sixth level spell may be imbedded.

16—Turquoise Candle (F) As *Grey Candle* except with turquoise wax; the caster creates a candle in which may be imbedded any poison of the caster's choice; determined upon the formation of the candle.

17—Blue Candle (F) As *White Candle* except with blue wax; the caster creates a candle in which a seventh level spell may be imbedded.

18—Wax Doll (F/M) After casting an *Enchant Wax* spell, the caster creates a small doll-like wax object, which must contain some bodily excretion from the target/victim (this may be hair, fingernail clippings, excrement, saliva, etc.). This wax doll is "keyed" to the target/victim. No matter where the target/victim goes, whoever holds the doll may control the target/victim. By concentrating, the possessor of the doll may cause the target/victim to follow some *Suggestion* (as in the spell on the Spirit Mastery list). Whatever damage befalls the doll also occurs in a similar manner to the target/victim (GM discretion). The only hope of the target/victim (other than waiting for the spell's duration to end) is to have either a *Cancel True* or a *Remove Curse* cast on the doll or on the target.

19—Purple Candle (F) As *White Candle* except with purple wax; the caster creates a candle in which an eighth level spell may be imbedded.

20—Black Candle (F) As *White Candle* except with black wax; the caster creates a candle in which a curse may be imbedded. Some curses are suggested in the Evil Cleric's List "Curses", but with a limit of 20th level.

25—Silver Candle (F) As *White Candle* except with silvered wax; the caster creates a candle in which a ninth or tenth level spell may be imbedded.

30—Wax-Shape (F) As *Wax Mask* except caster may also fabricate other body parts, as well, thus allowing caster to alter her entire body to the form of another humanoid race; adds 75 to Disguising.

50—Candle Mastery (F) As *White Candle* except with many waxes; the caster creates a candle which may contain up to one color/effect (see spells above) per ten levels of the caster. These different colors may be in swirls, stripes, layers, etc. for different effects ranging from sequential to simultaneous.

Coven Base Spell Lists

10.7 MENDING WAYS (Coven Base)

NOTE 1: *If any components are missing, the spells on this list will not work.*

NOTE 2: *Spells 1-5 and 14-16 deal with pliable plant and animal materials. Spells 6 and 17 deal with rigid plant material. Spells 7 and 19 deal with "soft" earthen material. Spells 8 and 18 deal with "rigid" animal material and include shells, exoskeletons, and chitinous materials. Spells 9-13, 20, and 25 deal with "hard" earthen materials. The 30th level spell "Mending True" would even mend a plastic item, for example.*

NOTE 3: *All spells apply only to non-living materials.*

NOTE 4: *This spell list was originally "researched" by a character looking to make money in a city. In fact, that seems to be this list's real advantage; almost everyone has an object they want repaired. Perhaps NPCs who know and use this list professionally might be called "Menders."*

	Area of Effect	Duration	Range
1—Mend String and Twine	1 string	P	touch
2—Mend Rope	1 rope	P	touch
3—Mend Parchment and Paper	1 sheet	P	touch
4—Mend Cloth	1 item	P	touch
5—Mend Leather	1 item	P	touch
6—Mend Wood	1 item	P	touch
7—Mend Earth and Ceramics	1 item	P	touch
8—Mend Horn/Bone/Antler etc.	1 item	P	touch
9—Mend Bast Metal	1 item	P	touch
10—Mend Common Stone and Glass	1 item	P	touch
11—Mend Precious Metal	1 item	P	touch
12—Mend Semi-Precious Stone	1 item	P	touch
13—Mend Precious Stone	1 item	P	touch
14—Mend Magic Parchment/Paper	1 item	P	touch
15—Mend Magic Cloth and Rope	1 item	P	touch
16—Mend Magic Leather	1 item	P	touch
17—Mend Magic Wood	1 item	P	touch
18—Mend Magic Horn/Bone/etc.	1 item	P	touch
19—Mend Magic Earth and Ceramics	1 item	P	touch
20—Mend Magic Stone and Glass	1 item	P	touch
25—Mend Magic Metals	1 item	P	touch
30—Mending True	1 item	P	touch
50—Mending Mastery	caster	1 rnd/lvl(C)	self

1—Mend String and Twine (F) Mends multiple rips in a piece of string/twine. All components must be collected together (i.e., must be within 10'R).

2—Mend Rope (F) As *Mend String and Twine* except mends rope.

3—Mend Parchment and Paper (F) As *Mend String and Twine* except mends parchment, paper, vellum, etc.

4—Mend Cloth (F) As *Mend String and Twine* except mends leather, hide, skin, etc.

5—Mend Leather (F) As *Mend String and Twine* except mends leather, hide, skin, etc.

6—Mend Wood (F) As *Mend String and Twine* except mends multiple breaks in non-magical wood.

7—Mend Earth and Ceramics (F) As *Mend String and Twine* except mends earth, ceramics, etc.

8—Mend Horn/Bone/Antler/Etc. (F) As *Mend String and Twine* except mends hard animal substances.

9—Mend Base Metal (F) As *Mend String and Twine* except mends iron, tin, lead, etc.

10—Mend Common Stone and Glass (F) As *Mend String and Twine* except mends ordinary stone and glass.

11—Mend Precious Metal (F) As *Mend String and Twine* except mends gold, silver, platinum, etc.

12—Mend Semi-Precious Stone (F) As *Mend String and Twine* except mends semi-precious stone.

13—Mend Precious Stone (F) As *Mend String and Twine* except mends precious stone.

14—Mend Magic Parchment and Paper (F) As *Mend String and Twine* except mends magic parchment, etc.

15—Mend Magic Cloth (F) As *Mend String and Twine* except mends cloth, rope, string, etc.

16—Mend Magic Leather (F) As *Mend String and Twine* except mends magic leather, hide, etc.

17—Mend Magic Wood (F) As *Mend String and Twine* except mends magic wood.

18—Mend Magic Horn/Bone/Antler/etc. (F) As *Mend String and Twine* except mends magic horn, bone, etc.

19—Mend Magic Earth and Ceramics (F) As *Mend String and Twine* except mends magic earth(enware).

20—Mend Magic Stone and Glass (F) As *Mend String and Twine* except mends magic stone and glass.

25—Mend Magic Metals (F) As *Mend String and Twine* except mends magic metal.

30—Mending True (F) Mends all facets of any one item. All components must be within a 50'R.

50—Mending Mastery (F) Allows caster to cast any of the above spells at a rate of 1/rnd.

11.0 ARCANE SPELL LISTS

11.1 PLASMA MASTERY (Arcane Spell List)

NOTE: *The spell list, Plasma Mastery, is intended for use as an Arcane list. Alternatively, it could be a Base Magician list which could be learned at increased cost. None have learned the spells relating to the use of Plasma to heal or give life; if so, the methods have not yet been revealed. Plasma is a combination of the six commonly known wieldable elements: Earth, Wind, and Water combine to give the Plasma its amorphous form; Fire, Ice, and Light lend power to the Plasma, which shocks and impacts even as it burns (though it feels cold due to soul-numbing effects) recipients of attacks with the raw element. Plasma Balls are the most dangerous form of Ball attack, as the element is attracted to metal yet able to seep through chinks in armor as well as react with it. Plasma Bolts are able to generate more sheer force and concussion than lightning bolts, though generally they are not as capable of inflicting lasting damage.*

	Area of Effect	Duration	Range
1—Detect Plasma •	10'R/lvl	C	self
2—			
3—			
4—			
5—Plasma Resistance	1 target	1 min/lvl	10'
6—			
7—Wall of Plasma	10'x10'x6'	1 rnd/lvl	100'
8—Plasma Bolt	1 target	—	100'
9—Eldritch Weapon	one weapon	1 rnd/lvl	touch
10—Plasma Ball	10'R	—	100'
11—Plasma Armor	1 target	1 min/lvl	10'
12—Plasma Bolt (300')	1 target	—	300'
13—Circle of Plasma	10'R	1 rnd/lvl	touch
14—Bind	1 target	1 hr/lvl	5'/lvl
15—Beam of Dissolution	1 cu'/lvl	P	100'
16—Alter State	100 cu'	P	100'
17—Plasma Ball (20'R)	20'R	—	100'
18—Plasma Bolt (500')	1 target	—	500'
19—Enshroud	5'R	1 rnd/lvl	self
20—Triad of Plasma	3 targets	—	100'
25—Nexus Gate	7'x4'	1 day/lvl	5'
30—Conjure Plasma Elemental	—	1 rnd/lvl(C)	10'/lvl
50—Soulfire	varies	1 rnd/lvl	self

1—Detect Plasma (P) As *Presence* on the Base Mentalist list, Presence, except only the presence of raw Plasma or Plasma spells may be detected.

5—Plasma Resistance (D) As *Resist Light* on the Elemental Shields list (Open Essence) except it protects against Plasma and allows a +5 bonus versus other elements.

7—Wall of Plasma (E) As *Wall of Fire* on the Fire Law list (Base Magician) except wall is formed of Plasma and criticals are 'A' (50%) or 'B' (50%) Plasma crits.

8—Plasma Bolt (E) A bolt of Plasma is shot from the palm of the caster; results are determined on the Plasma Bolt Attack Table 13.1 (*RMCIII*).

9—Eldritch Weapon (E) Caster's weapon (must be at least partially metal in order for the Plasma to bind) is enveloped in "Coldfire" and will inflict Plasma criticals of one degree less severity in addition to normal criticals when striking. Caster may only have one Eldritch weapon in effect at any one time. Any fumble delivers a 'B' Plasma crit to wielder.

10—Plasma Ball (E) A 1' ball of Plasma is shot from the palm of the caster; it explodes to affect a 10'R area; results are determined on the Plasma Ball Attack Table 13.2 (*RMCIII*).

11—Plasma Armor (D) As *Light Armor* on the Elemental Shields list (Open Essence) except it protects against Plasma and allows a +10 bonus versus other elements.

12—Plasma Bolt (E) As above except range is 300'.

13—Circle of Plasma (E) As *Circle Aflame* on the Fire Law list (Base Magician) except that criticals inflicted are Plasma criticals and the caster may increase the severity of the critical given by one for every additional 13 PP spent on the spell (to a maximum of 'E').

14—Bind (F) Target is imprisoned in chains of Coldfire. Physical attempts to escape result in a 'C' Plasma crit if successful **or** an 'E' Plasma crit if unsuccessful. Magical attempts to escape result in an 'H' Plasma crit regardless of success or failure (see Plasma Bolt Attack Table 13.1).

15—Beam of Dissolution (F) As *Unearth* on the Earth Law list (Base Magician) except the target matter (solid, liquid, or gas) is not destroyed but is converted equally into its other two states of matter. For example, if a solid material is targeted, then half of it is converted to liquid (usually water) and the other half becomes gas (usually air). Materials converted to solid state usually take the form of solid packed earth or sandstone.

16—Alter State (F) As *Stone/Earth* on the Earth Law list (Base Magician) except the target matter may be any type of nonmagical matter. The caster may control the final state of the matter (solid, liquid, or gas) and also the kind of matter if a sample is available and the value of the final material is no more than 5 gp/lb. Results are subject to GM approval.

17—Plasma Ball (E) As above except the area of effect is in a 20'R.

18—Plasma Bolt (E) As above except the range is 500'.

19—Enshroud (E) Caster's body is covered by Plasma. This gives the caster a +30 bonus versus Plasma attacks and he will take half concussion damage from such attacks. Anyone within 5' suffers an 'A' Plasma critical (no RR). Anyone in physical contact suffers a 'C' Plasma critical (no RR). Physical attacks from the caster that deliver a critical also deliver an 'A' Plasma critical. All of the caster's items are immune to the effects of Plasma for the duration of the spell but any ignitable/fragile material he contacts must make a RR or burn/break.

20—Triad of Plasma (E) As *Triad of Water* on the Water Law list (Base Magician) except *Plasma Bolts* are shot.

25—Nexus Gate (F) A Gate is opened to the "Elemental Plane of Plasma", 7' tall by 4' wide. Only creatures small enough pass through may pass, though unusually powerful creatures (20+ levels) may rip the gate to enlarge the dimensions enough to pass through. GM discretion is required.

30—Conjure Plasma Elemental (F) A Strong Plasma Elemental is conjured from the Elemental Plane of Plasma. The Elemental's *C&T* stats are: Lvl 20, MV100, Spt/10, VF/VF, L/LA#, 200 Hits, AT 12(-50), 150HBa(2x)(2D)/130HGr/[Plasma E]«, Berserk (NO). The Elemental will regenerate hits and damage in direct proportion to any elemental attack spell it is hit with, if the attacking spell fails a RR vs. the caster's level (e.g., if a *Firebolt* attack does 15D and fails a RR, the Elemental will regenerate 15 hits and will be healed of a medium or severe wound).

50—Soulfire (E) The caster taps Plasma directly, empowering him with several abilities for the duration of the spell: he can utilize a Plasma breath weapon 3 times/spell as a Great Drake: either a 130 OB using the Plasma Bolt Attack Table 13.1 **or** an area of effect cone of 300' length and 100' base. Due to the supernatural soul-numbing nature of the Plasma he will drain CO pts as an Undead in up to a 20'R (5 CO pts/rnd, -20 to RR); and he may use any one of the lower lvl spells (below lvl 25) on this list (1/rnd).

11.2 NETHER MASTERY (Arcane Spell List)

NOTE 1: *Nether is one of the primary elements that make up the foundation of the worlds. It has at times been mistaken to be as a cold darkness, but darkness is the opposite of light as heat is the opposite of cold. Nether is neither cold or darkness. Nether is neither light or heat. Nether is light and dark and cold and heat. Nether is not air, water, or earth. Nether is not spirit. Nether is nothingness. The point where light, dark, cold and heat meet. Nether is very difficult to learn to control and handle. This spell list requires x3 the normal development point cost to learn.*

NOTE 2: *The outer edges of Nether are black and void of color. While the inner mass of Nether is a black and slivery swirling mass of choatic flashes of bright and intense light and dark; radiating blast of cold and heat which burn and freeze all that is within it.*

Arcane Spell Lists

NOTE 3: *Any object which is stuck into a swirling mass of Nether must make a RR versus being pulledd apart at the point where it enters the Nether mass. For example, a sword is jabbed into a Nether mass; if the sword fails its RR, it is severed at the point where it meets the outer edge of the Nether mass. If a person's arm enters a Nether mass and that person fails his RR, the part of his arm in the Nether mass is separated from the rest of the arm. The arm does not bleed at the point of separation because the stumps are cauterized.*

NOTE 4: *If an object enters the Nether mass and makes it RR, normal Nether damage takes place. For example, the person mentioned above puts his arm into the Nether and makes his RR, he is not subjected to the limb separation but he is subjected to the normal affects of the Nether mass. In this case it would most likely be a* Nether Ball *attack with criticals being modified by to afflict only those parts of the body that are actual exposed to the Nether mass.*

	Area of Effect	Duration	Range
1—Detect Nether •	10'R/lvl	C	self
2—			
3—Nether Sight	self	1 min/lvl	self
4—			
5—Nether Resistance	1 target	1 min/lvl	10'
6—			
7—Nether Mass (1'R)	1'R	6 rnds	100'
8—Nether Summons I	elemental	1 rnd/lvl(C)	20'
9—Wall of Nether	10'x10'x6'	1 rnd/lvl	100'
10—Nether Bolt (100')	target	—	100'
11—Nether Resistance (10'R)	10'R	1 min/lvl	100'
12—Circle of Nether	10'R	1 rnd/lvl	touch
13—Nether Ball (10'R)	10'R	—	100'
14—Nether Summons II	elemental	1 rnd/lvl(C)	20'
15—Nether Bolt (300')	target	—	300'
16—Nether Armor	target	1 min/lvl	100'
17—Nether Mass (5'R)	5'R	8 rnds	100'
18—Nether Conflagration	1 blade	1 min/lvl	20'
19—			
20—Nether Ball (20'R)	20'R	—	100'
25—Nether Summons III	elemental	1 rnd/lvl(C)	20'
30—Triad Nether Bolt	3 targets	—	100'
50—Nexus Gate	10'x10'x1"	1 rnd/lvl(C)	20'

1—Detect Nether (P) As *Presence* on the Base Mentalist list, Presence, except only the presence of raw Nether or spells employing such may be detected.

3—Nether Sight (U) Allows the caster to look into the swirling mass that composes the Nether. This allows the caster to make out objects with the Nether mass.

5—Nether Resistance (D) As *Resist Light* on the Elemental Shields list (Open Essence) except it protects against Nether.

7—Nether Mass (1'R) (F) Creates a 1'R cloud of Nether matter: delivers 'C' Nether criticals on 1st and 2nd rounds, a "B" Nether criticals on 3rd and 4th rounds, and "A" Nether criticals on 5th and 6th rounds. One the first round of creation, any target(s) at the point of creation may make a 'Medium' maneuver to avoid contact. It drifts with the wind and affects all that come in contact with its radius.

8—Nether Summons I (FM) Allows the caster to summons a Nether Elemental. The Nether elemental will obey the caster, for one minute/lvl (provided the caster concentrates) and then the Nether elemental vanishes back to the Nether Plane. Treat as a Fire Servant that delivers Plasma crits.

9—Wall of Nether (E) As *Wall of Fire* on the Fire Law list except wall is formed of Nether and criticals are 'A' (50%)or 'B' (50%) Nether crits.

10—Nether Bolt (100') (E) A bolt of Nether is shot from the palm of the caster; results are determined on the Nether Bolt Attack Table 13.3.

11—Nether Resistance (10'R) As *Nether Resistance* except it provides protection for all within 10' of the caster.

12—Circle of Nether (E) As *Circle Aflame* on the Fire Law list (Base Magician) except that criticals inflicted are Nether criticals and the caster may increase the severity of the critical given by one for every additional 13 PP spent on the spell (to a maximum of 'E').

13—Nether Ball (10'R) (E) A 1' ball of Nether is shot from the palm of the caster, it explodes to affect a 10'R area; results are determined on the Nether Ball Attack Table 13.4 (*RMCIII*).

14—Nether Summons II (FM) Allows the caster to summons a Nether Elemental. Treat as a Weak Fire Elemental that delivers Plasma crits.

15—Nether Bolt (300') As *Nether Bolt (100')* except range is increased to 300".

16—Nether Armor (D) As *Light Armor* on the Elemental Shields list (Open Essence) except it protects against Nether.

17—Nether Mass (5' R) (FD) As *Nether Mass (1'R)* except that the radius is 5' and the Nether mass duration is increased to 8 rounds. Doing "D" criticals for rounds 1 and 2, "C" criticals for rounds 3 and 4, "B" criticals for rounds 5 and 6 and finally "A" criticals for rounds 7 and 8.

18—Nether Conflagration (F) Allows caster to envelope a weapon with nether matter. When the weapon inflicts any damage, the armor must make a RR; if it fails, the AT is treated as if it was AT one. After the duration of the spell, the weapon is completely destroyed. Any fumble delivers a 'B' Nether crit to wielder.

20—Nether Ball (20'R) As *Nether Ball* except radius is 20'R.

25—Nether Summons III (FM) Allows the caster to summons a Nether Elemental. Treat as a Strong Fire Elemental that delivers Nether criticals.

30—Triad Nether Bolt (E) As *Triad of Water* on the Water Law list (Base Magician) except *Nether Bolts* are shot.

50—Nexus Gate (F) A Gate is opened to the "Elemental Plane of Nether", 7' tall by 4' wide. Only creatures small enough pass through may pass, though unusually powerful creatures (20+ levels) may rip the gate to enlarge the dimensions enough to pass through. GM discretion is required for this spell.

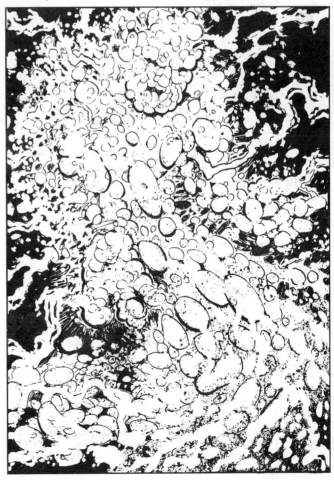

12.1 PLASMA CRITICAL STRIKE TABLE

	A	B	C	D	E
01-05	Tiny bubbles. +0 hits.	Fizzle out. +0 hits.	+1 hit.	+2 hits.	+3 hits.
06-10	+1 hit	+2 hits.	+3 hits.	+4 hits.	Stunned for 1 rnd. +3 hits.
11-15	Foe loses initiative for next rnd. Scary.	Spin foe. Loses initiative for 1 rnd. +4 hits.	Unbalancing blast. Foe must parry for 1 rnd. +5 hits.	Unbalancing blast. Foe must parry for 1 rnd. +6 hits.	Foe is stunned for 1 rnd. +5 hits.
16-20	Foe is spun about and loses initiative for next rnd. +5 hits.	Unbalancing blast forces foe to parry for 1 rnd. +5 hits.	Unbalancing blast forces foe to parry for 1 rnd. +8 hits.	Irritating burns force foe to parry for 1 rnd. +10 hits.	Zap stuns foe for 1 rnd. +10 hits.
21-35	Unbalancing blast causes foe to lose initiative for 2 rnds. +8 hits.	Minor burns. Foe must parry for 1 rnd at -10. +10 hits.	Crackling blast causes foe to parry for 1 rnd at -15. +10 hits.	Glancing blast. Foe must parry for 1 rnd at -20. 1 hit per rnd. +15 hits.	Strong blast reels foe. Stunned for 1 rnd. +20 hits.
36-45	Burns force foe to parry 1 rnd. +10 hits.	Disconcerted foe must parry for 1 rnd and loses initiative for 2 rnds. +9 hits	Blast forces foe to parry for 1 rnd. 1 hit/rnd. +15 hits.	Explosion stuns foe for 1 rnd. 2 hits per rnd. +15 hits.	Strike leg. Stunned for 2 rnds. Fights at -20 if no foot covering. +20 hits.
46-50	Distracted foe must parry for 2 rnds. +15 hits.	Staggering blast stuns foe for 1 rnd and inflicts 1 hit/rnd. +15 hits.	Sizzling blast stuns foe for 1 rnd. +15 hits. Add +5 to your next roll.	Foe is spun about. 2 hits per rnd. Stunned for 1 rnd. +25 hits.	Powerful blast. Stunned and unable to parry for 1 rnd; drops all held objects. +25 hits.
51-55	Burn stuns foe for 1 rnd. +10 hits.	Unbalancing blast causes foe to take 2 hits per rnd. Stunned for 1 rnd. +12 hits.	Hard blow stuns foe for 1 rnd. +12 hits. Add +5 to your next roll.	Foe is forced back 5 feet. Stunned for 2 rnds. 2 hits per rnd. Add +5 to your next roll.	Forceful blast stuns foe for 1 rnd. Stunned and unable to parry for 2 rnds. 3 hits per rnd. +20 hits.
56-60	Crackling blast stuns foe for 2 rnds. +15 hits.	Back blast spins foe; he takes 2 hits per rnd. All small metal items on foe's back are melted. +15 hits.	Foe is thrown back 5 feet and must parry for 2 rnds. +20 hits.	Hot strike. Foe stunned and unable to parry for 1 rnd. Fights at -10. +15 hits.	Blast floors foe; out for 2 rnds. 2 hits per rnd and fights at -10. +25 hits.
61-65	Powerful blow. Foe is stunned and unable to parry for 1 rnd. +15 hits.	Blow causes delivers 2 hits per rnd. Stunned and unable to parry 1 rnd. Fights at -5. +15 hits.	Leg strike; any metal greaves are destroyed; foe is stunned for 2 rnds. +15 hits.	Blast to shield arm. If no shield, arms are useless due to nerve damage, stunned and unable to parry for 2 rnds, +15 hits; otherwise, +20 hits.	Precision strike knocks foe down; fights at -20 and drops held objects. +25 hits.
66	Hammer blast shatters foe's shield arm; he is stunned and unable to parry for 3 rnds. +25 hits.	Strike shatters weapon shoulder. Stunned for 3 rnds. 5 hits per rnd if metal armor is worn. +20 hits.	Chest strike breaks both arms; foe is stunned and down for 3 rnds. Fights at -90.	Impact ruptures eardrums and kills foe if he has no helm; else he is out for 3 hours.	Direct hit. Surgical strike blows head into particles of matter which scatter into the wind.
67-70	Blow to back; foe is stunned and unable to parry for 1 rnd and fights at -5 due to burns. +10 hits.	Back strike. Stunned and unable to parry for 1 rnd. Fights at -5. +14 hits.	Snap breaks both arms; foe is stunned and down for 3 rnds. Fights at -90.	Focused blow takes foe down; out for 2 rnds. +20 hits. Add +5 to your next roll.	Blast to shield arm stuns foe for 1 rnd. If foe has a shield, it is broken; otherwise foe's shoulder breaks.
71-75	Blow to mid-section; foe is stunned and unable to parry for 1 rnd and fights at -10. +15 hits.	Strike to side. Stunned 2 rnds and unable to parry next rnd. 3 hits per rnd. +25 hits.	Back blow. Foe foe is stunned for 3 rnds and is unable to parry next rnd. Foe fights at -10 due to nerve damage.	Quick strike breaks shield arm. Stunned for 2 rnds. +15 hits.	Numbing blast. Arms are useless due to nerve damage. Fights at -25.
76-80	Weak strike to abdomen. Foe is stunned for 3 rnds and unable to parry next rnd. +20 hits.	Blow to feet topples foe. Foe is down and out for 2 rnds and takes 3 hits per rnd. +15 hits.	Strike knocks foe down. Foe is out for 2 rnds and fights at -15 due to internal bleeding. +15 hits.	Blast breaks weapon arm. Foe fights at -20. Stunned 2 rnds. +15 hits.	Awesome chest blast stuns foe for 10 rnds and knocks him down. Fights at -30. +30 hits.
81-85	Ripping backstrike breaks ribs and snaps cartilage. Foe is stunned and unable to parry for 1 rnd and fights at -25. +15 hits.	Horizontal strike fractures ribs and burns skin. Stunned for 2 rnds. Fights at -25. 3 hits per rnd due to burns. +15 hits.	Blistering blast sears skin. Foe is stunned for 2 rnds, fights at -25, and takes 3 hits per rnd. +20 hits.	Foe attempts to deflect blast with hands. Poor fool is down for 3 rnds and takes 3 hits per rnd. +25 hits.	Side strike rifles through organs. Foe dies after 6 painful rounds of inactivity. +35 hits.
86-90	Brutal blast knocks foe down. Stunned for 2 rnds. Foe fights at -50. +15 hits.	Calf strike burns muscle. Stunned for 3 rnds. Fights at -50. +25 hits.	Blast breaks thigh. Foe fights at -40 and is stunned for 3 rnds. +20 hits.	Blast squeezes abdomen. Foe dies in 4 rnds. +25 hits.	Heat wave. backbone is melted and foe dies of massive shock in 3 rnds. +35 hits
91-95	Crushing strike breaks hip. Foe fights at -50 and is stunned for 3 rnds. +25 hits.	Temple strike. If foe has helm, he is sent into a permanent coma; if not, he dies. +30 hits.	Strike twists and breaks hip. Foe takes 5 hits per rnd and fights at -60. +25 hits.	Red-hot fragments of jaw drive into foe's brain. Foe dies in 3 rnds. +55 hits.	Shock pulses through foe's nervous system. Foe dies in 6 rnds. +35 hits.
96-99	Strike contacts head and neck. If foe has helm, he is knocked out; if not, he dies in 3 rnds. +25 hits.	Wedge-shaped strike severs windpipe. Foe dies in 12 rnds. +30 hits.	Foe's feet are engulfed. Foe is stunned and unable to parry for 9 rnds. 6 hits per rnd. Fights at -75. +25 hits.	Foe receives a lungful of plasma. Foe dies in 1 rnd. +25 hits.	Foe's body is a pulped, smoking ruin. Add +20 to your next roll.
100	Head strike. If foe has helm, he is knocked out; if not, he dies in 3 rnds due to shock and fractures. +30 hits.	Blast withers body below neck. Foe is paralyzed permanently from neck down. +40 hits. Add +10 to your next roll.	Sizzling strike blasts through both eyes and into brain, killing foe.	Foe's lungs and heart burn and implode. +30 hits. Add +25 to your next roll.	Unfortunate foe is reduced to a molten puddle. Fetch a mop.

12.2 ACID CRITICAL STRIKE TABLE

	A	B	C	D	E
01-05	Only a drop. +0 hits..	Try again. +0 hits.	+1 hit.	+2 hits.	+3 hits.
06-10	+1 hit.	+2 hits.	+3 hits.	+4 hits.	Foe loses initiative for 1 rnd. +4 hits.
11-15	Foes loses initiative for 1 rnd. +2 hits.	Foe loses initiative for next rnd. +3 hits. Foe is spun about.	Foe is unbalanced and must parry next rnd. +4 hits.	Foe is unbalanced and must parry next rnd. +5 hits.	Foe feels burns. If foe has armor, he loses 1 rnd of initiative; if not, he loses 2 rnds. +5 hits.
16-20	Nearby splash gives foe +3 hits, foe loses 1 rnd of initiative.	Foe loses 1 rnd of initiative and takes +4 hits.	Foe is unbalanced and must parry next rnd. +5 hits.	Foe is unbalanced and must parry next rnd. +6 hits.	Foe is unbalanced and must parry next rnd. +7 hits.
21-35	Blast unbalances foe. He loses 1 rnd of initiative. +4 hits.	Foe must parry next rnd. +5 hits.	Light burns. Foe must parry for 1 rnd. +7 hits and 1 hit per rnd.	Minor burns. Foe must parry for 2 rnds. +8 hits and 1 hit per rnd.	Foe reels from blast. +15 hits and foe is stunned for 1 rnd.
36-45	Foe must parry for 1 rnd. +8 hits.	Blow unbalances foe. +9 hits and 1 hit per rnd.	Foe must parry for 2 rnds. +8 hits and 2 hits per rnd.	Blast stuns foe for 1 rnd and fights at -10 for 2 rnds. +10 hits.	Foe reels back 10 feet. +20 hits and foe is stunned for 2 rnds.
46-50	Light burns cause foe to parry for 1 rnd. +3 hits and 1 hit per rnd.	Foe loses 3 rnds of initiative. +8 hits and 1 hit per rnd.	Foe is unbalanced and must parry for 2 rnds. +10 hits. Add +5 to your next action.	Foe is spun about. +13 hits. Foe fights at -10 for 2 rnds.	Foe is staggered. +20 hits and 3 hits per rnd. If foe has non-magical non-metal weapon, it is destroyed.
51-55	Sizzling but weak blast stuns foe for 1 rnd. +6 hits.	Foe is stunned for 1 rnd. +8 hits and 2 hits per rnd.	Blast stuns foe for 2 rnds. +10 hits. If foe has leg armor, 1 hit per rnd; if not, 3 hits per rnd.	Blast stuns foe for 2 rnds. If he has helm, he take +8 hits and 2 hits per rnd. If not, he takes +11 hits and 4 hits per rnd.	Impact and acid stuns foe for 4 rnds. Foe takes 3 hits per rnd.
56-60	Foe is unbalanced and forced to parry for the next 3 rnds.	Foe is stunned for 2 rnds. Foe's clothing is destroyed.	Blast stuns foe for 2 rnds. +10 hits and all foe's clothing and leather are destroyed.	Strike to foe's shield arm. If foe has no shield or metal armor, he is knocked out for 1 day. +15 hits.	Strike to foe's weapon arm. Foe drops weapon. Foe fights at -10 and takes 3 hits per rnd.
61-65	Chest strike. If foe has metal armor, stunned 3 rnds; if not, stunned for 4 rnds. +6 hits.	Leg strike. Foe is stunned and unable to parry for 1 rnd. Fights at -5. +9 hits,	Upper leg strike. Foe is stunned and unable to parry for 1 rnd. +10 hits and foe fights at -10.	+10 hits. If foe has abdomen armor, he takes 2 hits per rnd; if not, 5 hits per rnd.	Leg strike, foe is knocked down. Stunned for 2 rnds. Cannot parry for 1 rnd. +13 hits.
66	Blast stuns all within 5' of foe for 1 rnd. Foe drops all he is holding. Fights at -15. +10 hits.	Foe is stunned 2 rnds. +15 hits. If foe is wearing organic armor, it is useless and he fights at -15.	Chest strike, if foe has non-magical, metal armor, it becomes fused and arms unusable; if not, knock out for 6 days. +15 hits.	Neck blast knocks foe out. Foe cannot speak for 2 months and takes 4 hits per rnd. +20 hits.	Head strike. If foe has helm, it is destroyed and foe is in a coma for 2 months; if not, foe's brain liquifies and he dies. +10 to your next roll.
67-70	Back strike. Foe is stunned and unable to parry for 1 rnd. +7 hits.	Back strike. Foe is stunned for 2 rnds, cannot parry for 1 rnd, and fights at -10. +8 hits.	Back blast stuns foe for 3 rnds and he cannot parry for 1 rnd. Fights at -15. +9 hits.	Back blast Foe is down for 1 rnd and 3 hits per rnd. Fights at -20. +10 hits.	Back strike. Foe is stunned and unable to parry for 4 rnds. Minor shock. Fights at -25. +15 hits.
71-75	Blast stuns foe for 3 rnds. Foe fights at -5 for 6 rnds. +8 hits.	Shield arm strike. If foe has a shield, he is stunned for 4 rnds; if not, arm is useless and he is stunned and unable to parry for 2 additional rnds. +10 hits.	Strike to shield arm. If foe has metal shield, he is stunned for 6 rnds and takes +12 hits; if not, +15 hits and foe is knocked down and arm is useless.	Strike to weapon arm. Arm is useless and foe is stunned for 3 rnds. +13 hits.	Shoulder strike shatters foes weapon arm, muscles and cartilage damage. Arm is useless, foe is stunned for 6 rnd and takes 3 hits per rnd
76-80	Strike to foe's upper chest stuns him for 2 rnds and he cannot parry for 1 rnd. +9 hits.	Arm strike burns foe. Stunned for 2 rnd and takes 2 hits per rnd. All cloth on weapon arm is burnt off and he drops all he is holding. +11 hits.	If foe has chest armor, he is stunned for 6 rnds, takes 2 hits per rnd, and fights at -5. If not, foe is knocked out for 3 days due to shock. +14 hits.	Foe loses the hand on his weapon's arm. Foe is stunned and unable to parry for 3 rnds and takes 5 hits per rnd. Severe Burns. +16 hits.	Chest strike knocks out foe due to shock, blood loss, and nerve damage. Foe take 3 hits per rnd. +18 hits.
81-85	Back blast stuns foe for 2 rnds. He is unable to parry for 3 rnds. +12 hits.	Back blast. Foe is stunned and unable to parry for 3 rnds. Muscles destroyed. Foe fights at -15. +13 hits.	Blast to thighs. If foe has leg armor, 2 hits per rnd and fights at -20; if not, massive leg damage (muscle/tissue) and fights at -85.	Lower back strike stuns foe for 20 rnds and adds 3 hits per rnd. +15 hits. Nerve and shock damage.	Foe inhales acid and he loses throat and lungs. Foe dies in 12 rnds. +20 hits.
86-90	Foe knocked down. If foe has metal armor legging, he loses use of legs due to nerve damage; if not, +15 hits and stunned/unable to parry for 4 rnds.	Leg strike. Any organic legging is dissolved causing 6 hits per rnd. Foe is stunned for 4 rnds. +14 hits.	Lower leg burns, foe loses foot but wound is sealed. Stunned and unable to parry for 6 rnds. 3 hit per rnd. Fights at -15. +23 hits.	If foe has abdomen armor, it is destroyed, foe is out, knocked down, and takes 2 hits per rnd. If not, foe dies in 12 rnds due to organ loss.	Foe lower body turns to mush. Foe dies in 9 rnds due to loss. +20 hits.
91-95	Hip strike. If foe has hip armor, +10 hits and stunned for 6 rnds; if not, stunned for 3 rnds and at -50 due to shock and nerve damage .	Head strike. Foe is blinded and fights at -95. If foe has organic helm, it is destroyed. If no helm, 8 hits per rnd and loses 50% of hair.	Upper leg burns. Foe loses use of leg due to tissue loss. Stunned and unable to parry for 7 rnds. 4 hits/rnd. Fights at -20. +25 hits.	If foe has full helm, his eyes are destroyed and he is in a coma for 2 days. If not, foe dies in 6 rnds due to massive brain damage. +20 hits.	Side strike melts foes lower body and internal organs. Foe dies in 6 rnds. +25 hits.
96-99	Neck strike. If foe has neck armor, stunned for 3 rnds; if not, stunned 4 rnds and +8 hits. If no head covering, splash into ear drives insane.	Neck strike destroys foe's throat. +20 hits. 12 hits per rnd and he is inactive for 9 rnds before dying.	Chest strike destroys foes heart and lungs. If foe has metal armor, it is fused to his chest and he dies in 5 rnds; if not, foe dies instantly.	Chest strike knocks foe back 10'. Massive nerve damage, foe dies of fatal shock in 3 rnds. +22 hits.	Chest strike destroys both of foes lungs. Blast throws foe back 10'. Foe dies in 3 gasping rnds. +30 hits.
100	Blast to head. +15 hits. If helmed, foe is knocked out & takes +1 per rnd; if not, foe drops into coma for 1 month, -85 to Appearance.	Blow to back of neck paralyzes foe from shoulders down. +20 hits. Foe is very mad.	Foe's head is no longer available for use. Acid smoke surrounds the body. +15 to friendly witnesses for 3 rnds.	Acid vaporizes foe's midsection. Destroys foe's clothing, armor & all he was carrying. Foe is cut in half and dies. Add +15 to your next roll.	All that remains of foe is a puddle of flesh. +20 to your next roll. YAH!

12.3 PHYSICAL ALTERATION CRITICAL STRIKE TABLE

	A	B	C	D	E
01-05	0	0	0	0	0
06-10	0	0	0	0	+1 hit.
11-15	0	0	0	+1 hit.	You gain initiative next rnd. +1 hit.
16-20	0	0	+1 hit.	You gain initiative next rnd. +1 hit.	Foe reels backward and must parry next rnd. +2 hits.
21-35	0	+1 hit.	You gain initiative next rnd. +1 hit.	Foe reels backward from hip strike and must parry next rnd. +2 hits.	Chest strike. Foe must parry next rnd. Add +5 to your next action. +3 hits.
36-45	+1 hit.	You gain initiative next rnd. +1 hit.	Thigh wound. Your attack stings your foe and he must parry next rnd. +2 hits.	Thigh strike. Foe must parry next rnd. Add +5 to your next action. +3 hits.	Thigh wound. Foe is spun around and must parry next rnd at -20. +4 hits.
46-50	You gain initiative next rnd. +1 hit.	Your foe is unsure of what's going on and must parry next rnd. +2 hits.	Back strike knock foe down. Foe must parry next rnd. Add +5 to your next action. +3 hits.	Back wound. Foe is spun around and must parry next rnd at -20. +4 hits.	Back wound. Foe is stunned next rnd. +5 hits.
51-55	Chest strike. 50% change. Your attack stings your foe and he must parry next rnd. +2 hits.	Blast leaves foe's chest smoking. Foe must parry next rnd. Add +5 to your next action. +3 hits.	Chest strike. Foe must parry next rnd at -20. +4 hits.	Chest wound. Foe is stunned next rnd. +5 hits.	Chest wound. Foe is stunned next rnd and fights at -10. +6 hits.
56-60	Leg strike. 60% change. Foe must parry next rnd. Add +5 to your next action. +3 hits.	Leg wound. 50% change. Foe is spun around and must parry next rnd at -20. +4 hits.	Thigh wound. Foe is stunned. +5 hits.	Leg wound. Foe is stunned next rnd and fights at -10. +6 hits.	Strike foe's leg. Foe is stunned and unable to parry next rnd. Foe fights at -10. +7 hits.
61-65	Arm strike. 70% change. Foe must parry next rnd at -20. +4 hits.	Minor arm wound. 60% change. Foe is stunned next rnd. +5 hits.	Forearm strike. 50% change. Foe is stunned next rnd and fights at -10. +6 hits.	Strike foe's arm. Foe is stunned and unable to parry next rnd. Foe fights at -10. +7 hits.	Forearm wound. Foe is stunned for 2 rnds and fights at -15. +8 hits.
66	Leg bender. 80% change. Foe is stunned for 2 rnds. Add +20 to your next action. +10 hits.	Weapon arm strike. 70% change. Foe is stunned 3 rnds. Add +20 to your next action. +12 hits.	Thigh strike. 60% change. Foe is stunned for 4 rnds. Add +10 to your next action. +15 hits.	Leg wound. Foe is stunned for 5 rnds. Add +10 to your next action. +18 hits.	Chest strike. Foe's lungs are filled with smoke and he is overcome and stunned for 6 rnds and fights at -40. +20 hits.
67-70	Neck strike. 90% change. Foe is stunned next rnd and fights at -10. +6 hits.	Strike foe's neck. 80% change. Foe is stunned and unable to parry next rnd. Foe fights at -10. +7 hits.	Neck strike. 70% change. Foe is stunned for two rnds and fights at -15. +8 hits.	Shoulder strike. 50% change. Foe is stunned for 3 rnds. Add +20 to your next action. +9 hits.	Shoulder wound. Foe is stunned and unable to parry for 2 rnds and fights at -20. +10 hits.
71-75	Thigh strike. 100% change. Foe is stunned and unable to parry next rnd. Foe fights at -10. +7 hits.	Leg wound. 90% change. Foe is stunned for 2 rnds and fights at -15. +8 hits.	Leg wound. 80% change. Foe is stunned for 3 rnds. Add +20 to your next action. +9 hits.	Leg wound. 60% change. Foe is stunned and unable to parry for 2 rnds and fights at -20. +10 hits.	Lower leg strike. 50% change. Foe is stunned and unable to parry for 3 rnds and fights at -25. +11 hits.
76-80	Shield arm strike. 100% change. Foe is stunned for two rnds and fights at -15. +8 hits.	Shield arm strike. 100% change. Foe is stunned for 3 rnds. Add +20 to your next action. +9 hits.	Shield arm strike. 90% change. Foe is stunned and unable to parry for 2 rnds and fights at -20. +10 hits.	Shield arm strike. 70% change. Foe is stunned and unable to parry for 3 rnds and fights at -25. +11 hits.	Weapon arm strike 60% change. Foe is stunned and unable to parry for 4 rnds and fights at -30. +12 hits.
81-85	Side wound. 100% change. Foe is stunned for 3 rnds. Add +20 to your next action. +9 hits.	Side wound. 100% change. Foe is stunned and unable to parry for 2 rnds and fights at -20. +10 hits.	Side wound. 100% change. Foe is stunned and unable to parry for 3 rnds and fights at -25. +11 hits.	Stomach strike. 80% change. Foe is stunned and unable to parry for 4 rnds and fights at -30. +12 hits.	Back wound. 70% change. Foe is stunned and unable to parry for 5 rnds and fights at -30. You only needed half a rnd. +13 hits.
86-90	Nail foe's back. 100% change. Foe is stunned and unable to parry for 2 rnds and fights at -20. +10 hits.	Back of head strike. 100% change. Foe is stunned and unable to parry for 3 rnds and fights at -25. +11 hits.	Hit on back of head. 100% change. Foe is stunned and unable to parry for 4 rnds and fights at -30. +12 hits.	Bruise to kidneys. 90% change. Foe is stunned and unable to parry for 5 rnds and fights at -30. You only needed half a rnd. +13 hits.	Leg wound. 80% change. Foe is stunned and unable to parry for 6 rnds and fights at -30. You only needed half a rnd. +14 hits.
91-95	Head strike. 100% change. Foe is stunned and unable to parry for 3 rnds and fights at -25. +11 hits.	Hip strike. 100% change. Foe is stunned and unable to parry for 4 rnds and fights at -30. +12 hits.	Chest wound. 100% change. Foe is stunned and unable to parry for 5 rnds and fights at -30. You only needed half a rnd. +13 hits.	Side wound. 100% change. Foe is stunned and unable to parry for 6 rnds and fights at -30. You only needed half a rnd. +14 hits.	Arm wound. 90% change. Foe's arms are struck numb and may not be used for 7 agonizing rnds. +16 hits.
96-99	Zap to the Head. 100% change. Foe is stunned and unable to parry for 4 rnds and fights at -30. +12 hits.	Bruise to cheek. 100% change. Foe is stunned and unable to parry for 5 rnds and fights at -30. You only needed half a rnd. +13 hits.	Neck wound. 100% change. Foe is stunned and unable to parry for 6 rnds and fights at -30. You only needed half a rnd. +14 hits.	Back wound. 100% change. Foe is struck in the back and is brought to his knees for 7 long rnds. +16 hits.	Chest strike. 100% change. Foe's heart stops momentarily. It takes 8 rnds before foe can do anything due to chest pains. +18 hits.
100	Throat burns. 100% change. Foe is stunned and unable to parry for 5 rnds and fights at -30. You only needed half a rnd. +13 hits.	Eye wound. 100% change. Foe is blinded and is at -90 for 2 rnds. Stunned for 6 rnds. +14 hits.	Head strike. 100% change. Foe's ears are blasted, staggers and falls prone for 8 long rnds. +15 hits.	Head strike. 100% change. Foe's brain is frazzled and is unable to cope with any action for the next 8 rnds. +18 hits.	Head strike. 100% change. Foe's eyes roll into back of his head. Foe awakens after 9 rnds and needs to reorientate (very hard). +20 hits.

12.4 DEPRESSION CRITICAL STRIKE TABLE

	A	B	C	D	E
01-05	0	0	0	0	Stunned for 3 rnds.
06-10	0	0	0	Stunned for 2 rnds.	Stunned 3 rnds. Mild depression. -5 to actions for 10 min.
11-15	0	0	Stunned for 1 rnd.	Stunned for 3 rnds. Mild depression. -5 to all actions for 5 minutes.	Stunned for 5 rnds. Mild depression. -5 to all actions for 10 minutes.
16-20	0	Stunned for 1 rnd.	Stunned for 3 rnds. Mild depression. -5 to all actions for 5 minutes.	Stunned for 5 rnds. Mild depression. -5 to all actions for 10 minutes.	Disorientated. Mild depression. -10 to all actions for 30 minutes.
21-35	Stunned for 1 rnd.	Stunned for 3 rnds. Mild depression. -5 to all actions for 5 minutes.	Stunned for 5 rnds. Mild depression. -5 to all actions for 10 minutes.	Disorientated. Mild depression. -10 to all actions for 30 minutes.	Disorientated. Moderate depression. -15 to all actions for 1 hour.
36-45	Stunned for 3 rnds. Mild depression. -5 to all actions for 1 minute.	Stunned for 5 rnds. Mild depression. -5 to all actions for 5 minutes.	Disorientated. Mild depression. -10 to all actions for 20 minutes.	Disorientated. Moderate depression. -15 to all actions for 1 hour.	Disorientated. Moderate depression. -15 to all actions for 3 hours.
46-50	Stunned for 5 rnds. Mild depression. -5 to all actions for 1 minute.	Disorientated. Mild depression. -10 to all actions for 20 minutes.	Disorientated. Moderate depression. -15 to all actions for 30 minutes.	Disorientated. Moderate depression. -15 to all actions for 3 hour.	Disorientated. Moderate depression. -20 to all actions for 6 hours.
51-55	Disorientated. Mild depression. -10 to all actions for 5 minutes.	Disorientated. Moderate depression. -15 to all actions for 30 minutes.	Disorientated. Moderate depression. -15 to all actions for 1 hour.	Disorientated. Moderate depression. -20 to all actions for 6 hours.	Disorientated. Severe depression. -20 to all actions for 24 hours.
56-60	Disorientated. Moderate depression. -15 to all actions for 10 minutes.	Disorientated. Moderate depression. -15 to all actions for 1 hour.	Disorientated. Moderate depression. -20 to all actions for 3 hours.	Disorientated. Severe depression. -20 to all actions for 15 hours.	Disorientated. Severe depression. -30 to all actions for 1 week.
61-65	Disorientated. Moderate depression. -15 to all actions for 30 minutes.	Disorientated. Moderate depression. -20 to all actions for 3 hours.	Disorientated. Severe depression. -20 to all actions for 6 hours.	Disorientated. Severe depression. -30 to all actions for 24 hours.	Severe depression. -30 to all actions for 1 month. Sad.
66	Foe falls unconscious. Suicidal depression. 15% chance/day of a highly suicidal act.	Foe goes into serious withdrawal from life due to an extremely low self-esteem catatonia.	Foe's mind goes elsewhere on an extended vacation. Coma.	The shock was too great to handle and foe's mind collapses. Coma. Death if no helm.	Foe's mind finds refuge in final surcease of everlasting Death.
67-70	Disorientated. Moderate depression. -20 to all actions for 1 hour.	Disorientated. Severe depression. -20 to all actions for 6 hours.	Disorientated. Severe depression. -30 to all actions for 24 hours.	Severe depression. -30 to all actions for 1 week. Enjoy the ride.	Foe is now manic-depressive for 6 months and is at -35 to all actions.
71-75	Disorientated. Severe depression. -20 to all actions for 3 hours.	Disorientated. Severe depression. -30 to actions for 24 hrs starting next rnd.	Severe depression. -30 to all actions for 1 week. Bummer.	Foe is now manic-depressive for 1 month. Lucky.	Foe is now manic-depressive. Suicidal. Permanent. 75%/day chance of suicide. Pitiful.
76-80	Disorientated. Severe depression. -30 to all actions for 6 hours.	Severe depression. -30 to all actions for 24 hours. Much sadness here.	Foe is now manic-depressive for 1 week.	Foe is now manic-depressive. Permanent. It could have been worse.	Mental Trauma. Roll 4 Random Insanities. Permanent. Time for the looney bin.
81-85	Severe depression. -30 to all actions for 24 hours.	Foe is now manic-depressive for 1 week.	Foe is now manic-depressive. Permanent. Life is now a rollercoaster.	Jolting. Roll 3 random Insanities. Permanent. Ugly.	Brain Fry. Roll 4 Random Insanities. Foe is at a -50 for all actions. Unconscious.
86-90	Foe is manic-depressive for 1 week.	Foe is now manic-depressive. Permanent. Life will continue to have its ups and downs.	Jolting. Roll 2 random Traumas. Permanent.	Suicidal depression. Permanent. 50%/day of suicide. Foe is now unconscious.	Catatonic depression. Permanent. Foe curls up to await Death.
91-95	Foe is manic-depressive. Permanent. Not a pretty sight.	Mental shock. Roll 1 random Trauma. Permanent.	Suicidal depression. Permanent. 25% chance/day of outright suicide.	Catatonic depression. Permanent. Foe attempts to get off the Merry-Go-Round of life.	Foe decides on a strategic withdrawal from reality. Coma.
96-99	Mental shock. Roll 1 random Trauma. Permanent.	Suicidal depression. Permanent. 25% chance/day of a suicidal action.	Catatonic. Permanent. Foe opts out.	Foe hides in the Darkest corner of his mind. Coma.	Foe stops moving and slowly sits down, closing his eyes. Death.
100	Suicidal depression. Permanent. 10% chance/day of a suicidal action.	Catatonic depression. Permanent. Foe wraps himself in a huddle and denys existence.	Severe depression. Too much for foe to handle. Coma.	Foe feels life is no longer worth living and gives up. Death.	Foe whimpers once as he falls to the floor. Death.

12.5 STRESS CRITICAL STRIKE TABLE

	A	B	C	D	E
01-05	Agony! +10 hits. Badly sprained back. -35 to all maneuvers.	Oh Pain! +15 hits. -50 on all actions. -5 to temp CO stat.	Racking Pain! +30 hits. -70 to all actions. -15 to temp CO stat.	Totally Paralyzed. +70 hits. -90 to actions after paralyzation is healed. -40 to temp CO stat.	+110 hits. You are at -100 to all actions and die in 12 rnds. -70 to temp CO stat, -20 to potential CO stat.
06-10	+4 hits. Pulled ligaments. -10 to all physical maneuvers.	Throbbing pain. +10 hits. -40 on all actions. -3 to temp CO stat.	Debilitating Pain. +25 hits. -10 to temp CO stat. -60 on everything. Uh Oh.	Crippling Pain from torn muscle tissue. -30 from temp CO stat. -80 to all actions.	Incapacitating Agony. +100 hits. Paralyzed (no action). -60 to temp CO stat, -20 to potential CO stat.
11-15	Sprained muscle -5 to all physical maneuvers for next 24 hours.	+7 hits. Ligaments and tendons damage. -30 to all maneuvers.	+19 hits. -50 to all actions -7 to temp CO stat. Nobody forced you.	+50 big hits. -30 to everything. -20 off temp CO stat.	Crippling Pain. +90 hits. -50 off temp CO stat. -15 off potential CO stat. -90 to all actions.
16-20	None	+5 hits. -10 to all physical maneuvers. Ouch!.	Terrible Agony. +14 hits. -40 to all actions. -5 to temp CO stat.	Prickly torment +45 hits. -60 to all actions. -15 to temp CO stat.	Excruciating Pain. +80 hits. -40 off temp CO stat. -10 off potential CO stat. -80 to all actions.
21-35	None	+3 hits. -5 to all physical maneuvers.	+10 hits. -30 to all actions. -3 to temp CO stat.	+37 hits. -55 to all action. -12 to temp CO stat. You did it to yourself .	+73 very real hits. -75 to all actions. -33 to temp CO stat. -7 to potential CO stat. Agony.
36-45	None	Pulled a muscle. -5 to all physical maneuvers for 24 hours.	+8 hits. -20 to all actions due to stinging pain.	+30 hits. -50 to all action. -8 to temp CO stat. Retirement ain't all bad.	+65 hits. -25 point off temp CO stat. -5 off potential CO stat. You are at -70 to do anything.
46-50	None	None	Bad Sprain. +5 hits. Pain. -10 to physical actions.	Pain lances through your body. +27 hits damage. -5 to temp CO stat. -40 to all maneuvers.	+55 hits. You are at -60. -20 to your temp CO stat. Time to retire, think about it.
51-55	None	None	+2 hits. That smarts You are at a -5 to physical maneuvers.	+24 hits. -1 to temp CO stat. -30 to all actions. Not good.	+50 hits. -18 to temp CO stat. Sprained 110 muscles, -55 to activity.
56-60	None	None	Sprain for the next 24 hours. -5 to all physical maneuvers.	+20 hits. Screaming muscles leave you -20. -1 to temp CO stat.	Lacerating Agony. +45 hits. -45 on all actions. -14 to temp CO stat.
61-65	None	None	None	+15 hits. Splitting pain in back bestows -15 to all actions.	+35 hits. -10 to temp CO stat. -40 to all actions. Scourging Pain.
66	None	None	None	+10 hits. Good Job. You are at -10 on all physical maneuvers.	Now that really hurt. +28 hits. -7 to Temp CO stat. -30 to all actions.
67-70	None	None	None	Dull Ache in joints. +6 hits. You are at -5 to all physical maneuvers.	+21 hits. -25 to all actions -5 to temp CO stat. Much Pain.
71-75	None	None	None	+3 hits. Smooth move. -5 to all physical maneuvers.	Gripping Pangs. +15 hits. -20 to actions. -2 to temp CO stat.
76-80	None	None	None	None	+12 hits. Throbbing Pain gives -15 to all actions. Not Pretty.
81-85	None	None	None	None	Sprained muscles and tendons. +7 hits. -10 to all actions.
86-90	None	None	None	None	+4 hits. -5 to all physical maneuvers.
91-95	None	None	None	None	Sore Muscles. +1 hit. -5 to all actions.
96-99	Beneficial Stress. +2 add to hit total (i.e., body development). Enjoy.	None	None	None	None
100	Very Beneficial Stress. +5 add to hit total (i.e., body development). You have initiative.	Beneficial Stress. +5 to temp CO stat (may not raise stat above potential).	None	None	None

12.6 SHOCK CRITICAL STRIKE TABLE 91

	A	B	C	D	E
01-05	None	None	None	None	1 rnd of stun.
06-10	None	None	None	Stunned for 1 rnd.	Stunned for 2 rnds.
11-15	None	None	Stunned for 1 rnd.	Stunned for 1 rnd.	Stunned for 3 rnds. Parry at half.
16-20	None	Stunned for 1 rnd.	Stunned for 1 rnd.	Stunned for 2 rnds.	Stunned for 4 rnds. Cannot parry. -5 for 1 hour.
21-35	Stunned for 1 rnd.	Stunned for 1 rnd.	Stunned for 2 rnds. Parry at half.	Stunned for 3 rnds. Parry at half.	Stunned for 5 rnds. -10 for 1 hour.
36-45	Stunned for 1 rnd.	Stunned for 2 rnds. Parry at half.	Stunned for 3 rnds.	Stunned for 4 rnds. Cannot parry. -5 for 1 hour.	Stunned for 6 rnds. Cannot parry. -15 for 1 hour.
46-50	Stunned for 2 rnds.	Stunned for 3 rnds.	Stunned for 4 rnds. Cannot parry. -5 for 1 hour.	Stunned for 5 rnds. Cannot parry. -10 for 1 hour.	Stunned 7 rnds. Cannot parry or change facing. -20 for 1 hr.
51-55	Stunned for 3 rnds. Parry at half.	Stunned for 4 rnds. Cannot parry.	Stunned for 5 rnds. Cannot parry. -10 for 1 hour.	Stunned for 6 rnds. Cannot parry. -15 for 1 hour.	Stunned 9 rnds. Cannot parry or change facing. -25 for 24 hrs.
56-60	Stunned for 4 rnds. Cannot parry.	Stunned for 5 rnds. Cannot parry. -5 for 20 minutes.	Stunned for 6 rnds. -15 for 1 hour.	Stunned for 8 rnds. Cannot parry. -20 for 1 hour.	Stunned for 12 rnds. Cannot parry or change facing. Disorientated. -25 for 3 days.
61-65	Stunned for 5 rnds. Cannot parry. -5 for 20 minutes.	Stunned for 6 rnds. -5 for 1 hour.	Stunned for 8 rnds. Cannot parry. -20 for 1 hour.	Stunned for 10 rnds. Cannot parry or change facing. Disorientated. -25 for 24 hours.	Stunned for 15 rnds. Cannot parry or change facing. Disorientated. -30 for 3 days.
66	Stunned for 10 rnds. Cannot parry or change facing. -25 for 24 hours.	Stunned for 16 rnds. Cannot parry or change facing.	Foe slams himself to the Floor for 4 hits. Coma.	Foe snaps rigid and slowly falls, the air whistling audibly from his lips. Coma. Death if no helm.	Foe collapses like card house in a stiff breeze. Death.
67-70	Stunned for 7 rnds. Cannot parry. -10 for 1 hour.	Stunned for 9 rnds. Cannot parry. -10 for 3 hours.	Stunned for 11 rnds. Cannot parry or change facing. -20 for 3 hours.	Stunned for 13 rnds. Cannot parry or change facing. Disorientated. -30 for 24 hours.	Stunned for 19 rnds. Cannot parry or change facing. Disorientated. -35 for 3 days.
71-75	Stunned for 8 rnds. Cannot parry. -15 for 1 hour.	Stunned for 10 rnds. Cannot parry or change facing. -20 for 3 hours.	Stunned for 12 rnds. Cannot parry or change facing. Disorientated. -25 for 6 hours.	Stunned for 14 rnds. Cannot parry or change facing. Disorientated. -35 for 3 days.	Stunned for 25 rnds. Immobilized for 3 rnds. Disorientated. -40 for 1 week.
76-80	Stunned for 9 rnds. Cannot parry or change facing. -20 for 3 hours.	Stunned for 11 rnds. Cannot parry or change facing. -25 for 3 hours.	Stunned for 13 rnds. Cannot parry or change facing. Disorientated. -30 for 24 hrs.	Stunned for 15 rnds. Cannot parry or change facing. Disorientated. -40 for 3 days.	Stunned for 30 rnds. Immobilized for 5 rnds. Disorientated. -50 for 1 week.
81-85	Stunned for 10 rnds. Cannot parry or change facing. -20 for 6 hours.	Stunned for 12 rnds. Cannot parry or change facing. Disorientated. -30 for 24 hours.	Stunned for 14 rnds. Cannot parry or change facing. Disorientated. -30 for 2 days.	Stunned for 16 rnds. Cannot parry or change facing. Disorientated. -45 for 3 days.	Foe spins about clutching his head and falls. +2 Hits. -60 for 1 week. Unconscious.
86-90	Stunned for 11 rnds. Cannot parry or change facing. -25 for 6 hours.	Stunned for 13 rnds. Cannot parry or change facing. Disorientated. -35 for 24 hours.	Stunned for 15 rnds. Cannot parry or change facing. Disorientated. -35 for 2 days.	Stunned for 17 rnds. Cannot parry or change facing. Disorientated. -50 for 3 days.	One last howl punctuates foe's collapse. +5 Hits. -75 for 1 week. Unconscious.
91-95	Stunned for 12 rnds Cannot parry or change facing. Disorientated. -25 for 24 hours.	Stunned for 15 rnds. Cannot parry or change facing. Disorientated. -35 for 2 days.	Stunned for 18 rnds. Cannot parry or change facing. Disorientated. -40 for 2 days.	Stunned for 21 rnds. Immobilized 3 rnds. -50 for 1 week. +2 hits.	Roll 3 random phobias. +7 hits. Coma.
96-99	Stunned for 13 rnds. Cannot parry or change facing. Disorientated. -30 for 24 hours.	Stunned for 16 rnds. Cannot parry or change facing. Disorientated. -40 for 2 days.	Stunned for 24 rnds. Immobilized 2 rnds. Disorientated. +1 Hit.	Random brain damage. +3 hits. Coma.	Foe crumples in an untidy heap. Death.
100	Stunned for 14 rnds. Cannot parry or change facing. Disorientated. -35 for 24 hours.	Stunned for 19 rnds. Immobilized 2 rnds. -45 for 2 days.	When foe awakes he is mindless drooling idiot. +2 hits. Coma.	Foe stops and remains in last living position. Pity. Death.	Foe's eyes glaze as he launches himself 10' backwards. Death.

12.7 DISRUPTION CRITICAL STRIKE TABLE

	A	B	C	D	E
01-05	A near miss. No extra damage.	Glancing blow. +0 hits.	+1 hit.	+3 hits.	+4 hits.
06-10	+1 hit.	+3 hits.	+4 hits. Add +10 to your next attack.	You may attack before this opponent in the next Fire Phase. +5 hits.	+6 hits. Foe loses his next attack opportunity.
11-15	You may resolve your fire before this opponent's next round. +2 hits.	Soft strike to foe's side. You may fire before this opponent for the next three rnds. +4 hits.	Minor disruption of foe's side. +7 hits. Foe takes 2 hits per round.	+6 hits. Foe is stunned for 2 rounds.	+8 hits. Foe is stunned for 2 rounds.
16-20	Foe is stunned next round, and must parry for the next two rounds. +3 hits.	Blow to foe's side delivers +5 hits. Foe must parry next round at -30.	Blow stuns foe for 3 rounds. +8 hits.	Minor side wound causes foe to take 3 hits per round. He is stunned next round.	Minor disruption gives foe 1 hit per round. He must parry for 3 rounds.
21-35	Foe must parry next three rounds. +4 hits. Add +5 to your next attack.	Foe stunned for the next three rounds. +5 hits, and foe takes 1 hit per round.	Disrupting strike hits foe along side of chest. Foe stunned and unable to parry for 2 rounds. Foe takes 3 hits per round. +9 hits.	Blast to foe's upper leg. +7 hits. He is stunned and unable to parry for 3 rounds.	Attack disrupts foe's side. +9 hits. Foe takes 3 hits per round and is stunned for 4 rounds.
36-45	Burst muscle in foe's lower leg. Foe stunned for one round and receives 1 hit per round. Move at -50.	Disrupt foe's lower leg. Foe moves at -50 and takes 4 hits per round. +6 hits.	Major wound to lower leg. Foe takes 5 hits per round and is knocked to one knee. He is stunned for 4 rounds.	Wound foe's groin. Shocked, he is stunned for 7 rounds and unable to parry for 4 rounds. +8 hits. Add +10 to your next attack.	Blow to leg shatters several bones and shreds muscle. Foe at -70 and takes 4 hits per round. Add +10 to your next attack.
46-50	Minor flesh wound along foe's back. +5 hits. Foe stunned for two rounds.	Disrupting blast along foe's lower back. He is stunned and may not parry for 4 rounds. +7 hits, takes 1 hit per round.	Blast across foe's back tears skin. Foe takes 3 hits per round and is stunned for 5 rounds.	Disruption of foe's lower back paralyzes him from the waist down. He is down and out for 20 rounds. +10 hits.	Minor disruption to foe's lower back. Foe is stunned and unable to parry for 5 rounds. He takes 4 hits per round. +10 hits.
51-55	Minor disrupting strike to foe's chest. Foe is stunned and unable to parry for three rnds and receives 3 hits per round.	Blow to foe's chest drops him to the ground. Foe takes 4 hits per round and is stunned for 5 rounds. +8 hits.	Disruption in upper chest drops foe for 3 rounds. Foe takes 3 hits per round. +10 hits.	Blast in chest collapses foe's lungs and breaks ribs. Foe operates at -50 for 4 rounds then slips into a coma. He dies 6 rnds thereafter. +12 hits.	Foe's chest ruptured. He takes 6 hits per round. In 3 rounds he drops, and after 3 more, he dies.
56-60	Minor thigh disruption. Foe knocked down and stunned for 2 rounds. +5 hits. Foe takes 3 hits per round.	Energy dissipation shreds foe's thigh muscle. Foe takes 4 hits per round. +9 hits. Foe moves at -50.	Pulverizing blast to foe's upper thigh. +11 hits. Foe falls and is stunned for 5 rounds. He takes 5 hits/rnd and moves at -75.	Blast in upper leg. Foe falls and takes 6 hits per round. He is at -90. Add +10 to your next action.	Major groin injury. Vitals destroyed. Foe stunned for 14 rounds and takes 2 hits per round.
61-65	Blast along forearm. +5 hits. Foe takes 3 hits per round and is at -25.	Blast to foe's forearm. Hand useless. +9 hits. Foe takes 5 hits per round.	Strike rips into foe's forearm. Arm useless. Foe takes 4 hits per rnd and operates at -40. +12 hits.	Forearm destroyed. Foe takes 7 hits per round and is stunned for 5 rounds. He is at -40.	Disrupting strike severs arm above the elbow. Foe takes 5 hits/rnd and is stunned for 8 rnds. He is at -50.
66	Non-weapon shoulder bursts from inside. Arm useless; will fall off if foe takes more than 25% activity; stunned no parry for 6 rnds, +10 hits, 5 hits/rnd.	Elbow in foe's weapon arm disrupted. Joint is destroyed and arm useless. +10 hits. Foe stunned and unable to parry for 10 rounds.	Foe's knee destroyed. He loses lower leg, and takes 5 hits per round. Foe drops and is out for 10 rounds. Afterwards he is at -70. +25 hits.	Blast to the face destroys foe's eyes, ears, nose and throat. He dies after 4 painful rounds.	Burst destroys lungs. Heart explodes. Foe falls and is inactive for 3 agonizing rounds before dying. +20 hits.
67-70	Break foe's collar bone. +6 hits. Foe is stunned for 4 rounds and may not parry for two rounds. Foe at -20.	Blow to foe's neck. Foe stunned for 6 rounds and may not parry for 3 rounds. Foe operates at -10. +10 hits.	Blow to collar area. Foe is stunned for 12 rounds choking. He operates at -80. +13 hits.	Massive cellular disruption in foe's shoulder. +14 hits. Foe stunned for 6 rounds and operates at -60.	Blast inside shoulder sends arm flying. Foe stunned and unable to parry for 12 rnds, +22 hits, 6 hits/rnd. Add +10 to your next attack.
71-75	Disrupt tendons in lower leg. Foe at -50 and knocked to one knee. Foe stunned for 3 rnds and takes 2 hits per rnd.	Muscles burst in foe's calf. Foe at -50 and receives 5 hits per round. +11 hits.	Foe's calf muscle destroyed, tendons disrupted and bone shattered. Foe is at -50; takes 6 hits/rnd. Add +10 to your next attack.	Blast destroys foe's foot. He is at -50 for 5 rounds before passing out. Foe takes 5 hits per round.	Shuddering blast scraps leg. Bone, muscle and blood vessels burst. Foe knocked down, stunned for 6 rnds. He takes 6 hits/rnd. +24 hits.
76-80	Disrupt foe's bicep. +7 hits, and 3 hits per round. Foe at -30 and stunned for 4 rounds.	Non-weapon arm disrupted. Foe at -40 and takes 6 hits/rnd. He is stunned and unable to parry for 7 rnds. Arm useless.	Non-weapon arm disrupted and useless; muscles destroyed; bone fractured. Stunned for 12 rnds; takes 4 hits/rnd. +14 hits.	Foe's non-weapon arm explodes and is messily removed from his body. Stunned and unable to parry for 18 rnds, 6 hits/rnd, +20 hits.	Foe's weapon arm bursts open. It is destroyed. Foe takes 6 hits per round, and is stunned for 36 rounds. +30 hits.
81-85	Strike foe in the side. Internal bleeding delivers 7 hits per round. Foe stunned 8 rounds. Add +10 to your next attack.	Blow to foe's side. +12 hits. Foe takes 8 hits per round. He is stunned for 12 rounds and operates at -40.	Blow to side of lower abdomen. +15 hits. Internal bleeding causes 6 hits/rnd. Foe fights for 24 rnds then dies due to organ failure.	Variety of foe's abdominal organs explode. He takes 8 hits per round and is at -80 for 4 rounds before expiring. +30 Hits.	Foe's backbone shattered by blast. He falls and dies after 6 quiet rounds due to massive organ failure. +40 hits.
86-90	Disrupting blast along foe's back. Foe takes 4 hits/rnd and is stunned for 5 rnds. +8 hits.	Strike to back of foe's head. The subsequent brain disruption kills foe instantly. +15 hits.	Shot pulps foe's brain. He dies instantly. +25 hits. Add +15 to your next attack.	Shattering blast destroys foe's kidneys and severs spine. +40 hits. Foe drops, then dies next round.	Strike disrupts hip joint. Leg is lost. Foe lapses into unconsciousness, dying in 6 rounds. +30 hits.
91-95	Blow off foe's ear. +9 hits. Foe takes 5 hits per round and hearing is at -50. Foe stunned for 10 rounds.	Blast disrupts hip, destroying the joint, +15 hits, stunned for 10 rnds before passing out. Add +20 to your next attack.	Foe's chest explodes from the inside. Heart destroyed. Foe drops then dies next round. +35 hits.	Disgusting strike guts through opponent. He is disemboweled and dies instantly. Add +20 to your next action.	Foe's arm and side destroyed by disrupting blast. He is stunned and unable to parry for 8 rounds, then dies. +35 hits.
96-99	Disrupting strike to middle of face, stunned and unable to parry for 12 rnds, 5 hits/rnd. Add +5 to your next attack.	Blast blows out side of foe's head. Foe drops and takes 5 hits per round for three rounds before dying.	Blast shatters backbone and exposes upper chest cavity. Foe dies instantly. +45 hits.	Back blow sends foe reeling. Broken in half, foe drops and dies next round.	Internal explosion sends rib fragments flying. Foe drops and dies immediately. Add +20 to all actions for the next 2 rounds.
100	Strike disrupts foe's neck, severing his head from the rest of his body. Foe dies immediately. +20 hits.	Head strike destroys brain. Foe is dead.	Foe's head explodes. He is very dead, permanently.	Head shot destroys brain in a gruesome display. Foe's lifeless, headless body tossed back 3 meters.	Foe's body ripped apart by cruel disrupting blast. He is no more. Good work.

13.1 PLASMA BOLT ATTACK TABLE

	20	19	18	17	16	15	14	13	12	11	10	9	8	7	6	5	4	3	2	1	
UM 01-02	F	F	F	F	F	F	F	F	F	F	F	F	F	F	F	F	F	F	F	F	01-02 UM
03-10	F	F	F	F	F	F	F	F	F	F	F	F	F	F	F	F	0	0	0	0	03-10
11-20	F	F	F	F	F	F	F	F	0	0	0	0	0	0	0	0	0	0	0	0	11-20
21-30	0	0	0	0	0	0	0	0	0	0	0	0	0	0	0	0	0	0	0	0	21-30
31-35	1	1	0	0	1	0	0	0	0	0	0	0	0	0	0	0	0	0	1	0	31-35
36-40	2	2	1	0	2	0	0	0	0	0	0	0	0	0	0	0	0	0	2	0	36-40
41-45	3	3	3	1	3	3	1	0	1	0	0	0	1	1	0	0	1	1	4A	0	41-45
46-50	4	4	4	3A	3	4	3	1	1	1	1	0	3	2	1	0	3	3	6B	3A	46-50
51-55	4A	5	5	5A	4	5	5	3A	2	2	3	1	4	4	2	1	5	5A	8B	5B	51-55
56-60	5A	6A	7A	7A	4	7	7	6A	3	3	6	3A	5	5	4	3A	7A	8A	10C	7B	56-60
61-65	5A	7A	8A	9B	5	8	8A	8A	4	4	7	6A	7	6	5	6A	9A	11A	12C	9C	61-65
66-70	6A	8A	9A	11B	6	9	9A	11B	4	5	9A	9A	8	8	6A	8A	11B	14B	13C	11C	66-70
71-75	7A	8A	10B	12B	7A	10	11B	12B	5	6	10A	11A	9A	9	8A	10A	12B	17B	15C	13C	71-75
76-80	7A	9B	12B	14B	8A	11A	12B	13B	6	7A	11A	13B	11A	10A	9A	13B	13B	19B	17D	15C	76-80
81-85	8B	10B	13B	15B	9A	12A	13B	16C	7	8A	13B	15B	12A	12A	10A	16B	15B	21B	19D	17D	81-85
86-90	8B	11B	14B	17C	10B	13B	15C	17C	8A	10A	15B	17B	13A	13A	12B	18B	16C	23B	21D	19D	86-90
91-95	8B	11B	15C	19C	11B	13B	16C	19C	8A	11B	17B	19C	15A	15B	13B	20B	17C	25C	23D	21D	91-95
96-100	9B	12B	16C	20C	11B	14C	17C	20D	9A	12B	19C	21C	16B	16B	15B	22C	19C	27C	25D	23D	96-100
101-105	9B	12C	17C	21C	12C	15C	19D	21D	10B	13B	20C	23C	17B	17B	17C	23C	20C	29C	28E	26D	101-105
106-110	10C	13C	19C	23D	13C	16D	20D	23D	11B	14C	21C	25D	19B	19C	18C	25C	22D	31C	31E	29E	106-110
111-115	11C	14C	20D	24D	14D	16D	21D	25E	11B	15C	23D	26D	20C	20C	21C	27D	24D	33D	33E	31E	111-115
116-120	11C	15C	21D	25D	15D	17D	23E	26E	12C	16C	24D	27D	21C	21C	23D	29D	27D	35D	36E	34E	116-120
121-125	12C	16D	22D	26E	16D	18D	25E	28E	13C	17D	25D	29E	23C	23D	25D	32D	29E	36D	39E	37E	121-125
126-130	12D	16D	24E	27E	17E	19E	26E	29F	13D	18D	27E	30E	24D	25D	28D	35D	32E	37E	41F	39E	126-130
131-135	12D	17D	25E	29E	18E	20E	27F	30F	14D	19D	28E	31E	26D	27D	30E	37E	35E	38E	44F	42F	131-135
136-140	13E	18E	26F	30F	19F	21F	28F	31F	15E	19E	29F	32F	27E	28E	31E	40E	37F	39F	47F	45F	136-140
141-145	13E	19E	28F	31F	20F	22F	30F	33F	15E	20E	31F	34F	29E	30E	34E	43E	41F	40F	49F	47F	141-145
146-150	13F	20F	30G	32G	21G	23G	31G	35G	15F	20F	32G	35G	31F	33F	36G	45G	43G	41G	52G	50G	146-150
UM 100	19G	24G	35H	27H	27H	30H	37H	41H	20G	26G	38H	42H	35G	38G	42H	50H	51H	49H	63H	60H	100 UM

Range:
0' — 10'	:	+35
11' — 50'	:	0
51' — 100'	:	-25
101' — 200'	:	-40
201' — 300'	:	-55
301' — up	:	-75

(For A,B,C,D,E use plasma criticals)

UM = Unmodified Roll

Result	Use Plasma	Use Cold	Use Electricity
F	E	A	
G	E	B	—
H	E	C	A

13.2 PLASMA BALL ATTACK TABLE

Roll	20	19	18	17	16	15	14	13	12	11	10	9	8	7	6	5	4	3	2	1	Roll
	F	F	F	F	F	F	F	F	F	F	F	F	F	F	F	F	F	F	F	F	
UM 01-04	0	0	0	0	0	0	0	1	0	0	0	1A	0	0	0	0	0	0	2	4	01-04 UM
05-08	0	0	0	0	0	0	0	1	0	0	0	2A	0	0	0	0	0	1	5	6A	05-08
09-12	0	0	0	0	0	0	0	2	0	1	1	3A	0	0	0	2A	1	2A	7A	8A	09-12
13-16	0	0	0	1	0	0	1	4A	1	1	2	5A	1	1	1	4A	2A	4A	8A	11A	13-16
17-20	0	1	1	2A	1	1	2	5A	1	2	3A	6A	2	2	2	7A	4A	4A	11A	13A	17-20
21-24	1	2	2A	4A	2	2	4	6A	2	4A	5A	8A	3A	3A	3A	9A	5A	5A	13A	14A	21-24
25-28	2	4A	4A	5A	3	3	5A	8A	4A	4A	6A	9A	5A	5A	5A	10A	6A	6A	14A	16B	25-28
29-32	4	6A	5A	6A	5A	5A	7A	9A	5A	5A	7A	10B	6A	6A	7A	13B	8A	8A	16A	17B	29-32
33-36	5A	8A	8A	9A	6A	6A	8A	10B	6A	6A	9A	12B	7A	7A	9A	14B	9A	9A	17B	18B	33-36
37-40	6A	9A	9A	10A	7A	7A	9A	12B	7A	7A	10B	13B	9A	9A	10B	17B	10A	10B	18B	20B	37-40
41-44	7A	10A	10A	12B	9A	9A	10A	13B	8A	8B	11B	14B	10B	10B	11B	18B	12B	12B	20B	21C	41-44
45-48	7A	11A	12A	13B	10A	10A	12B	14B	8A	9B	13B	16B	11B	11B	13B	19C	13B	13B	21B	22C	45-48
49-52	8A	12A	13B	14B	11A	11A	13B	16B	9B	11B	14B	17C	12B	13B	14B	21C	14B	14B	22C	24C	49-52
53-56	8A	12B	14B	16B	13A	13A	14B	17B	9B	12B	16B	18C	14B	14B	15B	22C	16B	16B	24C	25C	53-56
57-60	9A	14B	16B	17B	14B	14B	16B	18C	10B	13B	17C	20C	15B	15C	17C	23C	17B	17B	25C	26C	57-60
61-64	10B	14B	17B	18B	14B	14B	17B	20C	10B	14C	18C	21C	16C	16C	18C	25C	18C	18C	25C	28C	61-64
65-68	10B	15B	18B	19C	15B	15B	18C	21C	12B	15C	20C	22C	17C	17C	19C	26C	20C	20C	27C	29D	65-68
69-72	11B	15B	19B	21C	15B	15B	20C	22C	13C	16C	21C	23C	18C	19C	21C	27D	21C	21C	28C	30D	69-72
73-76	12B	17C	19C	21C	15B	16B	21C	23C	14C	18C	22C	24D	19C	20C	22C	29D	22C	22C	29D	32D	73-76
77-80	12B	17C	21C	22C	16B	17C	22C	23C	15C	19C	23C	26D	21C	21C	24D	30D	23C	24C	31D	33D	77-80
81-84	13C	18C	21C	22C	17C	18C	22C	24C	16C	20C	24D	27D	22D	22D	26D	31D	26C	26C	32D	34D	81-84
85-88	13C	18C	22C	23C	18C	18C	23C	24C	17C	21C	26D	29D	24D	23D	29D	34D	28D	28D	34D	34D	85-88
89-92	13C	18D	21C	25C	18C	18C	23C	25C	19D	23D	28D	30E	26D	24D	31D	34E	29D	30D	34D	35D	89-92
93-95	14C	19D	22D	23D	19C	19C	25D	26D	21D	25E	29D	32E	27E	26D	31D	36E	31D	32D	36E	37E	93-95
UM 96-97	16D	22D	25D	28E	21D	21D	27D	28E	23E	25E	31E	34E	30E	28E	34E	36E	35D	34E	36E	39E	96-97 UM
UM 98-99	18E	24E	27E	30E	23E	23E	29E	30E	26F	27E	33E	34F	32F	31E	36E	38E	37E	36E	38E	41E	98-99 UM
UM 100	20F	26F	29F	32F	25F	26F	31F	32F	29F	29F	35F	36F	34F	34F	38F	40F	35F	38F	40F	43F	100 UM

(For A,B,C,D,E use plasma criticals)

UM = Unmodified Roll

	Result	Use Plasma	Use Cold
	F	E	A

Range:
0' — 10'   : +35
11' — 50'   : 0
51' — 100' : -25
101' — 200' : -40
201' — 300' : -55
301' — up   : -75

13.3 NETHER BOLT ATTACK TABLE

UM		20	19	18	17	16	15	14	13	12	11	10	9	8	7	6	5	4	3	2	1		UM
UM	01-02	F	F	F	F	F	F	F	F	F	F	F	F	F	F	F	F	F	F	F	F	01-02	UM
	03-10	F	F	F	F	F	F	F	F	F	F	F	F	F	F	F	F	F	F	F	F	03-10	
	11-20	F	F	F	F	F	F	F	F	F	F	F	F	F	F	F	F	F	F	F	F	11-20	
	21-30	1	0	0	0	0	0	0	0	0	0	0	0	0	0	0	0	0	0	2	0	21-30	
	31-35	3	1	0	0	1	0	0	0	0	0	0	0	0	0	0	0	0	2	4	1	31-35	
	36-40	3	3	1	0	3	1	0	0	3	0	0	0	0	0	0	0	2	4	4A	3	36-40	
	41-45	5A	3	3	1	3	3	2	0	3	3	0	0	4	0	0	0	4A	5A	6A	5A	41-45	
	46-50	5A	5A	3	3	5A	3	2	2	5A	3	3	0	4A	4	0	0	5A	6A	7A	6A	46-50	
	51-55	7A	5A	5A	3	5A	5A	4A	2	5A	5A	3	3	5A	4A	4	0	6A	7A	8B	8A	51-55	
	56-60	7A	7A	5A	5A	7A	5A	5A	4A	7A	5A	5A	3	5A	5A	4A	4	6A	8B	9B	9B	56-60	
	61-65	9B	7A	7A	5A	7A	7A	6A	5A	7A	7A	7A	5A	7A	5A	5A	5A	7A	9B	10B	10B	61-65	
	66-70	9B	9B	7A	7A	9B	7A	7A	7A	7A	7A	8B	7A	7A	7A	7A	7A	9B	11B	12C	11B	66-70	
	71-75	11B	9B	9B	7A	9B	9B	8B	8B	7A	7A	8B	8B	7A	7A	9B	8B	11B	12B	14C	13C	71-75	
	76-80	11B	11B	9B	9B	11B	9B	8B	8B	8A	8B	10B	10B	9B	9B	11B	10B	13B	14C	16C	15C	76-80	
	81-85	13B	11B	11B	9B	11B	11B	10B	10B	9B	8B	10B	11B	9B	10B	12B	12C	15C	16C	18C	17C	81-85	
	86-90	13C	13B	11B	11B	13B	11B	12B	12B	11B	10B	11B	12B	11B	12B	13B	14C	16C	17C	19D	18C	86-90	
	91-95	13C	13C	13B	11B	13C	13B	14C	14C	13B	12B	13B	14B	13B	12B	14B	15C	16C	17C	19D	20D	91-95	
	96-100	15C	13C	13C	13B	13C	13C	14C	15C	13B	14B	14B	15C	13C	14C	15C	17C	17D	18D	20D	21D	96-100	
	101-105	15C	15C	13C	13C	15C	13C	15C	15C	15B	16C	16C	17C	15C	16C	16C	17D	18D	19D	21E	22D	101-105	
	106-110	16D	15C	15C	13C	15C	15C	15C	16D	15C	16C	18C	19D	15C	16C	17C	18D	19D	20D	22E	23E	106-110	
	111-115	16D	16D	16D	15C	16D	15C	16D	16D	16C	17C	18D	20D	17C	18C	18D	19D	20D	21E	23E	24E	111-115	
	116-120	16D	16D	17D	16D	16D	16D	16D	17D	16C	17C	18D	20D	18D	19D	20D	21D	21D	22E	24E	25E	116-120	
	121-125	17D	17D	18D	17D	16D	16D	17D	17D	16C	18C	19D	21D	18D	19D	20D	21E	22E	23E	25E	26E	121-125	
	126-130	17D	17D	18D	18D	17D	17D	18D	18D	17C	18D	19D	21E	19D	20D	21D	23E	24E	25E	27E	28E	126-130	
	131-135	18D	18D	19E	19E	18D	18D	19E	20E	18D	19D	20D	22E	20D	21E	23E	24E	26E	27E	29E	30E	131-135	
	136-140	18D	19E	19E	20E	18D	19E	20E	22E	19D	19D	21E	23E	22E	23E	25E	26E	27E	28E	30E	31F	136-140	
	141-145	19E	19E	21E	22E	19E	20E	21E	22E	20D	21E	22E	24E	24E	25E	27E	28E	28E	29E	31F	32F	141-145	
	146-150	19E	20E	21E	22E	20E	21E	22E	23E	22E	23E	24E	25E	26E	27E	28E	29E	30E	31F	32F	33F	146-150	
UM	100	25E	26F	27F	28F	26F	27F	28F	29F	28F	29F	30F	31F	32G	33G	34G	35G	36G	37G	38G	39G	100	UM

Range:
0' — 10'	:	+35
11' — 50'	:	0
51' — 100'	:	-25
101' — 200'	:	-40
201' — 300'	:	-55
301' — up	:	-75

(For A,B,C,D,E use Disruption criticals)

UM = Unmodified Roll

Result	Use Disruption	Use Stress
F	E	A
G	E	B

13.4 NETHER BALL ATTACK TABLE

Roll	20	19	18	17	16	15	14	13	12	11	10	9	8	7	6	5	4	3	2	1
01-04	F	F	F	F	F	F	F	F	F	F	F	F	F	F	F	F	F	F	F	F
05-08	0	0	0	0	0	0	0	0	0	0	0	0	0	0	0	0	0	0	1	1
09-12	0	0	0	0	0	0	0	0	0	0	0	0	0	0	0	0	0	0	3	4
13-16	0	0	0	0	0	0	0	0	0	0	0	0	0	0	0	0	0	1	5A	6A
17-20	0	0	1	1	0	1	1	3	0	1	3	4A	0	1	3	5A	1	3	7A	8A
21-24	0	1	3	4A	0	1	3	4A	1	3	4A	5A	1	3	4A	7A	2	4A	8A	10A
25-28	1	3	4A	5A	1	3	4A	5A	3	4	5A	6A	3	4A	7A	8A	4A	5A	10A	12A
29-32	3	4A	5A	6A	3	4A	5A	6A	4	4A	6A	7A	4A	5A	6A	10A	5A	6A	12A	13A
33-36	4A	5A	6A	7A	4A	5A	6A	7A	4A	4A	7A	8A	5A	6A	7A	12B	6A	7A	13A	14B
37-40	5A	6A	7A	8A	5A	6A	7A	8A	5A	5A	8A	9B	6A	7A	8A	13B	7A	8A	14B	15B
41-44	6A	7A	8A	9A	6A	7A	8A	9B	5A	5A	9B	10B	7A	8A	9B	14B	8A	9A	15B	16B
45-48	6A	8A	9A	10B	7A	8A	9B	10B	6A	6A	10B	11B	8A	9B	10B	15B	9A	10B	16B	17B
49-52	7A	9A	10A	11B	8A	9A	10B	11B	7A	7B	11B	12B	9B	10B	11B	16B	10B	11B	17B	18C
53-56	7A	9A	11B	12B	9A	10A	11B	12B	7A	8B	12B	13B	10B	11B	12B	17C	11B	12B	18C	19C
57-60	8A	10A	12B	13B	10A	11A	12B	13B	8B	9B	13B	14C	11B	12B	13B	18C	12B	13B	19C	20C
61-64	8A	10B	13B	14B	11A	12B	13B	14B	8B	10B	14C	15C	12B	13B	14C	19C	13B	14B	20C	21C
65-68	9A	11B	14B	15C	12B	12B	14B	15C	9B	11B	15C	16C	13B	14C	15C	20C	14B	15C	21C	22C
69-72	9B	11B	15B	16C	13B	13B	15C	16C	9B	12C	16C	17C	14C	15C	16C	21C	15C	16C	21C	23C
73-76	10B	12B	16C	17C	13B	13B	16C	17C	10B	13C	17C	18C	15C	16C	17C	22C	16C	17C	22C	24D
77-80	10B	12B	16C	17C	14B	14B	17C	18C	11C	14C	18C	19C	15C	17C	18C	23D	17C	18C	23D	25D
81-84	11B	13C	17C	18C	14C	14C	18C	19C	12C	15C	19C	20D	17C	18C	20D	24D	18C	19C	23D	26D
85-88	11B	13C	17C	18C	15C	15C	18C	19C	13C	16C	20D	21D	18D	19C	22D	25D	19C	21C	25D	27D
89-92	12C	14C	18C	18C	15C	15C	19C	20C	14C	17C	21D	22D	18D	20D	24D	26D	21C	23D	26D	28D
93-95	12C	14C	18C	18C	15C	15C	19C	20C	15C	18C	23D	24D	21D	21D	26D	27D	23C	25D	27D	29D
96-97 (UM)	14D	16D	20D	20D	16D	16D	20D	21D	16D	19D	24E	25E	22E	22E	27E	28E	24E	27E	28E	30E
98-99 (UM)	16E	18E	22E	22E	18E	18E	22E	23E	18E	21E	26F	27F	24F	24F	29F	30F	26F	29F	30F	32F
100 (UM)	18F	20F	24F	24F	20F	20F	24F	25F	23F	28F	29F	30F	26G	26G	31G	32G	28G	31G	32G	34G

(For A,B,C,D,E use Disruption criticals)

UM = Unmodified Roll

Result	Use Disruption	Use Stress
F	E	A
G	F	B

Range:

0' — 10'	:	+35
11' — 50'	:	0
51' — 100'	:	-25
101' — 200'	:	-40
201' — 300'	:	-55
301' — up	:	-75